Praise for Laurel Dewey

"Laurel Dewey has definitely earned a place in any discussion of the top mystery authors of the present day."
– Bookreporter

"Her characters are strong and interesting, and her protagonist, Jane Perry is just plain gutsy."
– Blogcritics

"Jane Perry is indeed an amazing character, and I can't wait to read more."
– Single Titles

"Jane Perry is a fabulous character. She's realistic and sometimes frustrating but you'll be rooting for her all the way!"
– Life in Review

"I don't know if Laurel Dewey is as widely known as Dean Koontz or James Patterson, but if she isn't she is definitely able to hold her own against the big boys. Her Jane Perry novels are written skillfully and engagingly making you constantly wonder what is going to happen next."
– Literary R&R

"Laurel Dewey is now among the best thriller authors I've read."
– My Love Affair with Books

Knowing

Knowing

A novel by
Laurel Dewey

THE
STORY PLANT

Also by Laurel Dewey

The Story Plant
The Aronica-Miller Publishing Project, LLC
P.O. Box 4331 Stamford, CT 06907

Copyright © 2012 by Laurel Dewey
Cover design by Barbara Aronica-Buck

Print ISBN-13: 978-1-61188-049-6
E-book ISBN-13: 978-1-61188-050-2

Visit our website at www.thestoryplant.com
Like Laurel Dewey on Facebook at https://www.facebook. com/pages/
Laurel-Dewey-Author/200115782067

First Story Plant Printing: December 2012
Printed in The United States of America

"A lion sleeps in the heart of every brave man."
Turkish Proverb

Acknowledgements

Many thanks to the cardiac nurses and physicians who generously gave of their time and helped me understand the intricate factors that go into a successful heart transplant surgery. I especially want to thank medical director of cardiac surgery, Loren F. Hiratzka, MD and cardiac patient Harry Wuest for their valuable information.

Additional thanks to my copyeditor, Sue Rasmussen, for going the extra mile. As always, a big thank-you to Lou Aronica and Peter Miller of The Story Plant for giving me the freedom to write from my heart.

"It is only with the heart that one can see rightly, what is essential is invisible to the eye."
Antoine de Saint-Exupéry

Dedication

To David.
My heart is always yours.

"What is this death but a negligible accident? Why should I be out of mind because I am out of sight? I am but waiting for you, for an interval, somewhere very near, just around the corner…."
Rosamunde Pilcher

CHAPTER 1

Sergeant Detective Jane Perry rolled to an abrupt stop in front of the gas pumps and checked the time. 7:17. It had been exactly seventeen minutes since she left her house on Milwaukee Street in Denver and headed south on I-25 but it felt like hours. Lately, reality had revolved in a surreal sphere, and Jane was looking forward to jumping off the mind-bending roller coaster and getting some heartfelt perspective on her life. But all that would have to wait now.

If Jane were still a smoker, she would have extinguished four cigarettes since she left her house. Even though it had been over eleven days since she was sucker punched by the news, the rawness of that first moment when she saw the truth in black and white was still fresh and stung like venom, hot and unforgiving. Nicotine would soften the edges but she'd made a promise to herself to quit, so she'd have to figure out how to steer through this oozing emotional wound without the comfortable dulling of pain.

That was proving more difficult as the days progressed. In one moment, Jane's world not only blew apart, but her entire identity split with it. She'd spent the past days dredging up her turbulent young life yet again—propelling her heart back into the chaos—searching for clues in the multitude of unspoken words and wondering how she missed the torturous secret her mother chose to keep. Unfortunately, her memories had been fogged by time and over twenty years of abusing the bottle. If there was any sign of what was hidden long ago, it was now buried in layers of regret and omission.

Jane rolled down her window and adjusted the side mirror on her '66 ice blue Mustang. She took in a deep breath, hoping it would abate her temptation for tobacco. The cool, mid-April breeze belied the promise of spring, even though March and April were known in Colorado as the wettest and snowiest months of the year. As Jane canvassed the flattened landscape so common for this section of the state, there was still no sign of the Isis of rebirth—no lush green panoramas to sink her teeth into and inhale the beauty. All that lay in eyesight were varying shades of taupe, edged by the blacktop of the frontage road. How was it possible for anything verdant to emerge from this lifeless topography? The sheer energy it took for Colorado to rise from the frozen ashes of winter never ceased to amaze and confound Jane. While the rains had abated over the last twenty-four hours, an uncommon moisture still clung in the normally dry morning atmosphere that lent a dampened spirit to her journey.

Jane leaned outside and caught her reflection in the side mirror. *No, it couldn't be*, she thought. Moving closer to the mirror, she parted her shoulder length brown hair and found a cluster of gray. When did this happen? Had she been so preoccupied with the events of her last case that she failed to notice the preamble to death painted on her crown? She studied her brown eyes in the mirror and noted the bags underneath—badges of a hard fought life where sacrifice trumped freedom. Crinkling her nose, Jane forced the lines around the corner of her eyes to deepen. She could chalk it up to too much smiling but anyone who knew her would disagree since Jane Perry's personality was not synonymous with grinning. She let out a hard sigh of resignation. How in the hell did she get so goddamned old in just thirty-seven years?

She leaned over and locked her Glock in the glove compartment on top of her badge. Even though her anticipated seven-day trip was purely personal, she never traveled without her service weapon. It was an anchor and a steel security blanket. Swiping her credit card, she selected the highest-grade gasoline for her cherished classic ride and filled the tank. A gust of wind blew across the service station, forcing Jane to button the collar of her leather jacket. She turned and surveyed the smattering of vehicles filling up at this early hour. Jane had always been a student of observation; always keenly taking in the minute details in front of her. That ability ran on autopilot and served her well as a cop when she had to recreate a homicide scene.

But lately, she'd taken to counting objects that were grouped together. It had almost become an obsession; something to indulge her addictive mind. At that moment, there were three cars, including hers, at the islands. There were seven islands, each with three options for fuel. But four of those fuel pumps were covered with yellow tape, marking them out of order. So, readjusting it, there were seventeen fuel handles available. *Ironic*, she mused. When she rolled into the gas station and looked at the clock, it was 7:17, which was seventeen minutes after she left her house. *Odd.*

She'd come to know these as *syncs*, clusters of seemingly disparate words, digital times on a clock, names, symbols or numbers that kept cropping up in such a way to herald a hidden message. While some of the *syncs* had been easy to decipher, most proved mystifying, leaving Jane to feel she either wasn't smart enough to understand the significance or that the message itself wasn't ready to be heard. This concept may have occupied illogical territory, but even the most logical human being has been guilty of latching onto a sign from above or below in an attempt to give meaning to an experience.

As much as Jane Perry primarily used her logic, these last few years had introduced her to phenomena that defied rational sense. The more she fought it, the more the strangeness attacked like a serpent, demanding to be acknowledged. More than anything, she couldn't escape the weird coincidences and *syncs* that plagued her daily life and infested nearly every homicide she worked. The constant dovetailing of events was so common now that she no longer questioned the mystical belief of entanglement with other humans, both dead and alive.

The fuel pump clicked but Jane kept squeezing the handle in an attempt to force every last drop of gas into her tank. She noted the signage on the pump warning against "topping off" your tank and some reference to "creating a cleaner, greener planet." *Fuck that shit*, she thought. She had a long drive in front of her and her hungry Mustang needed to be fed as much liquid "grass" as possible. When she finally filled it to overflowing, Jane removed the nozzle and hooked it back on the pump. Just as she did, she sensed the presence of the attendant behind her, ready to make a smartass comment. She turned, ready to verbally tackle him with her well-worn bravado. Yet to her astonishment, there was no one there. Jane spun around and scanned the immediate area, looking for any sign of an attendant in the vicinity but she came up empty. She chalked it up to a lack of sufficient caffeine, even though she'd already knocked back three cups of coffee in the last two hours. While gas station java swill wasn't her first choice, it would have to do.

Inside the small Quik Mart convenience store, Jane found four aisles stuffed to the gills with every known junk food. Besides the corpulent woman behind the cash register who crunched on a greasy pork rind, the only other occupants were a beefy biker and a scrawny teenage boy who was loading up on enough "crack in a can" energy drinks to keep him awake until he stroked out. A small television, located above the cash register, was turned on with the sound muted. Jane briefly glanced up as a booking photograph of a heavyset man filled the screen. His wavy brown, scraggly hair matched his unkempt beard and mustache. His name flashed underneath the photo: Harlan Kipple, age forty-two.

Jane knew all about Kipple, although she'd never met him. For almost fourteen days, he had been enjoying "three hots and a cot," courtesy of the Denver penal system. She would have caught the case but Kipple committed his crime southeast of Denver in Limon, Colorado and was only kicked to Denver because of his heinous, high profile crime and to insure he was secured prior to trial.

Kipple, an Interstate truck driver with only one past infraction of transporting illegal prescription drugs in his rig for his brother-in-law, had been accused of the macabre butchering of an unidentified black prostitute. It was your classic open and shut case since Kipple had been found in a dingy Limon motel, passed out in bed with the working girl, clutching a bloody hunting knife and covered in her blood. To make the case even more depraved, the poor girl had been gutted like a deer and her head cracked open, leaving her brain draped outside of her skull. As expected, drugs were involved and that part of the murder made Harlan Kipple nefariously notorious. Lab reports showed he injected the girl with ketamine hydrochloride—a PCP analogue used as an anesthetic in veterinary medicine but gaining popularity on the street as a date rape drug. Known on the club scene as "Special K," "Super K," "KO" and "Make Her Mine", ketamine was distinguished from other date rape drugs in that it produced a dissociative anesthesia, rendering the victim detached from all bodily sensations but often aware of what was being done to them and yet paralyzed and unable to respond. Picture being encased in a glass ball, while watching the unthinkable happen to you and having no way to fight back. It was the ultimate torture because if the victim survived the attack, they usually suffered from amnesia but were prone to subsequent, suddenly triggered vivid hallucinations that replayed the rape or attack, forcing the victim to question their reality. To Jane, ketamine was the epitome of a true mind-fucking drug that left its twisted mark on survivors for many years. As for the unsuspecting prostitute that Kipple mutilated, her last minutes were likely spent watching herself being raped and then filleted open until the grace of God separated her body from her soul.

But the incongruity of Kipple's case didn't end there. About two years prior to the grisly murder, he had been given a life-saving heart transplant—a surgery that nearly ensured him another healthy two decades of life. The fact that those years would now be spent confined to a cell and probably end in execution was God's little irony, Jane deduced. What a waste of a good heart, she recalled thinking when the story broke.

Kipple's face lingered on the television inside the Quik Mart. The press named him "Kipple, the Heartless Killer." Nothing works like an obvious alliteration when you're selling freaks to the public. Jane stared at his photo, searching out the darkness that always lingered behind the eyes of all psychos. But Kipple was a tough nut to crack. Instead of the penetrating evil, there was a strange softness and quiet sweetness that projected from his photo. Good God, was she losing her touch?

"Can I help you?"

Jane turned away from the screen to find the cashier staring at her, a speck of pork rind dotting her upper lip. "I need strong coffee."

The woman pointed her fat finger toward the back of the store, in the corner next to the bank of refrigerated shelves. Jane glanced outside to her Mustang and then quickly walked to the rear of the store. She selected the strongest brew available and the largest cup, filling it to the rim. Searching for the sugar, she tipped over the plastic bowl that held the packets. She counted them as she put them back in the bowl. Seventeen. She snapped the lid on the cup and carried it around the corner of the aisle, staring momentarily at the array of artery-clogging snack foods that lined the shelves. She looked up briefly to glance at her waiting Mustang before searching the selections for anything remotely healthy. It was another promise Jane made to herself after recently escaping what she assumed was a death sentence. She found herself drawn to the pine nuts, even though she never would have made that choice a few weeks ago. She squinted to read what was written across the front of the bag in green lettering: ENJOY THESE NUGGETS OF NATURE FROM THE PINECONE! The price was right for the small bag, a buck seventy.

Jane grabbed all eight bags on the shelf as she felt the burly biker walk behind her. For some strange reason, he hovered awfully close. She allowed the intrusion to continue for another few seconds before spinning around. But there was no one standing there. The biker was, in fact, on the opposite side of the store. Jane stood still, sensing a muscular thickness around her; a phantasm imprint that lacked clarity. A few years ago, she would have ignored this curious feeling but she'd learned the hard way that the more she pretended it away or chalked it up to booze, flashbacks, PTSD or lack of sleep, the more dynamic it became.

Knowing

Jane waited, looking into nothingness yet still clearly aware of the unassailable presence around her. She started to turn right but was drawn to the left. Moving around the aisle, Jane stood at the long magazine rack that framed the front windows. Cradling the eight bags of pine nuts, she made her way toward the cashier when she heard the soft brush of a magazine fall to the vinyl floor behind her. Jane turned to find a copy of *"The Q"*—a glossy, men's sports and outdoor magazine—splayed open, cover side up. She leaned down, picked up the magazine and replaced it on the shelf. Turning toward the cashier, Jane took a step and heard the magazine fall behind her again. She stopped. The phantasmal stickiness gripped her like a defiant child demanding her attention. Jane carefully turned toward the magazine, finding it sprawled in the same position as before. She leaned down, turned it over and stared at the advertising found on page seventeen. Against an indigo background lay a mountainous landscape with snowcapped peaks. Featured in the foreground was a woman's modest wristwatch placed upon what looked like a red satin cloth that stretched from one side of the page to the other. The hands on the watch pointed to 11:17. In the bottom left hand corner, there was an illustration of the "great and powerful" Oz from *The Wizard of Oz* peeking out from his purple curtained area. In bold, red block letters next to the image, it read:

IT'S TIME FOR A CHANGE, DOROTHY.

Jane searched on the page for the product or service being advertised and came up empty. She figured "time" related to the woman's wristwatch and Dorothy correlated to *The Wizard of Oz* but the rest of the ad was nonsensical. There were no website links or phone numbers that related to whatever they were selling. *Avant-garde garbage.* That's what Jane deduced as she inexplicably tucked the magazine under her arm and walked to the cashier. Suddenly, the presence that had hung so closely to her disappeared.

"That all?" the chunky woman asked.

"That'll do it."

The woman tapped her greasy finger on a greeting card stand to the left of the checkout. "We got Easter cards on closeout."

Jane regarded the woman with an incredulous stare. Did she actually believe Jane looked like a woman who would send someone an Easter card? Jane glanced at the nearly empty card stand and saw a glittery greeting with the

Archangel Gabriel blowing his trumpet. Who in the hell sends Easter cards? Jane peered around the card stand and saw liters of spring water. She grabbed four bottles and added them to her pile. "Okay. That'll do it."

"Thirty-three even." Jane handed the woman a fifty. The woman opened the register and handed Jane's change back to her. "Seventeen's your change."

"What in the fuck is going on?" Jane muttered.

"Excuse me?" the woman asked, offended.

"Not you." Jane's mind was elsewhere.

The woman dumped the purchases into a plastic bag. "Uh-huh," she replied, still affronted. "Hey…" Jane was still lost in thought as she tucked the seventeen dollars into her wallet. "*Hey*," the woman stressed, leaning forward.

Jane awoke from her slumber. "What?"

The woman pointed out the front window. "Isn't that your car driving away?"

Jane turned around just in time to see the back wheels of her ice blue Mustang squeal out of the parking lot. She raced outside, instinctively grabbing for her Glock and coming up empty. The only detail she could make out was the back of a man's head and his thick neck.

CHAPTER 2

"Un-*fucking*-believable!" Jane screamed as she stood on the edge of the gas station, watching the rear tires of her Mustang blow mud into the air.

She didn't lock the car door. She always locked the goddamned car door. *Always.*

Her mind raced, first taking into account all the items in her vehicle. There was the Glock and her badge, locked in the glove compartment. She figured the perp chose her older ride because it was easy to hotwire. Whether he could also jimmy the lock on the glove compartment and gain access to her shield and service weapon was another thing entirely. In the trunk was her luggage and laptop, which held hundreds of sensitive case files from past and open homicides. The more Jane quickly itemized everything in her Mustang, the more the weight of the world pressed down. The potential fallout from this was enormous. It was one helluva start to an already anxious road trip.

She tried her cell phone but there was no coverage. "Shit!" Jane exclaimed as she felt the walls cave in. There was no sure way to determine which direction the perp drove after he exited the frontage road, but Jane figured he was most likely headed southbound since that was the easiest entrance to speed onto from the gas station. She never considered heading back to Denver and aborting her trip. Jane had a small window of opportunity over the next seven days to lay eyes on the one person she never knew existed until eleven days ago. To turn back now because some asshole boosted her '66 ride was not an option. The only person she could have phoned for help was her younger brother, Mike. But he and his new wife were incommunicado, knee deep in the Amazon jungle for two weeks on a shamanic tour hosted by a guy named Bruno. The only other possible person she could call was Sergeant Weyler but Jane wasn't used to asking for personal favors, even though she knew Weyler would drop everything and come to her aid.

A thought briefly crossed her mind as she headed back to the Quik Mart. *Hank Ross.* That consideration actually made Jane stop in her tracks. They'd met less than one month before when she worked the Van Gorden abduction case in Midas, Colorado. But the connection they made—both sexually and emotionally—was still new and uncertain for Jane. But there *had* to be something there because Hank was the only one who knew where she was headed and why she had to go there. For the first time in forever, she actually trusted someone and allowed that unseen grain of vulnerability to exist and be laid bare. Yes, even though he was more than ninety minutes north of where she stood at that moment, she knew if she called him, he would show up.

But, no. She couldn't bring herself to do it. Like every other circumstance in Jane's thirty-seven years, she would figure it out alone. It wasn't so much pride with Jane Perry; it was a conviction that one is responsible for his or her own destiny and to depend too strongly on others often complicated one's fate. She got into this problem and dammit, she'd get herself out of it.

"I need to see the outside security video," Jane announced to the cashier as she blew back into the Quik Mart. Off-the-beaten-path joints like this one copy over their security video every twenty-four hours or fewer and Jane needed to examine the tape right away before human error took away that opportunity. The woman regarded Jane with a lazy drop of her mouth and said nothing. Jane leaned forward, irritation building. "I'm a cop," she stressed.

"Yeah?" the woman replied, in a stupor from inhaling too many pork rinds. "Where's your badge?"

"In the glove compartment of my car that's heading south right now."

She sat back, not seeming to understand the necessity for speedy action. "How did he steal your car?"

Oh, fuck me, Jane thought. "I didn't lock it."

"You didn't lock your car?" Disdain covered the woman's fat face. "If you're *really* a cop, wouldn't you know better than that?" The woman actually thought she was clever.

Jane reached her boiling point. She leaned forward, prepared to grab the woman's flabby arm. "I'm a homicide cop with Denver PD. I'm the one who shows up at 'Shop 'n' Robs' like this one when your cold, dead ass is lying in rigor on the concrete and your grieving family is standing just outside the yellow tape bawling like babies. So let's recap. Some son-of-a-bitch jacked my car in your fucking parking lot!—"

"You don't have to get huffy!"

"*Yes.* Actually, *I do*! I have important business to take care of. So, if you don't show me the goddamn security video and let me use your phone to call this in, I'll hold *you* personally responsible for grand theft auto. And believe me, lady, you do *not* want to get on my bad side."

Jane knew there was absolutely no way she could make the broad responsible for her bad luck, but Jane had always been able to toss out a threat with such authority that even domestic animals and house plants acquiesced. Fortunately, this dimwitted woman submitted. In a cramped backroom, Jane reviewed the security video, which was blurry with badly positioned cameras and jumped from one pump to another, leaving ten second gaps in the real time action on each fueling island.

"Jesus!" Jane exclaimed, frustration filling every pore.

"They told us they were gonna update the security system last year," the woman offered in a slow cadence.

"Is that right? I'll make a point to tell every perp to 'Google' this location." The video finally came to rest on Jane's Mustang. Unfortunately, the thief was already seated in the car and his face was obscured by the poor angle of the camera and the driver's front visor. Jane paused the video in an attempt to decipher any useable, identifying qualities about the male subject but it was useless. The only other video of her car showed it screeching away from the fueling station and out of the shot.

"Shit!" Jane muttered, standing up. "I gotta use your phone."

Jane valiantly tried to talk one-on-one with a local cop to try and gain some leverage but because the Quik Mart was located between jurisdictions, it started to get complicated and the clock was ticking. She then attempted to reach a couple cops she knew in Colorado Springs, located fifty miles south, but they weren't at their desks and Jane didn't feel it made sense to leave a scattered message on their voicemail. It became patently obvious to her that it was pointless to waste her time at the scene of the crime waiting for the cops to show up. Jotting down her name and the make and year of her ice blue Mustang along with the license plate, she handed it to the cashier with instructions to report the carjacking and deal with the cops when they got off their donut break and showed up.

Checking her wallet, Jane counted one thousand and seventeen dollars. Jane had allotted herself one hundred and fifty bucks a day for her seven-day trip. It was looking like that day's stipend would be spent on a bus ticket to Colorado Springs. The plan was to reach out to the two cops she knew there, file the grand theft charges and get them to put their eyes on the highway as quickly as possible.

After another labored conversation with the uncooperative cashier about where the closest bus station was located, Jane began a three-mile trek northbound on the frontage road. The day wasn't getting any warmer as the spring winds stung her face. She flashed on the warm, down coat sitting on the front seat of her Mustang and felt another wave of anger wash over her. By the time she reached the unmarked bus depot, she was told she could only travel twenty-five miles south before having to transfer to another bus that would take her to Colorado Springs. Jane paid the fare and boarded the bus. By the time they crossed the Castle Rock city line, Jane had devoured one bag of pine nuts followed by a half liter of water to cut the excessively salty taste in her mouth. She tried her cell phone several times, but coverage was spotty. A half hour later, the bus finally came to a stop on a flat, lonely frontage road. Awaiting her was the next bus, a small depot and a convenience store. She quickly exited, hoping her next ride wouldn't smell like bare feet and diesel fumes.

As Jane walked to the new coach—a polished, black luxury ride that featured a large luggage compartment—she noted the name on the side: *Anubus* with the number 121 below it. She recognized the name as a slight misspelling of the Egyptian God *Anubis*. Rising above the "n" was an illustration of what looked like the head of an Egyptian dog or jackal. *Lovely*, Jane mused. Jackals are known to scavenge dead bodies. She once looked up the symbology of *Anubis* after an intellectual killer she helped convict screamed the name out at his murder trial. The Egyptians believed *Anubis* guided souls to the underworld. Once there, assisted by the god *Thot*, *Anubis* supervised the weighing of the heart of the deceased. Jane wondered what the marketing mastermind was snorting when he chose such a loaded, ancient, death-driven moniker for the bus line. For anyone who studied Egyptian symbology, it didn't exactly suggest "safe travels."

Jane boarded the crowded bus and surveyed available seating. If a warm body didn't take up a seat, it was being used to hold additional luggage that wouldn't fit in the lower compartment. Jane meandered down the narrow center aisle, dragging the bag full of water, pine nuts and that strange *Q* magazine. A series of small televisions were located in the center of each row of seats, all tuned to a local Denver news program. Underneath each television was the bus number "121." Jane stopped, smelling something familiar but not connecting with the odor. Whatever it was, it had a rotting tang that made her gut queasy. The further Jane walked down the aisle, the more noxious the aroma became. Looking at the faces on the bus, she noted a strange pallor that inhabited each of them. Were they all being affected, she wondered, by this cadaverous scent?

Three rows ahead, she spotted an empty aisle seat. A Caucasian girl who looked about twenty years old occupied the window seat. She was wiry, dressed in a pair of black pants, a blue turtleneck and a gray hoodie. Her eyes nervously skirted the area outside her window. The kid was a textbook druggie and probably a hooker, although she didn't own the toughness required for the latter. Jane glanced up at the seat number. "Shit. That figures," she mumbled.

The girl quickly looked at Jane, her black eyes lined with thick kohl that emphasized the whites underneath the pupils. "*What?*" the girl anxiously said.

"Row seventeen," Jane replied, pointing to the aisle seat. "This seat taken?"

She stared at Jane for a little too long before responding. "No…" Fear edged the word.

Jane slid into the seat, securing her plastic bag between her feet. She could feel the girl's eyes study her and did her best to ignore it until it became irritating. "Look, I'd sit in another seat if there was one available."

The girl apprehensively looked down at Jane's bag. "What…what's in the bag?"

"Water," Jane said, scanning the rows in front of her in case she missed another empty seat.

"Is that all?" There was an obvious catch in her throat.

Jane turned to the girl. Sweat beads formed across her upper lip, which quivered slightly. "No. I got pine nuts and a magazine. You want any of that?"

The girl looked deep into Jane's eyes, searching…desperately searching. "No…No, I don't. My stomach is already too queasy."

Jane nodded. "It's that smell," she concluded. "Why do buses always smell like warmed over shit?"

"What smell?" the girl asked.

"You can't smell that? It's like rotting…something."

The girl sniffed in the air. "I don't smell anything."

Oh, great. Jane had experienced this odd phenomenon before and it always had a surreal conclusion. First the strangeness she felt in the Quik Mart and now this. And it wasn't even close to noon.

The girl turned back to Jane, hesitated briefly and then spoke. "Did…did *they* send you?"

Fuck, Jane thought. Why do the wingnuts of the world always choose bus transportation? "*They?*"

A small fountainhead of courage briefly emerged from the girl. "I just need to know. Okay?" Desperation clouded every whispered word. "Like you'd even tell me, right? It's just that you kinda resemble my mom and I thought maybe they'd send someone who looked like her just to fuck with my head."

Jane had been told she resembled a dyke, a slut and an angry young woman but she'd never been told that she looked like somebody's mother. Since there was nowhere to escape, she figured she'd come as clean as possible. "My name's Jane. My car got ripped off back at the 'Shop 'n' Rob.' I'm heading to Colorado Springs to file a report. That's my story. I don't know who 'they' are and I don't give a shit. So, let's just let it rest. Deal?"

The girl stared into Jane's eyes. "I *can* trust you."

"Look, if you're in trouble, maybe you should—"

"Shit!" the girl whispered, craning her neck and looking outside the window on the opposite side of the bus.

"What?" Jane asked with growing irritation.

The girl slunk down and peered outside the window next to her seat. "*Shit, shit, shit!*"

"What is it?"

"*Shh*! I swear I saw the red-haired dude out there wearing a black suit."

As much as Jane did not want to engage the girl or feed her paranoid delusions, she stood partly up in her seat and looked around the exterior of the bus. "I don't see any red-haired guy wearing a black suit." She sat back down. "Are you playing me? Because I'm telling you, I've had a fucked up morning—"

"Lilith."

"Huh?"

"My name's Lilith. And I doubt you'll believe a word of what I know. That's what *they* always count on. Make it so absurd so if you tell your story, you'll sound insane."

Jane regarded Lilith. "Are you high?"

Lilith turned away, her eyes silently canvassing the outside of the bus from her window. "Fuck off," she murmured.

Jane stared straight ahead. The television above her head flashed on the weather map of Colorado, showing a spring cold front entering the state. The bus driver boarded and faced the passengers. Jane noted that even though he'd been outside the entire time, he had the same sickly, gray pallor just like every other passenger on this black coach.

"Hey, folks!" the driver announced, "it's gonna be a couple more minutes. We gotta problem with one of the luggage compartments." He turned and left.

Lilith became increasingly agitated. "*Fuck!*" she said under her breath, nervously looking outside.

Jane couldn't take it anymore. She eyed the girl, speaking quietly. "Okay, if I tell you I'm a cop, will that change things?"

Her eyes widened. "For real?"

Jane nodded.

"But I thought you had your car stolen. How's that possible?"

Jane rolled her eyes. Lilith was the second person that day to question how a cop could be so stupid. "The two are not mutually exclusive. Look, in my job, I've heard some really off-the-wall stories. So, if you want to share whatever's freaking you out, I'll listen with an open mind."

Lilith turned her body toward Jane. It was as if she had found her savior. "I was headed to Denver this morning on another bus," she whispered. "I was goin' there to make a statement to a cop or whoever would listen to me." She swallowed hard, furtively peering around the bus suspiciously. "I was involved in a murder." Jane focused intently on her. "I *didn't* commit the murder," Lilith quickly added, "but I was *used* to make it happen."

"Who died?"

"One of my friends. Her name was Jaycee. She was a..." Lilith seemed suddenly embarrassed, "hooker."

"Okay," Jane said, nonchalantly.

Lilith chewed the flesh off her thumb. "I'm also a...hooker."

"Hey, I'm not your priest. I don't care what you do for a living."

Lilith slightly relaxed. "Jaycee was new in town. Like less than a week. I never even knew her last name or where she came from. But she seemed real nice so we hung out."

"How did Jaycee die?"

"I...um...had this guy ask me for a date. He was short. Like five six. And old. Like forty."

"Forty? Yeah, that's fuckin' ancient."

"Yeah. He had reddish gray hair. He drove up in a limo and I got in. There were two other guys in the back. Both were tall and thin and wore dark suits, thin black ties and had *really* red hair. I mean, like, fire red from hell, you know? And they had these piercing blue eyes, like glass almost. The guy on the left side had a weird bright crimson mark that covered most of the top of his right hand. It was like three inches long. It looked like he'd been in some kind of accident."

"Did you get any names?"

"Not from the two guys sitting across from me. But the guy who seemed to be in charge said his name was Mr. Ramos. I've entertained four guys named Ramos and they all had dark hair, so that was kinda different. I told him it was extra for a threesome but he told me he didn't want to do me. He wanted me to hook him up with Jaycee. He said he'd seen me with her. I told him to talk to Jaycee himself but he said he was nervous."

"Nervous?" Jane questioned.

"Yeah. It didn't make a lot of sense to me neither. I mean, trust me, this Ramos dude didn't look like a guy who was scared of *anything*. But then I figured, maybe he didn't want anyone seein' him with a black girl—"

"Jaycee was black?"

"As black as the darkest night. Seriously, I never seen no one that black. So, he tells me that he'd pay me good money if I bring her to a certain motel outside of the city but to keep it on the down-low with her 'cause he wanted to surprise her. He told me when he wanted to see her, the motel name and the room number. Told me there'd be a key waitin' for me at the desk and to bring her upstairs. Then, I was to go back outside and one of the guys with red hair who was in the limo would give me my money."

"None of this seemed a little freaky to you?"

"Oh, shit. Last week, I had a guy tell me to put on his mother's dress and then he nursed on my tit while he made me sing 'Three Blind Mice.' It's *all* freaky!"

Par for the course, Jane figured. "Go on," Jane insisted.

"I needed the cash. So, I agreed. If I'd have known…" Lilith shook her head as her eyes welled up.

Jane put her hand on the girl's arm. "What happened?"

"I did like he asked me to. I told Jaycee that there was this rich guy who wanted a date with *only* her. She was a little nervous but she liked the idea that someone thought she was special. So we drove down to the motel. And like Mr. Ramos said, the key was waitin' at the front desk. Room 170—"

"170?" Jane repeated, noting that damn seventeen again.

"Yeah. I take her up there and we go into the room. There was a vase on a table filled with dozens of narcissus. They were beautiful. It made the room smell real sweet. But when we looked on the bed, there was a guy passed out but it wasn't Mr. Ramos."

"How do you know he was passed out?"

"'Cause we tried to wake him up but he was wasted. His eyes would open but nobody was home, you know?" Tears fell from Lilith's eyes. "I should have never left her there. But she said she was okay. So, I walked out. I went downstairs and just like Mr. Ramos said, there was one of the red-haired guys from the limo...the one with the weird cherry mark on his hand? He handed me a fat envelope and told me to leave. I got in my car and drove home. That's when I counted the money. I couldn't believe it. Seventeen hundred bucks. I was rich."

Jane had to check herself momentarily to make sure she wasn't dreaming.

Lilith reached out to Jane. "But then...the next day, I watch the news and I hear about this dead working girl who they found cut up in a Limon motel... with her head split open..."

Jane was staggered. "*Hang on.* You're talking about *Harlan Kipple*?"

"*Yeah.* When they showed his photo on the TV, I realized he was the guy passed out on the bed." She leaned closer to Jane. "He didn't kill nobody! *Guaranteed.* He couldn't lift his eyelid, let alone a knife! He didn't even *have* a knife on him!"

"How do you know?"

"We wanted to check him out. See what his package looked like. We pulled back the covers. He was butt naked and there was no knife anywhere. Hand to God! Somebody set him up, just like I set up Jaycee!"

"Why Harlan?"

"How the fuck should I know? Bad shit happens to good people. But it's been eatin' at me ever since he got arrested and charged with murder. I couldn't sleep." She lowered her head. "I've never done nothin' in my life that's moral or good. And I figured maybe I could help him, you know? I didn't tell nobody what I was plannin' on doin'. I was goin' to Denver this morning and I was gonna tell whoever would listen to my story what I did and what I saw. And if they couldn't find who killed Jaycee, at least they could let that Kipple guy go free."

Jane waited. "Okay...so why are you now headed the opposite direction from Denver?"

"Didn't you hear what happened this mornin'?"

"No. I've been occupied."

"It was all over the news. I saw it on the other bus when we were drivin' to Denver. Harlan Kipple's lawyer took him to a hospital to get his heart checked out. And he escaped!"

Jane quickly recalled the muted TV in the Quik Mart and Kipple's face on the screen. "Wait a second. If someone is truly innocent, they don't escape. They talk to their lawyer. They build their case—"

"Hey, I ain't too smart, but this much I know: I don't think he's runnin' from the cops," Lilith said succinctly.

"Who's he running from? Ramos?"

"Maybe. Harlan *knows* he didn't kill Jaycee. He *knows* he was set up. Maybe he was threatened. Maybe he was supposed to die in that motel room? I'm sure as drugged up as he was, he doesn't remember anything that happened in that room, but somewhere down deep," she looked off to the side, lost in thought, "somehow he knows…in *here*?" She pointed to her heart. "Just like *I* know in that same place. It's a knowing. I should have had a knowing when I took Jaycee up to that room. She'd be alive today."

A million thoughts raced through Jane's head. "This Ramos guy only wanted Jaycee. You said she was new in town so why did he choose her specifically?"

Lilith shrugged her shoulders. "I don't know."

"Why would Ramos want to kill her? And why set up Harlan Kipple for the hit?"

"Hey! Which one of us is the cop here? I don't have a fuckin' clue." She moved closer to Jane. "But I *do* know one thing. I haven't felt like I've been totally alone since I met Ramos in the back of that limo."

"The red-haired guy in the black suit?" Lilith nodded apprehensively. "You think he's following you?"

"*I know* he is. About a week ago, outside of my place, there was a black sedan and the driver's window was cracked just enough that I could see red hair." Lilith grabbed hard onto Jane's jacket sleeve. "Whoever 'they' are, they gotta get rid of us who know about the murder. They took care of Harlan and got him in prison for it. But now that he's jumped, they're gonna go after him. I'm the only loose string left in this mess." She let go of Jane's arm. "I really *did* want to go to Denver and talk to a cop and make it right for Harlan. And even though I chickened out, you're a pretty good second choice right now." Lilith turned to the window as if she sensed someone standing outside.

"What is it?"

"It's weird. Even when I can't see him, he's in my head."

"In your head?"

She clutched the sleeve of Jane's leather jacket again. "Please don't think I'm crazy when I say that! It's the only way I can describe it. It's like…he's following me in my head." Lilith tapped the center of her forehead. Her eyes pleaded with Jane. "I'm scared to death. Can you please help me?"

Jane felt for the kid. She believed everything she said. More questions beat around in Jane's brain but her thought process was quickly hijacked by that overwhelming stench she smelled when she first got on the bus. Within seconds, Jane felt her gut seizing and ready to eject every last pine nut she'd ingested. She held her belly, trying to abate the nausea.

"You okay?" Lilith asked, concerned.

"You seriously can't smell that?" Jane asked, as her tongue began to tingle.

"No. I can't. What's goin' on?"

Suddenly, Jane recognized the same muscular thickness press against her that she'd felt back at the Quik Mart. There was urgency in the air, a million pinpoint spikes of electrical energy erupting at once. Jane could swear she felt her ass being pushed out of her seat. A wave of nausea hit hard. She rested a reassuring hand on Lilith's arm. "I'll be right back. I'm gonna be sick," she hurriedly said, grabbing her bag from the Quik Mart and booking it off the bus.

Jane tore into the nearby field with the dried stands of grass and large rocks. Ducking behind a sizeable boulder, she emptied every last ounce of her stomach contents onto the barren ground. As much as she used to get drunk and bear the consequences the next day, Jane never recalled being this sick, this fast. She tried to stand up but her knees gave out instantly. A strange ringing assaulted her ears, soft at first, then loud and unforgiving. For several moments, the world seemed to stop. She felt suspended in an unearthly cloak that protected her. When Jane emerged from that place, her head spun. She tried to stand up again, but she was forced back on her knees. The ground pulsed beneath her.

Still half outside of herself, she turned her head toward the frontage road and watched as the door on the black *Anubus* coach closed and the bus moved forward. Jane tried to yell and raise her arm but that damned heavy presence subdued her, preventing any sound from exiting her mouth. She watched helplessly as the bus rolled another hundred feet. Suddenly, a crimson flare detonated from the center of the undercarriage. Another ignition quickly burst in the rear followed by the final one in the front. In a millisecond, a cataclysmic, shock-and-awe explosion broke into the morning air as the bus blasted toward the sky. Shrapnel and blazing body parts rained down on the pavement, igniting small fires in the dried brush that skirted the road.

Jane covered her head and tucked her body as tightly as she could against the boulder. The hellish scene came to an uneasy rest within a minute. By then, a cluster of people ran out of the nearby depot and convenience store. The odd ringing in Jane's ears vanished, replaced by the hysterical screams and warnings to "stay back" from the terrified spectators.

Jane smelled the same sickly stench that sent her off the bus and into the field. But this time, she connected to where she'd smelled it before. It was the stink of decomposing bodies that she'd unfortunately grown used to at homicide scenes. Her senses had been so dulled by the sickening odor that when the aroma was outside of its deathly orbit, she couldn't pin it down. But crouching in that field with the burning chunks of debris smoldering against the human sacrifices, Jane realized that for some unknown reason, she sensed the tragedy before it happened. She even saw it in their faces—that ghostly, gray pallor that dwelled over the passengers minutes before their untimely death.

But there was something else. And that something still hovered to the side.

The small crowd of people moved around the debris field, some in shock, others calling on their cell phones for help. Jane grabbed her bag from the Quik Mart and warily stood up. A seat from the bus sat in the brush about twenty feet in front of her, engulfed in flames. Jane stared through the heat waves and spotted a black sedan parked across the highway, away from the wreckage. Leaning against the vehicle, was a tall, thin man in a dark suit with flaming red hair. His eyes, shaded with dark sunglasses, observed the scene with no emotion but appeared to vigilantly scrutinize the onlookers. Even from the distance between them, Jane noted the telltale, glaring, red mark on the guy's right hand that Lilith had recounted. For a moment, Jane could almost feel his thoughts. It was crazy, she said to herself. But just as Lilith confessed to her, it felt as though he was trying to worm his way into Jane's head. The hovering presence near her moved closer, offering an unspoken warning.

Knowing

Death surrounded her. Reverberations of regret, terror and shock lingered in the blackened air as the discarnate souls struggled to make sense of the void between worlds. Jane snuck a suspicious eye toward the red-haired man. Oddly, at that moment, death felt like a safer option.

She withdrew her wallet from her jacket pocket, removing her driver's license. Jane waited until the man turned, got into his black sedan and drove north on the frontage road. As she was programmed to do, she caught and memorized his license plate: AGA 171.

She skirted the burning wreckage until she came to a small spot in the grass that was untouched by the fire. There, she dropped her driver's license, face-up, making sure it would be easily seen. Crossing onto the frontage road, Jane headed south, a dead woman walking into the abyss.

CHAPTER 3

Everything was different now.

Almost three hours ago, Jane left her house with a nervous stomach but a determined heart to seek out and find the one person she never knew existed. For now, that quest would be on the back burner. As she walked south down the gravel frontage road, she began to regret her knee-jerk decision to toss her driver's license into the bus's burning debris field. With her Mustang possibly long gone and a belief by whoever found her ID that she perished in the explosion, Jane suddenly realized what a fucked up mess she'd created.

She surreptitiously turned around several times while she walked, checking to see if she was being followed by that strange red-haired freak wearing the dark suit and sporting the scarlet mark on his hand. As she replayed in her mind the story Lilith told her and relived the targeted sabotage of the bus, it started to feel like a nightmare from which she couldn't awaken. "Anubus," she whispered to herself. Given the deadly circumstances, it was ominous that a bus line named after the Egyptian god that guided souls to the underworld was the flashpoint for murder. But the world was full of companies and landmarks with Greek, Roman or Egyptian names, all of which contained often disturbing connections.

The longer she walked and thought about what had occurred, the more questions she had. Lilith's death was a hit, no doubt. And taking out an entire busload of innocent people was typical collateral damage to whomever ordered the job. Witnesses had to be killed. That much Jane understood. After her powerful and disturbing case two years prior when a Denver mob wreaked havoc on her personal and professional life, she was all too aware of the savagery of organized crime. But this felt different to Jane. The more she felt into the experience, the more extreme and atypical it became. This wasn't about some whacked-out group intent on hunting black prostitutes just so they could slice them open and crush their skulls while setting up a truck driver for the kill. The sense Jane got was that whatever group was behind it all—Jaycee's death, Harlan Kipple's set up for her murder and the mass killing of the bus passengers—they weren't amateurs and their ultimate goal was nefarious. But what was that ultimate goal and how many jagged rocks did Jane have to turn over in order to discover the answer?

An icy shiver interrupted Jane's focused thoughts. She wanted to chalk it up to the cold but she figured it was her body reacting to the reality of her situation. She was a blustery twenty-five miles from Colorado Springs. But that destination was useless now that she had sacrificed herself in the debris field. Her only job right now seemed to be lying low, just in case the red headed nutcase saw her or somehow knew she was still out there. But how in the hell could he know that, Jane thought to herself. She stayed as low as possible and out of sight and didn't move from the scene until he drove away. Still, she couldn't shake that eerie comment Lilith made to her on the bus about the disturbing fellow. "He's following me in my head," she confidentially told Jane. It sounded almost insane when she first heard it but now...*now* it crazily made sense. But *if* he knew, *how* did he know?

She turned around again, this time scanning the growing desolate area with precision. The cars zoomed by on the highway while the windswept western landscape to her left on the frontage road, bracketed by distant mountain ranges and vacant lots, stared back at Jane with an unforgiving glare. A wave of anger engulfed her. If she hadn't gotten her car jacked, she'd be well on her way to New Mexico. Jane threw down the bag of water and pine nuts and viciously kicked the gravel beneath her feet hard with her roughout cowboy boot. She silently vowed that if she ever laid eyes on the asshole who stole her Mustang, she'd eviscerate him and enjoy every minute of it. But as soon as that thought crossed her mind, she sensed the same thick presence circling around her that she had felt back at the Quik Mart and on the *Anubus*. It was neither angelic nor evil, but it sure as hell was demanding, seemingly ushering her forward with unyielding determination. Jane grabbed the plastic bag and continued walking at a faster clip as the western topography grew more rural. Two hours passed and she figured she'd traversed about five miles. Thankfully, the noon sun was bright and warmed her face. And yet, she still had no idea where she was going or what she'd do when she got there.

Her mind turned to Hank wondering what he was doing at that moment. Jane factored he was probably wiping down the counters at *The Rabbit Hole* bar and grill he owned and figuring out the lunch specials. *Lunch.* Suddenly, hunger overtook her. But the thought of ingesting another bag of pine nuts followed by a bottle of warm water from a plastic bottle quickly quashed her craving. If Hank knew where she was right now and the predicament she was in, he'd be in his truck and headed her way. What an uncommon person for Jane Perry to invite into her private world. It was odd, she mused. Instead of focusing on what in the hell she was going to do before the sun set, here she was irrationally thinking about a man she'd known for less than a month and who had gently worked his way into her steely heart. For a whisper of a second, she found herself wishing he was there with her. She shook her head, partly in an attempt to throw off that absurd desire. "Get a hold of yourself," Jane instructed herself out loud as she hastened her stride into nowhere.

About a mile further, the frontage road deviated from the highway, bending westward into the now amber and tawny terrain of sagebrush and dry grass that would eat fire if a spark were offered to it. To her right lay a graveyard of old trucks and burnt out cars, home now to nests of mice and birds. The road began to get steeper. Jane was just about to crest the first grade when she heard the sound of clanking metal ahead of her. Carefully, she crept closer, taking cover behind a stand of sagebrush. She knelt down and crawled twenty feet until she could see the source of the clatter.

She took in a quick breath. There was her ice blue Mustang no more than seventy-five feet away. All she could see was the left side of the vehicle. The trunk had been opened with a crowbar, which now lay across the ground. Her toolbox that she kept on the floor of the backseat, sat nearby. The perp who stole her ride was obscured behind the right front tire, seemingly tightening the lug nuts. *Karma*, she reckoned. Bad karma for him; good karma for Jane. But confronting him in this locale would be tricky, not knowing if he'd discovered her service weapon in the glove compartment.

She backed away from the scene to ensure a safe distance and time to think it through. The clanking of the tire iron continued in the background as she rapidly worked out various scenarios for overtaking the thief. The slamming of the Mustang's trunk made her turn around. That was followed by the subsequent clean connection of the ignition after being hotwired.

"Shit!" Jane grumbled, quickly returning to the sagebrush. But by that time, all she could see was the whirl of dust trailing her car. Standing up, Jane eyed her Mustang speeding toward what looked like a dirt road on the right hand side. She thought, *turn down that road, you son-of-a-bitch!* And as if her thoughts had wings, she watched the perp do exactly as she asked.

Jane stood there, momentarily stunned, as the thief drove carefully down the side road and disappeared into a grove of aspen trees that lay about a half mile away. She picked up her speed, jogging and then running toward the dirt road. Once there, she regarded the signage with a cautious eye. It was "County Road 17."

With the kind of single-minded purpose usually dedicated to wars or naval battles, Jane raced down the rural dirt road and kept a steady pace until she arrived at the stand of aspens. Her Mustang sat parked on the other side of the first large aspen, its engine still stuttering under the hood. Jane took cover behind the tree before carefully leaning away to check the scene. From that vantage point, she could clearly see that no one was inside the car. Scanning the area, she had to assume the perp walked away from the car and into the tight grove of trees.

Her heart raced but her pace slowed as she dropped the bag of water and pine nuts on the dirt and cautiously crept toward the passenger side of the Mustang. She halted momentarily on her haunches next to the passenger door, before gingerly lifting the door handle and inching it open. She noted the smell inside the car. It was a mix of fear and sweat. Removing the car keys from her jacket pocket, Jane watchfully opened the glove compartment and removed her badge and Glock. She slid the shield into her jacket pocket and lowered the service weapon with the business end pointed toward the earth. Before she stood up, Jane vigilantly turned around to make sure she was still alone. Satisfied, she snuck around the rear of the Mustang, this time anchoring both hands tightly around the butt of the Glock in combat mode.

Jane moved with skillful exactness, each step placed with purpose and taking care not to emit noise. When she reached the center of the aspen grove, she stopped, taking cover behind another large-trunked tree. The thief was kneeling in the dirt with his back toward Jane. Holding the Glock steady, she warily leaned just far enough around the tree trunk to observe the scene. Jane squinted toward the suspect, feeling bile burn into her throat. The perp had her heavy down jacket draped across his shoulders. While she shivered in her leather jacket, he was pleasantly warm.

She couldn't understand what in the hell he was doing. The palms of his hands clasped his large thighs while he rapidly murmured some sort of chant or prayer. Jane slowly ducked back behind the tree, pressing her forehead to the trunk. What in the hell was going on? She held her forehead against the white, chalky trunk with her eyes closed momentarily to try and get her own groove moving toward resolving this bizarre series of events but she came up blank. Opening her eyes, she guardedly leaned to the right to check out the scene again.

He was gone. Vanished. "What the fuck—" Jane whispered. But that was all she could get out before she felt a heavy arm encircle her neck from behind, dragging her backward. Jane almost lost her footing but quickly maintained her stance. It seemed like minutes but it was mere seconds as she felt her throat being compressed with an expert, military grasp. She strained to stay conscious and sustain control of her Glock but it was proving nearly impossible. Just seconds away from losing consciousness, she was suddenly filled with an inexorable power that stormed inside her body. In that slice of time, she lifted her right foot and, kicking backward and up, nailed the perp squarely in the kneecap. He released his grip and fell face first onto the dirt in pain, with his back to Jane. She spun around, Glock aimed straight on the center of the huge, fleshy center of the thief's back. Her eyes strained for several seconds to regain focus as he desperately inched away from Jane, grabbing his injured knee.

"Freeze or I'll fucking shoot you," Jane screamed, shaking off the dizziness.

"I'm not going back!" he yelled, never looking back and anxiously clawing away from Jane.

"I am *not* fucking with you! Move one more inch and I'll shoot!"

Her threats meant nothing to him as he continued his futile escape.

Jane trained the Glock inches away from the perp's left hip and emptied a piercing shot into the earth. The deafening sound rang against her eardrums. The thief froze, covering his ears from the numbing blast and screamed in shock.

"That was a warning shot," Jane declared, taking a step closer to him. "You will *feel* the next one. Now, turn your sorry ass over."

She could see his fat hands shaking. "Please, please," he stammered, "I can't go back there…" With that, he rolled onto his back.

Jane squared her Glock on his chest as a sliver of sunlight illuminated his face. Even though it was covered in dirt, she recognized him.

It was Harlan Kipple.

CHAPTER 4

"*Harlan Kipple*?!" Jane said, stunned. She withdrew her badge and flashed it. "I'm a cop."

"You ain't taking me back there!" he screamed, grabbing his knee in pain.

"Let me clarify," Jane replied, slipping her shield back into her jacket pocket. "I'm a cop…and that," she pointed to her Mustang, "is my car."

Harlan's head turned slowly toward the vehicle. Jane swore she could hear the wheels creaking in his brain as he processed the situation. "Oh, *hell*, no!" he shouted, slapping the dirt with his fleshy palm. "You have *got* to be kiddin' me!" He shook his head, seemingly in a world of his own. "I was fixin' on job-bin' that sweet little red pickup but my heart told me to take *your* car instead." He looked up at Jane. "So, you ain't one of them cops on my tail?"

Jane lowered the Glock and took a step back. "You're a real quick study there, Harlan."

His eyes turned suspicious. "Hang on. If you're really not after me, how come you were pointin' a gun at me?"

"Because you just tried to kill me, you fucking idiot!"

"*You* tried to kill *me*!" Harlan rubbed the left side of his neck. "You come up behind me and tried to stab me. What'd you expect me to do?"

"What are you, on crack? I was behind *this* tree the whole time. You attacked me *here*!"

Harlan shifted his gaze to where he had been kneeling in the stand of trees. "I'm all mixed up." Then, as if he came back to himself, he asserted, "*No*," he shook his head adamantly. "Not me. That wasn't *me* who attacked you."

Oh, shit, Jane thought. Harlan Kipple was schizo.

"Nah. *You*…You're the one who's nuts." It was as if he read her mind just then. "Risin' up and nailin' me like you did in my knee." He started gently petting his kneecap repeatedly as if it could brush away the pain.

Looking down at Harlan, the first image that came to Jane's mind was the Cowardly Lion in *The Wizard of Oz*. All crouched on the dirt, nursing his knee, with his corpulent physique, unkempt hair and tangled beard that sported debris from the ground. Her second realization was that she had no idea how she extricated herself from his death grip except that she recalled feeling that unstoppable muscle slide into her nearly cataleptic body before she assaulted Harlan. Sure, Jane studied self-defense and had used it enough times in her career, but she was never seconds away from unconsciousness when she employed the techniques.

Harlan glanced over to Jane's Mustang. "Your car's got a lot of juice." He turned back to Jane. "The tires are crap, though. They'd never put me in a rig with tires that wore out. I can't believe you set out on a trip with them on. Hell, I had to pull over just to tighten the lug nuts when I heard them rattlin' around. What were you thinkin'?"

What the fuck, Jane thought. "If I'd known you were going to jack my car, I'd have bought four new radials *and* had a cooler of cold beers and a case of Slim Jims waiting for you in the backseat," she sarcastically replied, securing her Glock inside the side of her jeans and lowering herself to the soft ground. Supporting her tired back against one of the budding aspens, Jane suddenly felt damn old and exhausted. But then, an out of control, cascading fountain of awareness washed over her, along with all the chaotic and dire possibilities that careened with it. "Holy shit," she murmured. "*Harlan Kipple!*" she yelled. "Just when I thought my day couldn't get any worse—"

"Hey!" Harlan interrupted. "You think *you're* havin' a bad day, officer? I've had a *shitty* day so far! Fact is, I've had *fourteen* shitty days *in a row*! And before that? Well, let's just say I'd come to terms with the fact that I'd gone *absolutely bat shit crazy!*"

Jane felt a need to keep sufficient distance from Harlan but she was also feeling a chill descend around the grove of trees. She pointed to her down jacket that had fallen off Harlan's back when he attacked her. "Toss that jacket over here. *Slowly.*"

Harlan looked crestfallen. "I ain't gonna hurt you." He carefully tossed the jacket toward Jane. "I'm not like that."

"Yeah, well. You tried to kill to me, so…" She slid on the jacket, never once taking her eyes off Harlan.

"I told you. That wasn't me."

"Is this that bat shit crazy part you mentioned?"

Harlan lowered his head. He shifted his huge frame on the dirt, jockeying for a more comfortable position. "Ever since my heart transplant almost nineteen months ago, I've never been the same. From the minute I woke up in the hospital…even when I was still cloudy on the drugs and anesthesia…even then…I felt weird."

"What?" Jane adjusted the collar on the jacket to cover her throat. "Sick?"

He looked up. "*No!* Strong! Unstoppable! *Fearless!*"

"Okay. So, why does that translate into bat shit crazy?" Jane watched as Harlan struggled with how to respond. "Just say it, Harlan."

"I don't like the same foods anymore. I used to love beer. And I mean *love* beer. I can't even be around the smell of it no more." He shook his head in embarrassment. "I was raised a Baptist but I don't relate to that no more. I'm drawn to *Eastern religion*, which I was brought up to believe was the Devil talkin'. I even bought a book on meditation! I say phrases and words that I've never said before. Like, 'be that as it may,' 'hazard a guess,' or 'it appears we have a situation.' I mean, who in the hell talks like that? Oh, and I black out a lot and wake up whispering these words and I can feel my whole body pulsating when that happens. It's like lyin' on one of them vibrating beds that cost four quarters that you can still find in some of the cheap motels on the truck route." He leaned forward toward Jane. "Sometimes…sometimes I know what people are thinkin' or what they're gonna say *before* they say it. I have a pretty good photographic memory and I have this ability to take a picture in my head of a room or area and know any detail you want to know." He stood up, still nursing his injured knee. "I'll give you an example. There are forty-eight aspens in this stand we're in. Of those forty-eight, thirty-five have large trunks. Two of the trees that have smaller trunks have a fungus on their bark. Not sure what that is but it's gonna kill 'em in short order." Harlan turned to Jane's Mustang. "It's exactly fifty-two steps from the driver's side of your Mustang to the spot in the center of the stand of trees where I knelt down." He eyed Jane, waiting for a reaction. "You want me to go on?"

Jane inched herself up to her feet. This guy was for real, she figured—real messed up and in real trouble. "Sure."

"I warn you, it gets weirder." Harlan leaned against an aspen, picking a few dead leaves from his scraggly beard. "I have dreams about a childhood *but it ain't my own.* In the dream, I look down and I'm about ten or eleven years old. I'm always runnin' through tall green grass that seems to go on forever. I hunker down, and I wait and I listen. Then suddenly, I realize I have a .22, single shot rifle in my hand and I lift up out of the grass and I nail a rabbit at one hundred yards!" He shook his head. "I'm a good shot but I ain't ever been *that* good."

Jane moved closer to Harlan.

"I have other dreams too. And I ain't no kid in them," he stated slightly bashfully. "I dream all the time about having sex with this woman whom I've never met before in my own life. She's got long, black wavy hair and boobs that just smother you." He seemed temporarily lost in that seductive vision. "And there's another woman in some of the dreams. She's beautiful and when I see her, I feel so much love I can't even explain it. I don't know her name but somehow I think it starts with an 'M.' But I don't have a clue why I know that." He drifted. "And yeah…there's one more woman after that. I…I've never seen her face but there's a weird scent that lingers around her." His mien grew grim. "But I also have nightmares. God-awful nightmares that I wake up from in a cold sweat and make me piss myself because I'm scared shitless." He began to shake. "I'm not sure what I'm scared about though because somehow I *always* block it out. But after it happens, my head hurts for hours, like it's fixin' to explode."

God, a cigarette would taste good right now, Jane mused. She kicked the dirt beneath her feet. "What does your doctor say about all this?"

He looked at her with his mouth agape. "Are you *kiddin'* me? *Seriously*? You think I would tell a *doctor* all this? Why don't I just check myself into the Pueblo hospital for loony tunes and tell 'em to strap me to a bed so they can put me on permanent lock down!" Harlan wandered into the center of the stand of trees.

Jane followed him, watching him with guarded curiosity. She felt a modicum of relief, partly because crazy people don't usually acknowledge that they're nuts and Harlan's use of ironic humor, even if it wasn't done on purpose, appealed to her. "How about the surgeon who did your heart transplant? Maybe everything you're experiencing is more common than you think with transplant patients—"

"He's dead," Harlan succinctly said turning to Jane briefly. "He and his wife were killed in a car wreck less than a month after my operation. The only person I've told any of this to is my buddy, Rudy. Well, he likes to be called *Rudolph* but *I* call him Rudy. I keep fixin' on a red nosed reindeer every time I say Rudolph."

"How about talking to one of your trucker buddies?"

Harlan looked at Jane, curling his lip irreverently. "Yeah. Right."

Knowing

"Where'd you meet Rudy?"

"He was a volunteer in the cardio rehab unit after my surgery. I couldn't have got through it all without his help." Jane silently cringed at Harlan's poor use of the English language. "And when I got out of the hospital, he volunteered to help me with whatever I needed. You know, food shoppin', doctor visits…and he never asked me for a penny. He said he did it 'cause he wanted to give back."

Do-gooders. Jane never trusted them. Everybody had a motive. *Everybody.* Even if that motive was to earn a seat in heaven, it was still a motive. "So, did Rudy tell you what you were experiencing was normal?"

"No. But he never laughed at me when I told him about stuff that happened. He seemed interested but he told me not to say anything 'cause nobody would believe me anyways. I told him not to worry 'cause I sure as hell wasn't gonna tell anyone!" Harlan's eyes drifted off to the side as a memory slipped into focus. "Hey…yeah…" he mumbled, seemingly floating away.

"Harlan?" Jane stated with a firm voice. He quickly turned to her trying to focus. "Was that one of those blackouts you mentioned?"

He shook his head. "No. The blackouts are different. This crap has only been happenin' since my living nightmare started fourteen days ago. I suddenly remembered just now that it was Rudy I was talkin' to at that bar."

"What bar?"

"The Blue Heron in Limon. Yeah. We were at the bar drinkin' a beer. Well," he rolled his eyes, "*I* was drinkin' *red wine.*" Harlan drifted again. "Everything's so damn foggy. I get bits and pieces of memories that belong to *me* but I feel like I'm hallucinatin' when I think about 'em so I can't be sure if they're real or not."

Jane immediately recalled that Jaycee, the black prostitute found in bed with Harlan, had been drugged with ketamine hydrochloride before she was killed. While she couldn't be certain, the memory issues Harlan described of "bits and pieces of memories" and feeling like he was "hallucinating" when pulling up a recent event, seemed to point to the possibility that he too had been drugged with ketamine. "How much do you remember from the bar?"

Harlan strained, seemingly trying to disentangle a memory from his weary mind. "I'd been tellin' Rudy for awhile about all these weird things I was feelin'…and seein'…I felt like I was on the verge of figurin' it out, I told him." Harlan suddenly remembered. "He said he wanted to help me!" The memory seemed to jar him. "*Yeah.* That's exactly what he said! Then…nothing. It all

48

goes black. The next thing I remember, is wakin' up in that damn motel and seein' that poor black girl…" He looked like he was about to vomit as he pointed with his left hand. "I heard footsteps comin' down the hallway outside and I quick, grabbed a chair and hitched it under the knob."

"Why?"

His eyes filled with terror. *"They were comin' for me."*

"They who?"

His face was desperate and grasping for elusive straws. *"I don't know!* Damn, I wish I could answer that for you! But all I remember from that god-awful moment is that I felt like a ton of bricks had dropped on me right then. I yelled real loud so whoever was on the other side of the door would go away and then I grabbed the phone and dialed 9-1-1. I read the address of the motel off the piece of paper under the glass on the table by the vase of yellow and white flowers, and then I guess I passed out on the bed. Next thing I remember, is bein' in the hospital and havin' some cop read me my rights. Hell, I thought I was still in the damn nightmare at that point. But I ain't woke up since."

Jane remembered Lilith telling her about the dozens of narcissus that made the motel room smell sweet. Who put the narcissus there, she wondered. If a man wanted to impress a woman, he would typically buy roses, not narcissus. It *had* to have meaning, she sensed.

"I didn't do it," Harlan suddenly said. "I didn't kill that girl."

Jane let out a hard sigh. "I know."

He looked confused. "Huh?"

"You were set up."

His pallor deepened. "Hang on, now," he stammered, backing away from Jane. "Who in the hell *are* you?"

"Calm down. I told you. I'm a cop. My name is Jane Perry. I'm a homicide detective with Denver PD."

"You been talkin' to my damn lawyer?"

"No. I talked to the damn girl who set up Jaycee."

"Who's Jaycee?"

"The black girl you're accused of butchering at that motel in Limon."

Harlan crinkled his brow. "Nobody ever told me her name." His eyes traced the ground. "Jaycee…damn…poor thing…" He grabbed his head between the thick palms of his hands. "Dammit to hell, I tell you, everything is just so jumbled up inside my head. It took me days to really wake up after I got arrested."

"You mean, come off the drugs?"

He gazed at Jane as if he'd finally found an ally. He moved closer to her. "Yeah. *Exactly*. Almost like the way I felt after my transplant surgery—"

"Ketamine will do that to you." Jane was now willing to wager a month's salary that Harlan had been drugged with the same stuff they used to disable and kill Jaycee.

"Seriously. You been talkin' to my no good lawyer? 'Cause you seem to know more about this than I do."

"I told you, Harlan. I had a conversation with the girl who admitted she was hired to bring Jaycee to that motel room. And when she dropped her off, they both witnessed you in the bed, naked and unconscious."

"Well, *hell*! What are we waitin' for? Get her in front of a judge!"

"She's dead."

He winced. "You sure?"

She nodded. Jane was not about to go into the grisly details of the bus explosion or the red-haired nut job in a dark suit with the strange crimson mark on his hand. And as far as mentioning the fact that Jane had wiped herself off the radar…well, she'd hold off on that little gem for a while too. "What about your buddy, Rudy? Have you heard from him since you were arrested?"

"No. He just fell off the face of the earth after that night." Harlan looked at Jane with grave fear. "He's probably dead too."

"Why?"

"It just feels like people who know me get dead real fast."

"Feels?"

"Yeah. *Feels*. My head don't tell me much anymore. I think with my heart more now. So, I don't *think* as much as I *feel*. And so far, when I do that, it never fails me." He moved closer to Jane. "Hey! Listening to my heart got me out of that goddamned hospital and away from my bastard of a lawyer!"

Jane was finally able to ask one of the questions that had been weighing on her. "If you're innocent, why run from your lawyer?"

"Aw, hell," he replied, sinking down to the ground and resting his back against a tree trunk. "If you don't already think I'm crazy, you will if I answer that."

Jane regarded Harlan with every ounce of cop insight she could muster. She'd stared into the eyes of murderers, rapists and con men. She'd also looked into the eyes of innocent people who had been accused of heinous crimes. There was often a thin line between the disparity of guilt and innocence and it was her job to detect which way the pendulum swung. The irony here was that after she'd exhausted all logic and weighed the facts, she listened to her heart to make the final judgment. Everything Harlan had told her so far—while a bit bizarre to the unseasoned observer in this world where the unseen often dominates the physical—came from an honest and terrified place. And her own heart told her he was neither crazy nor guilty. Jane sat on the ground across from Harlan so she could be on eye level with him. "I want to know, Harlan. I want to know why you ran." She could feel him silently sensing her sincerity. It was as if his eyes bore holes of insight into her core. "*Tell me*," Jane encouraged.

"My bastard of a lawyer appeared out of nowhere. He come to see me the first day I got transferred over to Denver from Limon. At first, I thought he was just grabbin' for a headline makin' case and as long as he got me a fair trial, I'd take him on. But, the whole time, my heart kept pullin' me away from him in a serious way. I mean, just a few minutes in his presence and I'd feel like I wanted to either run or kill him."

"You wouldn't be the first person who wanted to kill a lawyer."

"No, I'm serious. It was like hardwired into me." He stood straight up, holding an imaginary revolver in his right hand. "I wanted to creep up on the little worm and pop him right in the center of his skull! I'd leave a perfect hole in his head, with just the slightest trace of blowback from the powder around the edge of the wound." For a moment, Harlan oddly warmed himself in the bloody plan. Then, nonchalantly, he turned to Jane, quickly divested from the gory fantasy. "And I really ain't a violent man." He sauntered several feet away "It was a helluva lot more than I didn't trust him. But I could never fix a reason to it." He looked off to the side as a cool breeze swept through the trees and washed over him. "I went along until I knew I had to get away from him and this whole mess." He turned back to Jane, looking her straight in the eye. "Last night, one of the guards told me that my lawyer had called and he had arranged for me to go to the hospital and have my heart checked."

"Why?"

"Said he wanted to know what my physical status was…whether I was well enough to stand trial…" Jane's face showed apprehension. "Yeah, I felt the same thing, Detective. That's why I agreed to only go to the hospital as long as I had my bag with me."

Knowing

"What bag?"

"The bag I've been fillin' up with stuff since my operation. I don't know what the stuff means but I'm thinkin' it's a like a trail of clues to who this is." He pointed to his heart. "I don't have any idea what some of the things mean that I collect but I put them in the bag irregardless."

Irregardless. Jane shuddered.

"I got my notepad in there too," he added. "I've been scratchin' on that thing since damn near two days out of surgery. And it's one helluva clusterfuck of scribbles, pardon my French."

Jane held back a smile since she spoke "French" quite fluently and with obscene abandon at times. "Did they agree to give you the bag?"

"Yeah. My lawyer worked it out. It's in your car." Harlan let out a weary sigh. "When I woke up this mornin', I could feel it wasn't gonna be a good day. I was shackled in my orange jumpsuit and put in a van with my lawyer. The minute I got in that vehicle, I could taste it."

"Taste what?"

"*Death.* And I don't have a damn *clue* what that means, but I'm tellin' you, I was not comin' back to that place except in a body bag. I was so damn scared but ever since my operation, whenever I feel fear, it's as if this powerful understanding jumps into my bloodstream and I ain't afraid no more." He worked hard to make sure he explained it correctly. "And all I got to do is just let it take me where I need to go and I know I'll be okay. It's like…a knowing…so deep that to ignore it is to ignore the air or the sky or the ground beneath you."

Jane recalled Lilith's comment in the bus. "*I should have had a knowing…*" Odd, that sync, Jane thought. "What happened?"

"When they got me to the hospital, my lawyer said he was gonna check on somethin' and that he'd be back soon. They put me in a windowless room with a bed and cupboards full of drugs and needles. An orderly took off my wrist and ankle cuffs and told me to strip and put on a gown. He left me alone but outside my door, was a cop standin' guard. That's when I tasted death again. But this time, it was a *lot* stronger. I was trapped. But somehow…somehow I just *knew* what to do. I blacked out and when I come back inside myself, I was holdin' three syringes that somehow I'd filled up with this clear liquid. I don't remember doin' it and I didn't know what I was supposed to do with them. But then I must have blacked out again because the next thing I remember is sittin' back on the bed and holdin' my bag on my lap. It felt heavier and when I looked inside, there were boxes of the anti-rejection drugs I take every day."

He shook his head in amazement. "Somehow, I just knew they were in the cupboard." Harlan rubbed his head, the day suddenly catching up with him.

"How in the hell did you get out of there without anybody seeing you?"

"The doctor come in and brought the cop with him. *That* made no sense. My heart was beatin' like a bongo drum jacked up on steroids. I looked at the cop and I realized he weren't no cop. But he had a big ass gun and he brought it out of his holster and pointed it at my head—"

"Wait a second!" Jane interrupted. "What's the doctor doing during all this?"

"Absolutely nothin'! Standin' there calm as a cucumber, like he wasn't surprised."

"This guy's got a *gun* to your head and the doctor's not making a move?"

"*Yes, ma'am!* I ain't makin' this up! Like I said, I've had a *bad* mornin'!"

Jane settled back down. "Then what?" she calmly asked.

"I went all Kung Fu on them. I nailed the guy with the gun in the neck with one of the syringes. Then I did the same thing to the doc before he ever saw me comin'. They both went down but the fake cop with the gun kept stirrin'. I still had one needle left so it must have been meant for him. I nailed him in the neck again and he was out like midnight. I grabbed his gun and an extra clip I found on his belt, threw it into my bag, grabbed my shoes and ran out into the hallway. 'Course, I'm wearin' a hospital gown with my fat ass hangin' out the back. So, I ducked into the first room I could find and it was full of lockers. I found an open locker and grabbed this sweatshirt, jacket and these drab drawstring pants. Couldn't find underwear so I'm goin' commando."

"Thanks for the heads up," Jane offered. "I still don't understand how you got out of there without anyone seeing you or any alarms going off."

Harlan stared off to the side. "It happens sometimes. Ever since—"

"Your operation," Jane interjected.

"Exactly. From the moment I woke up from the anesthesia, I could feel this…this…" He struggled, trying to find the words. "Aw, hell. My words ain't gonna make any sense."

"Just say whatever comes to mind."

"Thickness."

"Thickness?" Jane felt a shudder down her spine.

"See? I told you my words wouldn't—"

"A muscular thickness," Jane quickly injected.

Harlan stared at her, stunned. "Yeah," he whispered.

Knowing

Jane felt the same sentient presence at the Quik Mart, on the bus prior to exiting it, and again, diving within her when Harlan attacked her by the tree. "Go on."

"I think it's protecting me," Harlan said. "And sometimes...sometimes it helps me become invisible." Jane scowled. "See! I told you it would sound weird! I don't mean like invisible on radar or security cameras," he quickly clarified. "I mean invisible in that moment. Invisible to those who might want to hurt me or stop my progress." Harlan looked Jane in the eye. "*That's* how I escaped from the hospital. I just walked out and nobody come up to me. I climbed in the back of a delivery truck and hid out under a pile of towels. And after a long bit when the driver stopped at a restaurant, I got out and started walkin'. I walked until I got to that gas station. God as my witness, I was gonna steal that sweet little red pickup but my heart told me to take *your* car instead." He let out a tired breath. "And here I am. I guess it don't get any freakier than this."

"Doesn't."

"Huh?"

"It *doesn't* get any weirder than this."

"Lucky me. I got an educated cop. Just like I had an educated lawyer. I hope you aren't as smarmy as he was." Harlan shook his head in disgust. "The day Mr. Ramos walked in was the day my doorstep darkened."

"*Mr. Ramos?*" Jane whispered. Harlan was wrong. It *did* get weirder.

CHAPTER 5

The gravity of Jane's situation took a hard turn south.

Given what she'd personally experienced that day and what she now knew after listening to Harlan, it was starting to look as if her demise was guaranteed. Death, it seemed, did appear to follow Harlan Kipple.

Death and Mr. Ramos, to be exact.

The problem was that Jane wasn't ready to die. After recently escaping a close call with the Grim Reaper, she'd actually begun to allow herself to live and even love. Since she was a child, she'd been holding her breath and lingering in the dark corners of her psyche. But now, she finally felt safe to exhale and breathe in life. No, death was not an option. Especially not now, *right now*, when she had a short timetable to connect with the person she needed to see.

But Harlan Kipple and his terminal trail of bodies were putting the *kibosh* on her plans. Why is it, she wondered, that every time you think your life is finally on track, a boulder slams onto the path and forces yet another diversion? *Fuck death*, she told herself. But then again, hadn't she already symbolically killed herself when she tossed her driver's license into the wreckage at the bus explosion? Wasn't that meant to create the illusion of her violent demise so the red-haired fellow would believe she was dead? *Just in case.* But then, she wondered, just in case what?

Jane walked into the center of the aspen stand, her mind spinning. She needed to get into her Mustang and floor it until she hit northern New Mexico. She wished she could pretend away everything that had happened over the last six hours. She begged to forget every numinous nudge she'd felt that day. But above all, she wished she'd never met Harlan Kipple because the longer she spent with him, the more empathy she had for his terrifying situation. When all was said and done, Jane Perry's job was to protect and defend the indefensible. It was simultaneously a ball and chain and her saving grace.

Knowing

The irritation continued to chafe as Jane's mind returned to the ostensibly evil individual known as "Mr. Ramos." Harlan wasn't the sharpest tack in the box but he could easily see that Ramos' name kindled an edgy ire from Jane.

"What is it?" Harlan asked, his bushy brown eyebrows narrowing. Jane hesitated. Harlan reached out and grabbed Jane's shoulder with his thick, calloused hand. *"What's goin' on?"*

She looked at him with a gut full of compassion. "You did the right thing, Harlan. Ramos is the one who set you up for Jaycee's murder. If he didn't kill her, then he's the one who arranged the hit." Harlan released his grip on Jane's shoulder as her words sunk in. She glanced to the side. "And then Ramos conveniently became your lawyer with the intention…I would have to assume… of arranging a hit on you when the time was right."

"Are you shittin' me?"

"Look, Harlan. I don't know what kind of mess you're in. But in my business, people are only after you if you know something, stole something or saw something."

He considered her words. "Well, I don't know shit, I'm not a thief and if I saw somethin', I sure as hell don't remember it."

"That's helpful," she deadpanned. "It doesn't make sense but you must be one helluva HVT."

"HVT?"

"High Value Target."

Harlan took in a quick breath.

"What's wrong?"

"I've heard that before but I can't remember where."

"Somebody called you that?"

"No. Not me." He buried his head in his hands. "Oh, shit. I'm gettin' all jumbled up again in my head. It's gettin' worse than ever now. I don't know who I am anymore! I don't know what belongs to me. I can't be sure what *my* memories are because they keep tanglin' up with his."

"His?"

Harlan pointed to his heart. *"His!"*

"How do you know your heart came from a man?"

"I ain't sure how I know, *but I know.* You remember them dreams I told you about? Sometimes in them I pass a mirror or a real still pool of water and I almost catch my reflection. And while I can't see it exactly, it ain't Harlan Kipple lookin' back. It's like when I'm runnin' in that field when I'm…*he…*

when he's a kid…with that .22? I'm so free. So alive." Harlan shook his head. "Goddamnit, I sound plug crazy, don't I?"

Jane would have agreed with Harlan a few years ago. But her own bizarre journey dancing between that thin veil of reality made her a believer. She still used logic as her first approach but the understanding and appreciation of what lurks on the other side was not far behind. "I don't think you're crazy, Harlan."

He looked relieved and let out a grateful exhale. "Thank you. It's hard to explain. You know when you got a guest in your house that you've never met before? Ever notice how it's like the edges around them are real sharp and unfamiliar so they stand out in your house? But if you feel a kind of harmony around them, the sharp edges melt and they begin to blend into the house as if they're part of it. That's the way I feel with him inside me. No sharp edges. He's not a guest anymore. He's part of my house now."

She considered his words, impressed by his explanation. "Maybe…I don't know…whoever's heart you have inside you is helping you sort out the chaos." Jane couldn't believe she said that. It was done to placate Harlan but then it sounded oddly rational.

He nodded. "Yes! That's what I've been thinkin' too." He approached Jane with urgency. "But I think he plays an even bigger role in all this."

"What kind of bigger role?"

"Like maybe there's a connection between *him* and everything else that can't be explained?"

"That's a stretch, Harlan."

"Why? My whole world has been upside down and inside out since I woke up from my surgery. Every day I feel like I'm walkin' a tightrope between different worlds!"

"I'm sure other heart transplant patients feel the same way—"

"No, no, no. Don't patronize me. This is deeper. There *are* connections and I aim to find them."

"How are you going to do that?"

Harlan measured his words carefully. "There are times he takes me over. It's happenin' a lot more now. And when it happens, I keep gettin' drawn to places and people and things that must mean somethin' to him," Harlan pointed to his heart.

Jane needed to tread lightly. "Okay. But maybe it's just left over memories that transferred over somehow when his heart was put into your body." Jane was open to new ideas but even she was wondering what in the hell she was talking about. "Why do you think it has to be bigger than that?"

"Because before I got my new heart, my life was as predictable as day followin' night. For nearly forty years, *absolutely nothin'* of any import happened to Harlan Kipple. Then, slap-bam, I get me a new ticker and I start to go nuts as my world gets crazier by the day. I mean, hello there, I *am* on the run for a murder I didn't commit! Have we forgotten that?! I ain't a smart man but I can put two and two together and it adds up that all this strangeness is connected to *this* heart." He wiped a few more errant leaves from his tangled beard. "Them dreams I've been havin'? They're tryin' to lead me someplace. When I was at The Blue Heron bar that night talkin' to Rudy and I told him how I felt I was on the verge of figurin' it all out, I was plannin' to take a road trip. I was hopin' he'd go with me cause he was the only one who believed me. But then, shit happened."

Road trip. Jane quickly recalled that that was how her day started out as well. And then, shit happened. "What kind of road trip?"

"If I'm gonna find any kind of peace in my life, I need to find out who this is inside me. How do I set myself free if I don't know who I am? Who he is? Who he was? I feel like if I put the puzzle pieces together, everything else will make sense."

"I don't understand. What pieces?"

"The pieces of his life," Harlan said, pointing to his heart.

Jane needed to inject a modicum of reality. "You're on the run for murder, Harlan. A brutal, stem to stern, braining-bashing, death penalty, *murder.* Now, I know you didn't do it, but that's going to be a tough sell now since you escaped custody. Your face will be plastered on every local TV news program. Your mug will be on the Internet and on posters throughout the state. Everybody from your next door neighbor to your first grade teacher is going to whore themselves out on national TV to talk about *you.* What you were like, who you hung out with, on and on. I don't think a road trip is prudent right now."

"I beg to differ." He looked surprised at himself. "There! *Right there!* Who in the hell says, 'I beg to differ'? Not Harlan Kipple! That's *him* talkin' right there."

Jane looked at Harlan askance. "Oh, fuck. You can't go on the run, Harlan! Look, somehow you need to get back to Denver and talk to someone who can sort this out—"

"No and *hell no*! That's *me* talkin'! Mr. Ramos or whoever he works for set me up for a murder I did not commit. And then he tried to off me with the help of a doctor and a fake cop this mornin'! I don't stand a chance in hell of goin' back to Denver and sortin' this out. It ain't the cops I'm mainly worried about. The cops ain't got *nothin'* on the psycho, sons-of-bitches who want me dead! Hey, if they can get a damn *doctor* to sign on to their plan, they obviously have friends in high places! How high up does that go? Lawyers? Judges? Maybe higher?"

"You sound a little paranoid there, Harlan."

"Ya think I might got a right to be?! I'm screwed six ways to Sunday, lady! If I went back to Denver, I bet you biscuits to a bankroll I'd be dead in less than twenty-four hours!"

Jane silently agreed, given the explosive footprint of the *Anubus* coach earlier that day. Yes, someone needed to kill Harlan Kipple and anyone close to him who knew a thing about his faux murder indictment. But why? No, no. She wasn't going to go there. This was not her problem. She had plans, dammit. Personal plans that had a deadline she intended on meeting. "Well, I don't know how you expect to work this out now, given the circumstances—"

"Ain't it obvious? I got your car and I got you...*a homicide cop*, no less! I understand now why my heart led me to jack your ride and not that crappy pickup." Jane stared at him in stunned silence. "We'll lay low tonight and then start out tomorrow...lettin' my heart lead the way. And little by little, I *will* figure out what's goin' on."

"Harlan, you really are delusional," Jane retorted, "if you think you're kidnapping me and my car so you can...find yourself! For God's sake, I've got a gun," she pointed to the Glock secured in the front of her jeans. "I could shoot you and end this right now."

"Aw, hell," Harland said softly, "I got me a gun too *and* an extra clip that I stole off that fake cop. I could shoot you too. But I ain't gonna and you ain't gonna shoot me neither." Harlan's insistence on gunning down the English language was like fingernails on a chalkboard to Jane. But no matter how guilty he was of grammatical dysfunction, his message was accurate. Jane wasn't going to plug him. She just wanted out of that damn aspen grove and away from the growing realization that she was between a rock and a very hard place. "Harlan, I've got personal business in northern New Mexico and I've got a short window of time to take care of that business—"

"That works out fine, actually. See, my heart is pushing me south of here. Well, kinda south and then southwest and then east again and then—"

"Harlan! If I take you with me, I'm harboring a fugitive! I've worked my ass off to get where I've gotten. I've waded through shit and hell to make it to this point. I'm not throwing away everything I've worked for on you!"

He was heartbroken. To Jane, he looked like a puppy—an obese puppy—you want to rescue but you know you'd end up regretting it later on. But then, his expression changed. It wasn't aggressive but it felt very focused and almost otherworldly. It was if he was boring into Jane's mind and rifling through the intricate web of her surging thoughts. "You don't have a choice," Harlan quietly stated, his eyes glazing over as he spoke with a different modulation. "You made your bed this morning. You threw away a part of yourself because you saw something that made you a believer. You're as much on the run as I am." His words appeared to shock him back into his body.

Jane looked at him with guarded courtesy. "How in the hell did you just do that?"

"I have no damn idea. But it looks like you and I are two peas in a dangerous pod."

Oh, shit, Jane thought, as she ran her fingers through her hair. The dye was cast and there was no looking back. Letting out a sigh, Jane resumed her all-business tenor. "You said you've been collecting stuff in a bag and writing down your thoughts? Well, let's see it."

Δ Δ Δ

Jane slid into the driver's seat of the Mustang while Harlan wedged his thick frame into the passenger side. He lifted a dirty burlap sack the size of a small gym bag off the floor of the passenger seat and removed a five-inch black spiral notebook with a faux snakeskin cover. Turning to the first page, he held it out to Jane. On the top of the page Harlan had drawn the letter "R" surrounded by what looked like a diamond. Beneath that was the rough drawing of an animal that looked like a vicious dog.

"What's that?" Jane asked, pointing to the animal.

"A wolf," Harlan said as if it was obvious.

"Of course," she said, rolling her eyes. "What does the 'R' stand for?"

"Hell if I know."

She examined the letter and surrounding diamond closer. "It kind of looks like a shield or maybe a family crest?"

Harlan regarded her with a blank expression. "Okay."

"What prompts you to scribble this stuff?" She glanced through the book.

"Prompts?" he asked with a quizzical expression.

Jane looked at him. "Yeah. You know? What triggers you to write all this?"

"Oh. I don't know. I don't remember drawin' or writin' any of it. But I can tell you that right before it comes through me, my head gets real quiet. I feel this pressure building between my ears and at the base of my head and then as quickly as that starts, it just stops. That's when I see the blue light special and hear the noon day whistle."

"Blue light special? What whistle?"

"It's like this bright, pinpoint of blue light that hovers in the air. And the whistle? Well, it's more like a high-pitched sound I imagine only dogs can hear. It starts in my left ear and crisscrosses over to my right and then somewhere in the middle, it feels like something lights up or gets ignited. Like one of them butane lighters? It feels like I got me a tiny flame in the center of my head and then it begins. I start writin' or doin' things I've never done before. Just like in that hospital this mornin'? Grabbin' the drugs, jabbin' them with the needles?" He rooted through the bag. "Speakin' of drugs, it looks like I picked up more than what I needed for my heart. I got me some Valium, Vicodin and some Oxycontin."

Jane turned to him. "You stole Oxycontin? Jesus, Harlan!"

"*I* didn't steal it—"

"Yeah, yeah, yeah. *He* stole it. Oxycontin? Well, add that theft to your growing list of felonies. That stuff is serious shit. It's synthetic heroin."

"No kiddin'? Wow. I bet it'll make a good tradin' item."

"Trading? What are you, Amish?" She turned her attention back to his notebook. "People who barter for Oxy are not the people we need to hang with."

"Well, I ain't throwin' it away."

"Then do me a favor. Toss it in the glove compartment."

Harlan complied. Sitting back in the passenger seat, he reached behind his neck. Using his thick first finger, he started digging his nail into a single spot directly under his hairline.

Jane glanced at him. "What in the hell are you doing now?"

"I feel like I got something stuck back there. Can you see anything?" He turned his large body in the seat.

Knowing

Jane checked it out but all she saw was a lot of surface irritation and redness from where he'd obviously been rubbing and picking at it on a regular basis. "There's nothing there, Harlan."

"It don't make no sense."

"Well, neither does your notebook." To Jane, it was like reading the mind of a mental patient who was on lockdown. The mysterious "R" framed in the diamond motif was repeated throughout the various pages. Another repeated drawing was a single circle with a dot in the center. Turning the first page, Jane found another rudimentary drawing of a human hand and wrist. On the inside of the wrist, Harlan drew what appeared to be a bird.

"That's a dove," he told her.

"Really? How do you know that?"

"I don't." He shrugged his shoulders. "I just do."

Jane shook her head at his bizarre reply. She continued to scan the notebook, stopping at a sketch of a picket fence with an arrow pointing to the word "blue." "What does this mean?"

"It means that if I'd had a blue colored pencil, I'd have colored that fence blue."

"Blue picket fence…None of this makes any damn sense, Harlan—" Jane turned the page and took in a slight breath. There on one single page, were two numbers repeated over and over again, one on top of the other. It was the number seventeen with the number thirty-three below it, both with a single accent mark after the number. No line separated the two numbers; they just free floated up and down and across the page. "Explain this to me," she said with a gruff tone, holding up the page for him to see.

"That's weird, ain't it? If I saw that in somebody's notebook, I'd think they was one taco short of a combo platter."

"It's got to have meaning. You devoted an entire page to it."

"Ain't got a clue. And I keep tellin' you that *I* didn't do it."

Jane flipped through the pages, stopping at a random spot. "Agna? Is that what you wrote?" She held the page up to him.

"Looks like it."

"Did you mean the name Agnes?"

"I don't know."

"Jesus, Harlan! Work with me, would you? Do you know someone named Agnes?"

He looked cornered. "I don't think so. Should I?"

Jane thought for a second. "Maybe it's the name of one of those women you told me you dream about?"

"Which one? The one with the big boobs? I don't think anyone would name that sweet young thing Agnes. If they did, she'd change her name, pronto."

Jane shook her head and put down the notebook. She stared into the grove of circling aspen trees. "Did you ever try to figure out who your donor was?"

"When I was in the cardiac rehab, there was this real nice nurse. She'd been with me in the recovery area the whole time. Her name was Stella. I *do* remember that name. Every single time I yelled 'Stella,' she'd come on over and ask, 'What is it, Stanley?' Poor gal had a hard time rememberin' my name—"

"Is there a point to this story?" Jane asked, irritation building.

"I'm gettin' there. I like to pace myself when I tell stories."

"Pick up the pace. You got a lot of people after you and I'm trying to help you."

"I had a lot of questions for Stella. I wanted to know when the next meal was goin' to get served because I was always real hungry. I asked her why I got lucky and had a room right across from the nurses' station. I asked her who that guy was who kept sittin' on the left side of my bed the whole time I was in recovery. I asked—"

"Wait. What guy?"

"Never found out. She said there wasn't nobody there and I had no visitors but besides forgettin' my first name, she also obviously couldn't remember my friend—"

"Friend? Why would you assume that?"

"I was out of it but I could tell he didn't mean me any harm. He was a big guy. Real muscular. Kinda thick in the arms and upper body, like he worked out every day."

Jane focused on the words "muscular" and "thick."

"He was like a cop or a bodyguard," Harlan continued. "But he never talked so I can't say for sure what his line of work was."

Jane's gut twisted. "Why would you need a cop or a bodyguard by your bed all the time?"

"Good question. It just felt like he was guarding me. I was pretty out of it when he was there."

"Describe his face."

"That's the weird part. Every time I reach up in my head to bring down his picture, it fades away like vapor. It's kinda like the same block I get with my nightmares. Every time I get to that door and start to turn the knob…"

Jane could see that Harlan was drifting far away. "Hey!" He jumped back to attention. "Did you ask her who your donor was?"

"I'm gettin' to that. I felt so good, so fast that I wanted to know. Stella said she had no idea, that it was hush-hush. But…"

Jane waited. "But what?"

"I think she knew. Maybe not his name but she was there when I had the operation. I can't imagine she didn't see him, even for a second."

"What's her last name?"

"Rich. But it's spelled different. I called her 'Richy,' 'cause that's how it looked on her nametag. But it was spelled R-I-C-H-E. Between Stella and Rudy, I was well taken care of in rehab."

Jane made a mental note of Stella's name. She checked the time. It was 2:30 and her stomach was rumbling from lack of food. "You hungry?"

"I guess. But I can go without food if I have to."

Jane reckoned Harlan could live off his fat reserves for days but she couldn't. However, figuring out how to skillfully find a food source and bring it back to their makeshift campsite was going to be tricky. She had enough water but the thought of eating another bag of pine nuts wasn't appealing. Still, it was better than nothing. She got out of the Mustang and retrieved the Quik Mart bag from where she'd left it on the ground. Sitting back in the Mustang, she rooted through the bag.

"You know, if we need to, we can live off what we can scrounge for 'round here."

"Huh?"

"You'd be shocked how much nutrition is packed in the wilderness. I started really gettin' into that about a year and a half ago. Bought me a bunch of field guides on wilderness foods—"

"Year and a half ago, eh?"

"Yep. Did you know that one cricket has thirteen jam-packed grams of protein? It's true. Did you know that there are approximately one thousand, four hundred and sixty two edible species of insects? Mealworms, included. Like the sayin' goes, 'Red, orange, or yellow, kills a fellow. Black, green or brown, wolf it down."

Jane regarded Harlan with a blank stare and a long pause. "And you know this because you've done this?"

"Once you get over the crunch of the cricket shell, it's all gravy from there."

"Gravy? You sure that wasn't the—"

"I think eatin' bugs was the gateway to my raw meat addictions."

"Oh, just shoot me. It'll be quicker," Jane murmured.

"They say you shouldn't even *touch* raw chicken with your fingers. Ha! I've scarfed half a raw clucker down and lived to talk about it!" He saw that Jane was not enjoying the conversational theme. "But I love *Italian* too and I never did before my operation."

"Italian?" She dug into the plastic bag. "Well, all I can offer you is some pine nuts." Jane handed him the bag.

Harlan regarded the bag in a quizzical manner. "Humph…" He took the pine nuts from Jane and then reached into his burlap sack. "That's one of the first things I put in my own bag." With that, he revealed the same bag of pine nuts. "I can't begin to tell you how many bags of these I ate before it dawned on me that it might actually mean something."

Jane was temporarily frozen. *What in the hell was going on?* Pine nuts are not what she'd call a common snack food and she could count on one hand how many times she purchased them.

"You okay?"

Jane reached her hand into the bag and pulled out *The Q* magazine. "You got that too?"

Harlan effortlessly removed an older edition of *The Q*. "What's goin' on?"

Jane felt a shiver vibrate down up her spine. "I don't know." Her mind raced as a gradual electric prickle engulfed her. "I…" Her head began to throb and her mouth went dry.

"Hey. You okay?"

As quickly as it began, it stopped. Jane tried to center herself. "Maybe you need to show me what else you have in that bag."

CHAPTER 6

Harlan dumped the contents on the dashboard of the Mustang. In addition to the bags of pine nuts, there was also an actual pinecone. A comical illustration depicting a Blue Heron walking tipsily across the road with a drink under his wing was next. A piece of lapis followed with a faux gold imprint of the Eye of Horus. Then came a dog-eared copy of *Autobiography of a Yogi* and a tiny bottle of sandalwood oil. An old cassette tape of a Patsy Cline album surfaced next on the dashboard, cradled in a ten-page newsletter with the name "Eco-Goddesses." An ordinary key was the final item Harlan placed on the dashboard.

"Where'd you get the key?"

"I just found it on the street. I don't think it opens anything because the teeth are too wore down."

"So, we have a key that doesn't open anything. That bodes well—"

"Wait, wait, wait. I forgot one." Harlan pulled out a glittery greeting card with the Archangel Gabriel blowing his trumpet.

Jane felt that damned electrical shiver crest her spine again. The tacky card was the same one she saw at the Quik Mart earlier that day. "You buy that card at the store where you stole my car?"

"Nah. When would I have had a chance to do that? I picked this up about a year ago."

It was just like the damn pine nuts, Jane factored. The odds that Harlan would have the same pine nuts she had purchased along with the identical greeting card she had just seen that day were ridiculously high. Her head throbbed slightly again. It was as though she felt herself being drawn into a web that she was powerless to fight. Part of her resented it and the other part welcomed the challenge. If anything, it might put off her original destination. And maybe that was for the best, Jane wondered. Maybe they weren't meant to meet and that's why this whole elaborate mess erupted. As soon as that inane reasoning swept into Jane's head, she realized she actually was somewhat grateful for this deleterious detour. She picked up the comical illustration of the blue heron walking tipsily across the road with a drink under his wing. "Blue heron. Didn't you tell me you met your friend, Rudy, at the Blue Heron Bar right before your life flip-flopped?"

"Yeah."

"Wouldn't you call that a drunk blue heron? *Blue Heron*? *Bar*? Jesus, Harlan, do I have to draw you *another* picture?"

He shrugged his shoulders. "I'm not clear on where we're goin' here."

"Maybe this has *nothing* to do with…" Jane hesitated. "With your heart or your donor. Maybe this is your subconscious remembering that night after somebody drugged you?"

"And Rudy. Don't forget about him. I'm sure he was drugged too."

"Yeah. That's exactly what this probably is," she cheerfully told herself, embarrassed that she actually entertained the remote possibility that this had anything to do with his heart transplant. "This is *you*!"

"Okay!" Harlan said agreeably.

"Yeah, you had a drink at The Blue Heron bar so you subconsciously found this illustration that represented that."

"Exactly!"

"And then you picked up the bag of pine nuts because after your surgery you were told to eat healthier foods and that was one of their recommendations!"

"Nope! Not at all! In fact, I hate pine nuts. On the Harlan Kipple nut tree, they don't even rank on the lowest branch."

"And now you can't stop eating bags of them," she stated with defeat.

"Yes, ma'am."

Oh, hell. Moving back to the nuttier possibility that there really was some sort of weird connection between his heart and him.

Harlan leaned toward her. "And beer? Don't forget how I can't stand beer now." He said with a wince.

Jane tucked the notebook in her leather satchel. "It all sounds crazier than shit."

"You think?" he said, with dripping sarcasm. "So you understand now why I don't really want to walk back into the police station and tell 'em my story? You think they might just speed book me right through to a prison cell or maybe the nut house?"

He was right. He didn't have a chance.

The hours passed and the sun moved closer to setting behind the Rocky Mountains. Jane felt bloated from two more bags of pine nuts and another bottle of water. Harlan seemed to be handling the food depravation pretty well. He was agreeable and almost childlike in certain slivers of moments. He was the kind of guy who makes the perfect victim. His hulking frame probably hadn't won him a lot of female attention and his solitary, nomadic life driving a truck on the road surely didn't secure a lot of tight friendships. With little education and a narrow view of the world, Harlan Kipple was fodder for anyone who needed a patsy. Even his name, Kipple, was easy to mock. It was as if he was born to be used, abused and then discarded while the plan was carried out with measured agony. Harlan trusted like a child trusted a stranger with a baby bunny. He was ignorance bathed in napalm. And when it all blew up for him, he probably said too much or not enough. Maybe he was so much in shock that he wasn't even aware what he was admitting to? After all, he *was* found nude and covered in the prostitute's blood. Explain that. Did it make sense that he killed her in a bloody rage and *then* decided to shoot some ketamine in his veins to chill after the bloodbath? Yeah, Jane mused contemptuously, that's the typical progression of sadistic killers. Go postal and then schedule a nap in the victim's blood. The fact that his lawyer didn't figure that one...Jane stopped herself in mid-thought. Yeah, his lawyer. The infamous Mr. Ramos. She shook her head. No, Harlan never had a chance.

Jane drew herself into a tight ball on the front seat of the Mustang while Harlan struggled to wedge his fat frame in the small backseat. She'd found two Bronco stadium blankets in the trunk and gave one to Harlan, along with a pair of ski gloves.

"You're like a boy scout," Harlan complimented Jane. "Always prepared."

"Yeah. I'm a boy scout. A boy scout with O.C.D."

Harlan tried to figure it out. "That would be a..."

"Very annoying boy scout," Jane translated.

The night grew increasingly colder forcing Jane to occasionally turn on the ignition and allow the heat to warm them for a few minutes. But the last thing she wanted to do was run out of gas, leaving them stranded. She wasn't tired and neither was Harlan so she struck up a conversation. "Tell me about that charge against you for prescription drug trafficking."

"You make it sound like I knew what I was doin'! I had no idea there were drugs in those boxes. I just picked up the shipment from the same storage unit my brother-in-law always sent me to before I headed to Florida—"

"Wait...what? You agreed to transport cargo that wasn't accounted for?"

"Yeah. I didn't see no harm in it. Besides my brother-in-law gave me five hundred bucks cash for every round trip. That gave me a little extra cash so I could take my wife out for a nice dinner more often."

"Wife?" Jane hoped Harlan couldn't see the shock percolating inside her. "You were married? When?"

"Almost twenty-two years ago. High school sweethearts. I was attracted to her walk and she told me she liked my hair. We had a pretty good run until that tiff with the law. When she found out I'd agreed to help her brother with the interstate deal, she said that was it—that I was no better than her worthless brother and she wasn't going to stay in a marriage like the rest of her worthless family. I was sort of hopin' that she'd reflect and realize that after nearly nineteen years at that point of a fairly predictable life that I was not, nor would I ever be just like members of her worthless family—"

"Harlan! Can we get back on point? Why would you take the hit for your brother-in-law? Why didn't you rat him out?"

"Hey, I was takin' five hundred bucks from him every time for doin' it! I didn't know what was in the boxes, but I *did* take that money. So, the way I looked at it, my hands weren't exactly clean."

"You could have explained all that to your counsel at the time and—"

"Hey, hey, hey, it's all in the past. My brother-in-law made a mistake and I helped him out. And it paid off. When I really was hurtin' and in the hospital, he told me that he'd pay for my operation, seein' as I didn't have insurance no more. And being that he's so damn rich—"

"He's rich? So jockeying up the money for your surgery would be like me buying you a coffee? He bought you and you allowed it."

"I wanted to live. Was I supposed to say 'no'?"

"He obviously survives off the backs of others who do his bidding."

"He knows people in high places. He's the one that got me in with that doctor of mine. I was in bad shape, Jane. I got so bad off, I would have had to perk up just to die. So, my brother-in-law come to see me at the house and saw the state I was in and said that because he owed me one for the rap I took, he was going to call in a favor and hook me up with the best transplant doctor in the business! And he told me I didn't have to worry because my number was going to come up real quick. And it was like he was a TV psychic because my number *did* come up real fast after that. The problem was that the doctor that did my surgery wasn't the same one he hooked me up with. The doctor I was supposed to have was sick or somethin' and so I got his wingman."

Knowing

"Wait…that's how you got your heart?"

"Yes, ma'am. Quite a story, don't you think?"

Jane's head spun. "Yeah. It is. You got preferential treatment. And maybe somebody didn't like that."

"That doesn't make any sense."

"But eating half a raw chicken because that's what your donor had a craving for makes sense?"

"Somebody set me up and wants to kill me 'cause I cut in line? I hope you plan on comin' up with somethin' just a little better than that."

"You said everything changed right after the operation—"

"Changed *inside* me. Not outside me. For nineteen months, nothing much happened. Rudy helped get me some steady work, I was payin' my bills on time, life was regular. Well, except when the nightmares started. I don't know what's behind that dark door but every time I reach down in the dream to open it, this cold sweat just covers me and I know if I open that door, I'm dead. Thank God for Rudy. He always talked me through it. Told me it would pass and gradually it'd all get back to normal.

"Rudy sounds like a fucking saint." Jane was starting to question Harlan's supportive little buddy. It was one thing for a woman to take on the role of a caregiver but men weren't typically genetically inclined toward that predilection. In this dog eat, dog eat world, a male with a penchant for propping up another man with words of constant encouragement and tactile therapeutic assistance tends to look like he has a one-way schoolboy crush. Outside of that possibility, he was overly attentive because he wanted something from Harlan. But it certainly wasn't an intellectual desire or financial strategy since Harlan lacked both attributes. Jane had a picture in her mind of Rudy, from his waiting white bread grin down to his buoyant optimism that was akin to Shirley Temple on crack. Why did Rudy *really* pay so much attention to Harlan Kipple? Between his brother-in-law who pulled the strings and pushed him to the front of the line and his chipper friend who was a little too cloying, the whole thing was beginning to feel surreal and yet strangely meaningful. Somehow, Jane strongly felt that these two individuals were connected to the outcome. "Your brother-in-law put you in the system by making you take the rap. And that prior you had made it easier for the cops when they nailed you for the working girl's murder."

"So, if I wasn't in the system, they would have let me off for the girl's murder?"

Jane stared straight ahead. She didn't want to look at him at that moment because the expression on her face would have melted glass. She explained it again to him but he still couldn't understand why Jane felt animosity toward his brother-in-law. Jane wasn't crazy about naïve victims and Harlan was as much of a sucker as anyone she'd met on the job. She was still attempting to wrap her head around the fact that he was married. Seeing as his wife made her decision based on his hair told Jane all she needed to know about the woman. A few hours passed and their conversation became more sporadic as Harlan started to doze.

"Hey, Harlan?" Jane reached in the back seat and nudged him gently.

He stirred, creaking one eye open. "Yeah?"

"What were you planning on doing before I showed up?"

"Runnin'. Just keep runnin'."

"What were you going to do when you ran out of your medicine?"

"I didn't think that far." He adjusted the Bronco blanket over his body.

"You got your sweatshirt on inside out. Did you know that?"

"Yeah. I ain't a Giants fan. The guy I stole it from must have been one though." He shifted in the seat and lifted the sweatshirt a little bit so Jane could see the front. "It's one of them celebration sweatshirts. Super Bowl forty-two. Giants win over the Patriots. Final score, seventeen to fourteen. Leading receiver was Plaxico Burress."

"What was Plaxico's jersey number?"

"Seventeen."

Jane shook her head. "Figures."

Harlan drifted off to sleep, his fleshy chest heaving up and down the further he fell into slumber. The snoring started shortly afterward; the kind of snoring that would make Gandhi reassess his pacifist bent. It was going to be a long, horrible night, Jane told herself. Reaching into her leather satchel, she pulled out a manila file. Rooting around under the passenger seat, she found her flashlight and lit up the first page in the file. It was a document Hank helped her score. The top of the page had the prison name in New Mexico and below that a booking photo of the dirty blond women with the vacant eyes staring back at Jane. Wanda LeRóy was her name. Jane knew the accent over the "o" was added as a dash of sophistication by Anne LeRóy, Wanda's mother. Wanda's father was named Harry Mills, a dashing gent who loved the ladies and paid particular attention to Anne. The only photo evidence she had of Anne and Harry was the 1967 black and white one paper clipped to the file.

Knowing

There was nineteen-year-old Anne with her lips pursed toward the "tall drink of water," standing in front of the Hayloft restaurant and bar in Midas, Colorado. Jane had memorized and digested every dot in that tiny photo for the last few weeks. Even though she'd somewhat accepted the fact that the tortured mother she always knew had lived a much wilder life prior to meeting Jane's father, she still couldn't believe that the tryst in 1967 between Anne and Harry produced a daughter. Jane had been the oldest member of her small family, looming over her brother, Mike, who was four years younger. But now there was an older, half-sister and as much as Jane didn't want to see any similarities in her sullen booking photo, she had to admit that Wanda and she shared similar eyes and mouths. Given up for adoption when she was two and living in an orphanage, Wanda probably never remembered her birth mother but she retained the name of LeRóy, possibly because it was erroneously believed to be her middle name and subsequently added on her adoption papers.

Based on the information that Hank and Jane found, Wanda had just been released from prison after serving a one-year sentence for theft and drug trafficking. She was living in a halfway house in northern New Mexico and that's where Jane was headed before her life spun out of control. There was a part of Jane that wanted to sit across from Wanda and talk to her. But there was another part that wanted to run from her. She may have been Jane's missing piece to her evolving puzzle, but that didn't make the reality of meeting Wanda and revealing her splintered family tree any easier.

Harlan let out a loud, terrified cry. Jane shone the flashlight in his direction but he was sound asleep.

"*No!*" he shouted. "No, no, no, no....." he mumbled. He held out his hand in front of him as if he were turning a doorknob and then quickly pulled back his hand. His breathing became labored as sweat beads formed across his forehead.

"Harlan!" Jane whispered with authority. He continued to make low grunts and open his mouth as if he were trying to take in more air. A word formed on his lips that sounded like French to Jane. She leaned closer, trying to hear it more clearly. "*Benieu,*" is what it sounded like. French, maybe? Harlan repeated the single word with more emphasis before shaking violently. Jane gently placed her hand on his leg in an attempt to calm him. Suddenly, a jolt of electricity pulsed through her body. A blurred series of staccato images raced in front of her. She quickly lifted her hand off his body and the pictures dissolved, along with the electrifying energy within her. "What the fuck…" she whispered. She stared at him for several long minutes as he shook, moaned and gasped in fear.

Retreating back to her fetal position on the front seat, Jane struggled with the reality of what she was up against. She could ditch Harlan the following day and trump up some story about how she found her Mustang abandoned on the side of the road when she returned to Denver. If her driver's license was ever recovered from the bus crash, she could explain it away with some craftily engineered story. She didn't have to help Harlan Kipple. But she knew that if she did ditch him on the side of the road, her conscience would never forgive her. His damn spirit would haunt her until the end of her days. And she'd spend the rest of her life asking, "What if?"

She sat up and snuck another look at him. He was settling back into peaceful slumber, temporarily relieved from the nightmare that gripped him. The foghorn snore resumed too, vibrating against the roof of the car. Jane let out a tired sigh. She thought again about how Harlan reminded her of a dim-witted puppy you rescue from the kennel. Against your better judgment, you take him home. But you know in the back of your mind you're going to regret it. You know that puppy is going to piss everywhere. You know he's going to forget where his dish is located. You know that when you throw the stick and tell him to fetch he's going to look up at you with those big eyes and that panting mouth with that sloppy tongue hanging out and not have a fucking clue what in the hell you're talking about. You'll tell him to "sit" or "stay" but you might as well be speaking in Norwegian slang because he'll never wrap his thick head around the concept. But by that time, you can't take the stupid mutt back to the kennel because you know nobody else is going to want him and all they'll do is euthanize the poor thing. So, you keep him around and you name him Killer or Rambo because somewhere deep down, you love the irony every time you call his name.

After a bit, you grow to love that dog, even though he eats you out of house and home and has to visit the vet every four months because he's swallowed another rock from the backyard and if the vet doesn't operate, he'll die. But by now, he's grown on you and you feel like nobody else can ever love him like you do. You know that if you were callous enough to dump him on the street, he'd be run over or poisoned from licking puddles of anti-freeze. And so the two of you dwell in the same space for as long as he's meant to live. You become his protector and he becomes your greatest lesson. And the day you have to put him down, you cry like a baby and have to take a day off work because you suddenly realize how much you really loved him, even though he never learned to fetch or stop eating rocks. You recognize that what he lacked in intelligence, he more than made up for with his endearing heart. Then it hits you that it was that heart that attracted you to him in the first place when you saw him trapped in that cage at the kennel. He was pure and somehow you recognized that when no one else could. As long as you live, you'll never forget him because you understand that anything or anyone with a pure heart is rare and should be cherished.

Jane settled back into the front seat. She brought out her cell phone and saw that there was still no coverage. It would take weeks if not months to identify all those burned and shredded bodies from the *Anubus* explosion. But when her ID was finally found in the debris field, Jane knew her cell would start ringing. And the first call would be Hank. He cared deeply for her and that scared the shit out of her. She couldn't really understand why he loved her. What was there to love? She'd been trained by her cop father to see the world as a battleground and every fight that was won only led to another fight. It was exhausting but it was the only truth she knew. She was taught to shut down and take whatever abuse was handed to her. After a while, Jane stopped feeling the physical pain, even though the scars were obvious. She'd been on her own emotionally since her mother died in her arms when she was ten and after that, she was her brother's keeper. But nobody took care of Jane. And that was acceptable because when you don't know what love feels like, you don't miss it. She might have seen the signs of love in a fleeting glance when she passed a couple holding hands or lovers locked in an embrace. But that was *their* reality, not hers. And so she spent the first thirty-seven years of her tortured life building a fortress that would protect her from love and the vulnerability that accompanied it.

Her detached heart had always been a quiet blessing to Jane. A cold comfort that reminded her of the dark world we spin around every day. It was easy to dive into a homicide case and use her mental prowess to solve it. Her heart was always present and engaged but stretching a healthy distance from the tragic interplays was vital for Jane's sanity. However, that consoling ritual of separation had destroyed any chance of a meaningful personal interlude. Trust had always been the enemy because for Jane to do such a dangerous thing, she had to ignore the arguments in her head and fall heart first into the void. And when she fell, there would be nothing there but faith to catch her and the prayer that this time, for the first time, it wouldn't end in a blaze of regret.

And yet, as hard as she fought it, it still happened. Somehow, the cosmos went off kilter and a planet must have turned retrograde, because out of nothing, Hank appeared in her life and gently worked his way into her caged soul. "You need an older man," he told her with that youthful grin. "You'd weaken a younger one." When she momentarily backed away from him, he would hold her and say, "Think with your heart, Jane."

As their accidental attraction turned into more than a passing infatuation, Jane did allow her heart to open. But now that they'd been apart for a handful of days, the enemy known as the mind began to question everything. He was too good, she told herself. Pain had been replaced by passion, but that was always short lived, she lectured herself. It was only a matter of time before it imploded. Her head didn't want to permit her heart to love. "Our fear of pain," she once read, "is stronger than our love of love."

So Jane did what she was programmed to do. She removed the battery from her cell phone and slid it, along with the phone, into the glove compartment. It was better this way, she told herself. Her ceremonial "death" was necessary, given the magnitude of the situation she was now committed to investigate.

Sleep came but it was sporadic and filled with cries and screams that didn't belong to her. The only thing Jane could vaguely remember was the sense of a giant net descending over her and an encroaching fear that her life was about to turn upside down.

CHAPTER 7

Jane felt the rising sun warm her cheek and stirred. Peering out the front window of the Mustang, the icy sheen of frosty crystals against the glass chilled her weary bones. A thin layer of spring snow covered the dirt. Within a few hours, it would be gone but Jane knew too well that April was a changeable month. Just when you think Colorado will accept the invitation, break the back of winter and cough up spring, it shows up to the party with a sudden blast of wet snow, crushing the warm days of renewal and promise. Spring is the gift for enduring winter's penance but one has to earn that gift. Letting out a sigh, she saw her breath. This was insanity. They couldn't hide out here another night. Besides food, Jane wanted a warm room and decent bed. She also desperately required wireless access so she could research all the cascading questions racing through her tired head.

The piercing sun streamed through the aspen grove, washing the white barked trees in a crystalline, golden light. Jane was drawn to one aspen tree and noticed what looked like an eye with Cleopatra kohl outlining it. Checking out the other aspens in the tight circle, she realized all of them shared the same mysterious, naturally occurring outline in the bark. How odd, she factored, that she'd never noticed it before. But now, the more she stared at the tall, slender trees washed in the luminous morning sun, that's all she saw. "Eyes" everywhere, rimmed with black and staring at her.

She sat back and felt the shallow breathing take over. It was a callback to the past when taking in too much air felt dangerous. Jane glanced in the rearview mirror at herself. Dark circles were evident as was a generally haggard appearance. She wasn't bouncing back from a rough night like she used to. While Harlan continued to snore and sleep in the backseat, Jane brought out a piece of paper and jotted down what they needed. She knew there would be a lot of eyes out there looking for her classic ride. Staying off the main highways was a necessity but that would sure as hell slow the trip down to New Mexico. But first things first. She nudged Harlan in the leg. It took another harder push to awaken him. "Come on, Harlan," Jane stressed. "Wake the hell up!"

After he relieved himself outside the car and stretched his rotund podgy frame, Jane directed him back into the back seat and covered him with blankets, coats and anything else she could find. "No matter what happens," she warned him, "stay under those blankets until I tell you it's safe."

They motored down the dirt path and back onto the frontage road. About a mile later on the left side, Jane stopped the Mustang and told Harlan to stay put. She grabbed a screwdriver from her tool chest in the trunk and turned to the acres of trashed cars and dead trucks that littered the area. Jumping the rickety fence, she entered the lonely lot and scanned one vehicle after another. When she found a relatively clean looking, out-of-state license plate, she removed it from the vehicle. By the time she returned to the Mustang, she had four decent plates from four different states. She decided on the one from California, and carefully peeling off the tags from her own plates, Jane reapplied them to the bogus ones. After screwing the plate onto her car, she stepped back to briefly admire her handiwork. This was the beginning of the subterfuge, she warned herself.

"We're making a stop in about half an hour," Jane told Harlan, who was still buried underneath the blankets.

"Food?" he mumbled.

"Later. We've got more important things on our plate."

It took longer than half an hour because all the side roads and back roads chewed up more time. She drove into the parking lot at 9:15 that morning where *The Tat Palace* was located and glanced around the vacant area. Like other areas, it had been hit by the economic downturn, leaving more abandoned businesses to choke out the ones that were still gasping for their financial futures. *The Tat Palace* was on life support but then again, just like bars, the customers don't normally congregate until afternoon or evening. From what she could discern from the solo pickup truck in the parking lot, Alex, the owner of the place, was the only one inside. Jane drove the Mustang around back and parked it in a shaded spot away from any prying eyes. She donned her leather jacket and pulled out a *Rockies* ball cap she found underneath the passenger seat. "Wait here one second," she advised Harlan, donning the cap and pulling it down so that it hid her eyes. She grabbed her leather satchel and got out of the car, tracing the building for security cameras. As Jane expected, there was only one by the side entrance. Returning to the Mustang, she helped Harlan extricate himself from the car and, after covering his head with a blanket so that only his eyes showed, she led him to the door of the business.

Knowing

Once inside, there was a small anteroom with a heavy black velvet curtain that separated them from the main room. Jane closed the door quietly and locked it, pulling down the greasy curtain for extra security and turning the sign so it read "closed." Using hand signals, she motioned for Harlan to wait for her and to be quiet. Peeking through the black velvet curtain, Jane could see that Alex wasn't in the main room. With stealthy precision, Jane entered the windowless room and waited. The walls were filled floor to ceiling with six-inch square cards that displayed the available artwork that Alex Delaney could ink onto your body for a ridiculously high fee. A small sign above the door to the back room read: I'D RATHER BE PISSED OFF THAN PISSED ON! Jane could hear the low hum of a radio playing heavy metal in the background and the sound of footsteps.

"Christ on a cracker, Perry!" Alex said, as he walked in. "What in the fuck are you doing here?"

"You sound just like my second cousin last year when I crashed the family reunion," Jane calmly retorted.

Alex stood his ground—all five foot seven of his tough, life-beaten body. The forty year old's greasy black hair was pulled back in a half-ass ponytail and his flesh was covered with so many tattoos that he looked like a walking mural. Even though Alex had been rotating in Colorado most of his adult life, he still retained the Boston edge in his voice. "Whatever the fuck it is, I didn't do it!" He started to retreat back into the back room.

"Hey! We're not done. I gotta talk to you!" Jane insisted.

He eyed her carefully. "You look like shit."

"Keep this up, Alex, and I'm gonna feel like you're my extended family that I never talk to."

"You look shook up. You back bending your elbow again?"

Jane regarded Alex with a thick-skinned stare. She turned slightly to the black curtained area, hoping to hell that Harlan couldn't hear everything. "I have no idea what you're talking about."

"Oh, come on. Word on the street was that you put down the bottle."

"The street, huh? Must be a slow news day on the street." She needed to move forward. "Look, here's the—"

"You used to buy whiskey by the case!"

Jane took several steps toward Alex. "You buy bread by the slice?" She scanned the area quickly. "We're alone, right?"

Alex eyed her cautiously. "Yeah..."

"You got cameras in here or in the back room?"

"Nothin' in the back. Got one in the corner over there." He pointed to a small camera in the corner behind Jane's head.

"Turn it off. And turn off the outside one while you're at it."

"What the fuck's goin' on here, Perry?"

"*Do it!*"

"*Why?*" Alex moved toward her. "What have you ever done for *me*?"

"Oh, hell, that's rich! If it weren't for me, you'd still be serving time for fraud. I went to bat for you with the judge. You got five years plus time served instead of ten years because of me. So, yeah, Alex, you *do* owe me."

"Motherfucker..." he mumbled under his breath as he flipped off the security feed. "Okay. It's off. State your business."

"My friend and I need some ID—"

"Are you fuckin' kiddin' me, Perry? I could go back to prison for this—"

"Well, we need to move past that—"

"*Move past that*? What? Have you jumped to the dark side?"

"Not yet. Look, how long is it going to take for a few IDs?"

He looked her straight in the eye. "I got out of the business."

Jane couldn't believe how obvious the lie looked. "Bullshit. I can smell your laminator in the back room!"

Alex pulled back, his eyes showing pinpricks of fear but his face doing everything to hide it. "Is this a set up? Is that what this is? You tryin' to trap me?"

"I don't have a lot of time, Alex. I need some good, fake IDs and you're going to make that happen for me."

"And if I don't?"

"Oh, fuck..." Jane hated having to dish out threats. "How about what if you *do*? Here's my offer. If you agree to help me—*and you will*—I will personally make the phone call and get your little brother transferred to a prison that is closer to you and your mother. It sucks driving more than two hundred miles to see him, right? And your mom? Last I heard, she's not doing well—"

"You fuckin' leave my mother out of this, Perry!"

"All I'm saying is that it would be easier for her to know she was only forty-five minutes or less away from her youngest son. I can make that happen for you, Alex. But first, you're going to do what I tell you to do. And you're going to keep your fucking mouth shut about it."

He stood there with steam coming out of his nostrils. "I hate it when people put me over a barrel."

Knowing

"Well, it beats getting bent over a barrel in Federal prison, which is exactly where you'd *still* be if it weren't for me! So, let's get started." She crossed to the black velvet curtain and motioned toward Harlan to walk into the room. "This is my friend, Alex."

Alex's mouth dropped open. "Holy fuck." He swallowed hard.

Harlan looked at Jane. "I never had anybody say that before when they met me."

"Shit, Perry!" Alex yelled, running his dirty fingers through his greasy crown. "What in the fuck are you doin' with—"

"This is Harlan Kipple—"

"I know who the fuck he is!" Alex screamed, as his Boston accent bled through. "It's all over the fuckin' TV!"

Harlan leaned closer to Jane. "He's real tight with that word, isn't he?"

Jane shot Harlan a look. "So am I—"

"Fuck yeah, asshole!" Alex bellowed across the room to Harlan. "There's a bounty on your head! I got a gun and I can shoot your mother fuckin' ass—" He turned to Jane. "You sure you're not back on the bottle, Perry? 'Cause these are the freaks you attract when you fall off the wagon!"

"How much is the bounty?" Jane asked, attempting to halt the intimidation.

"Twenty-five thousand bucks for information leading to the whereabouts of that fuckin' killer!" Alex proudly stated.

"That's all?" She turned to Harlan. "Man, I'd be pissed if I were you. Don't you think you're worth more than twenty-five grand?" She spun back around to Alex. "Shit, Alex, twenty-five grand is nothing when you consider the priceless cost of being a stone's throw from your little brother for the next fifteen years. What's that come out to per year?" She turned to Harlan who looked stumped. Jane worked the numbers out in her head. "It's around one thousand, six-hundred and seventy. That's…" She quickly worked the numbers, "That's a hundred and thirty or so a month."

"You're confusing me, Perry!" Alex insisted.

"It's just basic math, Alex. You are actually willing to take a measly one hundred and thirty bucks a month and turn this man in when you could be putting that cash toward gas in that same month to go see your brother." Jane moved closer to Alex. "Your mother doesn't have fifteen good years left, Alex. She doesn't have five and you know it. So why don't you get off your fucking high horse and think about your poor mother and how important it would be for her to see her youngest felon more often. Think of the memories she'll have, talking to him through the glass. Think about what that'll mean to *him* when she dies and he can know that *your* actions made it possible for him to see his sick mother on a regular basis before she left this world. Are you thinking about that right now? Because I am! I'm getting a fucking chill just thinking about it."

Alex looked completely baffled. He was trying to link point A to point B and then point C and still coming up short. "I have your word on this, Perry?" His voice was shaking for the first time.

"You have my word. The same word I gave you when I told you I'd talk to the judge on your behalf. That worked out pretty good for you. And this will too."

Alex threw Harlan a harsh glare. "I don't want to know anything. You hear me? I don't want to know nothing about why you're doing this. That way, when the cops question me—"

"Why would they question you, Alex? You're keeping your mouth shut, *remember*? You don't keep your mouth shut and your baby brother gets his ass transferred to Florida." Jane had no ability to make that happen but she was a better liar than Alex and followed up with a stern expression to lock in her threat. "Just the thought of that happening will kill your mother."

Alex sent fiery balls of hatred toward Jane. "Fuck you!"

"That's the spirit!" Jane clapped her hands and followed Alex into the back room while Harlan brought up the rear.

A small television was on in the corner of the room with the sound off. The small space smelled of burning plastic, toxic glue and cigarette smoke. Alex lit up a cigarette and headed over to his computer.

"You mind blowing that smoke in another direction?" Jane asked Alex.

"What are you talking about? You smoke like a fucking chimney!"

"I gave it up for Lent," Jane replied with an edge.

"Newsflash, Perry. Lent is over and you ain't Catholic. The day you turn Catholic is the day I grow tits."

"Hey!" Harlan interrupted. "Can you two catch up another time?" He pointed to the muted television. "I think we got more important things goin' on here!"

The screen showed Harlan's booking photo.

"Turn it up," Jane instructed him.

Harlan grabbed the remote and hit the volume button. The story cut to a woman being interviewed by a reporter.

"Aw, hell, that's my neighbor, Bonnie," Harlan said, slack-jawed.

"I'm telling you," Bonnie said, "none of this makes any sense! I've known Harlan Kipple for ten years. He's a good man with a good heart…"

"You hear that, Jane?" Harlan said, touching his chest. "A good heart."

"Why do you think Mr. Kipple escaped from custody?" the reporter asked Bonnie.

"I don't know! All I'm telling you is that Harlan Kipple is not capable of doing what they claim he did!" Bonnie stated with emphasis.

Alex selected the computer file he needed to make the IDs. "Yeah, right. I wish I'd had four more just like *her* when I got sentenced!"

"The difference is that you were guilty." Jane said.

Harlan glanced at Jane with a grateful look.

"If I was you, Perry," Alex said, carefully watching Harlan across the room. "I'd be sleeping with both eyes open. Jeffrey Dahmer didn't bother anybody either. Except for the people he ate, of course."

"I didn't do what they say I did!" Harlan pleaded. "I got set up!"

"Yeah, you and every other sick fuck—"

"Turn off the TV, would you?" Jane asked Harlan, who obliged. Alex grudgingly continued to search the templates on his computer to create the Colorado IDs while Jane studied the walls. There were more illustrations of tattoo designs, including a wall titled "The Top 20." Among the most popular were the usual doves, roses and barbed wire wraps. But there was one that looked like a vessel, another that appeared to be a long-legged bird, the Eye of Horus and a circle with a single dot in the center. Jane grabbed her leather satchel and retrieved Harlan's mysterious notebook. Turning the pages, she found the circle with the dot in the center and, in the bottom corner of the second page, a rough sketch that looked like the strange vessel on Alex's wall.

"What's this?" Jane asked, pointing to the vessel card on the wall.

Alex looked up from his computer. "Some Egyptian shit. That's what's popular right now. Fuckin' pyramids and the Eye of Horus. I had a guy come in here and ask me to ink the Eye of Horus right here." He pointed to the middle of his forehead.

"Did you do it?" Harlan asked.

"People are into making statements. I'm into paying my rent! Yeah, of course I did it!"

Harlan grimaced. "That'd be kinda weird, wouldn't it? When he's asleep, he'd always have that eye in the middle of his forehead that's open."

"It beats the hell outta what you did to that prostitute."

"Enough!" Jane yelled. "How much longer is this going to take?"

"My computer is slow," Alex replied with venom.

"What's the point inside the circle mean?" Jane asked.

"Fuck if I know," Alex mumbled.

"Bullshit!" Jane said. "You're going to tell me that you never ask these people what the symbols mean? They're having you permanently imprint them on their flesh. It means something to them and you never once were curious to find out why? How do you know you're not inking some sort of racist shit on them?" Jane purposely threw out the "r" word to elicit a response.

"The circle with the dot is not racist!" Alex countered, turning his attention away from the computer momentarily.

"So you *do* know what it means?" Jane stressed.

"Some woman told me it's a symbol for 'the focus within,' whatever the fuck that means. She was one of those Hindu chicks and she rattled on about the dot symbolizing the point of focus within the circle of the sun that blended the male and female forces." He rolled with eyes with exaggeration. "All I see when I look at that is a fuckin' eyeball staring back at me."

Jane looked at the wall again. Now that Alex mentioned it, she realized how much it did look like an eyeball. A delicate flower drawing caught her eye. "What's that one?" she asked, pointing up to it.

Alex squinted toward the drawing. "Narcissus."

Jane's antenna went up. "No shit? So why is that grouped in with the Egyptian-themed designs?"

"Apparently, it has to do with death and the underworld," he said with a roll of his eyes.

Another puzzle piece clicked into place. The set-up at the Limon motel with Harlan and Jaycee had ritualistic overtones. "And the long-legged bird? What's that?"

Alex returned to his computer. "It's got a strange name. Starts with a "B." Benet. Bennus—"

"Benieu?" Jane asked.

"Yeah. That's it. B-E-N-N-U. It's the Egyptian equivalent of the phoenix."

"Okay." Jane contemplated. She'd had a case a couple years prior where birds were used as metaphysical symbols.

"Let's get goin' on this," Alex instructed. "I want you outta here sooner rather than later." He grabbed his camera and looked at Harlan. "What's the fuckin' point of him looking like he does right now on a fake ID?"

Jane considered his point. "You're right. You got a razor and scissors?"

"I'd rather he didn't touch my shit," Alex said with a turn of his upper lip.

Jane took a menacing step toward Alex. "And I'd rather not be having this conversation with you right now, but here I am. Get me a fucking razor and a pair of scissors."

Alex retreated reluctantly to the bathroom, returning with an electric shaver and a scissors. Jane took them and handed them to Harlan. "Shave off your beard and cut your hair really short."

Harlan swallowed hard and walked into the bathroom. Jane sat down on a lopsided stool in front of a soft blue background screen and Alex took several headshots.

"You know what you're doing here, Perry?" Alex whispered to her.

"I got it covered," she stated.

"Am I going to turn on the TV in a couple days and hear that you're his next victim?"

Jane felt a shudder go down her spine. "He didn't do it. I have witness testimony to back it up."

"Then why are you running if you got a witness?" Alex kept his voice muffled.

Jane turned to the bathroom, hearing the buzz of the razor. "Because she's dead."

Alex stared at her. "Jesus, Perry. What have you got yourself into?"

Jane turned to the bathroom. "How's it going in there, Harlan?"

He peeked outside the door. Half his tangled beard was gone from one side of his face and the crown of his head looked like a weed-whacker had chopped off his messy locks. "It's goin'."

Five minutes later, he emerged from the bathroom, clean-shaven and with a shockingly different appearance. Jane grabbed the scissors and quickly sheared off more of his hair in order to make it look even. By the time she was finished, Harlan looked like a bowling ball secured on an Easter ham.

Alex took several photos of Harlan and, after importing them into his computer, he went to work creating the fake names and information. "We'll start with you," Alex said, pointing to Jane. "What name do you want on this?"

"Anne LeRóy. With an accent over the 'o.'"

"You came up with that name pretty quick," Alex said with an arch of his eyebrow as he input the information.

Jane rattled off an old address from the past to use on the ID.

"Weight?"

"Put one twenty," Jane said.

Alex added the finishing touches on the ID but Jane stopped him before he closed out the window with her photo. "I want another one. But this one is going to have the name of Wanda on it. Wanda LeRóy."

"You don't look like a Wanda," Harlan offered.

"She doesn't look one twenty either, but we're still slapping that on the card," Alex groused.

"Wait a second," Jane interrupted, "Change the name to Wanda Anne LeRóy."

"What's the address on this one, Wanda Anne?"

Jane gave it a thought. "Three eleven Harry Mills Street, Midas, Colorado. Put January 11th, 1972 as the birth date."

Alex complied. "Why January 11 of '72?"

"That's my birthday."

"Why are you putting your real birthday on a fake ID?" Alex asked.

"Be like Nike and just do it, Alex."

When it came time to concoct the ID for Harlan, there were a few minutes of discussion as to what fake name they should use. Alex suggested "Charles Manson" and then "Wilbur" in a mocking manner. Jane figured they needed a name Harlan could relate to.

"What was your dad's name?" she asked.

"Llewellyn Hartley Kipple," he replied.

Jane looked at Harlan. "*Hartley*? Are you kidding me?"

"What?" Harlan asked, totally lost. "I didn't name my dad."

"Switch it around," Jane told Alex. "Make it Hartley Llewellyn."

It took Alex another thirty minutes to transfer the computer images to the printer, layer the security imprints and then laminate them into incredibly realistic Colorado IDs.

Jane examined them with a critical eye. "You do great work, Alex."

"Thanks. Now get the fuck outta here."

Jane reached into her wallet and brought out two, one hundred dollar bills. She handed them to Alex who seemed shocked by the gesture. "You think I expected you to do it for nothing?"

Alex softened just a bit. "You still going to make that phone call and get my brother transferred?"

"I told you I would, didn't I?"

"People say a lot of things."

"Yeah, well, the difference is when I say something, I actually mean it." She gathered up the IDs, secured them safely in her satchel and motioned for Harlan to head toward the door. But before they left, Jane turned to Alex. "One more question." She brought Harlan's notebook out again and opened it to the first page where the mysterious "R" inside the diamond was located. She pointed to it. "Ever seen that?"

Alex took a long hard look at it. Without commenting, he carried the notebook to the counter and pulled out an enormous binder filled with tabbed sections. Turning to one that was labeled, "Roman Symbols," he scanned the pages until he found what he was looking for. Turning the large binder toward Jane, he stabbed the picture with his finger. "What about that?"

Jane stared at what looked like an ancient coat of arms. Awash in maroon colors and trimmed with golden yellow, a regal looking "R" filled the crest with a smaller depiction at the base of the letter that looked like a female wolf with her teats descending. The "R" had the same swirls and ornate look that Harlan drew in the notebook. "Harlan, come here," Jane said, ushering him quickly to the counter. "Does that ring any kind of bells for you?"

Harlan gazed at the page, seemingly being pulled into it like a magnet.

"Hey!" Jane said, punching his shoulder. "Don't do that. Don't disappear on me!"

Alex leaned closer to Jane. "I saw this kind of shit with a guy in a prison. They call it dissociation."

"Thanks, Alex. I got this," Jane replied in a tense tone.

"Something triggers him," Alex quietly stressed in a pseudo confidential manner.

"I'm aware of that!" Jane exclaimed. Turning back to Harlan, she forced him to look her in the eye. "Harlan! Does this mean something to you?"

He stared at the drawing. "Yes," he whispered.

"Where have you seen it before?" Jane asked.

He shook his head. "I don't know," he said, starting to slip away again.

Jane slapped him hard on the arm. "Stay with me, goddammit!"

Harlan snapped out of it. "Hey!"

Alex stepped back. "Fuck, Perry! Don't get him riled!"

She held the page up to Harlan's face. "What does this mean? What does the 'R' stand for? *Think*, Harlan."

Harlan's breathing became labored and he started licking his lips nervously.

"Jesus, Perry!" Alex cautioned. "He's gonna fuckin' blow!"

"Stop it!" Jane said to Alex before putting the drawing back into the binder. "Get him some water and let me use your computer."

Alex was more than happy to remove himself from the room. Jane dragged over a chair for Harlan and then spun around the counter to Alex's laptop. Pulling up the search engine, she entered "'R' maroon and golden yellow she-wolf." One entry came up and she clicked on it. It was the crest of "Roma," an Italian football club based in Rome. The colors were identical to the ones on Alex's drawing and there, at the top, was a more defined depiction of the she-wolf with two human babies beneath the animal, suckling on it. Jane turned to Harlan. "Does Roma ring a bell?"

Harlan stared into the air. "Rom—"

"What's that?" Jane asked with irritation.

He turned to her. "The word starts with 'R-O-M' but it's not Roma."

Alex returned with the glass of water and quickly gave it to Harlan before retreating behind the counter. "You need to get outta here, Perry."

"Give me a second," she said, scanning the page on the computer. At the very bottom were two short paragraphs.

The gold symbolizes God while the maroon symbolizes imperial dignity. The club's symbol is inspired by the myth of the creation of Rome. In that story, twin brothers, Romulus and Remus, are thrown into the River Tiber by their uncle. A she-wolf rescues the babies and suckles them, nurturing them as if they were her own.

As they grow into men, they take revenge on their uncle before Romulus kills his brother, Remus. Romulus goes on to become king of Rome—a city named in his honor.

Jane looked over at Harlan. She felt a surge of electricity bore through her before she even said the word. "Romulus?"

He quickly turned to Jane as if a light just went on in his brain. "That's it! *Yeah*. That's it!"

"Okay, you got what you needed," Alex said, reaching out and slamming down the top of his computer. "Get outta here!"

Knowing

Jane instructed Harlan to once again cover his head with the blanket. "Alex, even though you're a son-of-a-bitch, you've been a lot of help." She held out her hand to him.

He shook it warily, keeping one eye on Harlan the entire time. Leaning forward, he whispered in her ear. "Don't die, Perry."

"You're just worried something's going to happen to me and I won't be able to make that phone call for your brother."

"That's what I meant," he said, coolly eyeing Harlan across the room.

"For a second, I thought you were actually worried about me."

Alex looked at her and for a moment, it was as if he wanted to rescue her. But then his need to protect himself took over and he nodded.

She walked with Harlan to the black curtain. "Give us five minutes and then you can turn the security cameras back on."

Alex remained silent. But Jane detected a fear in his eyes that she couldn't shake for nearly a half hour.

Δ Δ Δ

Jane tore a blank page out of Harlan's notebook and jotted down a note to remind her about following up with Alex's brother. Harlan retreated to his hiding place on the backseat, under the blankets.

"So...how long you been off the bottle?" Harlan asked with shaded reluctance.

Fuck. Jane was not into dissecting her personal life with the few people she trusted, let alone someone she'd only known for twenty-four hours. "Going on sixteen months."

He peeked out from the blanket. "You're...pretty much...you know... over that problem?"

This was amusing. A guy accused of bashing in the head of a prostitute in a flop motel was uneasy about his rescuer's former lifestyle. "Let's just get it out in the open, okay? I was a drunk for a lot of years, since I was fourteen. As I got older, I couldn't stop at just one. If I drink one beer, I'll drink the bar. So, now I don't drink anymore. Any more questions?"

He thought for a second. "You miss it?"

Jane wasn't prepared for that question. "Yeah. Sometimes, I miss being able to disappear." The minute she said it, she heard the irony. Somewhere around the debris field left by the *Anubus* explosion was her discarded driver's license. She might not have had a drop to drink in more than a year but her addiction to running away was obviously still engaged.

"How come you want to disappear?"

Shit. If Jane sought out this line of questioning, she'd locate an A.A. meeting. She cleared her throat in an attempt to center herself. "Because it's easier than the risk of getting too close. You get too close and—"

"You start to care," Harlan said nonchalantly.

Jane silently agreed. "And then it ends." She looked out the side window. "And the pain paralyzes you."

He stared at her. "You really did get yourself hurt in this life, didn't you?"

She looked in the rearview mirror at him. "I don't know much else, Harlan."

"What do you mean? Are you dying? Are you sick? Are you convicted of a felony?"

"No."

"Then you're gold, Jane. If I were you, I'd start livin' and let yourself enjoy life. You never know when it's really gonna hit the crapper. I'd pay somebody right now if they could make me feel happy again."

She heard Harlan scrounging around. "What are you doing?"

"You got anything good to read around here?" he asked.

"I might have a few old newspapers or a magazine floating around somewhere." Jane cruised down a back road, making sure to keep at or just under the speed limit.

"Where to next?"

"Gotta get some food for us and other stuff. I'm keeping my eye out for a motel."

Harlan continued rooting around on the back floor for something to read. "I was doin' my countin' thing at Alex's place. There were three chairs in the front room and five in the back room. All of them were brown except for two that were black and had torn seat cushions. And he had one hundred and twenty one of them tattoo cards on his wall—"

"One twenty one?" Jane eyed Harlan in the rearview mirror. "You sure?"

Harlan regarded her as if she were a bit stupid. "*Yeah.* Why?"

She thought back to the *Anubus* the previous morning. Bus 121. "That number mean anything to you?"

"No."

"You *sure?*"

"Yeah, I'm sure. Why?"

The coincidences were getting too close together. Jane grabbed a pen and scratched "121" down on a scrap of paper. "I don't know. It's all gotta mean something."

"I had them nightmares again last night."

"I know. I tried to wake you up but you were pretty much gone." She almost mentioned the strange electrical pulse she felt when she touched him but decided against it. "You remember any of it?"

Harlan didn't answer right away. "I know you don't want to hear it but it's not me in the dreams or the nightmares. It's him."

"And you know this how?"

"Like I told you, the one with the young kid in the meadow shootin'? That's not me. I look down at my hands, and they don't look like what mine did when I was that age. Same thing with the nightmare. I'm turnin' that doorknob and it's not my hand."

"It's a nightmare. A dream. Why don't you tell yourself before you go to sleep that if you find yourself in that place again, to turn the knob and see what's on the other side of the door? It's called lucid dreaming—"

"No. You don't understand, Jane. I can't do that. Every time I touch that doorknob, I feel like every evil thing that ever existed in this world is movin' around me and tryin' to suck me into their darkness." He turned on his side to get comfortable. "It's *his* world, not mine."

They drove another five miles in silence until Harlan spoke up.

"You got kids?"

"No."

"Me neither. Not like the wife and I didn't try. But it's probably good it worked out that way, seein' how it's all turned out for me. You have a lot of friends, Jane?"

"No."

"Me neither. I don't understand a lot of people. I've tried but I just don't get 'em. That's why I liked my truck job. I was my own man out there and it was good. How come you don't have a ton of pals?"

"I don't think most people are worth investing time in. I'm not interested getting drawn into other people's dramas. I get enough of that on the job. Most people are only interested in getting what they need and so they use others to achieve that end."

"I see." Harlan thought about it. "You got a husband?"

Laurel Dewey

She came to a stop sign and rolled to a complete halt. "What do you think?"

He smiled. "Okay. You got a boyfriend?"

Jane hesitated and continued down the road. "I guess I do." It still seemed new. "Yeah. I do. His name's Hank. I think we're on our two-week anniversary. A regular streak, eh?"

"Did you call him when I jacked your car?"

"No."

"Why not?"

"I take care of my own shit. Besides, if I'd called him, I never would have found you and then what would you be doing right now?" She stole another look in the rear view mirror.

Harlan pondered. "That's nice and all but don't you think he's worried about you?"

"He's not worried. He knows I'm on a trip."

"Humph. You sure are." Harlan turned onto his back. "You think he can feel what you're feelin'?"

She eyed Harlan carefully. "What do you mean?"

"When people are real close, I read once how they can melt and become like one person. They can feel each other's fears and pains...even their thoughts."

Jane's mind drifted. She could count how many men she'd been with on one hand and have one finger free. While she shared an uncommon bond with one of them in her early twenties, it was a relationship bathed in drugs, booze and mutual incoherency. Being two souls who were independently drowning in their own tortured addictions, any chance of discovering a shared spiritual consciousness was not going to happen. But it was vastly different with Hank. Perhaps, Jane mused, that's why it scared her so damn much. There was nothing surface to their connection. From the moment he met her, he dove into her head and somehow fished out her fears and then showed them to her in a forgiving light. He wasn't afraid of her as so many others were. He had a knowing about her and she was beginning to allow herself to have the same for him. When Harlan asked her if she thought Hank could feel what was going on, she realized that on some level, he probably could. Without giving a second's hesitation, Jane silently sent Hank a message that she was okay and not to worry. And then, not a second later, she felt a consuming sense of longing. She wanted to touch him and make sure he was still real. She was only temporarily "dead," she told him with her mind's eye and she would resurrect when it was safe.

"My wife and I never had that kind of bond," Harlan continued. "I wish we had but she was a stranger to me most of our life together. She called me a stranger too when she found out what I did for her brother. I just can't imagine what she's thinkin' now, with all that's happened. One minute, I'm livin' the dream in Limon, Colorado and the next, I'm livin' in a nightmare."

Jane came to a four-way stop. She could see a large thoroughfare two blocks ahead. It was a dicey move to navigate in public like this but they needed supplies. "Harlan, you gotta stay under the blankets. No matter what happens, do not sit up."

She drove the two blocks and quickly found herself stuck in traffic that was funneling toward several banners and balloons hanging in the parking lot of a large strip mall. The muffled sound of someone talking on a megaphone could be heard coming from the parking lot, along with the strains of a rock band. This could work out fairly well, Jane figured, if she played it right. She headed into the crowded parking lot, swinging the Mustang away from the loud revelry and parked in a space between two large vans. A Kroger's Market stood about one hundred feet away. Security cameras would be everywhere so she slid her ball cap on and tucked her brown hair up into the cap. A pair of sunglasses finished off the covert ensemble. "I mean it, Harlan. Don't sit up—don't even move. I'll be back in fewer than ten minutes."

Inside the large store, Jane nervously grabbed a small cart and swept up and down the aisles, grabbing bags of apples, bananas, mixed nuts, lunchmeat, French bread, a jar of mayonnaise, cheese and a few other food items. Along the way, she tossed two packages of a camping cutlery combo in the cart, a large bag of ice, and a medium sized cooler. In the refrigerated section, she remembered that Harlan mentioned favoring raw foods. She put two-dozen eggs in her cart and added a gallon of milk. It would all keep in a motel mini-fridge she factored. Swinging the cart quickly down the next aisle, Jane noticed shelves of hair dye. It could come in handy and she chose a box labeled "Cleopatra Black." A few feet past that, was a wall of wigs meant more for a costume party than daily wear. Scanning the selections, Jane grabbed a short blond one called "The Diana." Moving speedily around the store, she snatched up several packs of batteries, twelve bottles of water and more lunchmeat. The adage came to mind that shopping when you're hungry is never a wise idea.

She started to head toward the checkout when she spied a display of pre-paid cell phones. The "throwaway" phones were always used by perps who needed to communicate without being traced. Jane snatched up three of the cheapest models and three, one hundred minute pre-paid cards. She wound her cart around and took one more trip down the aisle. Her eye traveled to a long shelf of beer selections. It wasn't the high-octane stuff since Colorado only allows supermarkets to sell 3.2 beer. But it was the perfect numbing amber Jane could easily score when she was underage and didn't want to risk her father finding out that she'd been pilfering his whiskey. She checked the time. 11:00. It was closing in quickly on the ten-minute window she promised Harlan. Racing to the checkout line, Jane bided her time behind two customers who moved at the speed of chewing gum. The clock kept ticking and with each passing minute, her anxiety level went up another notch. She needed to get out of that store. Five long minutes later, she finally reached the cashier. With the phones, the total was almost three hundred dollars. Slapping the cash on the counter, she helped bag the groceries and powered her way back to the car.

The band was playing even louder in the adjacent parking lot. Jane could hear a man on a megaphone telling everybody about how "Weller" would be arriving any minute. Jane ignored the rest of the announcement as she opened her trunk and hurriedly tossed the groceries into cooler. Once back inside the car, her mind slightly calmed down. "I'm back and we're going to have a good lunch," she stated. There was no response. Jane spun around in her seat. Harlan was gone. *The Q* magazine she'd purchased the day before was splayed on the backseat.

Jane's mouth went dry as her heart pounded. She tore out of the car and ran into the parking row, searching for Harlan the same way a terrified mother hysterically looks for her missing child. Jane couldn't call out for him, knowing that would attract unwanted attention. After rotating in circles for nearly a minute, she stood perfectly still and felt into the moment. When all else failed—when logic and proof strayed from the scene—Jane could always rely on her gut and let it lead her in the right direction. The clamor of the crowd rose, with chants of "Weller, Weller, *Weller!*" It was counterintuitive for Harlan to purposely walk into a mass of people when all the eyes of law enforcement were in hot pursuit of him. It was even more counterintuitive for Jane to run at breakneck speed toward that crowd in search of her erratic travel companion. The closer she got, the more discordant the sounds grew.

Knowing

When she reached the periphery, she ducked behind a tall hedge and counted four television cameras, each perched on a tall pedestal at opposite corners of the staging area. The overflowing crowd numbered at least three hundred, some holding homemade signs that read: RE-ELECT WELLER 4 CONGRESS! and WELLER IS THE WOMAN 4 THE JOB! Every damn person there had a camera. This was insane, Jane told herself.

And then she saw him. There he was, standing in the middle of the crowd in a complete daze. But the crowd was so into their effusive cheers, they didn't seem to notice the big guy with the weed whacker hair cut, wearing the inside out sweatshirt and looking like he was in suspended animation.

She had to get to him and she needed to do it as gently as possible. Moving through the eager crowd, Jane got within twenty feet of Harlan before the guy on stage with the megaphone screamed louder and the band swelled into an introductory riff.

"Okay, everyone!" he yelled above the din of drums and guitars. "I want you to put your hands together for the woman who makes sure your voice gets heard in Washington D.C.! Congresswoman Dora Weller!"

The crowd cheered, raising their signs and banners into the air. Jane glanced to the stage and watched the petite Congresswoman with blond hair and a conservative pink dress suit walk up to the microphone. It was the perfect distraction that would allow Jane to reach Harlan and lead him back to the car. But when she took a few steps further and got a bead on him, she stopped. He seemed to quickly come out of his daze and putting his hand to the back of his neck, he rubbed the irritated area he'd pointed out to Jane the day before. He then slid his hand to his ear, touching his lobe as if he had a remote earpiece attached. The crush of bodies grew in intensity as Weller waved to the crowd. Jane kept her eyes firmly on Harlan. Suddenly, he took his hand away from his ear, stared straight at the stage and then, inexplicably, turned his head all the way around to the right.

It was mere seconds before the single shot rang out.

CHAPTER 8

The crack of rifle fire blistered the late morning air. Screams erupted from the crowd as people ran in every direction to get away and take cover. Jane pushed her way into the crowd toward Harlan. He was standing there, staring at the stage, in a dissociative trance. Jane glanced quickly at the front area. It wasn't clear whether the bullet hit Dora Weller but swarms of security surrounded her and the stage. Jane grabbed Harlan by his massive arm and dragged him toward the car. But at one point while he was still in the crowd he stopped and turned back to the stage.

"Hey!" Jane screamed in his direction.

Harlan responded with a nod and trailed her back to the Mustang. Jane's agitation rose with each step. She'd occasionally turn around and angrily usher him forward. Once back at the car and safely hidden between the two large vans, Jane waited for Harlan to catch up. "What part of 'stay in the fucking car' do you *not* understand?" Jane seethed in a low voice. "What in the hell is wrong with you?! Are you trying to get caught?"

Harlan stared at her blankly. But just when Jane was about to rip him a new one, she stopped and looked intently back at him. His eyes were different. They had steely focus and razor sharp precision. Without a single movement on his face, he turned to his left toward where the shots rang out.

"I wouldn't have missed the target," he calmly stated.

Jane felt her body begin to shake. She'd been in the presence of evil in her life. And while this wasn't the same, it was an echo of the darkening vibration. Harlan turned back to her, expressionless. Then, she noticed a gradual fear entering him from behind his orbs, as if two spirits were occupying the same host. She slowly opened the car door and got into the Mustang. Harlan didn't move a muscle. The parking space in front of her was empty. She could easily drive forward, turn left and leave. This whole thing had become a catastrophic mistake. She'd let herself be drawn into another victim's drama and it was going south fast. She needed to get out of there and keep going. After all, there was a short window of time to get to New Mexico. Jane started the car. Glancing to her right, Harlan remained motionless. She rolled forward, edging out of the parking space. He could figure out his next move by himself, she told herself. Checking the rearview mirror, she saw him standing perfectly still, thoroughly committed to his own world. She rolled forward another few feet and then felt her foot move quickly to the brake. A gripping, nearly all-consuming presence filled the Mustang. A fist seemed to push against her sternum, forcing her into her seat. When she tried to lift her foot off the brake, it felt like it weighed fifty pounds.

Jane tried to fall into the energy in order to make some kind of connection, but the current was fractured between her and whatever was occupying the car at that moment. The only thing she thought she knew for certain was that whatever it was—*whomever* it was—it did not want her to leave that spot alone. She looked in her mirror again. He was still completely frozen. Jane made a silent agreement and suddenly her foot was freed from the brake pedal. Creeping in reverse, she inched the Mustang back to Harlan and unlocked the passenger door. Rapping her knuckles on the window, she screamed, "Get in!"

It took Harlan a few seconds, but he opened the door. Jane instructed him to crawl into the backseat and cover himself. He complied, the whole time remaining in a dull stupor. Jane drove the Mustang onto the main highway and then quickly detoured to the side roads that would take them far away from that strip mall. No words were spoken as Jane headed south, winding around the periphery of small neighborhoods and working her way into the mountainous clutches of south central Colorado. Ninety minutes later, and feeling secure in the fact that she'd carved enough space between them and anyone else, she pulled off the asphalt and drove for another mile on a pot-holed, dusty back road until coming to a hard stop under an enormous cottonwood. She turned off the ignition and spun around. Harlan was buried underneath the blankets. She could feel the pressure building inside her head. Jesus, a hit of nicotine would taste like heaven right now. Slamming her fist on the steering wheel, she reached between the seat and pulled out her Glock. Swinging open the door, she got out and popped the front seat forward. Jane raised the gun.

"Pull off the blanket, Harlan."

Slowly, he peeled the layers off his face but when he saw the working end of the Glock looking back at him, shock took over. "What's goin' on?!"

"Get out of the car! Now!"

He looked confused as he sat up. Glancing around, he twisted his face into a question mark. "How'd we get here?"

"I drove here, you fucking idiot! Get out of the car!"

He scooted his fat posterior forward as Jane took two precautionary steps backward. "No, no, what I'm sayin' is I remember fallin' asleep in the parking lot. Jane, why you got your gun on me?"

"Move faster!" she ordered him, taking another step back.

"This ain't makin' sense, Jane!" He struggled and then finally was able to extricate himself from the car. "Now what?"

Jane trained the gun on Harlan, moving to the right to get a better angle. "You don't have *any* memory of what happened back there?"

Harlan's breathing was labored. "I don't feel well," he whispered.

"*Nothing*? You recall nothing of what you did?"

His face showed terror. "Oh, sweet baby Jesus! What did I do?"

She delved into his psyche as best she could. It was the same thing she did when she was knee-to-knee with a suspect back at Denver Homicide. Most perps are guilty as hell and it is easy to see through their sloppy veneer. And then there are the few who appear guilty, have no solid alibis and maybe have wracked up a few minor past arrests but they didn't do the crime. They aren't easy to identify but Jane had trained herself over the years to read the small stuff. A perp's face is a roadmap of clues—everything from the way he or she looks down to the way he touches his mouth or lips when answering questions. And although it isn't written in any police procedurals, she'd created her own method for judging innocence or guilt. She couldn't teach it or explain it because it was akin to crawling inside someone's head and roaming around. For Jane, it was like diving into a shared subconscious where truth resides and lies cannot take root. The truly innocent ones are few and far between by the time they get into the interrogation room, but when Jane recognized that innocence, her instincts were always right. Right then, staring at Harlan down the short barrel of her Glock, she saw innocence. She also saw terror, confusion and desperation.

"Jane? *Please* tell me what I did."

She lowered the gun but gripped it tightly in her right hand. "When were you in the military?"

"I was never in the military."

This was dicey territory and Jane knew it but she continued. "*Think*, Harlan."

Knowing

"I can think all day long and I'm tellin' you I've never set foot on a military base."

None of this made sense. If he was who Jane thought he was, they had certainly chosen one of the most obtuse individuals for their job. "You have triggers, Harlan. I don't know the trigger that flipped the switch back there but I know it when I see it."

"Know *what*?"

Jane knew she had to tread carefully. "You are Harlan Kipple but you also have another personality buried in you."

He threw his hands in the air. "Oh, hell, Jane. I've been tryin' to get through to you about that."

"I'm not talking about your heart, Harlan! I'm talking about when a person experiences deep trauma, their personality can split into one, two or even a dozen alter personalities. I saw it in the parking lot back there. After the shooting you can't remember? Something took you over. It even stole your eyes."

"Wait, wait, wait! Back the hell up! *Shooting*? Somebody tried to shoot me?"

"Somebody took a shot at Dora Weller. The congresswoman? And you seemed to know exactly where that shooter was located because you turned toward him seconds before he hit the trigger."

Harlan sunk down onto the moist dirt and propped his frame against Jane's car. Heavy gloom descended over him. "I don't remember any of that, Jane. Damn, woman, I beg of you. *Please* believe me. I don't know why this is happenin' to me. But it's gettin' worse. I'm afraid I'm gonna wake up and I'm gonna be back in another strange room, with blood all over me and a dead person laying there." He rubbed the back of his neck hard. "Dammit! As sick as I was before my operation, I never experienced none of this stuff. I shouldn't have never agreed to let my brother-in-law push me to the front of the line! I should have waited for my heart like everybody else and dropped dead! Dear God, I wish you'd believe me when I tell you that this heart of mine..." He wavered, gathered his strength and spoke with conviction. "This heart of mine is leadin' me around. It's as real as being plugged into another person's body and mind." He worked his lumbering body off the ground and stood up. "Back there at the tattoo parlor, you as much as said that I was innocent. And you told me you talked to a girl who also said I didn't kill that prostitute! I don't know how else to say it and I don't know what else to do. So, why don't you take your gun and kill me right now." He moved toward her a couple steps. "I mean it! *Kill me*! Put me outta my damn misery! You got it in you to do it. I can see it in your eyes. You've killed a man before. Once you do it, it's easier the next time."

Jane stood there speechless. How in the hell could he know this? It had to be a guess or assumption. Just like every soldier who goes to war is assumed to have killed another person. She considered lying to him, telling him that he was wrong. But she also knew that was pointless.

"Hell, I'm a dead man already," Harlan yelled, waving his arms. "If the cops don't find me, my lawyer, Ramos, or whoever the hell he is, will track me down. That rat bastard already tried to have me killed *twice*! I've never met so many people in so little time who wanted to see me dead!" He took another menacing step toward her. "So, just pull the trigger. That way, you can get all the glory. Get your picture in the paper. Be the hero. And you can move on your way to wherever it was you were goin' before I stopped your progress. Go on, Jane. *Kill me*!"

Jane raised the Glock, aiming it at Harlan's heart. He didn't flinch. "I don't want my picture in the paper," she glared.

"Do it, Jane! Pull the damn trigger!"

They stared at each other for what seemed an eternity. She still kept the gun fixed on his chest. "How about this? We spend a few more days together. I'll do some digging for you. Maybe all that chicken scratch in your notebook will start to mean something. Maybe your heart…" she hesitated before continuing, "maybe it'll lead us somewhere." She lowered the gun.

Harlan's eyes filled with tears. "You believe me?" He jabbed on his chest. "About *him*?"

Jane let out a long sigh. "Please don't confuse my willingness to entertain any of this with the illusion of sanity."

"Huh?"

"I may consider it possible but that doesn't mean that we're not two people sharing a delusion!"

He tried to work it out in his head. "So…I'm lost. You believe me or don't you?"

Jane holstered her weapon. "You haven't sold me the goods yet but I'm leaning toward the purchase."

Knowing

Harlan smiled broadly and, quite unexpectedly, he wrapped his big arms around her. "I'm still a dead man walkin', Jane," he said pulling back. "But maybe...maybe somehow I can come out the other side and see the light."

She put a hand on his shoulder. "Think of me like your balloon, Harlan. And then ask yourself, are you the tether or are you the pin?"

He smiled again. "I ain't the pin."

"Then you have to do what I tell you to do. You can't be wandering off. You can't put yourself in a situation again where everything could implode."

He nodded in agreement. "Did that lady die back there?"

"I don't know. I'm sure it's all over the news."

Jane opened the trunk and removed two packages of lunchmeat, cheese and water from the cooler. She tossed a pack of lunchmeat to Harlan, along with a bottle of water.

"It's cooked," he said quietly.

Jane rolled her eyes. "Right." She returned to the trunk, pulled the eggs out of the cooler and handed them to Harlan. "Is that raw enough for you?"

He grinned, handing the lunchmeat back to her. "Perfect!"

Resting her backside on the hood of the car, she peeled off a piece of roast beef. Within seconds, she'd inhaled the whole package but her mind never stopped working. A cascade of ideas bounced in her brain, all needing the use of a phone and a computer to clarify.

"You know," Harlan offered, cracking an egg against his teeth and swallowing the yolk and egg whites, "I think he's tryin' to talk to you too."

"Please, Harlan. Don't push the cart too far down crazy road."

"You had pine nuts in your bag. And *The Q* magazine? What are the odds, huh?"

"The heart of a dead guy is telling me to buy pine nuts and a magazine?"

"Uh-huh. I think you can feel him too but you don't want to admit it. And he's obviously tryin' to tell me somethin' but I can't hear it." He knocked a couple more eggs into his mouth.

Jane glanced inside the car and saw *The Q* magazine splayed across the back seat. "You asked me for something to read in the car. Remember that?"

He nodded.

"You read *The Q* magazine. And then you got out of the car."

"Okay..."

Jane retrieved the magazine and turned it over. It was page seventeen and that odd, nonsensical advertisement. But suddenly, Jane noticed things on the page that stood out. The mountainous landscape with snowcapped peaks looked almost identical to the horizon that lay in the distance from the shopping mall that day. The woman's wristwatch featured in the foreground and placed upon a red satin cloth that stretched across the page showed 11:17. The bottom left hand corner illustration of the "great and powerful" Oz peeking out from his purple curtained area—the seeming orchestrator of the advertisement's focus—and the red block letters next to his image, "IT'S TIME FOR A CHANGE, DOROTHY," started making eerie sense to Jane. She thought back to the approximate time the shooting took place. Jane recalled looking at the clock when she was in the market and it was 11:00. It was conceivable that between the time it took her to go through the checkout line, walk to her car, put the groceries into the cooler, discover Harlan was missing and then walk across the parking lot to the Congresswoman's event, that the exact moment of the shot fired could have been 11:17. Then it hit her. The name Dorothy had a lot of nicknames, one of which was Dora.

What kind of magazine was this? Was it a primer for sleeper cell assassins who recognize the codes and are then triggered by the strange advertisements to follow through with the plans? Jane had to double-check herself once again. But the more she scanned that bizarre page, the more it felt like she had insight into a covert operation. As much as she wanted to dismiss her twisted theory, it was beginning to make strange sense. She'd heard of splinter groups clandestinely communicating with each other through classified advertisements, using phone numbers and code words so that only the criminals would understand the objective. It was the ultimate "hiding in plain sight" plan.

But *The Q* magazine was taking it to an entirely new, highly complex level. Some group—an underground, radical group perhaps—was using *The Q* magazine to communicate their objectives with their "sleepers." For that matter, it seemed that the dark deed was even being publicized ahead of time. But one had to understand the symbols, the play on words, the characters, maybe even the colors to comprehend what event would take place. Jane knew it wasn't just another far fetched, conspiracy theory because she'd seen taped interviews with high functioning suspects over the years who had a military background and were accused of a murder they couldn't recall committing. Every single one of them mentioned the word "triggers." One guy claimed a certain song set him off; another guy swore that a specific scent served as his alarm clock. But they all shared the experience of missing periods of time.

Knowing

It could explain why Harlan had no memory after he read the page and left the car. Something inside of him recognized the ad for what it was and that's why he knew when to turn his head in the exact direction, seconds before the shot was fired. But even though Jane had only encountered him twenty-four hours ago, she knew there was no way in hell he'd have the knowledge and competence to play for whatever nefarious team was involved in this. That left Jane with a preposterous possibility. But even suggesting it felt insane to her at that moment.

"Get me *The Q* magazine you kept in your bag," she asked Harlan.

He complied, not sure of her actions. "You find somethin'?"

"I'm not sure."

She checked the date of his issue. It was March of the previous year. Turning to page seventeen, she laid the magazine flat on the hood of her car. The page was filled with puffy clouds and a brilliant sun shining through them. One of the sun's rays connected to a small, private jet. In the bottom left hand corner was the same Oz character, pointing up to the plane. In red, block lettering, the "advertisement" read:

"IT'S CLOUD'S ILLUSIONS I RECALL..." MITCHELL.

Jane immediately noted that it was odd to not use the full name of the artist, Joni Mitchell. And while she wasn't a Joni Mitchell fan, she was almost positive that the correct line in the song was, "It's *cloud* illusions I recall..." Surely, the proofreader would have found that mistake. Unless, it wasn't a mistake. Jane stared at the page again. A private plane. "Cloud's illusions..." Mitchell. "Holy shit," she whispered under her breath.

"What?" he asked, cracking three more eggs into his mouth.

"You remember that private plane crash about a year ago? The one in Nebraska? Eight people were killed. One of them was Mitchell Cloud." Jane realized Harlan was clueless. "*Mitchell Cloud*? They called him 'The eccentric microbiologist who was obsessed with goats?'"

"If you say so—"

She looked back at the magazine. "Good God...Is this even possible?"

"Is what possible?"

"Who is this group? They covertly advertise hits on people...why?" She attempted to explain what she could to Harlan and while he listened intently, she saw he wasn't grasping the full impact.

"I don't get it," he said. "If I've never been in the military, how could that magazine trip me up—"

"*He* was in the military." Jane wasn't sure where that gem came from. But the statement felt honest and true.

Harlan leaned forward, intrigued. "*Okay*. What else?"

"Maybe he was a…" The minute she said it, she wished she could take it back.

"A *what*?"

"An assassin."

Harlan regarded Jane with a scowl. "Nah! This heart of mine doesn't feel dirty. It's pure and rehabilitated."

"Rehabilitated? That's an odd word to use."

"That's exactly the way I feel about him. Transformed. Yep, that's it right there. Baptized into his new life. That's who this is. There ain't no way I'm carryin' the heart of an assassin."

Jane knew if she was going to get to the bottom of any of this, she and Harlan couldn't be continually retreating to the wilderness. If she was going to help this lost soul, she had to start mixing it up with whomever might have some answers. Right now, she had one solid name and Jane was determined to check it out. They drove down the mountain road, stopping occasionally to check for wireless access. She found a pocket and stopped the car. Logging onto her computer, Jane went to a website that had never failed her when she was interested in profiling and getting background information about a witness or possible suspect. Typing in the individual's name, she easily found her, confirmed her photo ID with Harlan and discovered that the woman would most likely be at a specific Starbucks around 2:30 that day. Checking the time, Jane factored it would take about an hour to drive to the coffee house.

With Harlan ensconced in his usual spot on the backseat and hidden away, Jane gunned the Mustang down the gravel and dirt road. Curving around a bend, she came up on a large, colorful billboard that sported a smiling sun with the words, "SUNNY & SON FARMS—SPUD-TASTIC POTATOES SINCE 1937." Odd, she thought. This was such a remote stretch of road, why bother advertising with such a large billboard. Turning on the radio, she quickly found a news station and more information about the shooting of Dora Weller. The Congresswoman was shot in the attack and the shooter was still at large.

"How'd you know he missed his target?" Jane asked Harlan.

"What do you mean?" Harlan asked, peeking out from the blanket.

Knowing

Jane realized he had no memory of that eerie comment. "Never mind." She knew that since the rogue shooter was still at large, roadblocks could be set up anywhere at any time. Add one more complication to their jagged journey.

"In other news," the radio announcer said, "authorities are still going through the rubble at the site of yesterday's horrific bus explosion one hour south of Denver. Nobody is believed to have survived the fiery accident which is thought to have been caused by a leaking fuel line..."

Jane turned off the radio. There's no way in hell anyone could already know what caused that explosion. *A leaking fuel line?* That was a tidy explanation, Jane pondered. But as inaccurate as it was, Jane knew that people would hear that, feel badly for the passengers, maybe say a little prayer for their souls and move forward. Nobody would question it or consider any other options. Critical thinking, Jane believed, was a skill that was quickly becoming superseded by random acceptance of other people's inaccurate perceptions.

They rolled into the small strip mall and parked on the opposite side from the Starbucks. Jane rummaged through her glove compartment and brought out a pair of handcuffs. "Give me your wrist."

Harlan held out his right arm to Jane. She clamped the cuffs on his wrist and tightly secured the other end to the gearshift.

"Hey! What the hell—?"

"Like my grandfather used to say, "Run off on me once, fuck you. Run off on me twice, I'll fuckin' kill you."

"Damn, Jane. Your grandfather was a gangster?"

"No. He sold life insurance. But he knew where all the bodies were buried," she said with a droll tenor.

"What happens if I gotta pee?"

She felt underneath the driver's seat and handed him a stainless steel travel mug. "Just like those old instamatic cameras. Point and shoot." She pulled out her fake ID from the leather satchel, cracked the window and opened the door.

"An instamatic?"

Jane leaned back into the car. "Just point and shoot, Harlan. And *stay down*."

"Hey! You pickin' up food? I'll eat Italian. I *love* Italian food now."

Donning her jacket, ball cap and sunglasses, Jane made her way across the parking lot. Walking into the crowded Starbucks, she took a stealthy look around. The problem with rooting out a person based on their photo is that they usually look vastly different face-to-face. After studying everybody in the joint, she concluded that the woman wasn't there. It was a leap of faith, she silently agreed, but it was worth a shot. Jane was just about to leave when the fifty-four-year-old woman matching the photo walked up to the front door. She watched her carefully, knowing she had the right person because of her drab green scrubs. It didn't hurt that she also had a nametag that verified the I.D. Jane waited until the woman got her coffee and sat down at a small table tucked in the rear of the place.

"Stella Riche?"

Stella looked up from her Frappuccino and Kindle. Her short and no-nonsense hairstyle suited her profession. "Yes," she replied warily.

Jane pulled out the empty chair and sat down. "You and I need to talk."

Stella leaned back, clearly uncomfortable with the intrusion. "Who are you?"

"Who am I? Well, how about I say my name is…Julie Scott?"

Stella stared at Jane. "What's going on here? How do you know that name?"

"It's your daughter's name. The daughter who loves softball and plays in a pick up league? She hates polyester so her uniform has to be all cotton."

Stella swept up her Kindle, grabbed her Frappuccino and started to stand up. "I don't know who you—"

"Sit down, Stella," Jane said succinctly.

She looked around the Starbucks, seemingly for assistance, but everybody was too entrenched with their phones and computers.

"I'm not going to hurt you," Jane quietly said. "*Please*? Would you sit down?"

She lowered herself back into the chair, regarding Jane with distance. "How'd you find me?"

"I used my favorite magic website. It's called Facebook. The name 'Stella Riche' is spelled just oddly enough that you stand out from the pack. You're an ICU nurse for the small hospital right across the street." Jane pointed to the building. "Your eighteen month anniversary working there is coming up and you hope they celebrate the occasion with chocolate cupcakes from your favorite French bakery. You don't drive your car anymore but that's okay, because your husband, Marty, had to take early retirement so he drives you to work and picks you up. You love standard poodles, free downloads on Kindle, computer Blackjack and, of course, attending Julie's softball games." Jane smiled. "Go Tigers!"

"Oh, my God…"

"And your guilty pleasure is coming to this Starbucks at 2:30 every day for a Frappuccino…with extra caramel on the whipped cream. You even had the GPS coordinates embedded in the link to this place. A deaf monkey with one leg and a brain tumor could have tracked you down."

Stella looked at Jane in shock. "Shit…I've got to get off Facebook."

"So, here's the deal, Stella," Jane stated, shoving her chair closer to the table. "I need you to go back in time nineteen months ago and remember a certain patient in the ICU that you helped after his heart transplant surgery."

Jane watched as Stella's mind drifted back in time and then, something shifted. She licked her lips nervously and regarded Jane with a grave expression. "Who in the hell are you?"

"I'm part of an investigative team looking into a specific patient's history—"

"Give me a name."

She asked for a name so Jane tossed one out. "Anne."

"Anne?" she asked, full of doubt.

"Yeah. Anne." Jane pulled out her fake ID from her jacket pocket and laid it on the café table. "Last name is LeRóy. Accent on the 'o.' Gives it a little flair." She slid the ID off the table and back into her pocket. "So, now you have a name. As I said, I'm not going to hurt you. And I think I know why you're scared."

"Do you?" She was trying to be strong and brave but she was falling short.

"Well, you left that hospital about a month after his transplant surgery."

"I got a better job."

"Right. That little clinic masquerading as a hospital is probably paying you a third less than where you worked before and you're so busy there that you can pen in a daily 2:30 meet and greet with a Frappuccino. So, I'll ask you again, do you remember the patient's name?"

She let out a sigh. "Harlan Kipple. But I only knew him for three days before he was transferred out of the ICU and taken to the cardiac rehab unit."

"Have you been watching the news lately?"

Stella eyed her cautiously. "Yes."

"So, you're aware of the charges levied against Mr. Kipple?"

"Yeah," she said with a self-conscious shrug.

"That's it?" Jane said, mirroring the shrug. "Somebody you took care of—somebody who received a precious gift of life—is accused of such a heinous crime?"

She leaned forward, speaking quietly. "Nothing good will come of this."

Jane also leaned forward, parroting Stella's tenor. "This? You mean, you and I right here? Oh, I disagree. I think you're going to tell me everything you know. And that is a very *good* thing."

"Do you have a gun on me right now?"

"No, but I can arrange it if that compels you to talk."

Stella sat back, quietly contemplating her next move. "Dr. Keener's brakes went out on his Mercedes."

"Dr. Keener? He was the surgeon who stepped in when Harlan's primary surgeon was unavailable?"

She nodded. "I was the night nurse." Her mind traveled back to that day. "There was a lot of confusion."

"What kind of confusion?"

Dr. Keener was quite upset by the way the whole process unfolded. He was a very 'take charge' type of man. I heard about a conversation between Dr. Keener and other parties who were demanding he agree to do something he did not feel was right."

"And what was that?"

Her voice was so quiet, it was almost impossible to hear. "Mr. Kipple wasn't scheduled to have the heart transplant that night. There was another patient who apparently was supposed to get the donor heart. But Dr. Keener had misgivings about that patient."

"What kind of misgivings?"

"I wasn't there when the conversation took place. I heard all this second hand."

"From who?"

"Graham. The anesthesiologist. We went to the same church." Her lower lip trembled.

"Go on."

"Graham said that Dr. Keener was outraged—that's the term *he* used— that the patient scheduled for the transplant was not…in his expert opinion… in dire shape. Mr. Kipple was Status 1A."

"What's that?"

"He had less than one week to live. He was confined to the hospital on IVs and monitored constantly. When they determined he was a perfect blood and tissue match for the donor heart, they proceeded with the surgery and Mr. Kipple got the heart." Her body shook.

"Why are you shaking?"

She scanned the crowd nervously. "Because I don't want to get involved in this case. I don't want to go on record with any testimony."

"That's not going to happen. You're scared and it's not because you think Harlan Kipple is going to come after you and split your head open. In fact," Jane leaned closer, "you're positive he's not guilty."

"So? What if I believe that? What does it matter?"

"It matters because bad things seem to keep happening to people, and every single one of them started after that heart went into Harlan's chest." Jane sat back. "How about this. Give me Graham's information. I won't tell him I got it from you—"

"He's dead." Tears filled her eyes. "He died…in a freak accident."

Jane's mouth went dry. "What type of freak accident?"

"He drowned in his backyard pool. Did I mention he was also an Olympic swimmer?" Her tone was biting.

"Was that before or after the brakes went out on Dr. Keener's car?"

Sheer terror mapped her face. "After. What's your name again?"

"Anne LeRóy. But it doesn't really matter. You're not going to tell your friends about this meeting because you never told your friends anything about this mess to begin with."

Stella looked shocked at Jane's ability to read her so well. "Why would I purposely put anyone I love in danger? First I stopped driving and then I stopped swimming. Does that answer your question? Should I stop drinking coffee now? Should I worry about what's in this cup right here?" She stared at Jane with false bravado.

"These 'parties' you said were arguing with Dr. Keener? Did Graham ever mention what they looked like or who they were?"

"No. He never got any names. He just said one man had flaming red hair with some kind of red mark, like a burn, on his hand."

Jane cocked her head. "Like a burn, eh?" She felt her gut go queasy.

"And there was another man with gray, reddish hair. He was the one that Graham said was more forceful."

Jane factored the second guy had to be "Mr. Ramos." She leaned forward. "Does any of this make sense to you?"

She shook her head. "No." She took a careful look around. "Maybe somebody didn't get what they wanted." Stella eyed Jane cautiously.

Jane considered it. "So, they throw a psychotic temper tantrum?"

"You see? That's what makes all of it so easy to dismiss. The crazier it sounds, the more people will ignore it. I've said too much already."

"You haven't said anything—"

"My husband isn't well. If anything were to happen to me—"

"Nothing is going to happen to you—"

She threw an uneasy smile toward Jane. "Yeah, Dr. Keener and Graham thought the same thing." She got up, steadying herself on the table. "I'm leaving now."

Jane quickly slid the point of her cowboy boot out, blocking Stella's step. "Do you know who the donor was?"

Stella pursed her lips as she stared down at Jane. "No."

It took Jane only a few seconds to see the lie. "Yes. You do know. Who was it?"

"I have to go now." Stella strode around the café tables toward the front door.

Jane followed her out the door and onto the sidewalk. "Stella, come on!" She walked in front of her, halting her progress. "You have to tell me what you know!"

She came to a squeaking stop on her sensible track shoes. "What has this got to do with Mr. Kipple's murder charge?"

"I don't have a damn clue. I'm just a bottom-rung investigator. They never give me much info when they ask me to check into cases. It's very compartmentalized. We're like the CIA but without the dark suits and stony expressions. Stella, if I could just find out who the donor was—"

Stella quickly moved off the sidewalk and walked across to a grassy island in the middle of the parking lot. Jane followed close behind. "Are you wearing a wire?"

Jane opened her jacket and lifted her shirt. "No wire."

Stella took another furtive look around the busy parking lot. "He was in his early thirties. Extremely vital. Dr. Keener called him 'the most superior specimen' he'd ever seen. There were no signs of age-related decay that you often see even with people in their thirties."

"And how did our superior specimen die?"

"He was brought to the hospital by two men who said they found him alongside the road. He was brain dead but his heart was still beating. They put him on life support and you know the rest."

"They said they found him alongside a road?"

"He was shot. Apparently, it was what Graham called a 'miracle shot.' The single bullet lodged in the perfect spot so that he was still able to be a heart donor."

"A miracle shot, huh?" Jane thought for a moment. "How soon do you have to get the donor's body to the hospital?"

"Time is always of the essence. Seconds count. The longer they bleed out, the more chances the vital organs are going to weaken and possibly not be viable. Once we get the donor on life support, we can stabilize them."

"You have any idea how fast that donor was brought in after he was shot?"

"Graham said he heard Dr. Keener comment that the donor's injuries were 'horribly fresh.'"

Jane attempted to work out the scenario. Some guy in his early-thirties, who is the poster boy for fitness and health, is gunned down with one bullet that amazingly lodges in the best position that guarantees death while simultaneously protecting the 'superior' heart. He is then found within seconds of this tragic crime and driven at lightening speed to a hospital where his body is dropped off by these "heroes" who flee the scene. "Did you ever see any security tape of the two guys that dropped off the victim?"

"Of course, not. All of that happened down on the lobby entrance. We were up on the seventeenth floor."

"Seventeenth? Right."

"My break's almost over. I've got to go."

She touched Stella's arm. "Hang on." Jane looked her straight in the eye. "The donor had to have some ID on him. Come on...You had to hear some kind of name."

Stella tried valiantly to appear in control, but she was losing the battle rapidly. "It was some sort of Italian sounding last name. And it had an accent mark over one of the letters. I think it was over the 'o.' Like 'o-n-i' or 'o-n-e.' But..." She faltered.

"But what?"

"He had another ID on him as well. I thought that was odd."

"Do you remember that name?"

"I do. Werner Haas."

"Why do you remember *that* name?"

"Well, first off, I'm positive that wasn't the donor's name. He looked Italian, not German. And it's the same name as the famous classical pianist. My husband, Marty, actually has some of Haas' recordings from the 1950s. I have no idea why the donor would have a fake ID. Maybe he got into some mischief."

Mischief? Jane had to restrain herself from rolling her eyes. The more she talked with Stella, the more questions she had. "Does the name 'Romulus' mean anything to you?"

Stella thought for a second. "Isn't that part of the Roman mythology?"

Jane nodded. "Yeah."

"Means nothing to me. Why?"

"You said the donor's last name sounded Italian. Romulus? Rome?"

"That's over my head. Look, I gotta go—" She started back toward the hospital.

Jane followed, walking next to her. "*Anything else*, Stella? Come on! Think!"

Stella stopped walking. "Are you trying to save Mr. Kipple or condemn him?"

Jane gave that question serious thought. "I'm trying to save him."

"Well, good luck with that one." She started off again.

Jane suddenly remembered what Harlan told her about the "bodyguard" in his hospital room. Jane quickly pursued. "Hey, wait a second! You had access to his room—"

"It was right across from the nurses' station—"

"Tell me who the big, muscular guy was who was sitting by his bed."

Stella looked at her with a quizzical expression. "Did Mr. Kipple tell you that?"

"Yes. Who was the guy?"

"There was nobody in his room. He had *no* visitors. Trust me, I would have seen them."

"A big, muscular guy? Come on, how do you make that up?"

"Mr. Kipple was obviously hallucinating." She let out a soft sigh. "Look, when you're as sick as he was and you get a healthy heart, your life changes immediately. It's like you wake up for the first time again. Between the surgery, the anesthesia, all the drugs, the new heart, some people have a difficult

111

time with reality for the first few days. Hallucinations are common for anyone on that many drugs and sedatives. Mr. Kipple obviously imagined this muscular figure sitting next to him—"

"He specifically said he was 'guarding' him."

"Why would he need a guard? There was *nobody* in his room." Stella seemed to relax for the first time. "Look, a lot of transplant patients claim strange things happen to them after their surgery. They've even documented these cases."

"Like what?"

She appeared slightly awkward. "It's not something we talk about a lot. But when you spend enough time with heart transplant patients, as I have, you can't ignore some of the similarities of what they tell you."

"You mean he felt like he didn't know where he ended and his donor began?"

Stella looked at her in shock. "So, you *do* know about it?"

"I haven't researched it."

"Well, look into it. It's not as crazy as people seem to think it is."

"Tell me something. When people hallucinate after surgery, do they remember what they saw in a clear, concise way months after the hallucination?"

"I can't answer that."

"You said hallucinations can be common after surgery—"

"The drugs do it—"

"I get that," Jane stressed. "What I'm asking you is based on all the people you've helped transition through transplant surgery, do you recall any of them having a clear memory of what they saw days or even weeks after it happened?"

Stella let out a tired breath. "I can't say I have. It usually gets foggier the further they move away from the delirium." The sun's rays shone brightly in the center of the parking lot as Stella lifted her long sleeves to her elbows. "I really *do* have to go."

Jane glanced down at Stella's right wrist. There was a tattoo of a dove and a set of numbers. Her gut clenched again. It was exactly like the drawing in Harlan's notebook. "Can I see your tattoo?"

Stella held her wrist up to Jane. Underneath the dove was "17:33."

"Seventeen-thirty-three," Jane questioned. "Tell me what that means."

"It's from the Bible. Luke 17:33? 'Whosoever shall seek to save his life shall lose it; and whosoever shall lose his life shall preserve it.'"

"What does that mean to you?"

Stella looked off into the distance. "If you try to save your life by violating your conscience, you'll lose your life. But if you lose it in the name of God or all that is good, you'll live forever. The only way to preserve what we hold onto…this shell we call our body…is to always be ready to give it up. And then through the grace of Providence, you'll be protected for eternity."

Jane considered her words. "You follow that belief?"

"I try to."

"But you still don't drive or swim?"

Stella looked at her wrist. "This is there to remind me. It doesn't mean I don't have weaknesses or feel fear." She walked away and then turned back to Jane. "If I were you, I'd get as far away from Mr. Kipple as you possibly can."

"He can't hurt me."

"Oh, I know that. It's not Mr. Kipple you need to worry about." She eyed Jane with a mix of compassion and fear before turning and walking across the street.

Back at the Mustang, Harlan was still attached to the gearshift.

"Damn, I thought you were never gonna come back," Harlan groused. "You sniff out any Italian?"

She turned to him. "Possibly."

CHAPTER 9

"Are you shittin' me? He's *Italian*?" Harlan exclaimed to Jane after hearing about her visit with Stella.

"Apparently." Jane drove the Mustang onto a long ribbon of road that paralleled the highway.

"What's his last name?"

"She's not sure. 'Oni' or 'One.' With an accent on the 'o.'" Jane waited for Harlan's reaction. "That mean something to you?"

"Nope. Except it might explain how come I got twenty-two cases of Ragu and angel hair pasta back at my house." Harlan considered what Jane told him so far. "She really said he was a 'superior specimen'?"

"She did."

"Wow. That explains how incredibly good I felt from the get-go. See? I told you he weren't no assassin."

Jane scanned the area in search of a Mom and Pop gas station. "Yeah, about that...your donor was shot in the head and found on the side of the road. Miracle shot, she said."

Harlan's face dimmed. "What's a miracle shot?"

"It's when the shot makes you brain dead but leaves the heart pumping. And you have to know what you're doing to make that happen."

"I don't understand."

"Whoever shot him is most likely one of the two guys who dropped his body at the ER." Jane waited again for Harlan to catch up. Finally, her patience ran out. "It was a hit, Harlan! The assassin—your donor—was the target. The hunter became the hunted."

"Stop callin' him an assassin, Jane."

"You mentioned that you felt your heart was 'rehabilitated.' Maybe..." she thought carefully before she spoke, "maybe your donor had a change of heart."

"A change of *heart*?" Harlan stated, clearly getting the reference.

"A come to Jesus moment? Maybe he turned his back on the wrong people and when he wasn't looking, he was taken out?" Jane continued to concoct theories in her head. "Or maybe he was bad until the end and got taken out by a rival?"

"If a rival took him out, why would they care about dumpin' his body at the hospital?"

"Now you're thinking like a cop, Harlan." She spotted a small gas station on the right side of the road that only had two pumps. Scanning the low-rent location, it was clear there were no security cameras outside but just to be on the safe side, she pulled the Mustang to the second pump, farthest from the prying eyes of whoever was seated in the cashier's office.

Harlan sunk further under the blankets as Jane donned her baseball cap and observantly walked into the tiny side building. The odor in the ten by ten office was sickly sweet, thanks to an entire wall display of deodorizing, novelty "Christmas tree" air fresheners that are meant to hang from your rearview mirror. Jane never understood their appeal. If your vehicle stinks so much that you need to cover it up with a synthetic vanilla scented "tree" that induces migraines, maybe you should consider what's causing the stench. A preoccupied, pimple-faced kid in his late teens sat behind the counter, feet propped up, and head down on his phone, texting like a pro. A small television sat on the counter, blaring a loud commercial.

"Hey!" Jane said, after waiting for the kid to do his job.

He looked up from his phone, upset he had to stop in mid-text. "Yeah?"

"You giving away the gas today?" Jane asked with a serious expression.

He looked at her, completely lost. "Huh?"

She brought out a roll of cash and laid a few bills on the counter. "Fifty bucks."

"What pump?" he asked.

Jane looked at him and worried for our collective future. "You have two pumps. I'm in front of one of them. The other one is empty. Do the math." She started to turn when she heard the commercial end and a daytime news show begin.

"I couldn't believe it when I seen him."

Jane turned to the television. A guy wearing full motorcycle attire and a helmet was on the screen talking about his "shock" when he saw Harlan Kipple race out of the gas station in the blue Mustang. The sound bite and footage of the witness supposedly was taken right after the car heist. Speaking in a dopey southern drawl, the young man who looked to be around thirty, described in detail how he witnessed Harlan jump into Jane's vehicle and "tear out" of the area.

"Is there anything you particularly noticed about Mr. Kipple's demeanor?" the news reporter asked the man.

"Oh, yeah. His eyes. They were wild. Like a madman."

"How close did you get to him?" the reporter asked.

"I was at the pump right across from where the car was parked fuelin' up. He looked like a monster. That's the only way I can describe him. Like the devil incarnate."

Jane's antenna went up. She clearly recalled that there were seven islands at that gas station, but four of the pumps were covered with yellow tape, marking them out of order. And one of the out of order fuel pumps was directly across from where Jane's car was parked. Furthermore, Jane never saw any guy dressed head to toe in motorcycle gear when she was there. Something was seriously not right here. She wished she could play the quick interview back again to get a better look at the guy but before that thought cleared her head, the news program cut to the female anchor back in the newsroom.

"We have breaking news to report," the female anchor stated in a serious tone. "We are now learning the blue Mustang that was stolen from the Quik Mart south of Denver belonged to a Denver Homicide detective."

Jane froze. She eyed the kid who settled back into his seat and resumed texting.

"Detective Jane Anne Perry was last seen by the Quik Mart cashier yesterday morning and apparently witnessed her 1966 ice blue Mustang as it was being stolen…"

Jane Anne Perry? Jane cringed. She never went by her full name. Great. Now she wouldn't hear the end of it back at Headquarters. They'd be calling her "JAP" for months. The screen cut to the round-faced woman from the Quik Mart. Jane swore the chunky broad still had the greasy stains of yet another snack of pork rinds covering her shiny chin. Or as Jane surmised, "breakfast."

"She come on in here pretty full of herself," the woman explained to the reporter, "Said she was a cop but that didn't make no sense 'cause she wasn't smart enough to lock her car."

Jane wanted to punch the screen. The squirrely entitlement of the stupid and the clueless never ceased to amaze and infuriate her.

"She was all huffy," the woman continued to prattle on, "and ordered me to let her see the security footage…"

Ordered? Fuck her. More like suggested strongly, Jane told herself. She stole a glance at the kid behind the counter. He was still blissfully focused only on his phone.

The woman mentioned how Jane wrote down her name and the description of her vehicle and instructed the woman to call the cops as soon as possible. "She was real bossy," the woman said with great emphasis as she stared into the camera.

At that point, the TV screen filled with a BOLO alert. There was a photo some news hack found online of a dirty 1966 ice blue Mustang, along with Jane's license plate.

"Have you had a chance to talk to Detective Perry?" the studio reporter asked the on-scene guy.

"No, I have not. We did speak to Sergeant Morgan Weyler at Denver Headquarters who told us that the situation is 'fluid' and that an ongoing investigation is occurring at this time."

Jane's mouth went dry. She was aware Weyler was not revealing everything he knew. Telling the press that an investigation is "fluid" means that it's akin to a water main bursting and the euphemistic lifeboats are out in force, floating anywhere necessary to resolve the situation.

The studio anchor recapped the information about Jane's Mustang, just as the kid behind the counter looked up at her and then looked outside.

"Nice ride you got there," the kid stated.

"That's an ice blue, 1966 Mustang…" the anchor stressed.

The kid turned back to her and then looked at the car again. There was a moment of tension between them.

Jane stared out the glass door toward her car. "Mine's a '68."

The kid looked at her. "*Sweet!*"

Jane spied a pack of American Spirit cigarettes. She'd given up smoking—her last vice—but distraction was necessary. She pointed to the cigarettes. "I'll take a pack."

Outside, standing at the fuel pump, Jane flashed on Hank's face. It came out of nowhere and threw her off her game momentarily. He'd seen the news story and heard her name mentioned. She was sure of it. His concern was palpable but, strangely, also his awareness that she was okay. Still, part of her wanted to call him just to make sure he knew. But it was way too dicey now.

Knowing

After pumping every drop of fuel she could squeeze out of the handle, Jane quickly retreated back into the driver's seat.

"Golf Charlie…" Harlan muttered.

Jane turned around. "What?"

Harlan was sound asleep.

"What'd you say?" Jane asked.

There was a slight pause and then he spoke again. "Golf Charlie…"

"Hey, lady!"

Jane looked up and saw the kid standing about ten feet away and walking with purpose toward her car. "Fuck," Jane whispered, as she quickly tossed whatever she could find over Harlan's face. Plunging the key into the ignition, she started the car but the kid ran in front of it, with his hand out.

"You forgot your change!" he screamed at her, waving a few singles in the air.

"Keep it!" she yelled back, before peeling away from the pump.

She sped like a demon down the side road until she realized she better slow it down so she wouldn't attract unwanted attention. As much as she wanted to feel the beat of a hot shower across her tired back, there was no way they could safely check into a motel at this point. Glancing at her backseat passenger, she saw he was still slumbering. They had enough food in the cooler to last them a couple days maximum. Beyond that, she had no clue what was going to happen. But the idea of sleeping another night in that cramped car made her back ache even more. Pulling the Mustang over, she scanned the distant landscape. If she drove south to Highway 50 and headed west, she'd end up near the San Luis Valley. There, tucked into the mountains that shouldered the rural landscape and farmlands, were hunting cabins that more than likely were empty in April. While Harlan slept, Jane powered forward. But the farther she drove on Highway 50, the more she felt exposed. There was her blue bullet highlighted like a neon sign on that highly traveled, two-lane thoroughfare. All she needed was an eager cop and it would all be over. She factored where she might be able to locate a remote cabin and turned off the highway and onto a dirt road.

Harlan stirred and sat up slightly, checking out the topography. "Ain't that the Sangre De Cristos?" he asked, pointing at the mountain range.

Jane nodded and then explained her plan but Harlan seemed eerily drawn into the area.

"What's going on, Harlan?" Jane asked cautiously.

"I don't know. I feel…kinda sad all of a sudden."

"Hey, Harlan?" Jane could see he was in a slight fog. *Harlan?* He turned to her. "Does 'Golf Charlie' mean anything to you?"

"Nope. Did I say it?" His tone was nearly matter-of-fact.

"Yeah."

"You might want to start writin' these things down, Jane." He settled back under the blankets.

"Thanks for the advice," she mumbled under her breath. Glancing around the immediate area, she was surprised to see plenty of cell phone towers. Checking her phone, she had coverage. Could accessing the Internet out here be too much to ask for? The sun was setting in the far mountain range, casting a salmon colored glaze across the snowcapped peaks. With nothing but her headlights to guide her fairly soon, Jane knew she had to promptly locate a cabin for the night. The Mustang pulled the mountain road like a trooper, navigating around the rocky corners and forgiving Jane when one of its tires jogged into a pothole. She passed several vacant cabins but scratched them off her mental list because of either their exposure to the road or their obvious security system. Jane worried she'd have to tangle with the gearshift for another night of jagged sleep when she decided to travel down a gravel road. Less than one mile later and around two bends, she came up on the tiniest house she'd ever seen in her life hidden in a tidy circle of pine trees. She calculated the miniature abode at one hundred square feet but that was probably being too generous. If the seven dwarfs had a bungalow separate from Snow White, three of them would be fighting to stay in this place. After cautioning Harlan to stay put, Jane carefully got out to the car and moved around the property.

Looking inside the side window, the interior was surprisingly clean and well appointed with a leather couch, basswood dining room table, matching chairs and two recliners. An incredibly small woodstove stood against the opposite wall, a few feet away from a teensy alcove that held a kitchen. Neatly hung dishtowels, copper-bottomed skillets and a stainless steel kettle atop the two-burner stove completed the cheerful motif. Jane factored that if the dwarfs crashed here, it was Snow White who decorated the joint. She motioned for Harlan to get out of the car and then searched for any open doors or windows. But the place was locked up tighter than an overfilled matchbox. Jane turned back to the front when she heard the sound of breaking glass.

Knowing

"We're in!" Harlan offhandedly said. Reaching his thick, calloused hand through the shards of glass on the front door, he easily unlocked the door and walked in.

Jane shook her head at the mess. But as the cool, high country weather quickly swept across the secluded hideaway, she was more than happy to crunch her boots against the glass and join Harlan inside. There was a ladder and loft with a futon mattress covered in a comforter with an attractive pine needle design. Harlan opened the mini-fridge and rooted around.

"We're *not* stealing their food," Jane declared. She retrieved the cooler from the trunk and dragged it between the two leather recliners. "We'll sleep here," she said, pointing to the chairs.

"Close to the grub. Works for me."

Jane returned to the car to grab her leather satchel and computer, along with a small overnight bag. When she returned, Harlan had every light in the shoebox on.

"What in the hell are you doing?" she yelled, flicking off the lights one by one. "We don't want to light this place up like a landing strip." Searching through her bag, she brought out a large flashlight, turned it on and set it on the cooler.

"No fire either, huh?"

"No fire."

"Their last name is Peal," Harlan announced, pointing to a custom carved wooden sign that adorned the arch above the front door. It read: Welcome To The Peal's Paradise!

"Shit," Jane mumbled. "This isn't a hunting cabin."

"More like a love shack," Harlan stated, motioning to a framed photo on the wall that showed a gray-haired couple in their seventies holding hands and standing in front of their tiny mountain retreat. The matte surrounding the Peal's photo was shaped like a heart and across the bottom of the frame was a quote in gold relief: "The Opposite of Love is Not Hate. The Opposite of Love is Fear. Be Brave and Choose Love."

Jane stared at the photo a little too long. The couple looked deliriously happy. They were the type of people, Jane figured, who probably met and married in their early twenties and somehow managed to navigate life's ups and downs with grace and forgiveness. There was elegance in that design she mused—a rare and precious gift in our throwaway society. The longer she stared at the photo of the elderly lovebirds, the more she envied them. Love, it seemed, was effortless for these two.

Harlan gestured to the embroidered headrests on the leather recliners. One said "Millie" and the other, "Larry." They were happily connected, Jane decided. Joined at the hip and the heart. The kind of couple where when one dies the other follows soon after—not so much from grief, but because their lifeline has been severed.

"You want to be Larry or Millie?" Harlan asked.

Jane turned to the recliners. "How about if I'm the woman for a change?"

Harlan plopped his large posterior into Larry's chair and, like a pro, hoisted the chair back and the footrest up. "Now *this* is a comfortable chair."

Jane noted a small bathroom behind a partition. Next to the composting toilet was a shower that she figured half of Harlan could fit into. But she wasn't going to complain. They had a roof over their head, food to eat and a bathroom. Life was good. And when Jane turned to see a laptop computer on a tiny table near the kitchen, she factored that life just got better, thanks to Larry having Wi-Fi. Pulling out her computer, she was thrilled to find that there was enough of a signal to hijack. Harlan slammed eight raw eggs, a package of lunchmeat and a hunk of cheese while Jane eagerly made herself a hearty sandwich and washed it down with a bottle of water. She remembered the pack of cigarettes in her jacket pocket. Damn, that would taste like heaven, she thought. Nicotine fueled her thinking process, calming her while allowing better focus.

She hoped she still had a lighter somewhere in her leather satchel. As she rummaged through it, the manila file folder holding Wanda's photo and information fell out and splayed across the wooden floor. Jane went to grab for the photo page but Harlan swept it up first.

"Who's this criminal?" he asked.

"Nobody. Give it to me," she replied with an edge.

He kept staring at the photo and name. "Hey," he said, seemingly mesmerized. "She favors you, especially around the eyes."

Jane grabbed the sheet out of his hands and returned it to the folder. "This is none of your fucking business!"

Harlan studied Jane. "Is Wanda your cousin? It's okay if she is. I had a second cousin who did time for moonshine—"

"It's not my cousin." Suddenly, she felt flustered—a feeling she never allowed.

Harlan continued to eye her carefully.

"Stop staring at me, Harlan!"

But he kept staring. "Who is she? I can see you care about her—"

"I don't care. I don't even know her."

"Bullshit, you don't care! You wouldn't be actin' like this or carryin' her photo in a folder if you didn't—"

"She's my half-sister." As soon as the words fell from her mouth, Jane regretted it. "She's living in transitional housing in Northern New Mexico."

"You're goin' to see her, aren't you?"

"I was. And then you stole my car."

Harlan's mouth dropped open. "Aw, hell, Jane. If I'd known you were headin' out to see your kin, I'd never of jacked your ride."

"Well, no shit, Harlan."

Harlan considered everything. "So, when are we gonna see Wanda?"

"*We* are not seeing Wanda. *We* are more interested in figuring out who set you up and how to get your entire case thrown out."

He smiled. "You really want to believe that, don't you, Jane?"

"I do. Why in the hell would I still be here with you if I didn't?"

He looked at her with compassionate eyes. "I keep tellin' you I'm a dead man—"

"Stop saying that."

"It's true. Whoever's after me ain't gonna stop until they get what they want."

"And I explained to you before that people are only after you if you know something, stole something or saw something. And you tell me that none of that applies to your case. But it *has* to apply. You don't get the elaborate set-ups, Harlan, unless you are seriously wanted."

"All they want is me dead, Jane. They tried to do me twice. Once in the motel room and once in that doctor's office before I escaped."

"The motel was to set you up with the black prostitute."

"No, remember? I told you I heard footsteps comin' down the hallway outside the room and I grabbed a chair and shoved it under the knob. They were comin' for me, Jane! *Right then!* That's why I yelled like I did to make a scene and force 'em to leave. I called 9-1-1 and passed out. I'm tellin' you, they would have took me right then."

She shook her head. "*Why?* Why *you?* You're not an HVT, Harlan. You're not even…"

Harlan looked at her, waiting. "What? Smart?"

She turned away. "I didn't say that."

"I know. *I* said it. And it's true. I ain't smart. I'm the first to admit it, although it does seem that you're on board with that line of thinkin' too."

Jane couldn't believe how unabashedly secure Harlan was with his own mental shortcomings. "You're not the sharpest tack in the box."

He smiled. "I'm a few beers short of a six pack." He cogitated on that one. "*Damn*, I wish I still loved the taste of beer." He retrieved his bag of mystery items and sorted through it. The various prescription bottles fell out. "That reminds me, I got to take my pills." He knocked back his anti-rejection drugs with a bottle of water.

"How many of those do you have left?"

"Enough."

"How many days?"

He eyed the bottle through the orange plastic. "Four…maybe five weeks."

And then what? she wanted to ask, but she didn't. She pointed to the bag. "Let me see it all again."

Harlan handed it to her and she laid the contents on the wooden floor. There was the bag of pine nuts, a pinecone, the comical illustration of the Blue Heron, a piece of lapis with the faux gold imprint of the Eye of Horus, a dog-eared copy of *Autobiography of a Yogi*, a teeny bottle of sandalwood oil and an old cassette tape of a Patsy Cline album.

"Hang on, you got some more in here," Harlan told her.

He handed her the key he said he found on the street, the ten-page newsletter titled "Eco-Goddesses" and that sparkly Easter card featuring the Angel Gabriel. Finally, he handed Jane his small, black spiral notebook. Jane placed them in a neat row on the floor and then stood over them, looking from left to right and back again in search of any clues. The pine nuts and the pinecone seemed redundant but maybe that was on purpose. Perhaps Harlan was drawn to these two items because whatever was guiding him wanted him to make sure he recognized their importance. Her eyes drifted to the book. She picked it up and turned to several pages in the front. The spiritual classic was penned by Paramahansa Yogananda, an Indian visionary and Yogi who founded the Self-Realization Fellowship in Los Angeles, California in 1920. His life's work was to bring both awareness and appreciation of Eastern religion into the West.

Knowing

In 1952, according to the text, Paramahansa Yogananda knew his death was imminent, even though he was only fifty-nine and in good health. On March 7th of that year, he attended a dinner at the Biltmore Hotel in Los Angeles. At the conclusion of the evening, he spoke of a "united world" of peace and loving partnership between nations. He then read from a poem, "My India," and ended with the line, "Where Ganges, woods, Himalayan caves, and men dream God—I am hallowed; my body touched that sod." At that point, he looked up and slumped forward, dead. His followers insisted that he chose that exact moment to exit his body, citing *Mahasamādhi*, the conscious and intentional act of leaving one's physical body at the exact moment of spiritual enlightenment. While some conspiracy theorists claimed that the famous guru was poisoned by his enemies, his followers held fast to the understanding that their teacher left this life on his own accord.

Jane sat on the floor and flipped through the book, landing on a page that spoke about the bewildering months that followed Yogananda's death. As reported in *Time Magazine* in August of 1952, the mortuary director at Forest Lawn Cemetery wrote in a notarized letter that "the absence of any visual signs of decay in the dead body of Paramahansa Yogananda offers the most extraordinary case in our experience…No physical disintegration was visible in his body even twenty days after death…No indication of mold was visible on his skin, and no visible drying up took place in the bodily tissues. This state of perfect preservation of a body is, so far as we know from mortuary annals, an unparalleled one…No odor of decay emanated from his body at any time…"

Jane felt a shiver run up her spine. She instantly recalled the words of Stella Riche and how Harlan's donor was "the most superior specimen" his doctor had ever seen, even after being shot in the head and dumped at the hospital's front door. And there was that random comment Stella made about the donor's body having no signs of age-related decay. Jane worried she was reading far too much into Riche's comment but still…there had to be an odd connection between this book and Harlan's donor.

She picked up the "Eco-Goddesses" ten-page newsletter and flipped though it. On the last few pages, there was a large black and white photo of fifty people standing in front of a field of vegetables. A banner in front of them read: WORKING MEMBERS OF THE GREEN GOODNESS CSA. Jane remembered hearing about CSAs—Community Supported Agriculture groups. Individuals or families buy shares in the participating farms and enjoy weekly baskets of fresh produce. But these organizations require a lot of volunteers to make them work, including farm hands, who often intern with the various farms to gain real-world experience. Jane stared at the photo in the same manner she examined a piece of evidence back at Denver Homicide. The names of everyone in the shot were squashed together at the bottom of the photo, as if the typesetter wasn't given sufficient space to hold all the letters. Checking the address of the CSA, she noted it was located in the San Luis Valley, which was nestled in the Sangre de Cristo mountain range. While she couldn't be certain, Jane factored they weren't far from the farm.

"Don't you wish we had a cassette player?" Harlan asked her, distracting Jane.

"We do. I've got one in the car."

Harlan handed her the Patsy Cline tape. "Check it out, huh?"

She took the tape and shoved it into her jacket pocket. Leaning down, she picked up the black spiral notebook. There were pages she hadn't really examined that closely so she started flipping through it from back to front. Her eyes spotted a word and she returned to that page. "SUNNY" it read, in all caps and underlined. Jane's mind drifted to the billboard featuring *Sunny and Son Farms* and their "Spud-tastic potatoes." All caps and underlined told her that Harlan's subconscious needed to emphasize it. But why? She turned a few more pages and saw the picket fence drawing with the arrow pointing to the word "blue." Blue picket fence. Several pages after that was half of page of the letter "M," with a heart symbol after the last letter.

She held the page up to Harlan. "This 'M?' Didn't you say you had dreams about a woman whose name started with an 'M?' Someone you felt a lot of love for?"

"Yep. But so much more than love. I can't describe it, Jane. It's like we're one person. I never felt that with anyone in my entire life and here I am feeling it in a dream with a woman whose face I can't remember."

Jane turned to the next page. There was just one word on it. Mike. She turned back to the page of "M's" and then stared at Mike. "Shit…"

"What is it?"

"Military code. 'Mike' is code for 'M'" A sudden thought crept into Jane's head. "Golf Charlie," she said to Harlan. You said that in your sleep. 'G.C.' Maybe that's…" Jane stopped.

"What?"

"Your donor's initials?"

"Or the guy who's after me?"

"Possibly." Her eyes fell to the glittery Easter card. She felt her heart suddenly race. "Golf…" she whispered. Jane looked at Harlan. "Gabriel?"

125

CHAPTER 10

For a split second as Jane stared into Harlan's eyes, something shifted. It was so quick that anyone else would have missed it. But it was there and it was precise and deeply felt. It was acknowledgement fused with fear and then laced with gratefulness. Harlan slumped forward, his huge fingers working their way through his chopped hair cut.

"Harlan?" Jane said carefully.

He looked up at her. "That's his name. I can feel it," he quietly admitted.

Jane didn't want to believe it could be that easy. But there it was. With nothing but a feeling to back it up, she agreed. "Okay. Now all we need is a last name that starts with 'C.' An Italian sounding last name." This is when a cigarette was useful to Jane. She hadn't had a cigarette in weeks but the need for nicotine was starting to intrude on her ability to focus. A few puffs, she lectured herself, and then she'd toss it away.

Harlan announced he was going to take a shower. Since he was starting to smell rather ripe, Jane didn't have a problem with his plan. She stood up, feeling the ache of the last couple days settle in her low back. If sixty was the new forty, based on the way she felt, thirty-seven must be the new eighty. The walls of the tiny house felt as if they were closing in on her, so while Harlan took the five foot walk to the sliver of space Millie and Larry called their bathroom, Jane ducked outside with her computer.

Unable to find her lighter, she hunkered in the Mustang with the driver's door wide open, and shoved the car lighter into position. That was just one of the many advantages, she reasoned, for owning an old vehicle; car lighters weren't politically correct any longer and had been replaced with the jack for the iPod. All well and good, Jane thought, but you can't light a cigarette with an iPod. The lighter popped out of its socket, signaling it was ready with its glowing red tip. What a beautiful ritual, she reckoned, as she ceremoniously unwrapped the pack of cigarettes, lifted the top of the pack and pulled back the foil liner. Holding the pack to her nose, she drank in the fresh tobacco aroma, earthy and rich with subtle undertones of wet dirt. Sliding the cylinder from the pack, she stared at it a little too long. "I've missed you so much," she whispered to it as she pressed the tip between her lips. Returning the pack to her jacket pocket, she reached for the car lighter. There was a moment of guilt as she drew the burning red lighter toward her. Jane made a promise to herself that she would quit after her recent health scare. But it was organic tobacco, she reasoned. And yet, there was a slight giddiness—a sense of doing something bad—as she held the lighter to the tip of the cigarette and sucked in that first intoxicating hit. She closed her eyes and felt the nicotine bathe her nerves in a soothing blanket of serenity. Two more deep, invigorating puffs and she felt the familiar release of endorphins that spurred her forward and enhanced those powers of deduction.

Turning to her computer, Jane logged onto the bookmarked motor vehicle website that she used frequently on the job. She typed in "AGA 171," the plate she memorized off the ominous black sedan from the *Anubus* crime scene. The plate was registered to a private corporation called "ODIN" that had a fleet of automobiles. Jane first thought that ODIN was an acronym but after a quick Internet search, she realized the corporation was named after the ancient Norse God. One text stated that, "Worship of the god Odin was related to Norse and Germanic Paganism. His role as a Norse god was closely connected to war, bloody battles, victorious outcomes, death and rage while blending ancient magic and prophecy into the hunt." Jane fixated on that last word: *hunt*. Her eyes then drifted to the words "magic" and "prophecy." Reading further, she learned that Odin sacrificed his eye in order to gain the "Wisdom of the Ages." While Odin also had links with poetry and inspiration, he was more commonly associated with "fury, madness and the lone wanderer." Jane sat back and looked into the black sky above her. She was always blown away by some of the names people choose for their companies. When they dipped into names with less than admirable qualities, she questioned their intent. Nobody would seriously name their corporation, "Satan," "Hell," or "Chains of Torture" but they had no problem choosing a pagan god that carried the baggage of darkness and was known for "sowing strife and starting wars."

Jane recalled the number on the *Anubus*: 121. Strangely, when Harlan counted how many tattoo cards Alex had on his wall, it was also one hundred and twenty-one. These types of repetitive number sequences fascinated Jane. It always felt like the invisible hand that hung close by and attempted to direct Jane's progress by forcing her to see what she otherwise might not have noticed. Taking the bait, she opened a bookmarked site she'd used on another case that featured the occult symbology of numbers. It didn't take Jane long to uncover the meaning of "121." Next to the number was the Egyptian "Eye of Horus," the same ancient symbol imprinted on the piece of lapis in Harlan's mysterious bag. She felt her gut tighten. There was yet another *sync*. The text read: "121: The Age of Horus is a 2,000 year cycle beginning in 1904 in which the black *magick* master of evil, Aleister Crowley, stated the world would dive into 'a time of force, fire and blood…of unparalleled freedoms and rampant chaos.'"

Jane sat back in the driver's seat and took a hard drag on her cigarette. Between the nefarious ODIN and the fact that a bus incongruously named *Anubus* sported a number that was linked to chaos, she got the distinct feeling that whatever was on the other side of this insanity was veiled and treacherous. Jamming the cigarette between her lips, she looked up and saw Harlan cross in front of the light beam emanating from the flashlight inside the tiny house. Returning to the computer, she decided she needed to lighten the mood. She opted for a quick search on heart transplant patients who felt connected to their donors. To her shock, there were dozens of websites and articles that relayed stories of patients who openly conceded that they felt the "presence" of their donor "within them." One fifty-five-year-old woman received a heart transplant and quickly began craving beer and snack foods she hated prior to her surgery. She also started having dreams of running with a ball on a high school football field and feeling the hard tackle from behind. But the woman's next comment really got Jane's attention. "I had other dreams where I'd be making out with a seventeen-year-old girl," she wrote, "and I'm happily heterosexual." It wasn't until this woman was able to meet the family of her donor that things finally began to make sense. She found out she had the heart of an eighteen-year-old football player who died in a car crash after one of the biggest games of his short life. But none of it really sunk in until the family introduced her to their son's former girlfriend. She instantly recognized the girl as the one from her dream.

There were hundreds of these testimonials and Jane read through a few with growing interest. Their similarities were stark, all of them confessing to feeling as though they "shared a body with another soul." For some patients, this acknowledgment helped move them toward a greater spiritual spectrum; for others, it complicated their lives and made them feel as if their lives and memories had been hijacked by an intruder. For those patients, unexplainable fears and phobias plagued them. One man was convinced that his donor died in a boating accident because he became strangely terrified of open water and boats and had frequent nightmares where he was drowning. The fact remained that each of the donors was usually young, vibrant, relatively healthy and were either murdered or died suddenly in an accident. One case discussed a fifty-six-year-old man who was able to describe the exact manner in which his donor was murdered and could even draw the face of the murderer. Another startling case involved a five-year-old girl who received the heart of another child. Months after her transplant, she "recognized" the father of her donor in a shopping mall and ran up to him, calling him "Daddy."

"Maybe they don't know they're dead," one transplant patient wrote, "and they're continuing to live through me." A chill descended down Jane's spine. "It's like they're trying to talk to me," the same patient explained, "but I can't translate their thoughts and desires into anything I understand." A forty-nine-year-old woman who received a heart transplant went so far as to visit a psychic to discern what her donor was desperately attempting to convey. "The psychic held my hands," the woman wrote, "and she gradually felt the donor come through me and speak to her." Jane took another hit of her cigarette. "Jesus," she murmured, taking another look up at the house. Returning to the text, she read, "The psychic told me she saw images flashing in front of her and it took a few minutes to get them to slow down so she could understand them. But once she did, she could clearly describe to me what the donor's life was like and even how he died."

Jane took another hard hit on her cigarette. She recalled how just touching Harlan's leg the night before sent an electrical current through her and a blaze of blurred, staccato images in front of her eyes. This was crazy, she thought, as she sucked down another cool hit of nicotine. But as screwy as it seemed, the more Jane read about all these strange experiences, the more she realized Harlan might not be crazy after all. It *was* valid, even though many of the shared testimonials were given by people who refused to be photographed or did not want their last names to be printed. There was a still a social stigma attached to what these patients were silently experiencing. It trod in territory reserved for religion and higher spirituality but it still didn't neatly fit into any compartment.

She continued to research the subject, landing on a website that discussed the more spiritual aspects of the heart. "The heart has a unique intelligence," she read. "It holds memory and speaks to us in a language all its own." From what she gathered, the heart communicated "at the speed of light." When two people are deeply and faithfully connected to each other, an electromagnetic pulse—unseen by the eye or simple machines—bonds them together and affects the two of them forever, no matter how far apart they are. "Even death cannot separate them," Jane read, "for they have merged into one vessel." She swallowed hard. How incredible, she thought.

There were other articles that fascinated Jane. One of them had to do with Native Americans and other tribal groups throughout history eating the beating hearts of animals and humans after they'd been sacrificially slaughtered. "The ritual was meant to take in the imprinted energy of the deceased's heart," the article stated. "*Great power* is thought to result if you consume the heart of an animal or person who is considered profoundly wise and adept. Their soul joins inside you and operates in union." Jane cringed. She knew someone on the police force when she was starting out who used to take two weeks off every fall to hunt elk on the Flat Tops in Colorado. Upon his return to work one day, she recalled him regaling other officers with the usual hunting stories that involved driving for hours into nowhere, setting up camp, and then spending hours of silence in trees or hidden by bushes. But on this occasion, he vividly described nailing a six point elk and upon reaching the animal, found it clinging to life. He slit open the elk's chest, cut out the heart and ate it. "It was still warm and beating," she remembered the guy telling the group. He claimed he felt "invincible" after that experience. Jane quietly noticed the change too. But she also noted a strange impatience and jumpiness in him that hadn't been there before. Adrenal stress, she told herself at the time. When an animal doesn't fall after it's shot and runs for a while afterward, it's said that the meat is tainted with fear. The animal's last memory is of terror and running for its life and somehow, that changes the texture and flavor of the meat. Could it possibly also imprint that energy of fear and terror onto the person eating it, Jane wondered.

As gruesome as ritual sacrifice is, something about the primeval practice moved Jane to do a search. Her computer took a second to spit out the websites, as if the idea of the subject matter even disgusted her hard drive. The first few links dealt with the ancient Mayans and Aztecs but the sites further down on the page were eye opening to say the least. The BBC featured an article, reporting on how the ritualistic killing of children in Uganda "as sacrifices for wealth and good health" was on the increase. The practice, which was almost unheard of before 2007, suddenly had an upswing in 2008 with police investigating twenty-five ritual murders of children. In 2009, that number increased to twenty-nine. Who was instigating these horrific killings? According to the BBC, the country's "new elite" were the source, eagerly paying "witch doctors" large sums of money for the promise of health and wealth. One witch doctor charged $390.00 for an animal sacrifice. But the price was "steep" for "the most powerful spell—a child."

The ash began to lean heavily on Jane's cigarette. She tipped it outside the window before crushing the cigarette into the cold dirt with her cowboy boot. Taking another quick check toward the house, she determined that everything still seemed calm. She felt inside her jacket pocket for the cigarette pack and touched the Patsy Cline cassette tape Harlan gave her. The cover was missing, leaving just the bare, well-played tape with a song label lightened by age. She could barely make out the title of the album, "Walkin' After Midnight," and kind of distinguish a few of the songs. Turning the cassette over, Jane noticed a yellow highlighter pen had been used across one tune. It was right before "Honky Tonk Merry-Go Round" so Jane inserted the tape and forwarded it until she hit the highlighted song. Patsy's perfect pitch crept through the Mustang's speakers.

"If I could see the world through the eyes of a child, what a wonderful world this would be. There'd be no trouble and no strife, just a big happy life, with a bluebird in every tree."

She sat back and continued to listen to the tape.

"I could see right, no wrong. I could see good, no bad. I could see all the good things in life I've never had. If I could see the world through the eyes of a child, what a wonderful world this would be."

The song continued and Jane listened but she wondered what in the hell any of it meant. Maybe she was giving the song too much credit, she reasoned. Sure, it was highlighted but so what? But she kept listening and waiting for something to stand out and mean something. When it was over, she returned to her computer. She searched on the local news station's video feed for their interview of the helmeted motorcyclist who said he witnessed Harlan's escape in Jane's Mustang. Once she found it, she played it back repeatedly. After about the sixth re-run, she stopped focusing on the motorcyclist and began examining the background scenery.

"What the fuck—" Jane mumbled as she paused the video. Whatever gas station was used for this interview, it was *not* the same one where the crime took place. There were no roped off fuel pumps. In fact, from what Jane could tell, *this* gas station had only four islands, instead of seven. Eyeing the video even closer, the location of the Quik Mart building in the background didn't jibe with the proximity of where it was located at the actual scene. Jane sat back in her seat and shook her head in shock. It was clear to her that the "interview" with this motorcyclist was completely staged. But why? She repeated the video several more times, listening intently to every word he said. The interviewer, who was never seen, prompted the motorcyclist, asking about Harlan's demeanor. The descriptive terms of "madman," "monster" and "the devil incarnate" certainly painted a precise picture of what "they" needed to put forth into the public mindset. But just exactly who "they" were still baffled Jane.

She selected her home page. Dora Weller's shooting was at the top of both the national and Colorado news feed. Clicking on the link, she scanned the article. Weller was in critical condition but expected to live. To Jane, choosing Dora Weller as a hit made no sense whatsoever. Jane always considered her bland, white toast; a cheerful woman who wasn't too savvy but made up for it with a willing smile and a seemingly altruistic outlook on life. The only controversy that Weller was involved in was her denial of a Biotech firm's request to buy a thousand acres of rich grassland in Colorado. After a lot of controversies and headlines on the Denver news programs nearly every evening, Weller chose to uphold the loud and often subversive desires of the "Eco-friendly" activists who wished that the land be protected from "capitalistic development."

But that political issue certainly was not worth killing somebody over, Jane mused. Then again, there was that undeniable advertisement on page seventeen of *The Q* magazine with that ominous line: "It's Time For A Change, Dorothy." The ad did seem to have an "in your face" quality to it—something many of the anarchist, left wing groups enjoyed. Jane recalled the violent actions of "Eco-terrorists" over the years. One group firebombed a Vail ski lodge in 1998, causing twelve million dollars in damages. Jane checked into that story and discovered that the convicted group was indicted in connection with "seventeen acts of domestic terrorism." Jane read it again. *Seventeen*. This was getting stranger and stranger. Why would the Eco-Terrorists have anything to do with the shooting? Weller gave them what they wanted. And anyway, Jane figured, if she was going to play this scenario out, why would an Eco-Terrorist group be connected to the death of Mitchell Cloud, the unconventional microbiologist who spent over a decade of his professional life studying goats.

She returned to the home page and saw that there was a "Breaking News" update on the Weller event. Clicking on the link, she was greeted with a cell phone photo taken by somebody in the crowd during the mêlée after the shooting. There, standing in full view, was Harlan Kipple's image.

"Holy shit!" Jane yelled. She read the article quickly. They were tying him to the shooting, claiming he had gone "on a crazed killing spree." None of it made any sense to Jane. She desperately did more searches, looking for other photos from the scene that anyone might have uploaded to the Internet. From what she could find, she wasn't in any of the shots. But Harlan was easy to spot, especially now that he had the weed whacker haircut and no facial hair. "Fuck," Jane mumbled. Dying his hair at this point was futile. She was just about to start another search when she heard Harlan scream.

Ditching everything on her car seat, she raced inside the house. Harlan was on his knees, rocking back and forth and murmuring what sounded like a prayer. Jane leaned closer and heard every word.

"I will face the darkness, but I will not let it become me. Fear may be present but it will not possess me. I will face the darkness, as the knowing light within my heart and mind leads me home. And once again, I will be free."

He said it repeatedly and spoke each word with rapid inflections as if he'd been speaking those words his entire life. Each time he repeated it, his tension lessened and his body relaxed. By the twentieth repetition, Jane had the verse committed to memory and Harlan was calmer as he slumped forward onto the wooden floor. But when she lightly touched his back, he jumped up and onto his feet as if he had springs on his heels. The large flashlight rolled across the floor, casting an eerie shadow across the small room.

"What happened?" he yelled, struggling to breathe.

"You blacked out again. But you're back and you're okay."

He clutched his chest. "I don't think my heart can take this much longer, Jane."

"Sure it can. They loaded a superior specimen in there, remember?"

Harlan fell strangely silent and contemplative.

"Harlan?" Jane asked gingerly.

He walked to the leather recliner and sat down, cloistered by the darkness. After several minutes, he bowed his head. "I can't do this no more, Jane. It's killin' me."

Jane heard Harlan grab for a water bottle, followed by a rattling sound. She walked over to the overturned flashlight and shone it toward Harlan. He had a fistful of pills in his hand from one of the prescription bottles and he was just about to slap them into his mouth.

Jane lunged toward him. "Are you fucking out of your mind?!" she screamed at him, wrestling the pills from his palm.

"Let me do it, Jane!"

"Not on my watch!

Even though he had her by over one hundred and fifty pounds, Jane's blistering attack cowed him and he released the pills onto the floor.

She hovered over his corpulent frame. "Don't you *ever* do that again! You hear me?" Every fiber of her body shook as she stared at him.

He looked at her and his eyes softened. It was as if he bored inside her head and drew her terrified thoughts to the surface. "Okay, Jane," he softly said. But something in his voice sounded different.

She stepped back and observed him, shining the light on him like a back alley suspect. For a moment, she felt as if two people were staring back at her. Gradually, one of them drifted behind the other and Harlan's terrified eyes took over.

"What am I gonna do, Jane?"

She had an idea. A ridiculous idea. "Sit back and relax." She lifted up the cooler from between the two leather recliners and shoved Millie's chair closer to Harlan. Returning back to her car with the cooler, she put away her computer. The air was turning nippy, signaling another spring snowstorm on the horizon. Figuring the cooler would retain a bit more of the outdoor chill and preserve what food they had left, Jane propped it up on the hood of her Mustang. Grabbing a few blankets from the trunk, she locked the car and walked back into the house.

Harlan was still in Larry's chair, feet propped up, with a worried expression. "What are you plannin', Jane?"

After handing a blanket to Harlan, she slid into Millie's recliner and lifted the footrest. After a moment of thought, she spoke up. "Maybe I can help you."

"What are you talkin' about?"

She told him about the electrical shock she got when she touched his leg the night before and the strange disjointed images that pulsated simultaneously. "I can't promise anything," Jane explained, "but maybe I can...I don't know..."

"See what I'm seein'?" he asked, screwing his face into a curious twist.

The minute he said that, Jane grimaced. This was the kind of stuff people only do in Boulder or Crestone and even then, there are usually candles, incense, some sort of metal chime and monotonous, three tone music playing to accompany the event. "You want to just give it a shot?" She draped the blanket over her body.

"What makes you think you're even capable of doing this?" His tone leaned toward insulting. "You're a cop, for God's sake!"

"I've experience some pretty weird shit over the past couple years, Harlan. I can't explain it, except that…" She tried valiantly to come up with a suitable explanation. "I can't explain it. Maybe…I can be your eyes."

"What do I got to do?" he asked guardedly.

"Just lay back. Relax. Go to sleep."

He waited. "Yeah…Then what?"

"I'll just put my hand over your hand and close my eyes."

He stared at her with those obtuse orbs. "You ain't comin' on to me, are you?"

"No, Harlan. I'm not coming onto you. You want to give this a try or not?"

He let out a puff of air and settled back in the recliner. "Okay. Let 'er rip."

Jane turned off the flashlight, leaving them in total darkness, save for the subtle moonlight that crept across the wooden floor. It took Harlan about five minutes to relax and fall asleep. She waited until his breathing changed before gently cupping her right hand over his left hand as it rested on the arm of the chair. She closed her eyes and waited but nothing happened. Thirty minutes passed and she was still waiting while Harlan snored like a stuck foghorn. She finally opened her eyes and shook her head, silently belittling herself for entertaining such a bizarre plan. The day's events quickly caught up with her and exhaustion set in fast. Maneuvering her body into a more comfortable position, Jane let out a breath and, with her hand still cupped over his hand, allowed Morpheus—the god of sleep and dreams—to embrace her.

She felt herself floating as if on a cloud. Sinking deeper, she fell into a paralyzing slumber. And then it happened. First, Jane felt pinpricks of electrical energy sparking off the knuckles on her right hand. While she was conscious and aware of it on one level, another part of her was an observer. With her eyes still shut, a curious pinpoint of blue light appeared in the center of her vision. Yes, this is what Jane remembered Harlan calling the "blue light special." Seemingly powered by the electric connection between she and Harlan, the light expanded. Jane opened her eyes, expecting to see a blue light beaming into the house from an outside source. But there was only darkness and that cushion of moonlight in front of her. With her hand still on top of Harlan's, she closed her eyes again and let out a hard breath.

Within seconds, the electrical charge between them increased. She could hear Harlan's breathing become labored, signaling the onset of another chaotic nightmare. The blue light appeared once again and grew quickly until all Jane saw was a pulsating spectrum of intense sapphire luminosity. Just when she thought she couldn't take the intense glare, a high-pitched tone rang in her left ear and continued, as it moved through the center of her head and triggered the same tonal frequency in her right ear. A cyclone of energy felt like it was spiraling in the center of her brain. Jane likened the experience to being plugged into a jet that was about to take flight. Just like the rumbling of the jet's powerful engines as it speeds down the runway, the sharp tone lingered and intensified until when it reached a crescendo, she could swear something ignited inside her head. At the exact moment of ignition, the penetrating tone suddenly stopped and she was slammed forward into the sapphire light.

Strangely, Jane felt no fear as she looked down at the cool, wet dirt beneath her. Looking around, she saw an expansive farmland, cradled in a valley between two mountain ranges. The aroma of freshly harvested potatoes still hugging the dark earth enveloped her. Hearing footsteps through the tall grass, Jane turned. There was a dark-haired boy about ten or eleven years old with a round face and piercing blue eyes, carrying a small rifle. She watched him closely as he methodically hunkered down between the blades of green grass and, resting the rifle on his knee, took aim and shot. Following him through the grass that bent with the wind, they walked about one hundred yards until he stopped and picked up the body of a rabbit. She found herself wanting to say something but she couldn't speak. Somehow she understood that words were useless in this place and communication was only possible through the mind's eye. With that realization, she attempted to send the boy a message that she was there and watching him. To her utter amazement, he turned around and looked at her. Without moving his lips, she heard his young voice.

"Be brave, Jane."

In an instant, she was sucked out of that scene and catapulted through a veil of electric colors, each one holding a different scene. She chose one of them randomly and dove into it. A kaleidoscope of images flashed in front of her, none of them allowing her to focus long enough to interpret anything. In her mind's eye, she *thought*, "Slow it down!" and everything came to a halt. She was standing on a cheerful suburban street, filled with homes that sported clean picket fences and manicured lawns. Turning to her right, she saw a house with a blue picket fence. There was a mailbox with a last name on it. But she could only see the last three letters of the name: "SON." The smell of fermented hops mingling with evergreens overwhelmed her. The second she thought she couldn't stand the scent any longer, Jane was tossed into another rupture of light and color until she felt herself spit into another setting.

A perfume of roses replaced the nauseating odor as a sparkling setting spun around her. She was inside a house with lots of windows that allowed the warm breeze to freely move and mingle. In a far room, she could hear a man and woman whispering to each other and kissing. Everything around her ebbed and flowed with beauty and the spark of a new life being conceived. Jane wanted to stay in that exquisite spiral forever but as soon as she wished that, she was propelled out of the peacefulness and into a dark hallway.

Immediately, she sensed unmitigated doom. A tall, muscular man wearing a dark shirt and pants stood with his back in front of her. He moved down the unlit hallway with expert precision. Through the folds of darkness, she could see the pistol with the silencer clasped in his right hand. She followed him, somehow aware that he knew she was there. He reached a closed door at the end of the hall and stopped.

"Be brave, Jane," she heard his deep, commanding voice tell her.

The darkly clad man turned the knob and gradually opened the door. He moved inside confidently and crept to his right. Jane followed him through the door. The whole time, all she could see was his back. But around her, stood a wood paneled office with no windows. Stacks of files and papers were piled high on the desk and sundry tables that gave the room a cramped atmosphere. Reams of thick books with scientific symbols on the hard covers lay everywhere. Seated in the corner of the room at another desk was an old gray haired man. He, too, had his back to Jane. As much as she tried to see who these men were, she was unable to move past the one with the gun. Without flinching or hesitation, the man with the gun moved to the one seated at the desk. The silencer was pressed against the back of the old man's head and the trigger was pulled.

Blood splatter blew across the papers on the desk. Particles of brain matter slapped onto the paneled walls, drifting down the seams, driven by the warm blood. Jane observed the assassination without emotion. It was as if she was hooked into the psychotic matrix and felt indifferent to what just happened. But then a very odd thing happened, as if it couldn't get any stranger. The assassin holstered his weapon and stood over the man's desk. He stared for what seemed like an eternity before opening up files and going through the contents. He stacked one folder after another either to the right or left, as if he was separating the information he needed. Jane tried to move at that point but her feet were welded to the floor. Coupled with the sudden paralysis was the stark sense that she could easily feel the growing stress emanating from the assassin. The tension became so severe that her entire body felt ill.

The longer the man stood there, opening and closing files, the more her body ached, her head throbbed and her legs felt like jelly. The aura in the room was pure evil, Jane determined. A creeping, gut-churning, unrepentant malevolence that moves with a cunning gait and doesn't stop until its target has been conquered. It dripped with arrogance and greed, chewing through whatever it took to steal the exquisite prize. Her brain felt like it had been split open. The pain was unparalleled. She wanted to grab onto her head, fearing that her soul was being sucked from her body.

As the man continued to sort through the files, she sensed his repulsion grow with every word he read. After what seemed hours, he gathered a short stack of files and secured them under his tucked shirt. He then quietly moved toward a floor-to-ceiling bank of wooden file cabinets that stood six feet away. The cabinets were similar to those one might see at a high-end lawyer's office, except that instead of keys, there were touchpad code panels on each file cabinet. As he walked to the files, Jane was suddenly able to pull her legs off the floor. But when she tried to get nearer to the man's side to see his face and to also check out what he was scrutinizing, she was prevented from doing so. The best Jane could do was to maneuver her body several feet behind his frame the entire time. She watched as he placed the palm of his right hand over one of the keypads. After about thirty seconds, he ran his index finger over the nine numbers, up and down, back and forth, until he rested the finger on one number. He pushed it and repeated the strange back and forth on the keypad another five times, punching other numbers on the keypad until a soft click could be heard. The wooden file door popped open. Inside, there were two shelves. The bottom shelf was empty while the top shelf held a single medium sized white binder.

The man withdrew the binder and stared at the cover. Creaking it open, he stood and read the contents. Jane waited. Within seconds, she felt a biting pain in her heart. There was a sense that someone was taking a knife and slicing her chest open. Even in this altered state, the torture felt terrifying real. She endured it as long as she could until she heard herself screaming. The pain ceased instantly.

"What do you want from me?" she asked the man, using her mind to speak.

"Only what's necessary."

With that, he closed the white binder and held it to his side with the front cover facing Jane. She peered at the three letters in bold red ink: **IEB**.

The sound of waves quickly rushed through her head and a wooziness kicked in. There was a sense of falling off a tall building. She closed her eyes, allowing the sensations to envelop her. She felt no fear or anxiety, just a willingness to be released into the cosmos and flung at will until landing on terra firma.

Jane opened her eyes and was shocked to see it was morning. She was also aware that it was below freezing in that tiny house. And when she turned to Larry's leather recliner, Harlan wasn't there.

CHAPTER 11

Jane bolted from her recliner and headed out the door. The crisp blast of icy air gripped her as she stared at a fresh coat of fluffy spring snow. The first thing she noticed was the cooler on its side next to the Mustang. Food was strewn everywhere, with the tell-tail footprints of a raccoon outlined on the car's hood. Staring intently at the two-legged footprints, she followed them around the car and down a short rocky hillside. The footprints became easy to follow because along the way, articles of clothing had been dropped. First was Harlan's Plaxico Burress sweatshirt, followed by several undershirts, his pants and his shoes. Jane collected the clothing and continued to follow the barefoot prints in the snow, around several large boulders, until she saw Harlan in the distance. He had his back to her and he was completely naked.

Not wanting to yell for fear of attracting too much attention from possible neighbors, she made her way through the shallow, wet snow until she stood within several feet of Harlan. He was eerily still.

"Harlan?" she asked quietly, with trepidation.

"Yeah."

His voice sounded normal, yet strangely calm. "What's going on?"

"Adapt or die. I don't know where I heard that but it's true."

"Okay. Has that got something to do with why you're naked right now?"

"You gotta expose the body to extremes and then when you're put in extreme situations, it don't mean as much to you."

"Point taken. Put your pants on." She tossed him the pants and shirts.

He remained still. "I feel lighter, Jane. I feel lighter than I've felt since my operation. I always thought it took more energy to suffer than to give up. But if I gave up now, I'd spent whatever time I got left regrettin' that I didn't find out what he wants. He wants somethin', Jane."

"I know."

He slowly put on his pants and then the layers of shirts. "Thank you for what you did for me last night. I don't how you did it...but I feel like I got a new sun shinin' on me today."

She waited until he dressed and turned to her. "Well…you do have a new spotlight on you. They're liking you for Dora Weller's shooter."

He shook his head, almost expecting the bad news. "You believe me now, then?"

Jane nodded. "If DH was working this case, there's no way in hell we'd make that kind of leap or put out your name like that until we had enough evidence. We keep that kind of shit close to our vest and do our due diligence before parading a suspect in the media. They've got nothing to link you to the shooting except that you're on the run and you're a convenient fall guy. Your profile doesn't fit the Weller shooting. You don't allegedly butcher a prostitute and then take a shot at a congresswoman. They don't follow. Even if they are pegging you as a maniac, even maniacs follow patterns. Whoever fed that information to the media has a kind of leverage and power I've never seen. Whoever it is, they really want you badly and they'll distort you and your past as much as possible in order to turn everybody against you."

"Except for you."

"Except for me. And I'm just one person and I don't know what the hell I'm supposed to do for you."

"Did you find out what he wants?"

She hesitated a little too long.

"You *did*, didn't you?" he asked.

"I'm not sure. I have to do more digging."

"Damn, this is beautiful. He's been knockin' at my door, I just didn't know how to converse with him. Now we can."

Jane needed to check herself. "Jesus, Harlan, it's not that fucking simple. Good God! How did you make it this far in your life being so naïve? What I can or can't figure out will not make this go away. I have a feeling that even if we figure it all out, you're still not going to be safe."

He smiled. "Oh, hell, Jane. I've been safe my whole life. What did it get me? Now I've got the heart of someone who ain't lived a safe day in his life. I kind of like it now…except for the nightmares that make me want to piss my pants. Not sure why he got put inside of me, but crazier things have happened." He looked off into the distance. "You got any idea what it feels like to have the heart of champion in your chest? I never felt like I was worth anything, Jane. I never had that moment where someone told me I could do great things. But I feel different today. My heart has been freed."

Knowing

She motioned for him to follow her back to the tiny house. Back inside, Jane got on her hands and knees and collected every single pill that Harlan flailed across the room the night before.

"Grab a couple dishrags and figure out how to cover up that hole in the pane of glass where you broke in," she instructed Harlan.

He dutifully obliged, happy to be useful. She found the last pill and snapped the cap back on the bottle.

"Who do you know that killed himself?" Harlan asked her.

Jane was still on the floor, working her way up to a standing position. Her silence spoke loudly.

"You hear me?" he asked again.

"Of course, I heard you." She found a piece of paper and a pen. "I'm going to leave Millie and Larry a note with no names. And two hundred bucks. That should cover the damage."

"How come you don't want to talk about it?"

"It's nothing," she whispered as she jotted down a few rushed words to Millie and Larry.

Harlan used tacks he found in a bowl to attach the dishrag to the wooden slats between the glass panes. "*Nothing*?"

She finished the note and laid out two crisp one hundred bills. "That's right. Nothing. Grab the blankets and let's get out of here."

They walked out to the Mustang. Jane swept up the cooler and gathered up any uneaten food or packaging she could find into a trash bag she uncovered from the backseat. Once inside the car, she considered their next move.

"I have no clue how we're going to get more food. I gotta keep this car off the radar for now."

Harlan was working his big frame into his usual spot on the backseat. "Well…it's farm country down there, ain't it?" Harlan stated, jutting his chubby chin toward the road they drove up on. "Let's find a farm."

It was the most intelligent idea she had heard out of his mouth. Jane backed out of the driveway and headed down the narrow mountain road. Once they hit the lowlands, the high mountain snow was gone, replaced by miles of glistening, grassy fields and acres of well-turned dirt, patiently waiting for a seed. The Sangre de Cristo mountain range lay in the distance, as the early morning sun warmed Jane's face. After driving twenty minutes, Harlan spoke up.

"How come I feel so sad?"

"You said that last night when we drove through here."

"I know. I feel like my heart is breaking." He looked up at the passing scenery. "Hey! Up ahead there? Take that right turn where the sign is."

"Why?"

"I don't know. Just do it."

Jane reluctantly agreed, checking her rearview mirror to make sure no one was following her. Less than one mile down the gravel road he told her to stop. There was a small family farm about a quarter mile away, shrouded in a fence of cottonwood trees.

"We're gettin' out here," he declared.

"Hey, hey, hey! Are you nuts? It's open season on you!"

He sat up. "Farmer's season! You know what that is, right? No license to kill needed. You just shoot whatever wanders onto your property when you're sittin' on your porch." He smiled a goofy grin. "Come on, Jane. You're hungry, right?"

"What's in the field?"

"I ain't sure yet. Come on."

She was hungry and so she grudgingly agreed. Sliding under the barbed wire fence that surrounded the moist field, they wandered for several yards before Harlan reached down and snapped up something.

"Wild asparagus!" he yelled.

"*Shhh!*"

"Ain't nobody around, Jane."

"There's a farm over there."

"Who cares?"

"*You care*, Harlan! You might feel invincible but you're not. I bet you're now worth more than that twenty-five thousand dollar bounty."

"Yeah? You think?" he said proudly.

Jane shook her head. "Jesus, you are one goofy fucker." She came upon an unexpected cluster of wild asparagus and eagerly snatched it up. While it wasn't clear how Harlan knew this field existed, she wasn't going to bitch about free produce.

Harlan stayed close to her but kept his head down, searching in the vibrant spring grass. "You ever notice how when you're huntin' for wild asparagus, how it blends in with the blades of grass? It's kinda like a camo plant. You can be hoverin' over it, starin' right at it, and not see it. Wild asparagus is a very sneaky vegetable." He looked down in front of him. "Hot damn! I

143

found me the mother lode, Jane!" He snapped up the tender stalks, occasionally chewing on a few to test them. After several minutes in silence, he turned to Jane. "How come you said he was nothin'?"

Jane stopped in her tracks. "I never said it was a 'he.'"

Harlan looked at her in a strange daze. "But it was a 'he.'"

She stared at him. "Why is this so important to you?"

"'Cause I saw the look in your eyes last night. You took it personal. You couldn't save him and you'll be damned if anybody else is gonna do you like that again." He waited but Jane remained taciturn. "When you say it's 'nothin,' I don't believe you, Jane. I think you call things 'nothin,' 'cause you don't want to feel no more pain. But that don't mean it ain't still there."

"What do you want, Harlan?" Her tone was abrupt.

"You see, right there? That's what I'm talkin' about. Kinda knee-jerk. You gonna attack me before I attack you—"

"I'm not attacking you."

"And I ain't attackin' you. I'm just askin' you a simple question."

She hesitated and then spoke. "He was my boyfriend from college."

Harlan waited. "Yeah…Okay…Go on. What was his name?"

Jane snapped the end off an asparagus stalk. "Mark."

"And you loved him, right?"

Jane sighed. "We were mutually attracted to each other because of our shared addictions."

"You didn't answer my question, Jane. Did you love him?"

"Yes. I made that mistake."

"Mistake? How can lovin' someone be a mistake?"

"Because when you love someone, you don't let that person find you with a bullet in your brain! That's not love!" Her voice caught with emotion.

Harlan looked at her cockeyed. "You think Mark killed himself 'cause he didn't love you?"

She trod through the grass in search of more wild produce. "I don't need to hear you say his name."

Harlan stood still as Jane circled the meadow. "Mark…*Mark*…"

She spun around. "What in the fuck are you doing?"

"Why are you afraid of hearin' his name?"

She strode toward Harlan with angry purpose. "I don't talk about him. I don't think about him. So, *shut the fuck up*! It was a *long* time ago—"

"Hell, it can't be that long. You ain't more than…what? Forty-four? Forty-five?"

"I'm thirty-seven!"

"*Really*? Damn."

"Fuckin' take me out of my misery," she mumbled under her breath.

"If you're truly thirty-seven, we're only talkin' fourteen or so years ago. That ain't a long time, Jane. And you're lyin' when you say you don't think about him. You don't talk about him but you sure do think about him."

"Jesus! When I tell someone to shut the fuck up, they usually comply."

"Well, that's probably 'cause you got a loaded gun to their head," he offered, matter-of-factly.

She looked at him perplexed. "Why are you doing this, Harlan? Why do you care about any of this?"

"'Cause I like you and I think you deserve a good life. Maybe the first thirty-seven years could have been better but that don't mean the next thirty-seven are gonna hit the crapper."

"Nice. Real quaint. You ought to write greeting cards."

"And *you* oughta call Hank."

The comment came out of left field. "Are you able to comprehend what in the hell is going on with your life right now? Do you get what a fucking mess we're in?"

"What's that got to do with Hank?"

She was stunned and temporarily speechless. "I am begging you to stop being this stupid."

He smiled. "There ain't no 's' in 'tupid.'"

"Huh?"

"My granddad used to call me 'stupid' when I was a little boy. He said he didn't lose a testicle in the Big War and nearly a leg to give me the freedom to be stupid. But I didn't hear the word right. So, I said, 'I ain't tupid, granddad.' And he looked at me and he said, 'Well, boy, there ain't no "s" in "tupid."'"

"I don't get it."

"I don't either. Maybe you're 'tupid' too," he said with a mischievous grin.

They'd gathered enough asparagus to feed a small family and headed back to the car when Jane turned around.

"We need more food than this." She looked across at the farm. "Promise me you'll stay put in the car?"

Knowing

Harlan nodded and Jane set off across the perimeter of the meadow. It was barely eight o' clock in the morning but that was prime time for farmers. Jane surreptitiously approached the back acreage of the property and came up on a barbed wire fence. A sign warned her that she was encroaching on the private property of the Kirchner Family Dairy Farm and trespassers weren't allowed. But Jane Perry never let a little sign slow her down. Wiggling her way between the barbed wire, she managed to just make it through without getting hooked. But she didn't allow for the sloppy soil beneath her feet. When the sole of her cowboy boots hit a pocket of mud, Jane hit the muck hard. "Fuck me!" she whispered in defiance. Caked with dripping mud, Jane struggled to extract her body from the mess. But just as she was about to get up, she heard the sound of a man's voice in the distance.

"Sarah!" he yelled, angrily.

Jane hunkered down in the mud and low-lying grass. There was a large barn about fifty yards away, which Jane had to assume was the milking area. A tall, heavy-set man wearing a plaid flannel shirt and overalls led two cows toward the old structure.

"*Sarah!*" the man screamed again, with added frustration.

"I'm coming!"

Jane watched as a little brown haired girl about eight years old ran through the field toward the barn, carrying a baby goat. Almost simultaneously, Jane felt an insect work its way up the inside of her right pant leg. "Jesus!" she whispered, standing up quickly.

In that second, the little girl turned and stopped in her tracks, staring at Jane across the grassy field. Jane ducked back down but she knew the kid had already spotted her.

"Sarah!" her father yelled again. "Stop screwing around and get in here!"

Jane carefully looked up again from her crouched position. The child continued toward the barn but seemed more entranced with Jane than concerned. There were two options here, Jane factored. One was to continue to the barn and see what food she could grab and the other was to return empty handed to the Mustang. With her churning, hungry gut, the choice was obvious. By the time she reached the rear of the two-story wooden building, she could easily hear the loud scolding Sarah's father was delivering to his daughter.

"When I tell you to come here, I don't mean in five minutes!" he berated her. "I mean immediately! You understand?"

Jane carefully moved around the structure toward an open window.

"I don't want to hear any excuses out of your mouth, Sarah! We've got the Farmer's Market tomorrow. You know your responsibilities and I'm sick and tired of having to remind you! Is that clear? *You understand me?*"

Jane couldn't hear the kid's response but it didn't matter. Her triggers were igniting. "You understand me?" may have been three simple words to anyone else, but to Jane they sent her backward twenty-three years and into that chaotic household. That impulsive urge to strike out and attack the oppressor was there but the situation didn't allow for it.

"Smarten up, Sarah! Nobody in this world is going to give you anything! There are *no free lunches*! Remember that! You understand me?"

"Yes, sir," the child said, in a strong voice.

"Do your job!" With that, the man irately walked out of the barn and headed across the field.

Jane stood motionless for several minutes. She didn't hear anything inside the barn and so she craned her neck and glanced into the window. The kid was gone.

"Hi."

Jane spun around. "Fuck!"

Sarah stood behind Jane with a soft smile. "I didn't mean to scare you."

The awkwardness of the moment was only outdone by Jane's desperation. "I'm not gonna hurt you, okay?"

"I know you're not," the girl replied softly as she petted the goat's head.

Somehow the kid knew Jane was okay, although Jane had no clue how this child figured that out so quickly. "You got some milk and eggs in there?"

"Uh-huh," the girl nodded.

"Can I get some?"

The child checked around the corner. "Can you move fast?"

"Fast enough, kid."

Jane followed Sarah into the barn. On one side were the two cows in their milking stalls. Above them was a hayloft and to the side a long table with a red and white plastic tablecloth that appeared to be used for selling the farm's produce. Beyond that was a clothesline filled with shirts, a couple pair of overalls, canvas pants and towels.

"We keep all of it in there," Sarah said, pointing to an old refrigerator. She crossed to the large doors of the barn and acted as a lookout.

Knowing

Jane checked the items. Shelves of milk, cheese, yogurt, keifer and eggs filled the space. She snatched up one gallon of milk, three blocks of cheese, two-dozen eggs and a quart of yogurt. Sarah handed her a burlap sack to carry it. Sitting on a table next to the refrigerator were vacuum-sealed bags of homemade jerky. Jane quickly swept up six packages. Once it was all secured in the sack, she reached into her wallet and handed the kid a hundred-dollar bill.

"That should cover it," Jane stated.

"Just take it." She gently set the baby goat down on the barn floor.

Jane shook her head. "Like your dad said, there's no such thing as a free lunch." The girl stood there perplexed. Jane knew she had to beat feet out of there quickly. "What do you like to do in your spare time?"

"Read."

Jane shoved the hundred-dollar bill in the kid's pocket. "That'll buy you a few books. Tell your dad you found it on the road." She started to turn. "Or don't tell him," she said with a knowing glance.

"Tell him what?" the girl replied, wise beyond her years.

Jane looked at the clothing hanging on the line. "What size is that shirt and overalls?"

Back at the car, Harlan and Jane dove into the farm fresh food with gusto. Harlan was thrilled to have his raw eggs again and slammed six into his mouth before Jane even had the cheese unwrapped. As a dedicated omnivore, Jane knew she couldn't exist on just dairy alone so she plopped three raw eggs into a stainless steel coffee travel mug, added enough milk to dilute the yolks and swallowed it. To her shock, the concoction didn't make her gag. And it seemed to work because she began to gather more energy. She pulled out the flannel shirt and overalls she stole off the line and handed them to Harlan.

"You need to get out of those clothes. They look ridiculous and they smell."

"Yeah, and puttin' a flannel shirt and overalls on a fat guy makes him look even better," he sarcastically replied.

It was the first adroit comment Jane had heard from Harlan's mouth and she couldn't help but smile at his self-deprecating humor.

"What kind of trouble are we gonna get into today, Jane?" Harlan asked, powering through the carton of eggs.

She stared out into the fields that dotted the bucolic scenery. There was a sense of something close by—of family and home. But there was also a feeling of regret and unhappiness.

"What is it, Jane?"

"I feel that sadness too." She turned to the dairy farm and wondered if she was still hooked into that child's drama. But she wasn't. The melancholy came from another place. It was tinged with loneliness and buffered by years of disappointment.

"We ain't that far from the New Mexico border. Maybe we should get out of Colorado and head south? You still got to see your sister—"

"Half-sister," she corrected with an edge to her voice. "And I don't have to see her."

"Sure you do. Just like you're gonna have to call Hank," he replied, chugging a cup of milk and wiping off his face with the back of his fleshy hand.

Jane pulled up the memory of the night before. "Where's your notebook?"

He found it and handed it to Jane. Turning the pages, she scanned them quickly.

"What is it, Jane?"

"Just looking for something…" It was a stretch but she hoped it was in there. And it was, dead center, in the heart of the notebook: **IEB**. "Does that mean anything to you?" she asked him, pointing out the three letters.

"Nope."

Jane checked to see if her computer had any Internet coverage but she was out of range. "International…Environmental…Bureau?" She mused, taking a wild stab. "Investigative Election Board…"

"I Eat Bacon?" Harlan offered. "I Enjoyed Beer?"

Jane shot him a tired look. She needed to let her mind percolate a little longer on what IEB might stand for.

"Anything else in the bag?" Harlan asked, pointing to the burlap sack.

Jane was still deep in thought as she handed him the sack.

"Oh, shit…" Harlan murmured.

"What?" Jane asked, quickly coming out of her deliberation.

Harlan handed her an eight by ten color flyer. "This was folded at the bottom of the sack."

It was a flyer from the Las Animas County Sheriff's Office from the previous year, promoting the appointment of Undersheriff Joe Russo. Surrounding his smiling face were four cheesy color photos that were supposed to represent his professional interests. "Schools," "Community," "Family" and "Neighbors" framed Russo's mug. Harlan stabbed his first finger on the photo of a house in the "Neighbors'" shot.

"It's the blue picket fence, Jane."

"Holy shit." She eyed it closer.

"Did you see it too last night?"

"Yeah." It looked identical to what she saw in the vision. But Las Animas County was pushing one hundred miles east of where they were at that moment. Why in the hell this flyer was found at the bottom of a burlap sack in a dairy barn she just happened upon wasn't the biggest question Jane had. Her main quandary was how they were going to get to where they needed to be without tipping off a cadre of law enforcement. Checking a beat up map she found nearly glued under the driver's seat, Jane factored it would take about two hours to get to Trinidad, the county seat of Las Animas, if they took major roads and the highway. Opting for the most remote mountain back roads, she figured they would easily tag another ninety minutes onto the trip. After ducking behind a grove of trees to change into another pair of jeans, Jane secured the food in the cooler. With Harlan satiated in the backseat and snoozing under a heap of blankets, Jane turned the Mustang around and headed east.

CHAPTER 12

They rolled into Trinidad just after noon. Jane hugged every single side street she could find, sliding between vans and trucks whenever she could to avoid being detected. She had no clue where this house was located but she figured it was close to town and in a middle-income neighborhood. She came to a crossroad and didn't know which way to turn. Instead of locating a needle in a haystack, she was looking for a blue picket fence in a sea of houses. Jane stared at the flyer again. It was slightly blurred, but behind the house, she could see what looked like the top of a steeple on a church. Based on the point of view and assuming the steeple wasn't Photoshopped into the image, Jane cruised closer to the main drag and found the church. But she felt exposed out there in her ice blue bullet and quickly diverted down several side roads that led directly to a small, neat, middle-class neighborhood that looked identical to her vision.

She warned Harlan to stay down in the backseat as she drove up and down the streets. After five minutes, Jane pulled over to the curb to check the location of the church steeple. Three houses up, a woman walked out to her mailbox. She wore a silky pink dressing gown rimmed with faux feathers on the collar and sleeves. Her long black wavy hair flowed freely down her back, in stark contrast to her exquisite porcelain skin. There was a vibe about her that Jane instantly recognized.

Jane waited until the woman returned inside her house before inching the Mustang closer. There it was. A beautiful vine of tiny pink flowers draped over a blue picket fence. Jane backed the Mustang up and parked it a block away in a strip of greenbelt and hidden within a tight grove of spruce trees. Without even being asked, Harlan offered Jane his wrist.

"Better lock me in again. Just in case he gets the urge to roam." Jane clamped the handcuffs on Harlan's wrist and secured him to the gearshift. "What's your plan, Jane?"

She thought about it for a second. "I don't have a clue." Her gut starting gnawing, signaling her nerves going on high alert. She grabbed her badge and tucked it into her leather jacket. Reaching under the passenger seat, she rummaged around until she uncovered her Ruger .380 pistol snapped into its holster. Weighing fewer than ten ounces, it was the perfect concealed weapon and she'd looked long and hard before she found a holster that fit perfectly on her cowboy boot. After checking the clip and racking the slide, Jane attached the pistol and holster to her right boot. Harlan watched the whole thing.

"You think you're gonna need that?" he asked.

"Remember me, Harlan? I'm that annoying boy scout with O.C.D." Rummaging through the plastic bag from the previous day's shopping excursion, she removed the blond "Diana" wig and slid it over her hair. Tucking her brown hair under the wig, she gave the short hairstyle a quick once over before turning to Harlan. "What do you think?"

"I think you look like my ninth grade gym teacher. And that ain't a good thing."

She walked down the block, canvassing the neighborhood continually like an owl on sentry duty. The closer she got to the woman's mailbox, the easier she saw the name on it: Nanette Larson. Jane reached out and rubbed the three last letters, "s-o-n," moving back into the memory of what she saw the previous night. Scanning the front yard, it was immaculate and filled with romantically inspired statues of reclining fairies, tinkling metal chimes and multi-colored metal globes that reflected the blue sky. Rose bushes, still dormant, lined the clean, brick pathway that led to the white clapboard house. Above the front door was a wooden valance of carved roses—another purposeful romantic touch. Putting everything together, Jane understood Nanette's intention and the closer she got to the front door, the more she understood the woman who resided there. She took a deep breath, closed her eyes for a moment to get into the vibe and then knocked on the door.

It took about a minute before she answered, swinging the door open with gusto. "You're so early, sweetie!"

The minute she locked eyes with Jane, Nanette's visage went from false enthusiasm to trepidation. Her long black hair was still slightly wet from the shower and her face moist from the cream she had just applied. A sweet, aphrodisiac perfume of Jasmine oil wafted toward Jane. Romance and sensuality oozed off of Nanette's body, from her triple D breasts to her delicate feet that hugged pink, metallic beaded slippers. Jane figured she was about thirty-two and in exceptionally good health. This woman was not the town bicycle nor had she been passed around like a Netflix rental. She was a stunning goddess who made every single man believe he was the only one.

"Nanette Larson?" Jane said.

She froze. "Yes."

Jane quickly flashed her badge. "I'm with the local Sheriff's Department. We're investigating a crime and I'd love to ask you a few questions."

Nanette regarded Jane with growing fear.

Jane moved toward the door. "May I come in?"

Nanette stood to the side but her reluctance was apparent. "I have some-one showing up here in a few minutes," she said in a quiet, nervous voice.

Jane knew whoever was showing up wouldn't be there in "a few minutes" because Nanette had already given herself away with her effusive greeting. The woman was scared and it wasn't because she was afraid of getting busted for her chosen profession.

The living room looked like an ode to the antebellum period. Lampshades were adorned with clear crystals, a fainting couch upholstered in crimson and gold threaded fabric sat by the ornate white fireplace while the walls were wallpapered in a soft pink fleur-de-lis design. Two purple silk folding screens separated the front room from what looked like a small kitchen. But based on the carpet wear, the permanent pathway led from the front door and into a side room that Jane assumed was the bedroom.

Jane stood in the center of the room. "This won't take a long time, Nanette."

She closed the front door and kept her back to Jane, as if she was contem-plating her next move. It was obvious to Jane that Nanette was a gentle soul who didn't want any trouble.

Nanette turned. "I really do have someone coming."

Jane nodded. "Yeah, I know. You mentioned that already."

Nanette tensely studied the floor where the sheepskin rug lay in front of the fireplace. "Coffee?" she suddenly said, as if the idea was original.

Jane realized that a cup of java would taste pretty damn good. "Sure."

Nanette pulled her pink dressing gown around her chest, suddenly be-coming chaste, and walked between the two screens and into the kitchen. Jane followed her. The small white kitchen was banked with windows that flooded the room with sun and warmth. A back door led out into a small grassy yard rimmed with planting beds and more metal chimes that swung softly in the spring breeze. Nanette crossed to the coffee maker where a full pot of hot java was waiting.

"You like cream in your coffee?"

"No. I take it black."

"Okay. Then here you go."

With that, Nanette clutched the glass coffee pot and spun around. Jane quickly ducked out of range right before she launched the burning brew in her direction.

"Goddamnit!" Jane screamed, feeling the sting of a few hot sprays of coffee hit her hands. She backed up, hoping to avoid slipping in the puddle of brown liquid that now covered the kitchen floor.

Nanette quickly reached around and pulled out a steak knife from the wooden block. She lunged toward Jane, screaming in a strange, wispy tenor. Jane easily blocked the attack by grabbing Nanette's wrist and slightly bending it backward.

"Drop the knife!" Jane yelled.

Jane pushed hard on Nanette's wrist, trying to get her to drop the blade. But Nanette followed through with a hard slap to Jane's face with her left hand. Jane's instincts kicked into gear as she forced the knife to the floor and slammed Nanette up against the kitchen cabinets and held her in an easy chokehold.

"What in the hell are you doing?!" Jane screamed, inches away from Nanette's terrified face. "I just need to ask you some questions, for fuck sake!"

Nanette was breathing heavily as sweat beaded across her upper lip. "You're not from the Sheriff's office," she stated in a muted tone. "I know everyone who works at the Sheriff's office. The Undersheriff is my next appointment!"

Suddenly it made sense why Joe Russo used Nanette's house to define "Neighbors" in his colorful flyer. Nanette was working under the Undersheriff. "I'll let you go if you promise you won't attack me!"

Nanette's eyes filled with tears. "And let you kill me?"

"I didn't come here to kill you," Jane said, carefully removing her hand from Nanette's throat.

Nanette rubbed the delicate skin around her neck that was quickly starting to bruise. "Then what do you want?"

"I need to ask you some questions…" she hesitated, "about Gabriel?"

Nanette's eyes grew as big as saucers. "Please! I beg of you! Don't hurt me!"

"Am I fucking stuttering? I didn't come here to hurt you!"

"Then how do you know Gabe?"

"I don't! That's what I need to talk to you about!" Jane noticed the bruises getting more colorful on Nanette's neck. "Put some ice on your neck, would you? I don't want Joe thinking that your last client got too rough." She backed up to give the woman access to the freezer.

Nanette quietly brought out the ice tray and pressed a few cubes against her neck. "Where is he?" she asked Jane, her lower lip trembling.

Jane suddenly felt very sorry for the woman. It was obvious she was fond of "Gabe." "He's dead."

She put her hand to her mouth in shock. "Oh, my God. When?"

"About nineteen months ago."

Nanette bowed her head, clearly upset.

"When was the last time you saw him?"

"It's been just over four and a half years," she replied, daintily wiping her tears with her ring finger.

Jane was dumbstruck. "Jesus, the way you're acting, he must have made quite an impression on you."

"He captured my heart," she whispered. "He was a really wonderful man even though…" She bit her lip.

"Even though he did bad things?"

Nanette looked at Jane. For the first time, she relaxed. "Yes. Who are you?"

"I'm a private investigator. I was hired by his family to look into his murder."

"His family?" she regarded Jane with suspicion.

"Yeah. Why does that surprise you?"

"He told me he'd had no contact with his family for years. After he joined Delta Force, he said they wanted nothing to do with him. I think they're pacifists or something."

Jane's mind did somersaults. "Yeah, you're right. They are pacifists. But they still want to bring his killers to justice."

"I don't understand how you found me or what I have to do with any of this."

Knowing

Jane was asking herself the same damn questions. But the clock was ticking before Joe Russo showed up for his "nooner." "I need you to remember everything you can about Gabe as quickly as you can remember it."

"He'd be gone for months at a time and then he'd call me and we'd see each other. He always brought me a gift from wherever he'd been."

"Like what?"

"He brought me frankincense oil from Egypt once. Then there was the prayer rug from Iran. And the kilt," she said with a soft smile.

"The kilt?"

"Yes. He spent a lot of time in Scotland during the last times we were together."

Jane tried to make sense of it. Egypt, Iran and Scotland? "Approximately what time period was he in Scotland?"

She thought back. "Right around four and a half years ago, give or take a month or so."

"Right around the time before he stopped seeing you?"

"Yes." Her eyes drifted to the refrigerator.

"What is it?"

"Nothing…"

"Tell me."

"It's silly. He had cases of this special ale shipped to me from Scotland. It's the only alcohol he'd drink when he was here. I still have the last case in that closet," she pointed across the room. "And one in the fridge all this time, thinking he might just show up one day."

"What made that beer so special?"

"He told me it wasn't made with hops. It's made from an old Scottish recipe where they use pine needles to ferment it."

"Pine needles?"

"Yes."

"Did he ever tell you why he drank it?"

"Gabe always talked about how nothing is what it seems. How that if everybody found out what was really going on in the world, it would blow every single belief system apart. He told me once that everything we cling to is really an illusion that's manufactured by people who want to control us."

"This is the kind of pillow talk you guys would have?"

She smiled. "Sometimes…" She bowed her head again, clearly still affected by Gabe's death. "He was his own man. He didn't answer to anyone. But more than anything, he didn't want to be controlled, by any thing or any person. That's why he told me he only drank that beer."

"I still don't get it."

Nanette gathered her thoughts. "He said the first beers back in the 1500s were made from pine and other herbs that were…stimulating." She suddenly looked oddly embarrassed.

"Okay…"

"Apparently, they made men more talkative…more energized…more sexual."

"Really?"

"Gabe said that pine needles helped a man's testosterone while hops made a man tired and passive. And he said it was all by design. I remember the story because he told it so well. He said that five hundred years ago, the priests noticed how aroused and focused people were who drank the pine needle beers. And they weren't just sexually charged, he said, they were lively and a force to be reckoned with." Jane could see that Nanette took some comfort in the re-telling of the tale. "But the priests couldn't control them and the Church needed to take back that control. So, one day a priest noticed that the workers who were picking hops in the fields were always falling asleep and they were also impotent."

"How would the priest know the workers were impotent?"

She arched her well-plucked brow. "Do the math," she said succinctly.

Jane nodded. "Ah, right. The hypocrisy has landed. Go on."

"I guess the word came down that all beer from that moment on had to be made only from hops. If anyone made beer with pine needles or other energizing herbs, they were in violation of the Church's law and they were against God."

"The ultimate control," Jane said. "That story had an impact on you, didn't it?"

"Yeah. But I remember a lot of Gabe's stories. He was the most intriguing person I've ever met in my life and I was honored to call him my friend." She moved a step toward Jane. "He was a thinker. You don't run into those kind of people anymore, do you?"

Jane shook her head. "No, you don't."

Nanette checked the time. "Joe's going to be here any minute—"

"Where did Gabe live?"

"He didn't have a permanent address. He said there was no point. But his parents lived in Colorado, as you obviously know. Being pacifists, I don't think he related to them at all. And since he was an only child, he was good at being a loner. Gabe didn't need people around him. He was more like an island that was completely self-sufficient."

Jane wanted desperately to ask her if she knew the family's location but since she'd sold the ruse that they'd hired her that was off the table. "How'd you find out what Gabe did for a living?"

She studied the floor again. "One day when he was in the shower, I looked in his duffel. I found ten different passports, with ten different names."

"Do you remember if any of those names was Werner Haas?"

"No. I don't think so."

"How can you be sure?"

"I remember names with word associations. Helps in my line of work. I'd remember Haas because I like Haas avocados. I know that sounds strange—"

"No. Actually, I get it."

Nanette nervously licked her lips. "He knew I snooped in his bag. I don't know how he knew, but he did. But he didn't get upset at me for doing it. He seemed to know intuitively that I would never do anything to hurt him. He did tell me, though, that I needed to be careful. He used to sweep the house every time he'd show up. He said that if anything ever happened to him…" her throat caught with emotion.

"What?"

"That someone might come after me. Something about, 'cleaning up the loose ends'?"

That was a familiar requirement, Jane reasoned.

"And watch out for the 'gingers.'" Nanette added.

"The gingers?"

"Red heads. He told me to be cautious."

It seemed like a strange comment to Jane. Gabe sounded like a guy who was beyond the typical stereotyping and pigeonholing. The superstition about "gingers" being soulless and ruthless was born from the Vikings who purposely placed red headed soldiers on the front line because they were purportedly bred to be fearless and merciless when it came to killing the enemy. Jane was just about to discount Nanette's statement when she flashed on the red-haired creep from the bus explosion who had the strange crimson mark on his hand.

"So, has anyone come after you?"

"No. Just you."

Jane suffocated a smile. "You'll be okay. God knows you've got plenty of protection from Joe and the boys on the force."

Her eyes misted over. "Maybe Gabe's watching over me now?" She studied the floor again. "I think I knew he was dead because out of nowhere, I'd sometimes feel like he was in the room. I can't really describe it." She struggled for the right words. "It was like a…a—"

"Muscular thickness?"

She softened and her shoulders finally relaxed. "*Yes.* It doesn't make any sense, does it? But that's exactly the way it feels when I've sensed his presence." She smiled. "Adapt or die," she stated out of the blue.

Jane looked at her with a stunned expression. "Gabe said that?"

She nodded. "It was his mantra. You wouldn't believe some of the things he used to do to make that point."

"Like stand naked in the snow?

Nanette's jaw slightly dropped. "How did you—"

"You're not the first person I've interviewed who knew him."

"Oh. Of course." She checked the clock again. "I never caught your name."

"Anne," Jane replied quickly.

"Anne…"

Jane briefly wondered what strange word association Nanette was concocting at that moment. She also snuck a look at the time. "Look, I need to know if you are aware of who Gabe worked for? Was it the government?"

"I don't think so. I think after Delta Force, he was hired by a private contractor."

Private contractor. That was the new, politically correct way of calling Gabe a hired mercenary. It made perfect sense to Jane. From what little she knew about the man, he certainly didn't sound like someone with a strong desire to fit in. He was highly intelligent, strong, wired for the fight, an expert marksman and adept at rooting out the enemy. "You get a name of that private contractor?"

"No. I was smart enough not to ask that question. But I know he didn't trust them," Nanette declared. "He said the company who hired him was 'invisible.'"

"How?"

Knowing

"They answered to nobody. They blended into society and were embedded in every facet of our lives. It sounded like a lot of that conspiracy stuff you hear and disregard. But I could tell he wasn't lying. Sometimes, he'd send me postcards with photos of different foreign countries. It took me a while to figure out that within a week or so of receiving the card, the location featured in the photo would be in the news. And not in a good way."

"I don't understand."

"There was one with a picture of children from the Congo, dressed in their tribal outfits. Less than a week later, I saw a story on the Internet about a coup in that region and tribal leaders were slaughtered, along with lots of children. That got my attention."

Jane felt the clock ticking on their tête-à-tête. "You think Gabe was involved in that massacre?"

"I don't know. I can't imagine he would kill a child."

"But he *did* kill for a living?"

"I think…I think Gabe killed people who needed to die. I like to think he never touched the innocent ones."

"Did he ever mention the name Romulus to you?"

"No."

"How about Odin?"

"No. Never."

"What about IEB?"

"No. Why?"

Jane flashed on the white binder with the bold red letters on the front. Maybe IEB was the name of a job or a project Gabe was assigned to? "You never heard him use the term 'IEB'?"

"No. I swear he never mentioned it."

Jane factored that 'invisible' was the right word to describe his employers.

"Look, I know he killed people. But…he was exceptionally kind to me every time we met. He had a beautiful heart. I know people use that term a lot but I really mean it. He was better than what he did for a living. I always kinda hoped he would see that one day." She thought about her memories. "He could have done great things. He had abilities that other people do not have. I'm sure that's why he was so damn valuable to his boss."

"You paint him like a saint."

"No. He was better than that. If he could have changed his occupation and gone into the public sector, he would have done incredible things for this world. I know it! He was capable of making great strides. He had the charisma and perception to turn lead into gold. He would have been worshipped by millions."

"That's a helluva strong statement, Nanette."

"I don't care. It's the God's truth," she said matter-of-factly. "But I get the feeling that he couldn't leave his company ever. Even if he wanted to."

"Once a company man, always a company man," Jane echoed.

Nanette seemed to disappear within herself suddenly.

"What is it, Nanette?"

"Maybe," she whispered, as if Gabe's invisible "boss" was standing in earshot, "he did get out." She seemed locked in a strange place. "Maybe he got out because he couldn't do it any longer. It would explain that last card."

"What card?"

"It was a greeting card and inside, there was a photo of him. He was wearing jeans and hiking clothing. He had a backpack on and his body is turned away from the camera but he's looking back and you can just sort of see this look in his eye. It was like he was going away. Maybe, he was gonna go find himself?"

"I need to see that photo," Jane said with urgency.

"Hold on." She walked between the screens and disappeared into her bedroom.

Jane turned to the refrigerator and opened it. Scanning it quickly, she grabbed some apples and an orange, hiding them down her buttoned leather jacket. She started to close the door when she spied a peculiar label on a single bottle of beer. She picked up the brown bottle and looked at the green tartan label with the name, "Alba—Scots Pine Ale."

Nanette returned, holding a small Bible. With a sweet reverence, she slid the white envelope out of the Bible and handed it to Jane. There was no return address and no postmark.

"I found it in my mailbox one morning. I think he personally put it there."

Jane stared at the writing on the front of the envelope. A student of graphology, she'd learned many years ago to analyze handwriting and signatures in order to identify personality traits of perps and suspects. Gabe's handwriting was like a voice to his spirit. In Jane's mind at that moment, his personality was resurrected on that envelope. Part of his essence was forever fixed in the ink that stained the white paper. And through that energetic pattern—buried in plain sight between the "Ts" and the dotted "Is"—was a slice of his soul.

Knowing

Jane recognized his strength and dogged purpose. He finished what he started and was exacting on anything he pursued. The lines showed he demanded a lot from himself and was a confirmed loner.

Jane pulled the card out of the envelope. It was a museum photo of an Egyptian Pharoah's gold statue. In the center of his elongated forehead was a brilliant gem blazing with reflected light. At the bottom of the card was a quote from Matthew 6:22 "If your eye be single, your whole body should be full of light." Jane looked back at the Pharoah's golden face and back to the quote. It didn't add up. Who puts a quote from the Bible on a photo of an Egyptian "god"? Jane opened the card. Inside, Gabe inscribed in all caps: "I WILL FACE THE DARKNESS, AS THE KNOWING LIGHT WITHIN MY HEART AND MIND LEADS ME HOME." Jane's own heart began to beat like a drum.

"What is it?" Nanette gently asked.

"What he wrote here? It's the end of a prayer he used to say whenever he was in danger."

"Oh," she said with slight disappointment. "I thought he wrote it just for me."

"He did. He wanted you to know it. Just like he wanted me to know it." Jane looked at Gabe's photo as an electrical pulse charged down her spine.

"What's wrong?" Nanette asked, clearly concerned.

"Nothing." Jane stared into Gabe's eyes. It was as if she'd already known him for two days. She'd seen those eyes staring back at her. First, at the tiny mountain house the night before and again that morning outside in the snow. Gabe looked like he was about six foot two and was all muscle. His round face and taut jaw were set off by a tousle of black, wavy hair. But as tough as he looked, his eyes were probing, yet kind. Somehow, Jane understood that she was directed by an unseen hand to find this photo. "How old was he in this shot?"

"Thirty."

Somehow, he looked a lot older to Jane. Life and death had clearly taken its toll on Gabe. And yet, for all the killing he apparently carried out, there was a serenity on his face. That "knowing light" within his heart shown through those piercing eyes. He was an enigma wrapped in a puzzle, and somehow that essence was trapped in Harlan's chest. "I need to borrow this card and photo."

"Oh, no, no, no, you can't take that!" Nanette quickly argued. "That's all I have left of him."

"I promise I will return it to you. You have my word." She could see that Nanette was still concerned. "I'm trying to find out who killed him, Nanette. His family has the right to know."

"But certainly you have other photos of him? Why that one?"

Jane looked at the card once more. "I think he's trying to tell a story here. But it's coded and I need to figure out the code." She looked Nanette in the eye. "I *will* return it to you."

Nanette reluctantly agreed. "You should probably get going."

Jane looked down at the bottle of pine needle beer. "Hey, can I buy that case of beer off of you?"

Nanette regarded Jane with a curious expression. "I didn't buy it. Gabe did. Why do you want it?"

"It's another piece of his puzzle. How much do you want for it?" She brought out her wallet.

"Take it," Nanette offered in a sad whisper, pointing to the closet.

Jane crossed to the closet. "Oh, one more thing, we have various spellings of Gabe's last name. Would you mind jotting down how you think he spelled it?"

While Nanette grabbed a piece of paper, Jane recovered the case of twelve beers from the closet. She held back the cold brew from the refrigerator and replaced it with a bottle from the case. Nanette turned and saw Jane's gesture.

"I need twelve," Jane said. "You still need one."

Her eyes filled with tears. "You're very kind. I'm sorry I threw the coffee at you."

"It's okay."

"And slapping you and the knife—"

"Really, seriously, it's okay."

The front door bell rang. Nanette spun around quickly. "Here," she handed the piece of paper to Jane. "Go out the back door!"

Jane slid the paper in her jeans' pocket and cradled the case of beer. "Thank you. You've been a lot of help." She walked into the backyard and out the side gate, hugging the fence line until she knew Joe was safely inside with Nanette. From there, she quickly walked down the block and back to the car. It was turning out to be quite the day—free food in the morning and free beer at noon. She unlocked the passenger door and set the case on the seat.

Harlan peeked out from under the blanket. "Oh, hell, Jane. Did the stress push you off the wagon?"

Knowing

She was just about to answer when she heard the sound of a police siren. Turning to an upper thoroughfare that rose up from across the greenbelt, she saw two police cars with their lights flashing and heading down the road.

"Oh, shit," Jane murmured. "We got trouble."

CHAPTER 13

"Stay down!" Jane instructed Harlan, as she crept around the Mustang to the driver's side and got in.

"You think someone saw the car and called it in?" Harlan asked, clearly upset.

"I'm not sure." She slammed the car door and removed the fruit she stole from Nanette's refrigerator from inside her jacket. Her mind raced, strategizing several scenarios in her head but none of them seemed realistic. The sound of a bullhorn and someone loudly directing traffic in the distance could be heard.

"What are we gonna do, Jane?" Harlan was becoming increasingly agitated.

"I'll figure this out! Relax!" Peering out the side window and onto the upper road, Jane saw a long line of traffic meandering in a line. "We go up there and we blend into the traffic."

"Why can't we drive in the other direction?"

"Because that way," she pointed behind them, "is a dead end and that way," she pointed to her right, "takes us to the main highway. If the cops have eyes on our vehicle, they'll be stationed at the exits and onramps of the highway. We have no choice but to go up that direction." She looked at her gas gauge. "Shit."

"What now?" Harlan asked, his voice elevated a few octaves.

"We have enough gas to go maybe thirty miles."

"It's over, isn't it?"

"*Over*? Shit, Harlan, it's not even one in the afternoon. I never give up before eight." She slowly backed the car out of grove of spruce trees and traveled out of Nanette's enclave. The closer she drove toward the upper road, the louder the bullhorn sounded. She could see a third police car positioned at one entrance to the road. The staccato "blipping" of a siren every now and again startled Jane and forced a hard breath of air out of Harlan each time it erupted.

Knowing

Traffic quickly came to a standstill at a four-way stop. Jane's Mustang stopped three cars from the front. The sound of a motorcycle revving its engine came up quickly on Jane's side. She turned just in time to see a cop on his bike jabbing his gloved finger at her and then point it toward the right hand lane, ordering her to change lanes. Jane nodded but something didn't feel right. The motorcycle cop held back traffic, allowing Jane to easily switch lanes before motioning for her to follow him.

"What's happenin', Jane?"

"I don't know," she replied, hardly moving her lips. She followed the cop past the long line of cars, quickly picking up speed as he led her up the single lane and onto a crowded neighborhood street that paralleled the main drag and the center of the business district. The cop got off his ride and moved a road barrier so Jane could roll through. Once she passed the barrier, he closed it up again and walked up to the driver's side. Rolling down her window, Jane heard a band playing in the distance.

"You're really late," the cop told her. "You need to head down this block and turn right." With that, he got back on his bike and sped off in the opposite direction.

"What the fuck—?" Jane mumbled to herself as she motored down the street and turned right. When she saw the scene, she couldn't believe it.

"Talk to me, Jane!" Harlan whispered.

"I think we're going to be in a parade." In front of her were dozens of polished classic cars and every single one of them was a Mustang. A sign nearby read: "Welcome to the Mustang Sally Crawl." Jane maneuvered her Mustang in between two other cars that were lining up for the route. At the sound of a honk, Jane carefully slid the gear into first and began the slow journey down the parade route. Hundreds of spectators lined the street, clicking cameras and waving at the stream of automobiles. At one point, Jane rolled down her window and gave a demurred "Queen's wave" to the enthusiastic crowd. It was like an out of body experience and none of it made a bit of sense, and yet she kept a plastic smile on her face and her eyes trained. It was obvious to her that even with the television coverage of her ice blue Mustang splattered on the screen, nobody made the connection. And why would they? They were programmed that day to see exactly what they came to see. For them, it was all just a blur of metal and colors, loud engines, a band loudly playing "Mustang Sally", popcorn and peanuts and a pleasant diversion.

Jane was reminded of what Nanette told her about the "invisible" group that employed Gabe. *They blended into society*, she claimed. Jane waved at a little boy who was wedged in a small tree to get a better view of the procession. He enthusiastically waved back at her with a huge grin on his small face. The whole thing was becoming increasingly surreal and absurd. Fewer than five minutes before, trepidation hovered close by and now, she was waving to children in trees, followed by a trail of classic Mustangs that outshone hers by a mile. But nobody noticed that her car didn't fit in this group. They didn't see how dirty her car was compared to the others in the parade. They didn't recognize that the hubcaps on her wheels were not the originals. And none of those cheerful faces could ever comprehend that a wanted felon was hiding under blankets in the backseat.

She was just beginning to actually enjoy the bizarre diversion when the parade route ended and the cars in front of her turned in different directions. Jane followed suit and found a gas station a few blocks off the main drag. The pumps were crowded with a few other classic Mustangs, allowing her vehicle to easily intermingle without anyone noticing. Jane still put her ball cap on and kept her head down and away from security cameras when she paid for the fuel. But it became increasingly obvious that nobody cared. For a brief moment, she stood at the pump and took in the scene, silently shaking her head at how easy it was to hide in plain sight.

Looking across the street, Jane spotted an electronics store. A thought popped into her head and she decided to take further advantage of her apparent anonymity. After purchasing a large-size ball cap at the gas station that would fit Harlan's head, she went into the store and scooped up twenty infrared LED lights, wires, a roll of black electrical tape, two nine volt batteries and a couple "on and off" switches. Pushing her luck just a bit more, she drove to a 1950s style drive-in restaurant on the outskirts of town and ordered six burgers, three servings of fries, a bag of onion rings, a large chocolate milkshake for Harlan, a medium size one for Jane and two sixteen ounce black coffees. Jane drove out of town, heading east ten miles and into stretches of territory that looked as barren as a moonscape. Pulling off the road and parking the Mustang next to one of the many dilapidated old ranching structures that dotted the terrain, Harlan sat up in the backseat and dug into his meal. After two days of living on pine nuts, bottled water, lunchmeat and raw milk, Jane realized how good it felt to finally sink her teeth into a hot meal and sip a strong, hot cup of java.

Knowing

"Hey, I got something for you," Jane said, reaching into her glove compartment and bringing out a bottle opener.

"You keep a bottle opener in your glove box?"

"Yeah, so what?" Jane handed the bottle opener to him. "It used to live on the turn indicator," she replied with a wry smile, as she opened the case of Scottish beer and handed Harlan the cold one. "Go on. Try it."

"Jane, I told you already. Beer and me don't get along no more."

"Just take a fucking sip, would you?"

Harlan reluctantly popped the cap on the bottle and took a small sip. It was as if a memory washed across his face and another piece of his chaotic puzzle fell into place. "Aw, hell, Jane. That's like comin' home."

She smiled. "It's brewed with pine needles instead of hops."

"Pine? Humph." He took another sip. "How many of these babies did you steal?"

"I didn't steal them. She gave them to me. And there are only twelve of them so pace yourself."

He took another hearty sip. "Oh, my God. I think I died and went to heaven. Hey, you think this is what the pine nuts and the pinecone meant? Makes sense, right?"

Jane thought about it. "No, I don't feel like it is. I feel it's just another nudge. Another pine sync."

"I have no idea what you mean but I trust that you understand it." He took a healthy gulp. "And I thank you for this adult beverage." He grinned.

With all the excitement, Jane almost forgot about that little piece of important paper that was tucked into her jeans' pocket. "Hey…we were right. His name *is* Gabriel. Well, Gabe…that's what she called him. And I got a last name."

"You kiddin' me?"

Jane pulled out the piece of paper and unfolded it. She stared at the name for a moment before showing it to Harlan. "Cristsóne." Harlan's ICU nurse was right. The last name ended in "o-n-e" and there was the accent.

"Wow. Gabriel Cristsóne." He slightly shook.

"You okay?"

Harlan kept staring at the paper. "Yeah. I kinda feel like I'm finding myself."

"It's a part of yourself. Gabe may be your engine but you're still the driver."

Harlan sat back, clearly bowled over. "Cristsóne. It's official. I got the heart of a Dago."

"You also have the heart of a ladies' man." She enlightened Harlan about Nanette's relationship with Gabe. For a second, his expression was difficult to read, appearing as if he was shocked and disgusted simultaneously. But then a huge smile broke out across his chubby face. "*Wow!* Damn! You know how every guy thinks he's got a stud inside him? Well, *I really do!*" He leaned forward on the front seat. "I never had a lot of confidence with the ladies. I've always been on the chunky side. Never got the pretty girl. But this guy inside me? He's been laid, relaid and parlayed!"

Jane smiled. "That's one way of looking at it."

"I wonder what his line was."

"Line?"

"Every successful man has a line he uses to reel in the females."

"Is that so?" Jane said, grabbing a few fries. "What was your line?"

"'My name is Harlan Kipple. Ever been kippled'?"

Jane nearly spit out her fries. "*That* was your line?"

"That was my line!"

"God help you," Jane mumbled. With a pickup line like that, it was amazing he wasn't a forty-two-year-old virgin.

"You know, you told me that you had a dream about making love to a woman who had long black hair and big boobs."

"Hell, yeah.

"I'm pretty sure that was Nanette. But you also said there were two other women and one of their names started with an 'M'? You sure it wasn't an 'N'?"

He considered the question. "Nope. They are two different people." He thought about it a little more. "The one with the name that starts with the 'M'...that's real."

"Real? What do you mean?"

"It's deeper than deep. It's like a love I've personally never felt for any woman. I can't explain it, Jane. Just mentioning it makes my chest feel light and..."

"And what?"

He thought about it. "Indestructible. Like part of me won't never die."

Jane took a bite of her burger. "What about that other woman? You mentioned a third one to me? Maybe that's the mysterious 'Agna' or 'Agnes' you jotted down in your notebook?"

Harlan became quiet. "Nah. That ain't her name." He shuddered. "Pardon my language, Jane, but that bitch scares the shit of me. No joke. I can't look at her. That stench around her…it's like death."

"You gotta grow some courage, Harlan. I mean it. You gotta be willing to open your eyes and face whatever is shown to you. How are you ever going to figure out any of this if you refuse to look at it?"

"I thought you said you was gonna be my eyes, Jane."

She sighed. "Yeah, I know I did. But two sets of eyes are better than one. Stop being afraid, Harlan," she said with an edge. "They're counting on you to be terrified."

"They?"

"Yeah. The ubiquitous 'they.' The more scared you get, the more paralyzed you become, the more you don't want to see what's being shown to you…the more they can control you out of pure fear. And personally, I say, 'fuck 'em.' I don't have a clue why these people are framing you or why they're chasing you. But if you keep your head in the sand or continue thinking you're too stupid to give me some personal impressions of what you're feeling or seeing, then you're just another victim who doesn't give a shit about their life or their self-worth."

He was silent for a few minutes. "You're right, Jane. Nobody has ever expected nothin' from me. And I figured that was okay because those were the same people who kept tellin' me I was stupid. So, I just figured they knew best."

"Well, Harlan, I'm not one of those people. I don't give a shit if you murder the English language. And I don't care what your IQ is. But I *do* care if you keep wringing your hands and telling me that you're helpless. For God's sake, Harlan, you have the heart of a lion inside you! You hearing me? You have the heart of a warrior beating in your chest. Somehow, Harlan Kipple drew the long straw so I suggest you stop telling me you're an idiot and start acting like a guy who's got a fighter planted inside of him." She leaned closer to him. "Start showing some goddamned initiative!"

He swallowed hard. "Nobody's ever talked to me like that."

"Well, they should have. All of us are only as smart as our dumbest move. Raise your own bar, Harlan. You're smarter than your typical ape and they can teach those fuckers incredible tricks." Jane finished her burger and balled up the wrapper, tossing it on the floor of the passenger seat. "I have something else to show you if you think your heart can take it. I have a photo of Gabe."

Harlan's mouth hung open. "Damn! What kind of trance do you put people under to get names and photos?"

She brought out the envelope. "I think it's got more to do with my genteel and tactful approach," she replied sarcastically. Jane handed Harlan the greeting card. "Check out the face and body that went with your heart."

Harlan slightly hesitated.

"Go on, Harlan. Be brave. Don't you want to look into his eyes?"

Harlan took the card and slowly opened it. Removing the photo, he stared at it.

"So? What do you think?" Jane asked him.

"I can't hardly explain it, Jane. Between the beer and this, I don't know what to say....except thank you. You done real good." He read the words Gabe wrote on the inside of the card. "What does that mean?"

"That's the last part of your prayer. You don't remember it? You say it whenever you get nervous or feel cornered."

Harlan shook his head. "If you say so." He read the lines again. "What do you reckon he means when he says, 'I will face the darkness'?"

Jane pondered how she should frame her answer. "I think it relates to who he worked for." She laid out everything that Nanette shared with her about Gabe's employers. "I know you don't want to believe it, but Gabe really was a professional killer."

The light seemed to drain from Harlan's face. "Okay." He allowed that realization to gel for a few minutes. "Who'd he work for?"

"I don't know yet. But Nanette said that Gabe called them invisible."

"She used that word, eh?" Harlan's interest quickly grew.

"Yeah."

He nodded. "Yep. I know that to be true. The crazy thing is, Jane, that I can feel invisible too sometimes. Like when I left the hospital to get away from Mr. Ramos? Nobody looked at me. Nobody stopped me. It was like they couldn't even see me." He handed Jane the photo.

"Hiding in plain sight," Jane murmured. "I get it." She took another look at the photograph. "Maybe Gabe knew how to become invisible."

Harlan launched into his second burger. "For real?"

"Maybe. Or maybe he knew how to disappear off the map?" Jane reflected on a few key points Nanette shared with her. The card with the photo was not mailed to Nanette, indicating that Gabe personally left it in her mailbox. It was the kind of thing you do when you're leaving town quickly and you want to make sure you make final contact with the people you care about. Nanette commented that the last time she saw Gabe was just over four and a half years ago. If he was thirty in the photo, it would make him thirty-three when he was killed. Taking into account what Nanette told her, Jane knew Gabe was in Scotland right before returning to the States. Her comment that "maybe he got out" and that perhaps he was going to "find himself" felt eerily accurate. It was a leap on Jane's part but sometimes it was those leaps that often led her toward the truth.

Perhaps, she considered, something horrific occurred in Scotland—something that shook Gabe to his core. If her gut was leading her in the right direction, whatever happened had to be so viscerally haunting that he turned his back on the clandestine group he worked for and disappeared. Jane focused on the disconcerting scene that unfolded in her mind's eye the previous night. She replayed the entire disturbing vision moment by moment, realizing now she was strangely witnessing Gabe on one of his sinister missions. Walking behind him down the shadowy hallway and then following him into the room where he shot the old man behind the desk, Jane recalled the unrushed manner in which Gabe inspected the files and separated them into piles. Then there was the white binder with the curious "IEB" on the front and the chilling question she mentally sent to him, "*What do you want from me?*" and his unsettling reply, "*Only what's necessary.*"

Jane wondered if whatever was in those files and in that binder brought the gauntlet down on Gabe's career. Why else would she have been shown such a disturbing set of events if it meant nothing to the case? The fact that Jane was even seriously postulating about what she saw in that scene made her take a mental step back. Her entire career was built on formal investigation and facts. And yet, there was always that free-floating vapor of intuition that operated just outside her perception of reality. When all else failed, she could dip into that strange mist of infinite knowledge and somehow always grasp the truth. But to simply hold someone's hand and be privy to their dreams, nightmares and insights was pushing her usual abilities to a different level. If she was still a drinker, she'd blame it on the booze. If she hadn't experienced all the unexplainable events that had taken place over the last few years, she would chalk it up to stress, low blood sugar or any other suitable explanation that swept it neatly under the rug. The thought crossed her mind that all those odd encounters from the past years occurred so that she could easily wrap her mind around this bizarre case. It was like priming a pump so that once it was primed the water flowed freely. And through that, she could plausibly accept what someone else could not begin to concede.

Allowing that understanding to percolate, Jane hypothesized that Gabriel might have easily disappeared for up to three years before being killed. What occurred during those missing years could have a lot to do with why he was taken out. If he did know something that wasn't supposed to be revealed, he would be a defined target. She recollected the tried and true statement she'd mentioned to Harlan—*people are only after you if you know something, stole something or saw something*. If her indeterminate vision was accurate, Jane had to assume that Gabriel qualified for all three of those possibilities. Proving that conjecture was going to be a lot more difficult.

The story of the pine needle beer intrigued Jane. It wasn't just the sync with the pine nuts and pinecone that Harlan collected in his mysterious bag. It was the tale about how Gabe refused to drink any beer that he felt was created to control or destabilize a man's innate power. Jane felt that statement was not just relating to a man's sexual power; somehow it referenced power and control that subverts a person's will. Jane sensed that as much as Gabe may have cared for Nanette, he wasn't about to discuss his work with her in any depth. But that didn't mean he couldn't talk around the subject. His comment to her that "everything we cling to is really an illusion that's manufactured by people who want to control us," hit Jane hard. After her last case in Midas, she was patently aware of how *control* of another person's life and thoughts was critical if the goal was to usurp their power.

Since he was alone so much, Jane reasoned, Gabe had the need to unchain himself when he reconnected with Nanette. From her own experience, if you didn't have someone to unload on—even if full disclosure wasn't on the table—the chance of a person falling into a mental hellhole was more likely. You can repress your experiences with booze, cigarettes, drugs and sex but if you don't set them free just a little bit, the ulcers appear, the heart attacks happen, the depression sets in and your mind becomes a trap that destroys your soul. It was the reason why the average criminal talked to someone about what they did. It wasn't so much bragging rights, it was to relieve themselves of the burden that the event held over their psyche. Once spoken and released, they could live again and go about their day without the shadow of the darkened memory encroaching.

The more she contemplated the idea, the more she felt that this was exactly what took place between Gabe and Nanette. Somehow Gabe knew he could trust her. After all, when Nanette snooped in his duffel bag and found the ten passports with ten different names, he didn't attack her or stop seeing her. He just *knew* she would keep her mouth shut without him having to ask her. Jane sensed that Gabriel Cristsóne had the uncanny ability to know what people thought and how they would react, given various circumstances. That made him a valuable soldier and probably an invaluable asset and assassin for his employers. With his innate gift of perceiving people and their motives in a way that others were incapable of, Gabe was miles ahead of everyone else who still relied on fallible data and second hand information.

While Harlan continued to chow down on the drive-in food, Jane brought out the greeting card and looked at the front again. There was the gold Egyptian Pharaoh's statue with the brilliant gem blazing in the center of his elongated forehead. What was with all the Egyptian references? From the doomed *Anubus* to the popular Egyptian-centered tattoos at Alex's shop and then onward to the Eye of Horus etched into the piece of lapis, it was clear that Gabe's essence was screaming something at Jane but her ears weren't yet tuned to the frequency.

She read the quote again from Matthew 6:22: "If your eye be single, your whole body should be full of light." Jane peered at the golden Pharaoh and the solitary gem illuminated in its head. "If your eye be single..." she whispered to herself. She flashed on the Eye of Horus. That was a single eye, she figured. She recalled all the items Harlan collected in his bag—the pine nuts, solo pinecone, the *Yogi* book, the Patsy Cline cassette tape, a bottle of sandalwood oil, the Eye of Horus on the lapis, the key, the Eco-Goddesses brochure, the comical illustration depicting a Blue Heron walking tipsily across the road, *The Q* magazine and the Easter card featuring the Angel Gabriel. She grabbed her computer, hoping that somehow she could hijack a Wi-Fi signal out there in the middle of BFE but she came up short.

"We have to find a motel," Jane stated.

"But I thought we had to lay low—"

"I can't keep working out of this car, or break into mountain cabins or pray that we'll stumble upon another classic car show." She could feel the pressure building inside her. "If we're going to punch this investigation forward, I need to find us a shitty, low-rent motel that has Internet access."

About ninety minutes east of their location, Jane found exactly what she was looking for. It was called "The Shangri-La," but they should have called it "The Shangri-Low" because you'd have a hard time finding a motel that was much worse. The two-story structure looked like it was built in the 1950s and hadn't been renovated since the 70s. But it was in the middle of nowhere and just enough off the beaten path to accommodate their needs for the night. There were also only two other cars in the parking lot that surrounded the motel on all sides and one of those cars was leaving. After checking in under "Anne LeRóy" and getting a room with two single beds, Jane drove the Mustang to their first floor room, #9. At least it wasn't number seventeen, Jane mused. But it was on the corner of the two-story building, and well out of view from the main office. Jane parked the Mustang in a space three doors down and unpacked the car before telling Harlan to carefully remove himself from the backseat and follow her into the room.

Once inside their room, Jane quickly closed the grimy curtains on the only window in the place. Turning on the lights, they surveyed their temporary digs. It looked like a slightly remodeled storage unit, thanks to the cement walls and bunker-like quality. The twin beds were supported on a permanent concrete frame and separated by a night table that was bolted to the floor. A brown and red shag carpet covered the floor, complete with various holes where it looked like someone had dropped a hot iron skillet and singed the nylon fibers. A bureau that looked like it came out of Goodwill stood at the foot of the beds with an analog television that featured a DVR recorder. There wasn't even a coffee maker or mini-fridge in the room but the ancient TV had a DVR remote control.

"Don't drop anything on the carpet, Harlan. We'll never find it."

"If these walls could talk, they'd scream," Harlan offered with a straight face.

"If these beds could talk, they'd beg to be vaccinated," Jane added, removing her blond wig and sauntering into the cement-blocked bathroom. The shower looked like something you might find in a remote village while on a Peace Corps mission. The towels appeared as if they just came out of a trauma unit. It was the type of motel where you lay your head on the pillow and wake up an hour later with a non-specific sore throat. The kind of place where bed bugs remain bloated on their immovable feast. Where simply brushing against the sticky remote control produces a crimson rash and pinprick pustules. But with everything going against it, it was still better than another cramped night in the Mustang and safer than breaking into a remote mountain cabin.

As much as Jane wanted to dig into her computer, she realized that she could use a hot shower and some soap. The small showerhead put out a powerful blast of water pressure that soothed her aching muscles and slowly renewed her spirit. She washed her hair and was just about to get out when a thought crossed her mind. Standing under the intense jet, she quickly turned the hot water off and allowed the icy cold stream to pelt her skin. At first, the shock didn't register. There was a moment when the heat and ice felt fine. For those few seconds, everything seemed like it would be all right. But then the shock of the frigid water hit her hard and she wanted to jump out. But she let out a hard breath and allowed the arctic gush to cascade down her spine and then across her face and hair. After several minutes, she'd adapted to the frigid water and even began to disregard the chilly temperature. By the time she toweled off, a wave of heat engulfed her skin as well as a renewed sense of energy and purpose. She dressed in a long-sleeved t-shirt and comfortable sweatpants and joined Harlan back in the room. While he showered, Jane turned on the television to wait for the local 5 p.m. news broadcast. She muted the sound and turned on her computer.

But the sound of loud voices and occasional pounding coming from the room directly above them distracted Jane. Given the fact that the motel was built like a bunker, it was incredible to Jane that she could hear anything. But the murmuring voices and erratic pounding continued until she finally had enough. Grabbing the room key, Jane walked outside and climbed the outside stairs to the second level. The voices coming from the room were even louder. She approached the room and checked the number. "Room seventeen—that figures," she said to herself. Inside, a man and woman were engaged in a heated argument. Jane edged closer to the front window and was able to clandestinely observe the two. It was clear that the woman, who towered above the man by at least eight inches, was in charge. Jane couldn't determine whether they were married or not, but the way the woman belittled the guy and occasionally slapped him on his arm or the top of his head gave Jane the impression that she wasn't in any danger. The guy, however, probably wasn't as lucky. Jane turned to go back downstairs when the decibel level coming out of the room doubled in intensity. She wasn't about to endure another crappy night of sleep and so Jane trod back to the room and pounded on the door. To her surprise, the yelling didn't stop, even when the woman unlocked the door and swung it open.

"Yeah?" the strident female bellowed.

"Hey! You're kinda loud," Jane stated. "Can you keep it down?"

"Who in the fuck are you?" the woman asked with a strange snarl.

"I'm the one in the room downstairs who can hear you through cement walls."

"Fuck off!" the woman yelled, starting to swing the door shut.

Jane caught the door. "Hey! It's called fucking common courtesy!"

The diminutive man walked forward in a menacing manner. "You looking for trouble, bitch?"

Jane had to hold back her instinctive, knee-jerk response. But then she couldn't help but see the bulge poking against the idiot's crotch.

"You come up here and bother us again," he said, suddenly acting as though he was tall, "and I'll call the fuckin' cops!"

"Never mind," Jane said with a shake of her head. "Have at it!"

Jane stormed back to her room and plopped on the bed with her computer. Harlan was still in the bathroom and the whacked out couple upstairs was still making enough noise to wake the dead. Doing her best to block out the distracting sounds, Jane logged onto her account with CBI and ran background checks on Gabriel Cristsóne, using variations of his name and spellings. But it was evident that his digital footprint didn't exist. She had no access to the FBI site and her contacts there weren't top shelf. For that matter, she couldn't call them anyway, considering her situation. Jane ran a general search on Gabriel, adding the word "Colorado" to the search field, in hopes of locating family members, but she came up empty again.

She thought about Werner Haas, the name Gabe used at least once. But all she found was the well-known pianist that Stella Riche alluded to. Somehow Jane knew that name had portentous meaning. It was far too obscure and the fact that Gabe continued to carry that fake ID several years after disappearing from his job made it even more compelling. Jane tried variable searches, even plugging in the word "Romulus" and "IEB" next to Haas and found nothing. Her thoughts turned to *The Q* magazine. Recalling Gabe's tenure in Scotland four and one half years prior, she took a leap of faith and went online to *The Q's* avant-garde website. Draped in an ominous black and purple design, the website featured subscription information as well as several articles from recent issues. Jane had to keep reminding herself that this was supposed to be a high end, men's sports and outdoor magazine, but it was so heavy with ads and so light on content that she wondered why anyone would bother subscribing to it. There was a link to archived issues and the site gave the viewer a one-time pass code to view an old issue. Jane counted back four and half years and then, allowing for one or two months, chose an issue. With all the artwork to download, it took a few minutes before she could view page seventeen. But the minute it began to load on her screen, her heart began to race.

At the top was a pastoral scene that looked like the Scottish Highlands. Tiny dots that looked like either goats or sheep grazed in the verdant rolling hills. An old timepiece hung in the lower half of the full-page ad, with its hands pointed to 10:10. And in the center was a single sentence: THERE COMES A TIME WHEN ALL GOOD THINGS HAAS TO END.

Jane sat back on the bed, still slightly shaking. Page seventeen really *was* a subversive kill directive. And from what Jane could tell, the entire magazine seemed to exist solely as a primer for traveling silent assassins who somehow found their own triggers embedded within the ads and acted upon them as required. She looked at the cover again and wondered why, "Q"? Did it stand for a certain word? Was it a play on words and mean "The Cue" as in The Cue to Kill? And then she realized what it stood for. "Q" was the seventeenth letter of the alphabet.

Jane reviewed the ad again. And after checking out a few other ads in the magazine that actually did appear to relate to a product, she observed how bizarre and unconventional they all were. In fact, the quirkier the ad, the better. It was simple, Jane deduced, to bury an assassin's next hit amidst the idiosyncratic pages of this disconcerting glossy publication. If everything else made no sense, why would page seventeen stand out? Based on Nanette's timeline and the old watch featured in the ad, Jane made the assumption that someone by the name of Haas met his maker on October 10th of that year. But now there were even more questions left unanswered. If Haas was the target, why in the hell would Gabe go to the trouble of creating a fake ID with Haas' name on it? Why in God's name would he want to advertise the name of the man he was sent to kill?

Jane located the greeting card and Gabe's photo. She stared into his eyes as they peered back at her. When that shot was taken, Gabe Cristsóne had possibly killed dozens of people. By Nanette's account, he only killed those who "needed to die." And while Jane agreed that there were people taking up oxygen on this planet who were more useful fertilizing daisies, the question of who or what group makes that final assessment was clearly significant. The sweeping up of souls who no longer had alleged value to the cause and who might have always had an early expiration date next to their name seemed like a sickening solution. But it was obviously one that the clandestine group known as Romulus or Odin had no difficulty issuing.

She returned her attention to Gabe's photo. There was purpose in his orbs. A reckoning. A desire to even the odds. But there was also a need for absolution, a purposeful mission into the wilderness to wash away his sins and uncover the answers to his questions. She drew the photo closer to her, wishing his voice would seep from the paper. "Talk to me, Gabriel," Jane whispered. She'd stared at hundreds of photographs of dead victims over the years, boring into their eyes in search of resolution. And sometimes, if she stared at them long enough, she could hear them speak. But that was only after months of working a case that struggled to be unraveled. She'd only been involved in this nightmarish case for three days and time was not on her side. If Jane was going to figure out any of this and remove the stigma that followed Harlan, she was going to have to get answers quickly and she was going to have to sharpen her intuitive eye.

She gazed at the photo one more time. Gabriel Cristsóne had done what many people in this world fantasize about. He'd removed himself from the world but stayed within it, ducking in and out of different characters and names, hanging around just long enough to finish a job and find some entertainment before moving on. From what she could figure out so far, Gabe continued this pattern after leaving his employer, walking into the world with nobody and no system to answer to.

It was a romantic notion and one that Jane had considered more than once. But instead, she disappeared into the amber liquid and nearly drowned. Now, starkly sober, the probing urge to disappear surfaced. To walk blindly into the void and live a life that blended self-satisfaction with self-sufficiency sounded like a plan. Sure, she wouldn't be able to indulge in personal relationships that held any future but somehow, Jane was willing at that point to give that up in order to retreat into what she perceived as freedom. The more she imagined what Gabe's life was like, the more she envied him. He may have agreed to do the devil's bidding but he also appeared to have an understanding of what the broader picture entailed. And he wasn't afraid of or cowed by the evil cabal who paid his salary. If anything, he stayed one step ahead of them, escaping their clutches for over three years. She pictured him hopping from one obscure island to another during his lost years, interrupted by sojourns atop mountain peaks and one-night stands in the local villages. He had only what he could carry on his back and no timetable in which to accomplish his objectives. It was life in the purest, rawest form, with consistent, trusted intimacy the only thing absent. The more Jane mused on Gabe's rogue lifestyle, the more she wanted to belong to it. It was easy to run and she knew how to do it better than most people. All she needed was the trigger—the situation that would allow her to flee without regret.

Of course, it would help to have enough cash to sufficiently support this escape. How would that work, she contemplated. Maybe Gabe created fake bank accounts all over the globe that he could dive into? He could have depended on an underground group of people to aid his progress but somehow Jane didn't feel that was entirely accurate. No, Gabe wouldn't take off like he did and then lean on others, while possibly putting them in danger. Even though Jane never met the man, she knew him. She felt his power and his independence. He wasn't afraid to die but he fought to live. He did what was needed to survive but he never harmed those who were innocent. Somehow Jane sensed that he plugged back into his pacifist upbringing and used it to stay alive. But somewhere down the road, he must have decided to re-emerge back into society and it was then that he was taken out. The question was *why*? What propelled him out of his sanctuary of solitude and back into the matrix of chaos?

Harlan was still ensconced in the bathroom, humming to himself off-key. Jane started to turn back to her computer when she sensed something odd outside. Sliding off the mattress, she crept to the curtained front window and carefully peeked out. The sun had set across the flat eastern plains of Colorado, leaving an Armageddon haze of orange and gray striations hanging in the upper atmosphere. The world out there felt dangerous. There was a heartbeat of anguish and torture that Jane could not rectify. But it stayed close to her, as if it was trying to get her attention. She pulled back the dirty curtain a little more and peered outside, gaining a broader view of the empty parking lot. Had they been detected? she wondered. Were the inscrutable "they" hiding in the bushes and behind the cement barriers, waiting for Jane and Harlan to emerge so they could gun them down and then hide their bodies forever? Although she had checked and doubled-checked her routes, while continually monitoring her surroundings, she questioned whether they just *knew* where she was. Jane needed to check herself again. She was starting to sound like Lilith on the *Anubus*, rambling about, "Even when I can't see him, he's in my head." It sounded insane when the poor girl said it but now it was beginning to make a lot of sense.

Jane scanned the quickly darkening parking lot one more time before securing the curtain against the window. Returning to her computer, she did a quick search for the meaning of the name "Gabriel." She questioned why she was wasting her time but then she found a curious website that had several pages of spiritual and mystical references to the fateful name. "Strength of God" and "The Divine is my strength" were two meanings attributed to the Archangel Gabriel. "Those who call on the Angel Gabriel," one text wrote, "will find themselves pushed into action that leads to beneficial results." Jane arched an eyebrow when she read the next passage. "Gabriel can bring messages to you through visions which will help to guide you on your course." She re-read it again, shocked at the statement. "If your third eye is closed and your spiritual vision is blocked," the passage continued, "Gabriel can open these portals, allowing one to receive prophecies of the changes on the horizon."

She stared at her computer screen. A comforting warmth crept around her, stretching its arms around her body and enveloping her. For a few minutes, she rested inside it, aware of its light and rectitude. There was profound power within it but there was also a sense of time running out—an urgent intensity that demanded to be heard. After it passed, Jane looked up at the television. The sound was still muted but a commercial played showing a woman who Jane figured was younger than she, pointing to her face to show the spots where age was encroaching. Jane turned on the sound and listened to this young woman gush about a new face cream that helped turn back the clock after six weeks of daily use. Jane would normally ignore such an ad but she was drawn to it. The only thing age offered was the possibility of wisdom through suffering and experience and the acceptance of what could and could not be changed. But other than that, Jane saw no other benefits to burning down one more candle each year. The ache in her back grew each month, the bags under her eyes matured and there were those strands of hair that were lighter than the rest of her brown locks. Her eyesight wasn't what it used to be just a couple years ago and she found herself starting too many sentences with, "These kids today…" When did she let herself get so fucking old?

The early, local news program began with a "Breaking Story." Dora Weller was still hospitalized after the shooting incident but expected to make a full recovery. However, her political team was making a major announcement. The camera cut to a microphone where a group of five men and women were lined up in the background. A man who looked to be in his early thirties approached the microphone. He wore a sharp black suit that made his shock of red hair stand out even more. His demeanor was quite serious as he spoke without the use of notes.

Knowing

"I want to thank everyone for coming here today on such a short lead time. It's been a tough couple of days for Congresswoman Weller but rest assured, we have been told by her incredible medical team that she will make a full recovery. However, after discussing the situation with her team and her family, Ms. Weller has made the decision to step down from her Congressional seat."

Jane heard the water shut off in the bathroom. She hit the PAUSE button on the DVR remote control and looked closer at the TV screen. Something felt completely off. "What the fuck?" She turned back to her computer and pulled up her history. Finding the right link, she clicked on it. She opened the video interview she watched of the motorcyclist who allegedly witnessed Jane's car being stolen outside of the Quik-Mart. She waited until the camera focused on him before pausing the video. Carrying her laptop to the television, she held it up to the TV screen to make a visual comparison. Even though the motorcyclist had his helmet wedged tightly down across his forehead, it didn't matter. Comparing the two faces, it was obvious to Jane that it was the same man. What in the hell was going on? She hit the Play button on the DVR TV remote and continued listening to the announcement.

"Her trusted aide, Steve Crandall, has been chosen as her successor. At this difficult time, we hope everyone allows us to effect a smooth and effortless transition as we move forward and continue with the many objectives that Congresswoman Weller believed in so strongly." He smiled a crooked grin. "Without further ado, let me be the first to introduce to you, Mr. Steve Crandall." The red-haired man motioned to the side of the screen.

Jane quickly punched the PAUSE button on the remote control. There was the indelible, bright crimson, three-inch mark on his right hand—the same way it looked from a distance at the *Anubus* explosion.

Harlan opened the bathroom door and emerged wearing the overalls and flannel shirt. He rubbed the back of his neck as he said, "I look like a damn pig farmer in this get up, Jane." Turning to the TV and the still image on the screen, he stopped in his tracks. "What in the hell, Jane?" He pointed to the television. "He's alive! My buddy, Rudy, is alive!"

CHAPTER 14

Jane was still trying to figure out what was going on. But Harlan's statement forced her jaw to drop. "*That's* your friend from the hospital?"

"Yeah," Harlan sat on the edge of his bed and stared at the screen. "He cleans up pretty well, eh? Never saw him wearin' a suit."

Jane buried her head in her hand. "Holy shit, Harlan." She steadied herself. "Tell me again how you and Rudy met."

Harlan kept rubbing the back of his neck. "He come to me when I was in the rehab unit. Said he was a volunteer and wanted to help me get back on my feet."

"Is that right? Stayed real close to you?"

"Oh, yeah. Hardly ever left my side—"

"Told you to call him day or night, no matter what?"

"You got it, Jane. They don't make a lot of people like that no more."

"Yeah, actually they do. They call them psychopaths."

Harlan turned to Jane, his face twisted in confusion. "Huh?"

A wellspring of anger rose up within her. "You've been set up from the very beginning." The realization sent Jane backward, flat on the bed. "Who in the fuck are these people?" she whispered to herself.

"I don't get it, Jane."

She gathered her thoughts and sat up. "You really couldn't tell that he wasn't your friend, Harlan? *Really*? Look at him!" She jabbed her finger at the TV screen. "Can't you see the darkness dripping off this asshole?"

Harlan looked at the screen. After about a minute, he finally spoke up. "He was my friend, Jane. He sat up with me when he didn't have to. He stayed late at the rehab unit just to hang out with me. He brought me groceries when I got home and never asked to be paid back. He treated me real good."

Jane looked at Harlan. It was like hurting a child but she had to. "He was with you at the bar before you blacked out and woke up in that hotel room with the dead, black prostitute." She waited for him to get it but he was still struggling. "You were so worried that Rudy was in danger? Are you kidding me? Hell, *he* was the one who most likely put something in your beer that night to knock you out. Just like your Mr. Ramos? He may have a law degree but that's not his first occupation. Rudy—or whatever name he goes by—is part of the same group that is trying to kill you."

Harlan was not wrapping his head around any of it. "No, no, no. This don't make no sense. Rudy was a—"

"Remember when I told you about that woman I met who cleared your name? The one who admitted that she set you up? The one who is now dead?"

Harlan nodded. "Yeah. You never said how she died."

"She was blown up in a bus explosion. I watched it happen. And that man right there," she pointed angrily to the TV screen, "was leaning on a black sedan, just outside of the debris field. I ran the plates on his car and they belong to a private corporation that goes by the name of ODIN. I think it's got to be a cover corporation for Romulus. I'm starting to think that the Romulus crest you drew in your notebook…the one with the female wolf suckling the two human babies, Romulus and Remus—" Jane stopped. "*Remus*! Fuck! Sounds a lot like *Ramos*, doesn't it?" It made sense, Jane deduced. Lilith's comment to her about how she had "entertained four guys named Ramos and they all had dark hair," while *this* Mr. Ramos had "reddish gray hair." And the way that people made assumptions about how names are spelled based on how they sound would account for the often-sloppy translation of *Remus* to *Ramos*.

"Hang on, Jane! Who's Remus?"

"It's not his real name, Harlan!" Jane reopened the window on her computer where she found the meaning of Gabriel's name. "You said Rudy liked to be called Rudolph, didn't you?"

"Yeah."

She plugged in the name "Rudolph" and waited for the website to spit out the meaning. "What in the hell is going on?" Staring back at her on the screen were two words: Famous Wolf. "Romulus," she whispered. The whole thing was a strange combination of Occult symbols blended with ancient lore. Nobody used their real names and the names they chose seemed to impart some hidden significance. "If Mr. Ramos is acting as Remus and Rudy is the wolf—"

Harlan kept staring at the TV screen. "I just want to know why Rudy's in a suit."

Jane paced around the room. "It doesn't make sense. Rudy must not be the one in charge of all this."

"How do you know that?"

"You don't put the guy who is truly in charge in front of the cameras. The people who pull the strings in this world require a wall between them and the ones they fuck over. They don't run for public office, they don't have their names plastered in the papers, they don't advertise their existence. They stay in the background and operate behind a lead curtain." Jane glanced back at the video that was paused on her computer screen. Rudy was the go-to guy. He was the chameleon who could act according to whatever was required of him. She thought back to the sequence of events over the past few days, beginning with her car being heisted. Realizing now that the video of Rudy dressed in the motorcycle gear was shot at a different time and a different location but intentionally made to look like the actual Quik-Mart, Jane reached the only logical conclusion in this increasingly illogical case: every single part of the scenario was planned except for Harlan stealing Jane's car. That required a fake interview that was somehow fed to the local news stations. But Dora Weller's shooting was looking more like a set-up to oust her and replace her with whomever they needed to manipulate in that slot. However, what Weller's shooting and Harlan Kipple had to do with each other was still a mystery.

Jane hit the PLAY button on the TV remote and watched the news conference continue. Steve Crandall approached the microphone while Rudy retreated behind him, yet still remained in the camera frame. Steve looked like your typical affable local political figure who had been forged from chewing gum, then molded and stuck into whatever position his handlers felt he could cope with. He was weak, Jane realized from the few seconds of watching him. As he spoke, Jane tried her best to educate Harlan on some of the visual and audio "tells" she witnessed from Crandall. He hesitated a microsecond too long before he spoke. His inflections curved downward, indicating someone who wasn't sure of himself, as opposed to those whose inflections were upward rising, denoting confidence and a firm grasp on what was being said. He was scrawny too, barely filling out his uninspired suit. A strong wind could blow Steve over and she was positive that he startled when trains tooted their horns. *Malleable.* Easy to control. Yes, that's what Jane knew about Steve Crandall.

Turning her attention to Rudy who was still featured in the camera frame, she realized that as criminal as he was, he also didn't have the right vibe to be the guy in charge. On the psychopathic scale of ruthlessness, Jane put Rudy at about a five or six out of ten. He certainly could easily control and handle Steve Crandall with his crimson marked hand tied behind his back. But he seemed to fit more into the management branch on the psychopathic tree of death, skillfully organizing those below him but still answering to the top echelon that hovered far above him. His name that meant "famous wolf" could easily have been a tip of the hat to Romulus. But as far as him being the epitome of the she-wolf depicted in the Roman myth, that theory felt completely false to Jane. Whoever seized that top position within this nefarious band of psychopathic henchmen had to have a much deeper skill set; a heartless sensibility to accomplish the job at hand. Like any true psychopath, Jane understood that the top dog knew where all the bones were buried but had never lifted a shovel of dirt to cover them up. That's what the lemmings like Rudy and Mr. Ramos were good for. Whoever was the ringleader of this unholy circus was damn near invisible, just as Gabe explained to Nanette about his mysterious employers. And if the group known as Romulus was anything like the handful of corrupt "private contractors" who were hired to do the bidding of an elite few, they would be almost impossible to penetrate.

Jane let the news conference play in the background but she'd already tuned it out. Her tenure at DH had given ample opportunities to engage with psychopaths who murdered family, friends or complete strangers and never uttered a breath of compunction. She knew the beast very well. They aren't always rotting away in a solitary prison cell. The fact is, psychopaths inhabit every occupation on earth. From law enforcement and politics to education and science, their ilk is embedded in the fabric of our daily existence. Starting with her own tarnished bloodline, Jane was aware of the flint-like intelligence that often accompanies those who are hardwired to create destruction and eschew peace and harmony. Too often, they are the ones who are admired in their chosen professions, considered to be irreplaceable and honored for what is perceived as their "steely resolution." But what the ignorant masses never realize is that "steely resolution" translates into targeted chaos, torture, cheating, lying, maneuvering and meting out enormous suffering upon others without feeling a spark of remorse. From the true psychopath's point of view, people are either commodities that can be traded or they are pawns on a chessboard, easily moved and used with impunity. A man or woman's usefulness is measured by what they can deliver, and once their worth is sucked dry they are discarded. "Security through domination," Jane remembered once reading about the psychopath's mindset. Peace through war. Freedom through devastation. Psychopaths in places of power perfect Orwellian speak and whenever possible, encourage their followers to mindlessly repeat their slogans so that their messages could be broadcast on a wider platform.

Their collective approach is so carefully planned and executed that they can often go unnoticed in public. The psychopaths wear their masks of normalcy, they know the right buzzwords because they invented them, and they understand how to use those words with assurance so that everyone in earshot will believe that all is fine. But it's a grand deception meant to undermine everything that is good and optimistic. Optimism is the enemy of the psychopath's ultimate agenda. Opportunity is born from devastation and the greater the damage, the better the opportunity for profit and power. A well-trained psychopath will always play on fear and if they have to manufacture the fear, so be it. In fact, Jane recognized how the worst psychopaths—the ones who operate in elite industries or within other public arenas—are held up by their colleagues as "movers and shakers" and "guys who get things done." The idea that the end justifies the means is accepted and a blind eye is often turned if the "end" is lucrative.

The fact remains that the higher one climbs up the ladder of "success," the more likely one is to interface with one of these sharply dressed snakes. And while they might not get their hands dirty like their brother and sister psychopaths who cling to the lower rungs, their resources are far reaching and able to exact terror on a whim. And yet, the naïve souls who orbit in their murky realm never really accept the vicious power their bosses are capable of generating. Even when the innocent ones are in their presence and held hostage in those iron fists, none of them seem to see the cool, soulless, calculating side of these monsters. Nobody cares enough to look into their eyes and see what is so obviously staring back at them.

And if those innocent ones allow themselves to contemplate for one second that the person in front of them is evil, they usually doubt themselves for even considering it. The perfect psychopath makes sure of that through the waves of manipulation and mind games he enjoys. His razor-sharp intellect produces a personality that can outthink anyone and maintain that level of acumen indefinitely. The seasoned psychopath knows how to penetrate another person's mind. They understand with pinpoint accuracy what motivates another person to act and respond and they exploit that knowledge to their benefit. They understand all of this and more because they study the human mind. In fact, they are obsessed with the mind and how breakable it can be.

Knowing

Even though psychopaths are certainly members of the human race, Jane knew they perceive themselves as vastly superior and removed from the rest of us. They aren't just separate from the unwashed masses; they are detached from humanity. And thus, through this belief that they are extraordinary beings, they regard the rest of the world as nothing more than amoebas—single celled consumers who live in a Petri dish and deserve the same treatment given to a flea on a pig's ass. They conduct random experiments on humans as if they are running a rat through a maze and charting how long it takes for it to get to the cheese. They proclaim edicts from their executive thrones that serve only themselves, but they expertly give the impression that through these proclamations everyone will benefit.

It is a "brilliant evil," as Jane saw it. Nothing is left to chance. The true psychopath has all their bases covered and is adeptly prepared for the first person to rise up and accuse them of atrocities. But instead of eluding their accuser, they confront them head-on. That is part of the game for the psychopath. There is a devilish fun in staring someone in the eye and lying so skillfully that it sounds like the harp strings of truth. The experience is useful to the psychopath because it keeps their muscle memory alive and tunes them into new tricks so they can fight and win with greater resolve the next time they are confronted.

But Jane was well aware that the psychopath's greatest power lies in the cozy belief that he either doesn't exist or that his intentions are not as catastrophic as others fear. True evil, unto itself, is difficult for the average person to contemplate. For many, it's a radical notion that there are people born into this world who want nothing more than to inflict pain and suffering on others. Furthermore, the idea that wickedness could somehow be burned into a person's psyche before they take their first breath is controversial. All those well-intentioned neophytes who need to feel safe desperately cling to the idea that if these psychopaths really do exist, all they need is a gentle hand and someone to love them. That type of stupidity infuriated Jane. She'd seen the glint of real evil too many times to deny its existence and she knew that rehabilitation was a joke. She'd felt the full brunt of their torture and insanity and lived to suppress it. And she also understood that trying to explain this level of moral turpitude to someone else who does not want to conceive of it is like banging your head against the proverbial brick wall—it only feels good when you stop. Thus, through the blind ignorance and denial of others, the gifted psychopath is given a wide berth that allows him to exact his ruin without being held responsible.

While it seems the psychopath has everything going for him, he does lack a few important traits. The first thing he lacks is a conscience. Jane had seen it too many times on the job that a true psychopath understands absolutely nothing that the human heart is normally wired to perceive. Somewhere down the line, the internal connection that links their heart with their mind was severed. And from that, the psychopath moves through life without fear of reprisal. But their built-in need to control others and outcomes carries its own problems. And from that, Jane discovered the one thing that psychopaths despise.

They hate spontaneity.

Whether it is a sudden "act of God" or a random interloper who comes out of nowhere, spontaneous events put a cog in their wheel. Their well-crafted scenarios are always planned to the last breath. While they allow for the occasional unexpected blips, they are usually not able to navigate their ships when they encounter waves of unplanned rebellion. Artificial rebellion is one thing because the true psychopath recognizes it for what it is and knows it will never result in any groundbreaking change. But honest mutiny that happens naturally is what the psychopath fears. They would never admit it, of course. And they will call out their attack dogs to suppress it in all ways possible. This is when their cool confidence often slips; this is when they grit their teeth and sometimes make mistakes.

More than anything, the psychopath needs to always be in control of others and he holds onto that control as if it were his own breath. The psychopath does not want his minions to wake up. Their slumber is necessary in order for him to enact his crooked schemes. An unchecked uprising could create the opening for other minions to wake up to the psychopath's ruse and that could never be tolerated. If themes such as love, compassion, forgiveness, integrity and honor are promoted too much, there wouldn't be enough energy left to hate, destroy, and create chaos. It is a requirement that the human spirit be squashed in order for the psychopath to continue his terror unabated. It is necessary for people to believe that the only power they have comes from whatever the psychopath allows them to believe they earned.

"Gingers," Jane said out loud.

"What's that?" Harlan replied, turning the TV on Mute.

"Gabriel told Nanette to watch out for them. It was an odd comment from a guy who seemed pretty free-thinking. But he wasn't talking about red heads in general. He meant these guys," she motioned to the TV news conference that was about to end.

Harlan continued to rub the back of his neck.

"Why do you keep doing that?" she asked.

"You sure I don't have somethin' stuck back there?" he asked, turning his back to Jane.

She looked again. "You've rubbed it so hard, you've got a blister forming."

He growled. "I just want to get a knife and dig at it."

"Jesus, Harlan. Get a hold of yourself."

He stopped rubbing his neck and stared at the television. The news conference was wrapping up and Rudy put his hand on Steve Crandall's back as if to guide him out of the room. But the gesture imparted a lot more than guidance to Jane. It looked more like a man putting his hand up the back of a puppet.

She shook her head. "You really couldn't see through him, Harlan?"

"I was raised not to judge people."

"Oh, fuck. It's not judgment, Harlan. There's a huge difference between judging someone's lifestyle and looking into their eyes and seeing their truth." She turned to Harlan. "Or their lies. Or their sickness. Or their intentions to hurt you.

"How do you figure out people, Jane?"

"I observe them. Every single day I watch them and I keep little notes in my head about things I see and then I sort the little notes into some little files. Generally, everybody who is in the same little file usually has the same big issues. Finally, I filter my observations even more and break the files down until I'm able to see between their lines."

"You mean *read* between their lines?"

"No. I mean *see*. It's hard to explain. I've read all the psych books but there are things you can't really put into words and if you did, it would sound bizarre. You have to see it and when you do, you understand it because you've seen the same colors and shapes before in someone else."

"Like what?" Harlan asked, truly interested.

"I know what abuse looks like. That's an easy one. I know what being told you're no fucking good looks like." She hesitated, drawing up a dark memory from her past.

"How?"

"It's in the way they walk. They're really tentative, not wanting to invest themselves in the next step because they've been told so many times they're a fucking failure."

"How do you help them, Jane?"

"You can't help most of them."

"How come?"

"Because they don't want help. They're too fucked up by the time I meet them. I know that when I deal with a woman who has been repeatedly physically abused by a long line of partners, she keeps attracting the same assholes because she believes she deserves the abuse. She likes the drama that comes out of it. Hell, she feeds off of it. She loves playing the victim and she'll never change. Because the dirty little secret is that on some level, she actually craves abuse. It's the only time she feels alive and loved. She never got the memo that in all relationships, the woman is *always* in charge. Even the ones who are on the floor getting the shit kicked out of them, even *those* women are still in charge of the relationship."

"You mean that?"

"Harlan, I've seen it a million times. Women rule every single relationship, even the ones that are toxic. The abused woman has the power to leave but, because she thinks she's a piece of shit, she chooses to stay with the bad guy because a good man is weak in her eyes. A good man hates the drama. A bad man requires it."

"Humph," he said. "Never thought of it that way." He paused for a second. "Can you walk into someone's house and figure them out if they ain't there?"

"Sure. I do that all the time. You can tell a lot about a person from being in their house. Somebody once said that a person is only as good as what he or she does when nobody else is watching. That's true. But since that's unseen, it's my job to perceive what other people either can't see or refuse to look at."

He leaned on his thighs. "Like what?"

"You can determine a lot about a man or woman by how they treat their animals and their houseplants. If the dogs are cowering and the plants are dead or need water, that's a 'tell.'"

"Ha! That makes sense."

"I don't trust people who are happy all the time. And the ones who are deliriously happy 24/7? Those are the ones who are hiding the biggest secrets. I don't have a lot of confidence in a man who always has a clean desk. They're usually very sterile individuals. A cluttered desk shows me a mind that is engaged in more than one pursuit and interested in many. I prefer people who drink their coffee black. They aren't afraid of tasting something bitter. When I meet someone who insists on dumping sugar into their brew, I know they need to sweeten the bitterness of their life. And those who pour cream into their coffee need to dilute the bitterness of life. Those are the ones who don't want to believe that life can be acrid and unpleasant. If you want a no nonsense person who can deal with a problem head on, find a coffee drinker who takes it black."

"You drink it black, Jane?"

She smiled. "I drink it black."

"What if they prefer tea?"

"What kind of tea?"

"Sweet tea?"

"That a cultural thing. But a man who opts for chamomile tea at night over decaf leans toward being a pacifist. Those are the people pleasers—the ones who have a difficult time making a decision because they're afraid of offending others. Lots of Libras, Pisces and Cancers love chamomile tea at night."

"What about the folks who don't drink tea or anything else?"

"You mean the purists?"

"Yeah. The teetotalers."

"The ones who brag about how liquor or drugs have never touched their lips? I don't like them. They see themselves with a false superiority. They like to believe that if they don't dip into the coal, they'll be removed from the soot. But they don't realize that it's the soot that creates the character and the compassion and fills all those nooks and crannies with hard-earned mistakes and lessons. The purists are so afraid of soiling themselves that they don't see the payoff from the redemption. I like people who have allowed alcohol and drugs to pass their lips and gone into the bowels of hell and then come out the other side. I like them when they stop the drink and drugs and find their souls. Because unlike the purists, the ones who have seen hell and survived it will never judge those who continue to struggle. The purist will judge from sheer ignorance because he's allowed himself to believe that there is some sort of prize gained from abstention. But he limits himself to a rose colored world that isn't real and holds no fire. A man or woman with no fire is easily manipulated

Harlan, and they'll believe whatever supports their narrow-minded agenda. But you want to know the ones I really stay clear of?"

He leaned forward, clearly intrigued. "Who?"

"The ones who like to tell you that there's no 'I' in 'team.' I'm aware of that fact and, in my opinion, therein lies the problem with that word." She smiled.

He laughed. "Hell, Jane. I've never met nobody like you before."

"Well, Harlan, ditto. Right back at you." She glanced at the TV screen. A graphic showing the *Anubus* crash flashed on the screen. Jane quickly turned on the sound.

"Police tell us there will be an update in the next few hours regarding the bus explosion that occurred south of Denver several days ago. The horrific accident that claimed all passengers on board is still thought to be caused a faulty fuel line."

The news shifted to another story and Jane muted the sound. So, they were sticking with the faulty fuel line ruse. Who paid off the investigators, Jane wondered. Or were the investigators specifically chosen because they were already bought and paid for? She could easily see how all-consuming this deception could become. In order for it to work, you'd have to have people in place who were from all walks of life and in all kinds of employment. It must be like a giant Rolodex, Jane determined. Each time a fire had to be put out or started, the man at the top spun that Rolodex and like Russian roulette, pulled the trigger on the next asset in the complicated chain.

"Hey," Harlan said. "You hear that? No more hubba-hubba comin' from the second floor."

Jane nodded. "Don't get too excited. They're probably just resting before the bell rings on round two."

Harlan found the rest of his chocolate milkshake from the drive-thru and finished it. He enthusiastically knocked back six raw eggs after that, along with half of the yogurt from the dairy farm. He capped off his odd meal with a bottle of the pine needle beer, smacking his lips like a satisfied glutton. By the time Harlan was through, he rubbed his bloated belly and lay back down on his bed. Seconds later, he was snoring like a seasoned pro.

Jane brought out the two ball caps, along with the LED lights, wires, electrical tape, switches and batteries she purchased. Using a knife to poke ten holes in the seam right above the visor, Jane then wrapped the wires onto the LED lights with the proper positive and negative connections confirmed before poking them through the various holes on the cap. She then taped the loose wires together, affixing them to the nine-volt battery, which she secured in the back open seam of the hat. She repeated the same thing with the second hat. In fewer than thirty minutes, she had the perfect foil for the standard security camera. Her creation wouldn't be effective for blowing through the NSA, CIA, FBI or any other alphabet organization. But for the typical, run-of-the-mill security camera at gas stations, supermarkets, etc., this would do the job very well. Jane had to give all the credit to a smarmy little two-bit hack she'd met on the job during one of DH's investigations. When she noticed his ball cap was lit up, she asked him about it. He informed her that the LED lights blind cameras, creating a ball of light around a person's face when they are on camera, thereby making it impossible to clearly identify them. With the advanced facial recognition software that Jane knew was out there, this low-tech answer to becoming invisible seemed like the perfect plan.

She ate the last hamburger, even though it was cold, and drained the last of her chocolate shake. Looking over at Harlan, he was sound asleep. Jane wished she could do the same but her head raced too much for sleep to overtake her. She eyed the case of beer that sat next to Harlan's bed. That always helped her sleep. Sure, it took at least six of them, followed by several generous shots of Jack Daniels to guarantee the results. But it slowed her head down and that was worth its weight in gold. She glanced at Harlan again and then carefully reached down to the case. Opening the flap, Jane slid one of the tartan labeled bottles out of the box. Cradling it between her palms, she felt the sensuous slender neck of the bottle between her fingers. That's where she'd always hold the bottle between her first and second fingers. It was comforting right then. Almost too comforting.

She turned to Harlan and saw the bottle opener that had fallen into the folds of the comforter. A strange, high-pitched whistle began to ring in her right ear. She quickly shut off the television, thinking it was coming from there but the whistle continued unabated. *One is too many*, she heard in her head, *and a thousand is never enough*. Why that old AA saying suddenly crept into her consciousness was anybody's guess. But there it was and it kept repeating in her head like a broken record. Finally, she put the bottle back into the case and held her ear. The whistle stopped and the pain disappeared. Jane turned back to the case and leaned toward it again. The whistle commenced again and she sat back on the bed. The whistle stopped, this time with a defined finish.

Jane glanced around the room. The air felt curiously thick and probing. Harlan continued to snore, happily lost in deep sleep. She pushed the pillow into her low back and sat up, still canvassing the room. It looked as if the light was dimming slightly. She waited and watched and then waited a few minutes more before she spoke. "Gabriel?" she whispered, feeling somewhat insane at that moment. The light in the room appeared to gradually return to normal. She donned her refurbished ball cap and pulled it low over her forehead. Flicking the switch that was attached to the nine-volt battery, the pinprick LED lights glowed softly against the fabric. She sunk down against the headboard, squashing her body against the pillow and imagined herself invisible.

After about a half hour and with Harlan still sleeping, Jane turned the television back on. Maybe, she thought, if she watched some bad TV, she'd drift off to sleep. Scanning the channels, she landed on an obscure cable channel from Europe and a show titled, "The Future Is Now." From what Jane deduced, the program featured segments where the host—an affable, if not quirky, freckled guy in his mid-forties—traveled the globe and reported on individuals and companies who were dedicated to developing new products and innovative breakthroughs. Some of the inventions were ridiculous and some were clever. But the segment that got Jane's attention had to do with something called a "spider goat." She learned there was a spider that spun a silk thread that was stronger than Kevlar. The idea was that if there was enough of this exceptional silk thread, a fiber could be created that was stronger than steel but very flexible and could revolutionize the materials industry. The silk could also be inserted into the human body to strengthen or support ligaments, tendons and limbs.

The problem was that the spiders were cannibalistic so they couldn't be farmed for their silk. But researchers figured out how to bypass this pesky issue. In the lab, they genetically altered a goat's embryo with the DNA of the spider and proudly produced what they called a "spider goat." It looked just like a regular goat but when these genetically modified animals lactated, they produced a "spider milk protein." When the milk was filtered in a lab, the proteins were separated, leaving clear strands of silk, visible to the naked eye. Jane leaned forward, staring in stunned disbelief at the TV screen. It seemed impossible but there it was—silk fibers coming out of a Frankenstein goat. Talk about a commodity, Jane thought. It was one thing to breed a sheep to get superior wool or to breed a chicken that laid huge eggs. But in her mind, there was something quite disturbing about creating a four-legged creature that shared its body with another species.

But that fact didn't seem to bother the scientists who gushed about the "breathtaking potential of innovation." Jane sat back on the bed. All well and good, she said to herself, but who's keeping checks and balances on the ones who are envisioning these genetic freaks of nature? That wasn't brought up during the show. Jane kept waiting for someone to raise that question but it was as if this development was the new normal and people just had to get used to it. One doctor on the program said, "Our scientific pursuits are only restricted by biological truths and our vast imaginations. If we can conceive it in our minds' eye—even if it sounds impossible—we know we can create it in a lab." There was an arrogant confidence in his tenor, a sort of "ethics be damned" attitude.

But when the program's host left the spider goat farm and journeyed to NASA's *Ames Research Center*, Jane realized she was blissfully unaware of how fast technology had jumped into a brave new world. Visiting the medical director at the research lab, the freckled-face host excitedly faced the camera and explained that the future of our world lay in the hands of Biotech companies who were "engineering our lives for the better." There was technology that allowed NASA scientists to develop organisms and cells that could be converted into therapeutic molecules. These molecules were then injected into the body of astronauts to combat the potentially fatal poisoning that happens from exposure to the sun's intense rays when they travel in space. "Like it or not," the host proclaimed, "the future is here *right now* and *this* is just the tip of the iceberg!" And he said it with a strange, gleeful cadence that struck Jane as being damn near pathological. The program never brought up the moral issues around these experiments. Nobody once asked, "What happens if the spider goats get loose and mate with other goats? Won't we eventually have a world of spider goats, thereby erasing any memory of an original and true goat?" It didn't matter to any of them. At least that's the way Jane read them. These white-coated men and women couldn't wait to produce the next genetically modified anomaly and state that it was another "new normal" as well as "a benefit to mankind."

Jane clicked off the TV. She'd seen enough. In her quest to find something boring that would induce sleep, she had instead stumbled upon a group of freaks who were probably right now crossing a Chihuahua with a gnat and creating a dog that was even more annoying. She checked the time. 8:00. If she could get to sleep right away, she might be able to grab eight hours of rest. And if the couple upstairs kept it down, she might even be able to enjoy an uninterrupted slumber.

Turning off the light, Jane slid under the covers and closed her eyes. She willed herself to sleep, demanding it. After a few minutes, she felt her body floating over itself. Yet, it was odd because instead of falling into a void, she suddenly felt very awake. There was a moment of feeling suspended in mid-air right before she was rocketed through the darkness and dropped onto a walkway. Jane couldn't see her feet or anything around her. The only thing visible was a brilliant spotlight in the near distance and a simple folding chair. She walked toward the spotlight and sat down in the chair. It didn't feel like a dream. There was a palpable urgency surrounding her as if a thousand people suddenly needed to talk to her all at once. She heard footsteps coming toward her. The way the soles hit the ground, Jane knew it was a man. A figure appeared at the edge of the spotlight and sat down on another chair that appeared out of nowhere. It was her partner on the job, Sergeant Morgan Weyler. He was dressed in his usual dapper, navy blue suit with the crisp soft blue shirt underneath. His ebony skin looked brilliant under the light as he leaned forward on the chair.

"Hello, Jane."

"Boss?" she said, using her pet term for him. "How'd I conjure you up?"

He smiled. "You called my name?"

Jane was perplexed. "I didn't call your name."

He looked at her, peering into her soul. "Think about it."

She stared into his eyes and realized it wasn't Weyler's eyes staring back. "What's going on here?"

"I thought it would be easier for you to hear my words from someone you knew. Someone you felt comfortable with?"

Jane looked around the area but all she saw was pitch-blackness. "What is this place? Where am I?"

"Let's call it your mind."

"Let's call it whatever in the hell it is." She could feel her heart racing.

"Calm down, Jane. There's nothing to be afraid of."

She looked at him, diving into his orbs. "Is that right? I'd say there's a helluva lot to be afraid of. Given the situation I'm in?"

Knowing

"You're smart. You're very smart. You'll figure it out. I had to do a lot of things without any computer or phone or car." He sat back in a relaxed position. "So, what was it you wanted to ask me?"

"How many questions do I get?"

He smiled. "This is not a fairy tale. You get as many as you want."

"Who is after Harlan?"

"You already know that."

"I do?"

"What else?"

Jane wanted to believe this was a dream, but it wasn't. "Who shot you?"

"Some expert shooters they hired to track me down."

"Did you know you were going to die?"

He smiled. "Of course."

"Why?"

"Because they falsely put out the info that I died when I chose to disappear three years before. When they call you 'dead,' it's a done deal. Even before things happen in real time, they always talk about it like it's already happened. They believe that secures the energy for the actual physical event and assures its success."

Jane contemplated everything. "Did you know you were going to die that day?"

"Oh, yeah," he said matter-of-factly. "It had to be on that day."

"Why?"

"Lots of reasons. Most of which you won't believe."

Jane had heard it all and she was somewhat offended. "Try me."

"They love numbers. They love seasons. Then they like to combine those two. It's *all* about the energy, Jane."

"They dabble in the Occult?"

He shook his head. "They don't dabble, Jane. They're drowning in it."

Her head spun, trying to decipher his clues. "What? Are they Satanists?"

"Satanists are weekend warriors," he said calmly. "*These* people do what they do because it's in their blood. It's all they know."

"Okay, so they're into the occult?"

"You're trying to attach what you think is a meaningful word to explain darkness. But you're falling into the trap. Occult simply means 'hidden.' It doesn't always mean evil."

She was starting to get angry now. "So, they're into hiding things?"

"Don't approach this with anger, Jane. If you do, the rage will prevent you from seeing the subtleties. And yes, it's very much about hidden information. *Why* do they agree that certain things *need* to be hidden?" He leaned forward, resting his arms on his thighs. "Because the individuals who understand the way the world *really* works do not believe that everyone else can grasp what they have understood for a very long time. Knowledge is passed down from generation to generation within the hierarchy. Secrets are embedded in the fabric of their existence and they accept it. They explicitly understand that coveting those secrets gives them power that others will never have. And through that power, they believe they will never fail. Why? Because as long as they make the rules, they'll *never* lose."

Jane considered his words. "And you worked for these people?"

"I did."

She stared into his eyes. "And you killed for them."

He sighed. "Yes. I did."

Jane kept checking herself because the entire scene was challenging her sense of reality. "What in the hell do they want?"

His visage grew serious. "The two most precious things." He pointed to his chest. "The heart," he drew his finger to his temple, "and the mind." He pointed back to his chest with emphasis. "*The heart*," and again to his temple, "*and the mind*."

Jane sat back and let out a hard breath. "Are you going to keep throwing metaphors out at me or are you going to give me a little more help?"

He was silent for several long seconds. "You're not hearing me, Jane. Maybe if you heard from someone else?"

Suddenly, he was swallowed in a pool of darkness. Within a split-second, another spotlight shown on a chair within arm's reach of Jane, and in it was her younger brother, Mike. He was wearing a Bronco's sweatshirt and jeans. A signature crooked grin crept across his face, causing his face to soften and make him appear fifteen years younger than his hard fought thirty-three.

"*Mike?*" Jane asked in a stunned voice.

"Is this better?" he asked.

It was Mike's face but it wasn't his eyes or his voice. "No. It's creepier than shit! What *is* this, for God's sake?!"

He reached over and grasped her hand. "The heart and the mind, Jane."

"Mike, I—" she stopped herself, "I don't know what that means!"

Knowing

"There's a war but it's not fought for freedom. It's fought for ownership. And the ones who own the essence of a man and the soul of a child are the winners."

"Essence of a man? Soul of a child? I don't understand…" She looked around the area again, hoping for a doorway out. "My God, what in the hell is this?!"

"Pay attention, Jane!" He grabbed her wrists tightly. "The heart and the mind!"

"You said that already and I still don't know what in the fuck it—"

The image of her brother vanished and in the blink of an eye, Hank sat in the chair in front of her, illuminated in a cylinder of beautiful light. Taking her hands gently in his, he dove into her eyes with exquisite love. For several, intoxicating seconds, she only saw Hank staring back at her. Then the glaze of the other eyes engaged. But there was a part of her that wanted desperately to believe it was truly Hank.

He lifted her hand to her chest. "The heart," he said before lifting her hand to her forehead, "and the mind."

She wanted to fall into his body, even though she knew it wasn't him.

"Jane! Are you listening?"

"Heart and the mind," she whispered.

She tipped her forehead against his. "I just want you to know that I'm okay—"

And with that, she opened her eyes and stared into semi-darkness that filled The Shangri-La motel room. Darting up in bed, she breathlessly checked the time. 10:30. Harlan was still asleep but something wasn't right. She heard the low rumble of a car engine slowly rolling by their room and heading a bit farther before stopping. Jane slipped out of the bed and moved the curtain back just enough to be able to see. It was the police and for the first time in her life, she wasn't happy to see them.

CHAPTER 15

She dove across to Harlan's bed, jarring him out of his hard snooze. "Harlan!" she said quietly but forcefully. "Wake up! We've gotta get out of here."

Harlan struggled to consciousness. "What? What?"

Jane stumbled around the room in the semi darkness, shoving clothes back into bags and grabbing all the food. "Cops! Outside!"

"Aw, shit, Jane."

She grabbed the pair of jeans she'd tossed across the floor, a random shirt from her bag and her boots and ran into the bathroom. She could hear Harlan dragging the bags and the cooler to the door. Her mind raced with various scenarios, none of which were appealing. Then a thought crossed her mind that was so devious it might just work. Zipping up her jeans, she strode back into the room and found her leather jacket. Searching the pocket, she came up with one of the prepaid cell phones nestled against her wallet. She turned to Harlan. "Keep packing. And don't say one word, no matter what you hear me say! Understood?"

He nodded nervously, grabbing everything around him and plunging it into bags. She returned to the bathroom and shut the door. Pounding on one of the walls, she confirmed that it was pretty much a cement bunker and noise proof. Jane paused briefly, closed her eyes and quickly got into character. She then dialed 9-1-1.

"9-1-1. What is your emergency?" The operator said.

"He's gonna kill me!" she whispered loudly with a strange southern twang. "Oh, my God, help me, please!"

"Ma'am, where are you? I can't tell from your phone."

"I'm at The Shangri-La motel," Jane said breathlessly, rattling off the address she located on the back of the toilet. "I'm trapped in the bathroom. He's got a gun and he said he's gonna kill me and the baby. Please hurry!"

"We have a unit already in that area, ma'am. What room are you in?"

"Room seventeen! Second floor. North side. Please hurry before he—" She hung up quickly and darted out of the bathroom.

Knowing

"Gee, Jane. You are startin' to scare me," Harlan said with a slow cadence. She carefully peered out the window. "You got everything ready to go?" He nodded.

"Okay. When I point to you, open the door and we're outta here." She continued to play sentry for a few more seconds until she saw the single cop respond to his radio call. Once he raced up the side staircase, she signaled Harlan to open the door.

Jane unlocked the car and Harlan quickly wedged his body into the backseat as she piled the bags and cooler into the vehicle. Retrieving a sheathed knife from under the driver's seat, she snuck a look around to make sure the cop wasn't in view. Without hesitation, Jane stabbed the right rear tire of the patrol car with several damaging gashes. Racing back to the Mustang, Jane put it in neutral and rolled down a low incline that spilled onto the darkened, desolate, two-lane road.

"I've always wanted to do that," she said with a mischievous smile. Turning on the engine, she skimmed down the deserted road without her headlights until she was a quarter mile away.

"What's the plan, Jane?"

"Right now, we drive and we keep driving until I can figure something out." She checked the gas gauge. She had just under half a tank left. Heading east, the territory became increasingly barren. About thirty minutes later, she rolled down her window and chucked out her disposable phone. Between the sham 9-1-1 call, the slashed tires and ditching the cell phone, Jane figured she was getting oddly comfortable rotating on the other side of the law.

Continuing for another thirty minutes, she came upon a small town on the far southeastern plains. It was one of those "if you blink, you'll miss it," towns. About a mile later was a lonely bowling alley sitting out in the middle of nowhere.

Harlan extricated himself from the blankets and bags that filled the back seat and sat up. He was wearing the rigged ball cap Jane made for him with the LED lights adorned across the front. "Stop, Jane! Pull in there!"

"The bowling alley? Why?"

"Just do it!" he said with urgency.

"Harlan, we have to—"

"Just do it, Jane!"

She stopped the Mustang and turned back to him. There was a strange look in his eyes. "Oh, fuck. What now?"

"I have to go in there."

"The bowling alley?" She checked the time. "It's coming up on midnight."

"You told me to start takin' some initiative, right?"

"Initiative *I* have some control over. Why do you need to go in there?"

He started to move his large frame toward the door. "Fine. I'll get out and walk."

She spun the car around. "Oh, shit, Harlan." The parking lot was nearly empty but the lights were blazing inside the large building. Jane drove around to the back of the building and parked the car in a far corner that was littered with empty quart amber bottles of Tecate Mexican beer. Before the key was out of the ignition, Harlan was chomping at the bit to get out of the car. Once he pried himself outside, Jane reached into the glove compartment to retrieve her Glock, tucking it into the back of her waistband. She found the orange prescription bottle of Oxycontin that Harlan stashed in there. For some odd reason she couldn't fathom, she felt compelled to grab it and shove it into her jacket pocket. She turned back to find Harlan heading toward the bowling alley. "Hang on, Harlan!" Finding her Ruger .380 and holster, she quickly locked it onto her boot and bolted out of the car.

When she turned the corner around the bowling alley, he was nowhere to be seen. "Fuck!" she screamed, scanning the near empty parking lot. Heading inside the building, there was one lane open and two guys who were clearly inebriated. She glanced around and didn't spot Harlan. Seeing a bar in the far corner of the bowling alley, Jane ran toward it. A red neon sign above the entrance welcomed her to *The Dystopian Lounge*. The pungent scent of tobacco filled the air. To the left was a long bar and a lonely bartender leaning against the shelves of booze. Three very drunk patrons sat at the various tables, none of them paying any attention to the large man on stage with the microphone in his hand, wearing overalls, a plaid shirt and a ball cap that was lit up like a Christmas tree.

Jane had no clue what to do except slide up against the back wall and watch everything unfold. The bartender, who was doing double duty as the Karaoke host, called out to Harlan, asking him what song number he wanted. Jane observed Harlan closely and realized part of him had symbolically left the building. In an altered state, he turned to the bartender and instructed him to play song number "one forty-four zero." Jane focused on the bartender. He suddenly took extreme interest in Harlan as he moved to the console that sat on the top of the bar and plugged in the four-digit code. Jane hung back and waited as the canned music started. At first it sounded like cheesy cocktail music, peppered with a little piano, drums and a Moog synthesizer. And then, without referring to the "cheat screen" where the lyrics rolled, Harlan began to sing. It was Tony Bennett's "Just in Time" and he sang each word with pitch perfect rhythm.

"Just in time, I found you just in time. Before you came, my time was running low…"

Jane hugged the back wall and cringed. If this was Harlan's idea of an ode of appreciation, she didn't need it.

"I was lost, the losing dice were tossed, my bridges all were crossed, no-where to go!"

Harlan continued to sing and Jane turned to the bartender. He was still intently focused on Harlan with a penetrating stare. Jane worried he identified Harlan from his TV mug shot. But there was something else—something in the way he watched Harlan that generated a kind of all-consuming fear.

"For love came just in time," Harlan continued. "You found me just in time. And changed my lonely life, that lovely day!"

Jane observed Harlan and realized he wasn't looking at her. In fact, he was focused far away, and seemingly singing to another person. The instrumental interlude began. Jane trained her eyes on the bartender as he walked over to the wall phone and dialed seven numbers. He kept staring at Harlan as he spoke into the phone with what looked like extreme urgency. In fewer than twenty seconds, he hung up and leaned against the bar, hanging on every word coming out of Harlan's mouth. When the tune was over, Harlan nonchalantly set down the microphone. The boozed up customers managed a few rounds of applause before returning to their nightcaps. As if he was on automatic pilot, Harlan crossed to the bar and sat on the stool in front of the bartender.

Jane couldn't stand it any longer. She walked over to the bar and sat next to Harlan, looking directly at the bartender the entire time. The second she sat down, the bartender regarded her with a confused expression. He looked at Harlan and then back to Jane. Harlan said nothing. He just sat there and waited. Without uttering a word, the bartender set three empty shot glasses in front of Harlan in the form of a triangle. Turning back to the shelves of liquor, he got up on a stool and reached up on the third shelf and back behind the last row of bottles. He brought out two bottles, both with ornate designs. Returning to the bar, and without saying a word, he set the two bottles in front of

Harlan. Jane peered over and saw that one bottle was an expensive vodka and one a cheap whiskey. Harlan didn't look at the two selections. He just tapped his chubby finger against the cheap whiskey bottle. The bartender filled the three shot glasses, corked the bottle and set it to the side. But he didn't move away from the bar. He just stayed in place and waited. Harlan didn't hesitate. He lifted the first shot glass and swallowed it without flinching. He snagged the second shot and repeated the gesture.

The third shot glass, positioned at the tip of the triangle, remained. Harlan didn't budge; he held the bartender's steely glare for what seemed like an eternity, before turning to Jane. Jane looked into his eyes and felt compelled to pick up the remaining shot. She held it to her nose, smelling the burnt bouquet that screamed "cheap." But she let it linger there a little longer than she expected. She was transported back to her fourteenth year, sneaking out to the back of the house at night to steal a few sips from a bottle of cheap whiskey she'd gotten a neighborhood reprobate to buy her. She remembered the naïve anticipation and the sense that she was doing something dirty and bad but increasingly necessary. It was the fun before the fall. It was the lie before she realized it had her in its clutches. It was everything that came before and nothing that followed. It was the innocence that just one more sip would be enough. Jane closed her eyes and felt her will force strengthen. She opened her eyes and set the shot glass down on the bar to the far right of the other two empty glasses.

Harlan still appeared as if he was in an altered state. The longer he stared at the bartender, the more confused and frightened the bartender became.

"How ya doin'?" the bartender asked Harlan with tension lacing his voice.

"How do you think I'm doin'?" Harlan replied, his voice sharing another's.

The bartender cheated a glance toward Jane who never took her eyes off him. "This is a new twist. How come I wasn't informed?"

Jane realized that this was not about identifying Harlan Kipple. She waited for Harlan to speak but when he stayed silent, she piped up. "It's on a need to know basis only." She was shocked at how genuine her words sounded, even though she had no idea what in the hell was she was talking about. Waves of apprehension swept between the bartender and Jane. "So," she offered, "you got something for us?"

The bartender creased his eyes just enough that she could tell this wasn't the way it usually worked. His anxiety level decreased slightly but was still apparent. "Yeah. Sure. Of course, I do. Give it thirty minutes."

Knowing

Jane's heart began to race. Was there something in the special bottle of cheap whiskey that would take effect in thirty minutes? She suddenly felt trapped and realized there was no way out of this scenario except to play it out to its conclusion.

The bartender stepped away from the bar and leaned against the shelves of booze. The only time he took his eyes off Harlan was to quickly take a probing look at Jane. She felt like they were caged zoo animals that just showed up from the jungles and the zookeeper didn't know what to do with them. She watched the clock and when thirty minutes passed and nothing happened, her nerves took it up a notch.

"It's thirty minutes," Jane announced. She turned to Harlan who seemed to be blissfully lost in his own world as he stared straight ahead. "I'm not waiting any longer." She started to get off the barstool.

"Give it a couple more minutes," the bartender said, swallowing hard.

"I know a trap when I smell it," she said, her courage re-emerging. She turned to Harlan. "Come on, we're leaving."

But Harlan didn't budge.

"*Seriously*," Jane stressed, wrapping her hand around as much of Harlan's large arm as she could. "*Let's go.*"

"Where you goin'?" the voice asked from behind her.

Jane turned to find a wiry fellow standing there. His brown hair was cut into a sharp, military buzz that made his lucent light blue eyes appear peculiarly intense. He wore black jeans and a plain blue t-shirt under a black leather coat that looked like it'd been pummeled under a desert tank. His mannerisms indicated a guy who thought he was extremely valuable. But Jane could easily see behind his façade. To her, he was a borderline idiot, an elevated water boy, a guy with more muscle than mental acuity and someone who shot before he thought. As far as Jane was concerned, these were some of the more dangerous individuals because their lack of intelligence blended with their puffed up self-importance made them impossible to reason with.

She positioned herself in front of him to show a modicum of dominance but not to overwhelm. "You're late," Jane said to him with false bravado.

He glared at her. "And you're unexpected. So, shut the fuck up."

This wasn't a game. Jane could see the focused intensity and irritation coming from the guy. Whatever mess Harlan had "initiated" would likely open a few windows into the hidden world of Gabriel Cristsóne.

The guy turned around, and then back to Jane and Harlan. "*You comin'?*" he asked forcefully.

Harlan swung his large frame off the barstool and walked over to the guy, casting a long shadow over him. Jane followed behind them as they walked into the parking lot. It was just past 12:30 and the stillness in the cool air lent an added precautionary flavor to the moment. They approached a black SUV with smoky windows. The guy opened the back door. Harlan walked up to him and the wiry fellow grasped the back of his neck. But a look came over the guy's face that suggested something wasn't right. Harlan crawled into the back of the SUV. The guy looked at Jane and she stepped forward. He repeated the identical neck grab with her, along with the same perplexed look. She stepped into the backseat and sat wedged next to Harlan. There was nobody else in the SUV. The guy got into the front seat and closed the door. He sat there motionless for about a minute, occasionally checking Harlan and Jane out in the rearview mirror. Jane could almost hear the wheels turning in his head, and in her opinion the wheels were in desperate need of oil. She could engage him in witty repartee or suffocate him with ego-vaulting compliments but she knew it would be useless. Why bother? It would be like giving Stevie Wonder a flashlight. It's a nice gesture but what's the point?

The guy reached across to the glove compartment and removed something but Jane couldn't detect what it was. He held the item in his lap for about fifteen seconds before he quickly turned around and pointed two targeted beams of red light at Harlan and Jane. The last thing Jane remembered was the sense of falling down a dark hole.

∆ ∆ ∆

There was a stony silence. Everything around her was out of focus and she knew she was unconscious. She willed the scenes around her to become clearer. And as if her thoughts had a voice, the people and places sharpened until she could clearly see everything. The first image was the man she witnessed Gabe killing in the darkened house. He was very much alive and bent over a long wooden desk in his study, coolly studying what appeared to be medical books. Jane caught quick glimpses of illustrations in the book that looked like the brain. She moved toward him and he turned as if he sensed her presence. Jane peered over his shoulder and saw a clear drawing of the cranium split in two pieces. The distant sound of tribal drumming was heard coming from the other side of the office door. Jane turned to a door and opened it. Walking across the threshold, she was thrust into another country. Dry grass crunched below her feet as swirling globes of dust and dirt spun around her. The drumming intensified and she calmly walked toward the syncopated, pounding sound.

It was an African village and the elders sat in a circle on the ground, beating their drums in unison. A huge fire burned in the center circle. A windstorm swept through the village, kicking up dust and debris. Jane heard the sound of young children screaming in the lattice-roofed mud huts around the periphery. She ran toward one of the huts but the second she crossed the threshold, the scene changed dramatically. Suddenly, she was back in the old man's office. The floor of the office was covered with hundreds of plastic syringes, all filled with a golden serum. The old man stood at his desk, facing Jane and holding the white binder with the stark **IEB** written in bold red ink on the cover. He placed his hand over his heart and then rested it across the top of the white IEB binder. He then placed his index finger on his forehead, holding it there for a few seconds, before lowering his finger to the floor and pointing to the hundreds of syringes. "The heart and the mind," she heard him say without moving his lips. "Are you hearing this, Jane?" He then held out the white binder to her, encouraging her to come forward and take it. She kicked the syringes out of the way to make a path, but the closer she moved to him, the farther away he appeared. Jane reached out to grab the binder but it was always inches from her grasp.

The smell of moist dirt in an old shed surfaced. She immediately recognized the nauseating aroma and was catapulted back to her father's workshop twenty-three years ago. The throbbing pain in her stomach felt acutely fresh. She could feel herself back there again as if it was happening at that very moment, laying on the cold, damp dirt, feeling the sticky blood flow from the repeated blows. She knew if she opened her eyes, he'd be standing over her, waiting for her to show the first sign of weakness. So, she gathered every ounce of strength and promised herself that when she opened her eyes, she'd fight back. Jane counted, preparing herself for the violence. One, two, three…

She opened her eyes. Hovering over her was the buzz cut idiot that came to the bar and escorted Harlan and Jane to the SUV.

"Wake up!" he demanded, kicking her hard in the thigh.

Jane winced. Her hands were tied with rope behind her back and her face was half-planted in the sandy dirt. Scanning the area with one eye, it looked like a cement-lined storage container that could accommodate a large truck. No windows. One door. And it smelled moldy and dank.

Δ Δ Δ

"Well, looky what I found in your waistband?" the guy announced, producing Jane's service weapon. He pointed it toward her face. "Ya know, ya really need to holster these things."

Jane turned slightly on her back, stealthily checking whether her Ruger was still holstered to her boot. From what she could tell, it was still there. "Where's Harlan?" she asked, her voice sounding raspy and tired.

"Where's Harlan?" he said in a mocking tone. "I bet you'd like to know that."

Jane may have been just coming to, but her attitude was fully present. "That's why I asked you, you fucking moron."

His countenance darkened and before she could protect herself, he slapped her hard across her mouth. "You shut your mouth, bitch!"

"Where is he?!" she screamed, undaunted by him.

He slapped her even harder across the mouth, this time breaking her lip open. "I told you to shut the fuck up! Who's the stupid one here, huh?"

Jane licked the blood off her lip and stared at the fool.

"That's better," he said, all puffed up. "You do what I tell you or I'll kill you with your own gun and everybody will think you offed yourself when they find you on the road with a bullet in your brain and your gun in your cold, dead hand." He let out a weird celebratory hoot.

"When you do that," Jane stated, feeling her lip throb, "make sure you put in my left hand."

He looked at her with a quizzical expression. "I don't get it."

"That's a shock."

He grabbed her by the hair and pulled her head off the ground. "What'd you say, bitch? I can't hear you! You think I won't shoot you?" He pressed the tip of the Glock into her cheek. "I've kilt lots of people. You'd just be another notch on my bedpost."

"You mean belt," she said, grimacing.

"Oh, somebody in this room thinks they're really smart, don't they?" He let Jane go and stood up, straddling her body. "I let my gun do my talkin'."

Jane figured that was probably a wise idea since this inbred jackass couldn't string together a single intelligent sentence.

Knowing

Hovering over her in an intimidating stance, he pointed the tip of the gun at her head. "Hell, I was born with a gun in my hand!"

Jane looked up at him. "Is that right? So, I guess that means you were a C-section?"

"Huh?"

It was the answer she fully expected. Pearls before swine. "Never mind."

"You mockin' me?"

"Nah. I bet you're hung like Einstein and smart as a horse."

He smiled broadly with pride because he stopped listening when he heard the word, "hung." It was like having a heart to heart with a squirrel. You want to believe they understand you, but deep down, logic tells you that it's jetting over their heads. She looked up at him, so full of himself, and she wasn't scared one bit. The thought crossed her mind that there was an up side to growing up with the devil in her house. She knew what true evil looked like and it sure as hell didn't resemble this freak. This jerkoff was just another fucker with a gun. She'd put book on it that he didn't live to see his thirtieth birthday. Jane could always determine the people who were destined to have a short shelf life. Somebody with a few more brain cells would cap his ass. And when the cops come to scrape his body off the pavement, they'd be chatting about whatever game was on that night or who got traded to another team. He'd get shoved into the drawer at the morgue with a toe tag that said John Doe. And when they looked in that drawer at him, they wouldn't see a tough guy. They'd see just another fucking asshat who rose to his level of incompetence right on schedule.

He continued to straddle Jane, pointing the gun at her the entire time and making threats, each one sounding more insane than the last. Finally, Jane had enough and piped up.

"Hey, you get off on Oxies?" she asked him.

He shut up and stared at her with his tongue slightly dangling from his mouth, like a dog waiting for his dish. "Yeah…Why come?"

"Well, I'll tell you why come. I got me a full bottle in my jacket pocket. You can eat 'em or you can sell 'em. Either way, it's gonna be a lucky day for you."

He let the gun lazily fall to his side. "You pull out the bottle first," he instructed her, thinking he was quite savvy.

"How can I do that? My hands are tied."

He stared at her, licking his lips with anticipation. "Oh, yeah."

"It's in my right pocket. Go on."

With his mouth slacked open, he gingerly patted her jacket pocket and smiled when he felt the prescription bottle. Reaching in, he brought out the orange container and stood up, still straddling Jane's body. "Whooo-wee!" he whooped.

"Yeah!" Jane said, eyeing him carefully. "Hillbilly heroin, huh? That should kill the pain, right?"

"What pain?"

"This pain." Jane drove her cowboy boot into his groin.

He fell backward, grabbing his jewels and sending her service pistol to the side.

Jane rolled herself up to a standing position and moved closer to him. "Where in the fuck is Harlan?"

He tried to stand up but the pain was too much. "I'll cut your throat!"

"I thought you were gonna shoot me in the head. Make up your fucking mind!"

"Fuckin' bitch—" he started toward her face when the door opened.

Jane turned around just in time to see a looming figure come toward her. He'd swept up her discarded Glock and before she could react, he had her in a firm chokehold.

"You try one fucking thing and I'll kill you!" the man said with a thick cockney accent. He turned to the idiot still nursing his testicles on the dirt floor. "Get up, you fucking shit-hawk!"

He struggled to his feet, sweating and trying to get his breath. "She's a mouthy bitch!"

The other man swung Jane around to face him. Looking up at him, this guy was a whole different ball of wax. He towered over her with his imposing, six-foot-three-inch frame. Jane factored he was in his late sixties and had led a brutal life. Craters of pockmarks filled his ruddy face. His deep-set black eyes held decades of rage and bloodshed. His crown was cleanly shaven, adding another level to his sadistic appearance.

"Who in the fuck are you?" Jane asked, undaunted.

"See what I mean?" the imbecile added.

"Shut up!" the man ordered his minion.

He shoved Jane out of the cement building. It was still pitch black outside as the three of them walked through the cold night air, down a gravel path, around a corner and into a house. The one-story house had an open floor plan, making the fifteen-hundred-square-foot space seem cavernous. Against the far wall was a kitchen set up, to the right sat a few couches and chairs and to the left was an elaborate bank of six computers scattered atop tables that looked like they'd been purchased at the Salvation Army. Two chairs faced each other in the center of the room and Jane's ass was firmly planted in the one with the rickety leg that forced her forward. It was the oldest trick in the book, she recalled from her early days on the force. You bring in a scared perp to the interrogation room and put him in a chair that has one leg shaved down just enough to give him the perception that *he* is off balance. But Jane knew how to shift her left foot in front of her to steady the chair so that she didn't fall flat on her face.

"Where's Harlan?" she asked in a demanding tone.

"Turn around." The man instructed her as he sat down across from her.

With her hands tied behind her back it wasn't easy, but Jane twisted her body and saw Harlan lying on a futon in the corner of the large room.

"He won't come to," the man declared. "*Nothing* I've done brings him out of it. So, I know you've got the fucking codes. Give me the one that wakes him up."

This was different, Jane figured. Suddenly she was Harlan's handler. Checking out the vibe between the guy seated across from her and dimwit standing next to him like a Labrador on point, she factored that their relationship was akin to master and slave.

"Untie me," Jane demanded.

He leaned forward in a menacing stance. "I'm not fucking around here! *Give me the code!*"

"Are you gonna untie me?" she asked again, echoing his intimidating posture.

He sat back and observed Jane. After a long minute, he lurched toward her and then quickly stopped but Jane didn't flinch once. Just inches away from her face, he stared into her eyes. His stale, toxic breath was overpowering. But she was unmoved. Jane steeled herself the way she'd taught herself to do when she was a kid. When you've experienced the worst, everything else is a cakewalk. Evil didn't inspire her to fall into the vacuum of fear. She saw the beast for what it was and understood that all monsters have their weaknesses that a trained eye can exploit. All she had to do was pretend that she wasn't afraid to die and keep the conversation going for as long as necessary. He brought out a long knife and quickly cut the ropes, freeing her hands. Sitting back in his comfortable chair, he observed Jane a bit more before he tipped his head to the side.

"Did you hear that Mary had a little lamb?" he asked her as his eyes sent a penetrating gaze toward her.

Jane kept her face frozen. "Fleece was white as snow?"

He shook his head, seemingly becoming more agitated. He leaned forward, this time with urgency. "*Did you hear that Mary had a little lamb?*"

"Baa, baa, baa?" Jane retorted.

"Stop fucking with me!" he yelled. "Go deep!"

"How deep?" she asked, realizing this was a one-sided conversation.

His little psychotic buddy leaned over to him. "I think her alter split."

The man turned to him with rage and spoke in what sounded like an odd, garbled mix of German and Chinese. He snapped his fingers and, like a trained seal, the dolt dropped to his knees and bowed his head. The man looked at Jane again. "Her alter didn't split!" Bewilderment colored his face as he tried one more approach. Leaning toward her again, he screamed, "Zero, one, one, two, three, five, eight!"

Jane stared him down. "That your phone number?"

His agitation peaked. "Goddammit! *Zero, one, one, two, three, five, eight!*" he screamed in her face.

"You can scream at me all fucking night. It's not gonna work!"

He peered into her eyes. "There's still life in those eyes. What in the fuck is going on in there?" He leapt to his feet and grabbed the back of Jane's neck, as if he was searching for something important. "Where is it?!" he yelled. "We've checked him already," he said, motioning to Harlan. "It's red and blistered on him where it should be. Is he a stupid sod? Did he cut it out? Did you cut *yours* out too?"

Jane recalled Harlan's comment about wanting to get a knife and "dig out" whatever was irritating his neck. "That's possible," she said.

"Well, it doesn't make sense! You don't bloody cut it out! You lose your connection, for fuck sake! And I know there was a connection because you went into the fucking bar. He sang song number one forty-four zero. The shots at the bar? Wake the fuck up! How would you know the code? And why are there two of you instead of one? There should only be one and he's been dead for over four fucking years!"

That's all she needed to hear. Jane felt her gut churning. She pretended to slump forward as if she was sick. But once she was in reach, she quickly hiked up the right leg of her jeans, slid the Ruger from the boot holster and stood up, kicking the lopsided chair to the side. Simultaneously, the two men produced 9mm handguns and pointed them at Jane's head. And there they stood, the three of them no more than four feet apart and with enough firepower to pepper them all into Swiss cheese.

"My name is Jane Perry. I'm a cop! And so far, you've made two mistakes. The first one was promoting that pinhead beyond his evolutionary capabilities," she declared, jutting her chin toward his dimwitted associate. "The second mistake was kidnapping a cop. Last time I checked, kidnapping is still a crime."

"Is that right?" the man said, still aiming his gun at Jane's forehead. "Well, for starters, the rules don't apply to us. Rules are just for reference purposes. And second, I know who the fuck you are already! I took a photograph of you and scanned it into our system. You work at Denver Homicide. And as of last night's announcement, you are officially dead."

She stared at him with vengeance, never lowering her pistol. "What in the hell are you talking about?"

"It was on the late news last night. You died in an unfortunate bus explosion. Your adoring Sergeant almost broke down on live television when he made the announcement."

Jane's world crumbled around her. She steadied the Ruger but the news clearly dimmed her aggression.

The man shifted his stance toward Jane, never moving the gun an inch from her forehead. "I have to assume you understand the significance of that breaking news announcement? So, here's what I need to know. How long has Denver Homicide been involved?"

Jane knew she had to cut off any conspiracy connection at the knees. "They're not involved. It's just me."

"Don't piss down my neck and tell me it's raining!" he yelled, still holding his gun on her.

"I'm telling you the truth! Harlan stole my car. I tracked him down and he told me his story."

He continued to hold his gun on her but she could easily see that his interest was piqued. "Lower your gun," he said.

"You and your little buddy first," Jane countered. They didn't move. "I can stand here all night."

"And I can kill you in half a second," the man rejoined.

"But you won't. And you won't kill Harlan either. We're the hiccup you weren't expecting. Spontaneity sucks, doesn't it?"

"Give me your gun," the man demanded.

"You already have my Glock."

"And now I want your Ruger."

"I can't do my job without a fucking gun!"

"You don't have a job to go back to, you bloody cunt! *You're dead*! Didn't you hear what I said? Once they make the announcement, it's a done deal! Now, give me your fucking gun!"

Jane stared him down but it was pointless. If she took a shot at one of them, she'd be mowed down. She lowered the Ruger and handed it to the man. "Give me a chair that you haven't fucked with," she said, her courage re-emerging.

The man turned to the dolt and motioned for him to holster his gun and get Jane a chair. Once she was seated, he set his pistol on a nearby table within arm's reach.

"You know my name," Jane offered. "What's yours?"

"Call me John."

"John what?"

"John Burroughs."

She smiled. "Really?" It was the first coded fake name she understood. John Burroughs was the name Elvis Presley used when he traveled and checked into hotels to remain ingognito. "Is that the best name you can come up with? Or do you just like to joke that Elvis has not left the building?"

"Oh, you're a funny little twat, aren't you?"

"What his name?" Jane asked, pointing at his hypnotized subordinate.

"I only know him as 'S.B.'"

"What does that stand for? Stupid bastard?"

"I haven't got a fucking clue what it stands for."

Jane licked the open cut on her lip. She could feel it starting to swell. "You got some ice in this joint?"

"No," John said with an evil grin, "we lost the recipe."

She sat back. He didn't have a splinter of compassion and why would he? Jane observed that people really *do* take on the grime of their associations and actions. It was impregnated in this guy's cells. It never fails. What we've seen and what we've done washes over us and colors the aura that shadows us. "Okay, fine. Let's cut to the chase. Are you Romulus?"

Knowing

For the first time in their short relationship, John showed trepidation. "What in the fuck are you talking about—"

"It's a simple question, John."

"You should know the bloody answer!"

"Okay. So that's a 'no,'" Jane stated.

"If you don't have a clue about Romulus, how in the hell do you know anything about them?"

"You just confirmed it," Jane said with a tinge of sarcasm.

"You never make light about Romulus!" he bellowed, fear imprinted in his tone. "*Never*! You can joke about Jesus, Buddha, Moses, Mohammed, dead babies, rape, cripples and retards but you *never, ever* joke about Romulus." He sat back. "I don't get it. That beached whale is an escaped felon. I never heard of him until I saw him on the news a bit ago. So, what in the fuck is *he* doing in the *Dystopian Lounge* singing song number one forty-four zero? Only one person in this world ever knew that trick. Your podgy traveling associate had to know somewhere deep down that we'd show up, even though it's been over four years since the last meet up with the other one. And the only reason we show up is to get codes for the next job. So, if you don't know the codes and he's unconscious, what am I to make of all this?"

Jane shuffled every possible answer in her head. "You wouldn't believe me if I told you."

He laughed. "Oh, sweetheart, you'd be shocked at what I'm willing to believe."

She glanced back at Harlan, still blissfully asleep. "He was mistakenly re-cruited into your group."

"*Bullshit*! They *never* make mistakes!"

"Well, they did! And they did it big time. Now they're trying to fix it. And when I say 'fix it,' I think you know what I mean."

He leaned forward. "*They don't make mistakes*, Perry."

"Oh, come on. You seriously think they are going to recruit a truck driver with a low IQ?"

"They recruit rapists, murders, pedophiles, thieves, racists, sociopaths, derelicts and mental patients. I'd say a truck driver with a low IQ is improving their stats."

Glancing between John and S.B., Jane figured that between them they hit the criterion from the former category. "Look, I have witness testimony that proves Harlan Kipple was framed."

"I'm sure he bloody well was! That's the way it works, you stupid cow. Sometimes you get framed first before you get taken out. It all depends how they decide to spin it."

His statement sounded like psychotic logic. "For fuck sake! Look in my eyes! I'm not lying to you! He was never part of your group."

"That he can remember!" He shook his head and pointed to S.B. who was conspicuously silent. "I can send this bloke cross country for a hit and when he returns, he can't remember any of it. Wiped clean from his scrambled little fucked up mind! And if something goes wrong along the way, he's got a suicide trigger in place so he doesn't lead anyone back here." He laughed. "You telling me that Mr. Kipple has no bloody memory is not an answer! If he's not one of us, then how in the hell did he know the codes at the karaoke bar?"

A sudden idea came into Jane's mind. "Well, there's only one reason I can think of." She gathered her thoughts. "Harlan told me that about four and a half years ago, he picked up a hitchhiker on the road during one of his Interstate hauls. The guy's name was Gabriel Cristsóne."

The look on their faces was hard to judge. But Jane could easily see that S.B. was obviously affected by Gabe's name. As for John, his face showed traces of alarm before a gradual scowl took over.

"Well, well, well," John replied, sitting back in his chair to ruminate on the news. After a hard minute, he leaned forward. "That changes a lot now, doesn't it?"

"I don't know. What does it change?"

"Four and a half years ago, you say?"

"That's what Harlan told me."

"I see." The wheels were turning in his head like a windmill in a hurricane.

"And why would he bother mentioning about this random meeting four and a half years ago with a complete stranger?"

"Because he never forgot him. Harlan said Gabriel was quite the enigma." She checked herself, realizing Harlan would never use a word like that. "They talked for a couple days as he drove across the country. Harlan called it a real heart-to-heart discussion."

Jane couldn't determine what John was thinking at that moment. He was well trained to keep his thoughts from translating across his countenance. But there was a sense of indignation and a hint of resentment. "Gabriel died around four years ago. He was killed."

Jane managed a raise of her eyebrow to effect slight shock. "Oh, my god... Holy shit! You order his hit?"

"Where in the bloody hell did that come from?"

"Did you?"

"I'm not high enough on the food chain to order that kind of hit."

"Okay. Did you kill him?"

"Oh, that's rich! I don't off the HVTs."

High Value Targets, Jane understood. "Okay. Did you know him?"

John screwed his pockmarked face into an ugly twist. "Yeah, I knew him. Thought a lot of himself, that one. Real elite. They plucked him out of Delta. I heard they tested him to see how far they could push him before he broke. *They* gave in before he did." He rolled his eyes like a teenager who's jealous of the high school quarterback. "He was the best shot they ever found. But that was the least of his talents. They found out he could pick up most languages without hardly trying. He had a photographic memory. And he could recite a conversation back to you verbatim, even if it occurred years before with no notes or recordings. He also had a keen ability to play different roles—a farm worker, priest, oil rig worker, executive. But there was something else. Something..." He reached for the elusive word and fell short.

"A knowing?"

He regarded her with wariness. "Yes. That's exactly it. It was uncanny. He could look at a person or just their photo and tell you everything about them. He knew their personality, their favorite foods, their sexual fetishes, their secrets. And he was never wrong. While I didn't personally witness it, I was told that he had the ability to see into the future. Apparently, he would describe events that hadn't happened yet and how they unfolded. I suppose that alone made him a valuable asset to the group. Nothing like manipulating a timeline that hasn't occurred yet."

Jane was stunned. "Oh, come on. You're saying that was done?"

"No. Of course, not. Then again, how in the fuck would we know?" He let out a hearty laugh but it quickly died down. His face washed with derision. "Paid that fucker fifty thousand for each hit. Then after a year, he got double. That doesn't include, of course, the ten grand a week they handed him for expenses when he did a job." He grabbed his groin in a crude gesture. "He was the fair-haired son, that one. Kept to himself. Didn't rub shoulders with anyone. Except for that quirky little fuck, Monroe."

Jane nodded, fully engaged in the subterfuge. "You think Monroe's quirky? I don't."

"You've met Monroe?" he asked, peering at her suspiciously.

Jane hoped she hadn't dug herself a deep hole and that Monroe was actually six feet under. "No. Just heard a lot about him from my sources."

"If you've never met him, then how do you know he's not quirky?"

Jane decided to go for it. "After Harlan dropped off Gabriel, he found some notes that had fallen out of his backpack."

"Notes?" John's interest was apparent. "What type of notes?"

"Just some random correspondence between them." She leaned forward. "It wasn't love letters."

"Knowing Gabriel, I don't suspect they were," he said dryly.

"You know, Harlan would love to meet Monroe. Any chance you can tell me where I can find him?"

John leaned forward. "And why in the fuck would he want to meet him?"

"Harlan's a very curious guy."

"Is that right?" He cheated a glance toward Harlan. "Last I heard Monroe lives north of here, out in fucking nowhere."

"Can you be more specific?"

"Outside of Sheldon Springs."

Jane nodded. "So, why do you think Gabriel was targeted?"

"Why do you care and what has that got to do with a bloody thing?"

"Well, obviously, Gabriel said things to Harlan on their road trip. Things that maybe he shouldn't have said. Like the codes at the bar—"

"I have a very hard time believing that Gabriel was as chatty as your little friend makes him out to be," John interrupted, his voice dripping with disgust.

"Well, he was. How else would a guy like Harlan know about the codes at the bar? Maybe Gabriel knew he was going to get killed and so he unloaded on the first stranger he thought he could trust. But all that did was put Harlan in the crosshairs. And here we are."

"And here we certainly are," he mocked. "Tell me something, Perry. Why do you care about that piece of shit lying on the floor behind you? Why don't you just plug him and get on with your life?"

"Because I'm crazy. Haven't you heard? Sixty is the new forty and crazy is the new sane."

"Crazy, my ass." He leaned forward, diving into her eyes. "You still have your soul, sweetheart. That's your problem. You should behave like a machine. You learn that and your options for destruction are limitless. People think the term 'selling your soul' is just a phrase. It's not. It's fucking real. And it's done with bloody abandon every single day. It's a beautiful thing, Perry. Wouldn't you love to live with no rules or laws or moral codes? You're a cop, so it shouldn't be tough to make that leap."

Jane remained undaunted. "Did Gabriel sell his soul?"

John sat back looking irritated when Gabe's name was brought up again. "No," he said succinctly. "Gabriel thought he was better than the rest of us. But that didn't stop him from doing the Devil's work."

"Why'd they put out a hit on him?"

"I wasn't privy to that."

"Did he have the wood on somebody?"

"Fuck. In our work, you have the wood on everyone so you can use it when necessary."

"I'm not talking about blackmail. I'm talking about something deeper. Maybe he uncovered a significant plan? Something that Romulus is involved in—"

"You know what gets you killed?" John angrily countered, lunging forward.

"What?"

"Audacity. Gabriel had the audacity to believe he was better than he was. He thought he could win against them and that was his fatal mistake."

Jane considered it. "But if really could see the future, like you said, he already knew he would be killed."

"Unless he believed he could manipulate the outcome."

Manipulate the outcome. It was an odd statement to Jane. "I don't get it. How would he do that?"

"I don't know." Threads of jealousy were woven into his tenor. "But if anyone could do it, I imagine he would be the one who could pull it off."

Jane tried to make sense of it all. An expertly trained, high-level assassin possibly uncovered stunning information and clearly understood the depth of what that information meant. But on some strange, intuitive level, he also knew his life would end because of it. Jane quickly recalled the IEB white binder. "Ever heard of 'IEB'?"

"No clue. Why?"

"Gabriel mentioned it to Harlan on the trip. You sure you never heard of it?"

"I'm fucking positive! His clearance was far above mine."

"You never heard about IEB or—" Jane suddenly saw a flash of the African village and the elders seated in a circle pounding their drums. "How about Africa?"

"Well, you're all over the place now, aren't you?"

Jane pulled up the comment that Nanette made regarding the postcards Gabriel sent her when he was gone. She mentioned that one postcard featured children in the Congo, dressed in their tribal outfits. Less than a week later she read a story about a coup in that region where the tribal leaders were slaughtered, along with lots of children. "The Congo?" Jane asked tentatively, feeling some sort of veiled significance the minute the word left her lips.

John stared at her. "The Congo?" He looked interested even though he was doing everything possible to hide it. "What did he tell Harlan about the Congo?"

She couched her words carefully. Something told her he was trolling for information and had nothing of import to offer her. "He took photos of the kids in their native garb," she offered, winging it as she went. "He told Harlan they'd never seen a digital camera before so they were thrilled to see themselves in the monitor." Jane wasn't certain where all this bullshit was coming from.

"Is that right?" he replied, not caring one bit.

"Yeah, he said something like, 'We take all of this for granted, but through the eyes of a child…'" She stopped, hearing the words she just uttered. It was the exact title of the Patsy Cline song on the cassette tape that Harlan carried in his bag.

"Through the eyes of a child, *what*?"

A wave of terror gripped Jane and then subsided. But a sense of dread hung close to her.

"Hey!" John yelled. "I asked you a fucking question!"

She came back into herself. "You can see forever," she replied, not sure what she meant.

He regarded her with derision. "Fuck! What a load of tripe. What else about the Congo?" John asked in an irritated tone, fishing for information.

She shook her head. "That's it. Just the kids. Does it mean anything to you?"

He snorted contempt. "The few times Gabriel reached out and we made contact, he never said a word about what he saw or was involved in. But it

221

wouldn't have mattered. They change names of projects all the time. They compartmentalize us on purpose. So Bob doesn't have a clue what Bill's doing. But then again, by the time Bob is on the scene, Bill is probably dead. So, problem solved there, eh?"

Jane could see that John took her bait and she let him talk.

"There are organizations within organizations," he continued. "Secrets within secrets. And it's all buried so deeply that one arm doesn't know what the other is doing. It's all by design. It's so no one has any idea of what the master plan is except for those in charge. And *those* people are so few, you'll never meet them." He picked at his front tooth with his fingernail. "I only know what I'm asked to do. I don't know what came before or what happens after. All I know for certain is that the people I work for invented the darkness. They own the bloody patent. And their hand is in every single major organization on this planet, even the ones that appear entirely altruistic. They leave nothing to chance, you see? Every gesture is planned to the last motion. They don't do anything that isn't *significant*. There's no wasted effort. Every breath is programmed and considered before inhaling. Dates, locations, seasons…they are all important. And above all else, ritual is king. Without ritual sacrifice, there's no point to the process because it's through the ritual that they gain and maintain their power."

"So, you're saying Gabriel was sacrificed?"

"Yes. I'm certain of it. His death knell probably kept their gods satiated for quite a while."

She let it sink in. "Because of his abilities?"

"Oh, shit. It went far beyond 'abilities,'" he mocked. "He had raw, impenetrable *power*." He cocked his head to the side. "And when you kill someone like that, it's like throwing a large stone into the water. The waves of energy produced from that death can be significant. It's the way it works. Someone always has to die so someone else can prosper. Sacrifice is what it's all about, sweetheart. You can't sacrifice enough people or beliefs. Because with each sacrifice, the more supremacy is attained. Through someone else's blood, one can use that death to attain greatness." He eyed Jane carefully. "Don't think you're so above us, Perry. If you had to, you'd sacrifice someone in a bloody heartbeat."

Jane thought about it. "Only if it meant saving them."

"Killing someone to save them? That's a novel idea. Gotta remember that one." He looked at her with a handler's eyes, modulating his voice in an attempt to mesmerize Jane. "Don't you want to know what greatness feels like? You could be a fantastic asset to us, Perry. I mean it. This could be one of those out-of-the-box opportunities for you. Everyone thinks you're dead. The timing is brilliant. You change your identity, alter your appearance, maybe have a little cosmetic surgery? We don't have a lot of women in our ranks. Who knows how far you could climb up the ladder? You've already killed at least one person in your career. I can tell. I can always tell that. Once you've taken the life of another human being, it's stamped on your psyche. So, the next one and the one after that shouldn't be difficult at all, eh?" He smiled broadly. "Yeah. I see the potential of greatness in you."

She looked around the sparse house and its meager trappings. "Greatness, huh? You've killed a shitload of people. I don't see that it's working out for you."

He scowled, shaking his head with disdain. "I thought you were smarter than the average cunt. But you have no fucking idea." He observed her like a lab specimen. "You've bought into the falsehood that with goodness comes an inevitable reward. But that's bloody untrue and you know it! Look around and tell me what goodness gets you. It doesn't propel you forward. It traps you in the promise that with every wonderful deed you accomplish, somehow you'll gain a gift. But that's a false belief system. Because no matter how many stellar actions you initiate, the evil in this world is overwhelming and will always defeat you."

He moved his chair closer to hers. "You're like the rest of the sleeping masses who enjoy believing that all nursery school teachers are virginal and all preachers are faithful." His tone was eerily calming. "But the truth is nothing like that. Yet it doesn't stop people from trying to convince themselves that goodness still exists. The stupid fucks have no clue that goodness died a quick death years ago and has been replaced with all that's left."

She looked him in the eye, unmoved by his words. "You're wrong. There still is goodness in this world. You just don't attract it."

He waved his hand at her in a dismissive manner. "Fuck off! Have you taken a hard look at the world lately, sweetheart? You tell me that there hasn't been a precise objective over the years to propel the shit to the top of the heap. It's been done on purpose, you stupid bitch, and there's nothing anybody can do to stop it! Ninety-nine percent of the human drones out there cannot wrap their minds around the idea that there are a chosen few in this world who will stop at nothing to gain whatever it is they believe they need. And if that means destroying people, places, ideas, concepts, morals and the lot, so be it. They achieve their goals through creating chaos! They love it. They feast off it for breakfast, lunch and dinner. And all the fear that's produced from that chaos? They thrive on that! It's their manna from hell." He leaned back, displaying a certain amount of pride. "Some call it 'driving the wedge.' I like to call it the Chaos Quotient. Throw enough chaos at anyone and they shut down because they can't process anything thoroughly. Too much is happening all at once so nobody can focus on any one thing before the next 'unexpected' thing happens. And so everyone's running around just trying to make it through their day and juggle all the distorted information their primitive mind questions but their rational mind accepts based on what they've been told." He smiled like a feral Cheshire cat. "You see how it works? Hit them with a blast of madness and convince them that it's sanity. Tell them that this is the new reality—a reality that doesn't allow for contemplation or critical thinking or even common sense. And do it all in plain view and if someone is smart enough to figure it out, you just label them crazy, unhinged, mentally unstable, in need of medication and then give them whatever it takes to get them so bloody numb that they shut the fuck up." He smiled again. "It really is quite humorous to watch especially when you know how the game is played."

"You can't continue chaos forever," Jane stated.

"Of course, not. The ones who create the chaos are the same ones who come up with the solution. Brilliant, eh? So no matter what happens, *they* always win. Trust me, *they will always win.*"

Jane turned back to Harlan who was still sound asleep. She sat back and glared at John. "So, what's the plan?"

"What do you mean?"

"Are you going to kill us or not?"

He met Jane's intense glower. "You're already dead. Remember?"

She sat forward on the chair. "Right. So, I think we're done. What happened here is between us. I won't breathe a word of it."

"Dead men tell no tales."

There was a thick silence between them that seemed eternal. With no more words, John snapped his fingers toward S.B., who dutifully handed him two black blindfolds. He tied one around Jane's head as she heard S.B.'s footsteps trod toward Harlan. She was gruffly pulled to her feet by S.B. and taken outside into the cold, early morning air. After being handcuffed and then locked onto what felt like the side mirror of the SUV, she heard S.B.'s feet retreat back into the house. Before she'd figured out how to escape the cuffs, she heard John and S.B. return, grunting as they walked. She felt Harlan's large body brush against hers as he was lifted into the backseat of the SUV. Her cuffs were removed and she was shoved into the SUV. The ride lasted half an hour. At least, that's what Jane factored as she quietly counted in her head. No words were exchanged the entire time. For all she knew, they were driving in circles just to throw her off. But thirty minutes later, the SUV came to a halt and the back door was opened. Jane was grabbed first and hauled out of the backseat before being thrown onto the asphalt. About one minute later, she felt Harlan's body fall next to her. She waited, knowing they were still hovering close by. One of them stepped toward her and removed her wallet from her jacket pocket.

"Oh, fuck, you've gotta be kidding me!" Jane argued, straining against the blindfold. "You're ripping me off?"

"I never bet against the team," John replied. "So I like to improve my odds whenever possible."

He stuffed the wallet back into her pocket and leaned close to Jane's face. The hot, venomous stench of his breath nearly overpowered her.

"I'll let them finish what they started," he whispered in her ear. "Don't ever believe you can outsmart them, Perry. They always get what they want." He dug into her jacket pocket again, removing her car keys.

Jane heard him heft the keys across the parking lot and their soft landing in dirt.

"That'll slow you down in case you're stupid enough to follow us," John sneered.

There was a tense moment before Jane heard John and S.B.'s feet trail back to the SUV. She waited until she couldn't hear the vehicle's engine any longer before removing the blindfold. They were back at the bowling alley, lying next to the Mustang. Jane quickly pulled out her wallet and found that everything was still there except for one thing: all the cash. She untied Harlan's blindfold and nudged him in the shoulder. He didn't respond.

"Harlan!" She nudged him again with more urgency but he didn't move. Leaning closer to him, she said the first two words that came to mind. "You're safe."

Harlan immediately opened his eyes and looked at Jane. Looking around the scene, he shook his head of the cobwebs. "Oh, shit," he mumbled. "What'd I miss?"

CHAPTER 16

Jane brought Harlan up to speed, which didn't take long since she left out most of what transpired. "What's the last thing you remember?"

He thought about it. "Drivin' into this parkin' lot."

She sighed. "You don't remember singing, 'Just in Time'?"

"What's that?"

"Oh, gee, Harlan," she stated wryly, "And I thought you were singing those words just to me."

"It ain't funny, Jane." Suddenly he became serious. "None of this is comical. We're outta money. How in the hell are we gonna buy gas and food?"

"We have about half a tank left. I have an emergency hundred-dollar bill stashed in the glove compartment. And there's still enough food in the cooler if we ration it." Her attempt at Pollyanna optimism quickly disintegrated. She turned to Harlan. "Okay. We're fucked." She worked herself up off the asphalt, gingerly avoiding the broken beer bottles. Her car keys were sitting out there in the dark somewhere, probably closer to dirt than pavement based on the sound she heard when they landed. Jane walked around the Mustang and realized something was wrong. Peering at the right rear wheel, it was completely flat. "Oh, fuck." This was instant Karma—ethereal payback for slicing the cop's patrol car tire.

Harlan heaved himself up. "You got yourself shitty tires, Jane. I tried to tell you that when we first met." He rubbed his hand across the top of the tire. "You got an air pump and a good spare?"

"Good enough."

"Well, finally somethin' I can actually help you with!" he said with pride.

After Jane found the keys lying in a landscaped island next to a small, decorative tree, she popped the trunk and Harlan went to work changing the tire. Jane grabbed a cigarette, promising herself just two puffs. She checked the time on the clock. It was 3:11. "Shit," she whispered. If this was a cosmic joke, she wasn't laughing. How many times had she seen 3:11 staring back at her during her last case in Midas, only to find out it happened to be Wanda's birthday. She took another drag on her cigarette and walked into the empty parking lot. How long had she been gone? Six days? No. It was coming up on four. How in the hell was that possible? Based on what Hank and she had learned, there was only a short window of time before Wanda moved from her halfway house to another location. After that, tracking her down might be more difficult, especially if she ghosted herself like a lot of addicts and fell back into her old life. Jane tried to persuade herself that she didn't need to meet or talk with Wanda but Hank convinced her that if she didn't make the trek to Northern New Mexico she'd always wonder about her half-sister. "That'll dog you forever, Jane," he warned her. And he was right. She hated that fact but it was true. But it was also a fact that Wanda didn't have a clue that Jane existed. Here Jane was, focused on the woman, like she had been a couple weeks before, and realized that she could think about Wanda 24/7 but it didn't mean they had any purposeful connection. Right now, it was a one-sided relationship. Jane lectured herself that if she wanted to, she could blow it off and never look back.

She took another hit of nicotine, hoping it would ease her nerves. But there was a gradual shaking that crept under her skin that felt like a thousand electrical outlets buzzing simultaneously. Jane looked into the coal darkness. She heard the distant horn of an Interstate truck, miles away from their desolate location. But she didn't feel one bit alone. Were they watching her, she worried. Had John made a call and improved his odds even more by tipping them off to their whereabouts? Between the cops and the mysterious Romulus, Jane knew she had to make some serious adjustments in their plans if she was going to be able to continue and figure out how to remove Harlan from this mess.

Her lip started to throb where she'd been slapped. Rubbing it gently, she noticed some of the dirt from the floor of the cement blockade was firmly embedded in her inflamed cut. All she needed now was an infection to cap off her night from hell. She turned back to the Mustang in time to find Harlan stashing the dead tire in her trunk. Letting out a hard sigh, she knew what she had to do. It wasn't going to be easy and she'd have to wing it, given the enormity of her situation. But her back was against the wall and as much as she wanted to continue being the lone wolf, she was aware that either the cops or Romulus would devour her unless she got some help.

Trekking back to the car, Harlan was waiting for her.

"They may have jobbed your two guns, Jane. But I still got one," he beamed, tipping his head toward the backseat. There was the 9mm he'd grabbed when he escaped from the hospital days before. "Extra clip, too, don't forget."

Jane looked at him. He was so proud that he could fix her tire and now he was thrilled that he could offer a gun and a clip. "Thank you," she offered.

He licked his lips nervously. "We're gonna be okay, Jane. Right?"

She nodded, still formulating her plan.

"Hey, can I ask you somethin'?" he said.

"What?"

"How'd you wake me up? What'd you say?"

"I said, 'You're safe.'"

"Yeah?" he smiled. "Humph. It's funny. I didn't hear you say it, but I remember relaxin'. And I knew I was gonna be okay."

Jane searched through the car and found her last remaining disposable cell phone. She stared at the phone, willing herself to dial the numbers. "We are going to be okay, Harlan." Looking at the haphazard collection of items in the car, she sighed. "We need to get this all organized so we can transfer it easily."

"Transfer it where?"

"To another vehicle. This one is too much on the radar. Could you take care of it for me?"

"Sure," he said, happy to have something to do. "But, you really think we should add car theft to the list?"

Jane wished it could be that simple. "Just take care of it, would you?" She squashed out the cigarette and lit a new one. Fresh tobacco was required. She turned and walked back into the pillows of darkness that hugged the parking lot. Somehow, having this conversation in the shadows of night was fitting. She stalled for five minutes, lighting her cigarette and puffing on it like a fiend. Then she dialed the number halfway and stopped, going over her appeal out loud, changing the wording to sound less desperate. After half an hour and down to the butt of her cigarette, she let out a long breath and with a shaking hand, dialed the number. It rang twice before he picked up.

"Jane?"

She was stunned. It was a disposable phone. How could he know it was her?

"*Jane?*" he asked again, his voice raising a nervous octave.

"Yes," was all she could utter. Hearing his voice somehow overwhelmed her.

"Where are you?"

"I'm okay, Hank."

"Where are you?"

"Can you get to Sheldon Springs sometime today?"

"Sheldon…Jesus, how in the hell did you get down there? Yeah, yeah. Of course."

She arranged to meet him at the only motel she remembered in that area. If memory served, there was a wooded area one block west of the motel that would come in handy. Jane gave him her cell phone number and asked him to call her before he got there and she'd relay the room number.

"I need some stuff," she added. She could hear him grabbing a paper and pen.

"Are you going to tell me what in the hell is going on?"

"I will when you get here."

"Has this got to do with Wanda?" he asked in a probing manner.

She smiled. "God, I wish. You have that pen ready?"

"Yeah," he said, not satisfied. "Shoot."

"I need five hundred bucks. I'll pay you back."

"I don't give a shit about that. What about your credit cards?"

"I lost them."

"Uh-huh." His voice was tense. "Jane, what in the hell is going on?" he asked, dredging up his past law enforcement tone.

"I'll fill you in when I see you. The next thing I need is food. Lunchmeat, apples, cheese, chips, two dozen eggs…no, make that three dozen—"

"*What?*"

"You writing this down?"

"Three dozen eggs. Got it. You want four pounds of butter? How about a skillet? Should I pack some dishes and cutlery? Need any salt?"

His sarcasm was oddly calming to Jane. God, it felt good for her to hear his voice. "Nah, just the eggs will do. I could also use a couple disposable cell phones."

He scratched his pen on the paper. "This is getting interesting."

She touched her cut lip, feeling heat emanate from it. "Is that aquarium store still in business south of Midas?"

"*Aquarium* store? Yeah…"

"Good. When they open this morning, could you go down there and pick up some fish antibiotics?" She heard his pen drop.

"*What?*"

"Just look for Fish-Mox Forte," she replied in a serious tone. "It's amoxicillin. The same shit humans use, just packaged differently."

"Is that right? How many bottles do you need, Jane?"

"One will do. I figure that a single capsule a day treats a ten-gallon aquarium and there's 100 capsules in a bottle—"

"Jane! What in the hell is going on?!"

"Will you get these for me?" she stressed.

He let out a tired breath. "Fish antibiotics. Check. What else?"

"I need a rental car. Something on the larger side."

"How large? A four door sedan or a van?"

She thought about it. The idea of tooling around in a van gave her the chills. But it would be a helluva lot more comfortable for Harlan and it would give them an adequate place to sleep at night without having to rely on seedy motels. "Get me the van. Something really plain and boring."

"Plain and boring van. You want GPS?"

"No. I hate GPS. I like to see where I'm going. I'll take a good map, though."

"A good map. Anything else?"

She thought quickly. "Maybe a box of 9mm ammo?"

"Ammo. Of course. Makes sense. Right. Is that it?"

"Yeah. That's it."

"So, let me read this back to you because I think you need to hear this. You want five hundred bucks, lunchmeat, apples, cheese, chips, three-dozen eggs, a couple disposable cell phones, one bottle of fish antibiotics, a vanilla van with a good map and a box of 9mm ammo."

She went over everything in her head. "Yeah. That covers it."

"*Seriously*, Jane?" He sighed. "You realize that anybody else would get the authorities involved?"

"You're not 'anybody else.' That's why I called you."

"Why didn't you call me four days ago when you got your car stolen?" For the first time his voice sounded angry.

"I sent you a message," she offered in a soft voice.

"What do you mean?"

"The day after my car was jacked. I sent you a mental message, letting you know I was okay."

"You know that's not the kind of message I'm talking about, Jane."

"Yeah. Well, you must have gotten the message."

"Why's that?"

"Because you said my name when you answered the phone tonight. And if you believed for one second I was dead, you wouldn't have done that. Am I right?"

There was a hard pause on the other end of the phone. "Okay. I'll give you that. But goddammit, Jane, you should have called me. The old fashioned way? You can't leave me hanging here! I need to know what's going on."

"I'll talk to you when I see you. My minutes are running out on this crap phone," she lied. They said a rushed goodbye and she hung up. Part of her felt weak for having to phone him and ask for help. But another part of her was aching to touch him. He'd reduced her to rubble, she decided. Where once had stood an independent, self-sufficient person, there now was a lost soul standing in a dark parking lot at four in the morning, counting the hours until she could hold him in her arms. She hated herself for it. Needing anyone was a sign of weakness in her eyes. One starts depending on another and before they know it, they've lost their drive and vulnerability becomes their fulcrum. While she'd allowed herself to be vulnerable with Hank over the past month, it wasn't etched into her psyche. And the longer they'd been apart, the more she'd convinced herself that it was wise to leave a door open or at least a large window in order to escape if necessary.

Taking advantage of the cloak of night, Jane drove north to a twenty-four hour gas station. She secured her ball cap on her head as she got out of the Mustang and did a quick check around the area. She added air to her tires and checked the oil level under the hood. Using the rainy day, hundred-dollar bill she'd been holding back in the glove compartment, Jane put twenty-five bucks of fuel in the Mustang. If the plan was going to work, she wanted to make sure he could drive straight back without stopping. That's assuming Hank would agree to do it.

Checking the time, she figured that traveling on the highway might be safer and certainly quicker than the bumpy county roads and back highways. But the closer she drove toward I-25, the more she felt the walls caving in on her. A few blocks later, she saw flashing lights and what appeared to be a checkpoint up ahead. Her paranoia kicked in and, putting two and two together, wondered if the cops at the Shangri-La put out a BOLO for her Mustang. She pulled over to the side of the road, keeping her engine running.

"Why you stoppin', Jane?" Harlan asked from under the covers in the backseat.

"I don't know how to get to Sheldon Springs on the back roads. I'm not sure there even are back roads. What'd you do with the map I had in the glove compartment?"

He lifted his head and scanned the interior of the car. "I saw it 'round here somewhere."

Headlights crested the hill behind her. "Get down, Harlan," she ordered him.

He obliged. Jane watched the headlights loom closer in the rearview mirror. As it approached, the vehicle slowed. She kept her eyes pinned in the mirror, her heart racing faster as it moved closer. And then, the flashing lights came on.

"Fuck!" Jane exclaimed, as her mouth went dry.

"What's goin' on?" Harlan asked.

"Whatever you do, whatever happens out here, *do not* make a sound or move a muscle. You hear me?"

"What's happenin', Jane?" Harlan stressed.

The patrol car eased up behind the Mustang.

"*Don't move a muscle,*" Jane said quietly, as waves of anxiety crested. She spied the 9mm tucked into the side of the passenger seat. Moving her hand carefully, she lifted the service weapon, took off the safety and racked the slide.

"Jane?" Harlan whispered with fear. "What are you doin'?"

"*Shut up,*" she whispered, feeling part of herself drift away. Securing the gun under the driver's seat, she watched the cop get out of his car. At first glance, he appeared young by the way he moved. She sensed slight apprehension from him, indicative of how a rookie ambles up to a vehicle late at night. Catching sight of herself in the mirror, she concocted the first stunt that entered her mind. Burying her head on the steering wheel, she pressed on her cut lip until it opened and blood shot out. She heard the tap-tap on the driver's side window and saw the harsh flashlight beam entering the car. Forcing herself into character, she left her cop vibe behind and assumed the role of a victim.

"Ma'am?" the youthful voice asked.

Jane turned to the window, blinded by the flashlight. "Help me!" she cried, rolling down the window.

"What's wrong, ma'am?"

Jane saw that he indeed was as green as they come. He didn't look over twenty-three and while she couldn't be certain, he looked more scared than she was. She opened the driver's door. "My man…he beat me up. He cut my lip. See?" She got out of the car as crocodile tears welled in her eyes.

The cop backed up and shone his flashlight in her face. "Have you been drinking, ma'am?"

"*Drinking*? Oh my, God, no! I'm just tryin' to get away from him so he won't do me like he's already done me tonight."

The officer pointed the light into the backseat of the Mustang. Jane quickly fell to the asphalt in a crouching position. She knew if the cop was trained correctly, he would keep his focus only on her.

"Ma'am? Please get up!"

"I just want to get north of here but I don't know how to do it," Jane cried.

"Please, ma'am," he said with an uneasy tone, "you have to get up off the ground. Come on!" He offered her his hand.

She took it and slowly worked her way back up. "Thank you. You're very kind, officer."

He turned to the Mustang in an inquisitive manner. Observing him, Jane realized he was a fucking pup. He was too tentative. She knew she could overpower him in less than a second, grab his gun and knock him out. His eyes continued to linger a little too long on her car. A fire began to boil in her gut. She could take him down. One good pop to the back of the head and he'd go down hard. She'd cuff him and stuff him in the back of his own patrol car. Yes, she could do it.

He turned back to her. "This a '66 Mustang?"

She never took her eyes off him. "No. It's a '69." She inched closer to him. "It's the only thing of value my deadbeat man owns. When he finds it gone, he's gonna come after me. That's why I gotta get outta Dodge and head north. But I don't know how to do that. I'm all turned around, you see?" She looked deeply into his eyes. God, he was innocent. The inferno inside strangely tamped down. Out of nowhere, she heard three words. *Manipulate the outcome.* Looking up, she saw a vehicle crest the hill behind them. "Oh, god!" she screamed, running into the center of the road.

The cop turned around. "What's wrong?"

233

"It's him!" Jane screamed, moving farther away from her car.

"Ma'am! Get outta the road!"

"He's followin' me! I can't let him catch me!"

The cop rushed toward her and quickly pushed her to the opposite side of the road. "You can't be running into the road like that, ma'am."

The approaching car slowed and then passed them.

"Oh, sweet Jesus!" Jane exclaimed. "You see what he's turned me into? I'm all paranoid!" She grabbed his sleeve. "Can I ask you for a huge favor?"

"What's that?" he replied, visibly overwhelmed with her antics.

"Would you please escort me to the highway that heads north?"

"Well, I—"

"I beg of you, officer. I don't have no map! Please? If you could just lead me to the highway and drive with me a little bit, I'd feel so much safer."

He was so confused by this point, Jane wasn't sure if he even knew which way was north. He nodded nervously. "I can do that for you, ma'am."

Jane returned to the Mustang and followed the patrol car around the checkpoint and onto I-25. For ten miles, she trailed him until he waved her forward and exited the off ramp. She didn't stop shaking for another half hour.

Δ Δ Δ

The rising sun was minutes from cresting over the far mountains when Jane rolled into Sheldon Springs. She checked out the wooded area west of the motel to ensure it was still densely cloistered and would work. Satisfied it would serve the necessary purpose, Jane swung the Mustang toward the far end of the motel and told Harlan to wait for her. She barely had enough cash for one night and the look on the front desk clerk's face when she handed him every coin in her pockets was priceless. Jane specifically asked for a room in a section of the building that was vacant, explaining that she'd been on the road for days and needed to sleep soundly. The clerk happily obliged her, directing her to the second floor and the corner room, explaining that there were only two other guests staying in that section.

Jane returned to the Mustang as the morning sun filtered through the cottonwoods that lined the parking lot of the motel. She quickly motioned Harlan to get out and together they quietly ascended the stairway and went into their room. Jane figured it would do just perfectly. Before going back to the car, she quietly walked past the rooms on that side of the building. Only two of them had their window curtains covered. The rest Jane could easily peer into and see that they were empty. She noted the room number two doors down from their location. Number fifty-one. Satisfied, she returned to the car and unloaded everything out of it, including every box from her trunk and each item from her glove compartment. Taking care to be exceptionally quiet, she gingerly walked up the stairs and stuffed the sundry items into the room's spacious closet. There was only one thing left to do. Heading downstairs again, she drove the Mustang to the wooded area about one block west of the motel and parked it in the shadiest section she could find. Before walking back to the motel, she took one last look at her beloved ride and said a quick prayer.

Once settled back at the motel with Harlan, she sat down on the bed next to him and explained her plan.

"I get it, Jane," Harlan said, after hearing the whole thing. "You need some time alone with him. I got no problem gettin' out of your hair for a bit."

Jane wanted to tell him that it wasn't just about being alone with Hank; it was more about keeping Harlan hidden. As much as she hated lying to him, the truth remained that nobody could discover him. Not even Hank.

Jane wisely used the free hours before Hank showed up. She hopped into the shower and washed her hair. After re-organizing the luggage, she pulled out clothing that needed to be cleaned. Turning the motel's bathtub into a large washing sink, she pummeled and scrubbed a couple shirts and her muddy pair of jeans. Figuring Harlan's lone flannel shirt could stand to be freshened up, she had him remove it and then added it to the wash water. Hanging everything on the bathroom hooks, Jane turned on the fans and heat lamp and willed the clothing to dry quickly. She heard Harlan call her name with urgency.

When she walked back in the room, Harlan had the television tuned to the local Denver news morning show.

He pointed to the television. "That's my ex-wife, Jane!"

Jane looked at the forty-ish woman. She was maybe five feet tall and probably tipped the scale at two hundred pounds. She didn't look smart but she didn't look mean or vengeful. The banner beneath her face read: Arlene Kipple, ex-wife of fugitive Harlan Kipple.

"She's lost weight," Harlan offered, obviously taken back by the whole thing. "I expect it's 'cause of the stress." He stared at the TV screen, his mouth slightly ajar.

Knowing

"I ain't seen him for a while now," Arlene told the reporter, her eyes tearing up. "But I don't care what anybody says, the man I knew was not capable of the crimes they are sayin' he did. I want that information to get out there!"

Harlan began to tear up. Jane sat next to him on the bed and put a comforting hand on his back.

"I ain't never heard her stand up for me like that," Harlan whispered.

"If your husband is watching this, Mrs. Kipple," the reporter asked, "is there anything you'd like to tell him?"

Arlene gave the question a good amount of thought before answering. She turned to the camera with every ounce of love she could muster. "You was a good man, Harlan. I should have given you another try. Maybe you wouldn't be in this mess if I'd done that."

That wasn't what the reporter expected and all attempts by him to manipulate Arlene into vilifying her ex-husband were met with nothing but positive words for him.

"*Anything* else you'd like to say to Mr. Kipple?" the reporter stressed, eager for a crumb of denigration.

"Be smart, Harlan. Don't do nothin' 'tupid," she smiled weakly.

Harlan choked up and managed a sad smile. "I won't, Arlene," he said back to the television. He flicked the TV on mute and turned to Jane. "I wonder if she still likes my hair."

Jane took the bait. "Speaking of your hair, Harlan. I think we need to alter your look even more."

"Break out that black dye you bought—"

"No, not the dye. I'm thinking you ought to shave it off."

He looked at her, aghast. "All of it?"

"No, just a stripe down the center," she sarcastically replied. "Of course, all of it!"

"I don't know, Jane. That's gonna look weird."

"You look like you stuck your head in a lawn mower, Harlan. How much worse will it look?"

He stood up and stared into the mirror above the bureau. "I'll look like a Q-tip," he scowled.

"Nah. Not a Q-tip," she assured him, quietly surmising a polished marble on top of a giant puffer fish was a better analogy. "Trust me on this one, okay? There's a razor and shaving cream on the sink in the bathroom."

He reluctantly nodded. "You do have a plan, right Jane?" His voice sounded desperate for the first time.

"Of course. I always have a plan and then I have a plan that backs up that plan," she assured him. The truth was she had a marginal plan and an even sketchier one behind that. But she was able to sell the statement with such confidence that Harlan was satisfied enough to gather more strength and move past his temporary panic.

He retreated to the bathroom. Jane felt the mounting tension creep up her spine and stiffen her neck. She lay back on the bed and stared at the ceiling. Checking the time, she factored that Hank was figuring out what else to bring her besides the lunchmeat, chips and other food items. Knowing him, he was whipping together his famous chicken salad and wondering how to keep one of those incredible hot dogs she loved to eat from his sports bar, The Rabbit Hole, looking good during the long drive. He was such an uncommon person to be able to read Jane so accurately. It took tremendous courage for her to fall into his comforting charms. She'd become so used to the physical or emotional abuse that past lovers dealt out, she had no idea how to navigate a relationship that wasn't built on a foundation of turmoil. There were many nights over the past month when she'd lay awake and wonder why he loved her. What in the hell did he see in her? She didn't acquiesce like so many other women. She didn't bat her eyes at him and play dumb. She never sat by the phone waiting for his call. But there she was in that hotel room lying on the bed and unable to get him out of her tangled mind.

She turned the sound up on the TV to take her mind off of him. The news anchor teased the next story, featuring an announcement that Congresswoman Dora Weller's replacement, Steve Crandall, was scheduled to make. The camera cut to an outdoor location that looked like Northeastern Colorado with miles of grassland in the distance. Crandall approached the microphone in a tentative manner and read poorly from his notes.

"I want to thank you all for coming out here today," Crandall said in a weak voice. "First, I want to let you all know that Congresswoman Weller is doing great and her doctors are telling us that there shouldn't be any lasting issues from the incident."

The incident? Jane shook her head. It was a shooting, not an "incident." But the word "shooting" was most likely erased from this puppet's vocabulary by the people who pulled his strings. Jane was highly tuned into the dialect of those who agree to work under someone else's thumb and do their bidding.

Knowing

Their pronouncements are always filled with sterile, "soft" words that sanitize discussions and never allow for forthright honesty. Honesty and candor are the red-haired stepchildren of politics as usual; they have to be beaten to a pulp and replaced with tolerable terminologies that train the public to accept illogical answers. Considering that Weller was shot, Jane was pretty sure she wasn't "doing great" and that there *would* be "lasting issues from the incident."

There was a frightening coldness attached to that throwaway statement by Crandall. But then again, he didn't write it. This guy was so out of his element, it was pathetic. He stumbled on his prepared statement several times and repeatedly rubbed his forehead in a way that suggested he was totally lost. But as the camera pulled out, Jane saw Rudy standing in the background with several other officials. He never took his eyes off Crandall and from Jane's point of view, it appeared as if he had Crandall on a very short leash.

"We're here today to talk about the future," Crandall said in a way that made Jane believe whatever "future" he was about to discuss was not his creation. "We have a lot of natural resources here in our great state of Colorado and I know that Congresswoman Weller agrees with me that we should not waste those resources."

Jane frowned. The whole thing was bullshit. This idiot wasn't having any deep discussion with Weller. While Jane never looked at Dora Weller as being part of any brain trust, she was very clear in her voting record and actions that she sought to protect land rather than exploit it.

"These are tough times for many of us in Colorado and around the country," Crandall continued. "It's vital that we attract established companies and promote our state as one that is forward thinking. With that said, I'm here today standing in front of rich grassland that is currently not be used to its full potential. I'm aware that the approximately one thousand acres seen behind me has been hotly debated in the news and is a point of contention with many environmentalists as to how this ranch land might be utilized. I realize that Congresswoman Weller dealt with a lot of these issues already and made the decision to let the land stay as it is, preferring to opt for an open space agreement. However, after an extensive overview, that agreement was found to have various loopholes attached to it that could complicate the fair use of this acreage in the future. Obviously, we do not want to embark on any agreement that could potentially excise this valuable area from future use.

"Now, I'm fully aware of the environmental concerns many of you have regarding oil and gas and fracking. And let me be clear that this is *not* what is being considered for this acreage. We think we've created a sustainable solution that will put this land to good use and not create any damage. In fact, our plan will actually improve the integrity of this area and be quite sustainable."

Sustainable. He said it twice, two sentences in a row. Jane knew it was a loaded word and that whatever followed, usually carried a caveat. "Sustainable" could mean anything—from actually improving and maintaining the land while protecting it from misuse, thereby "sustaining" its integrity, to turning the land into a zone where no human are allowed.

"I want to introduce to you Mr. Andrea Bourgain. He is the CEO of The Wöden Group. He's flown all the way to the United States from his home in Belgium. Please welcome him!"

Crandall turned the microphone over to a handsome, gray-haired man in his late sixties. Bourgain spoke with a peculiar accent that blended French and German intonations. Jane quickly brought out her computer and did a search on Wöden. But the first few links that popped up had nothing to do with the Belgium company. Jane clicked on one link and read the first sentence:

"Together with his Norse counterpart, Odin, Wöden is a major deity of Germanic paganism." Jane stared at the word, "Odin." It was a little too coincidental that it happened to be the same name of the corporation that was attached to a fleet of automobiles, one of which just happened to be driven by Rudy and parked near the *Anubus* crash. While Bourgain prattled on about how wonderful it was to be "in your beautiful state," Jane did a further search on Wöden. "For the Anglo-Saxons," the story acknowledged, "Wöden was the *psychopomp* or carrier-off of the dead." Jane shook her head. Of all the names a company can come up with, why in the hell would they choose a name that historically was connected to a pagan god known for carrying off the dead?

Jane called Harlan to check on him. "You okay in there?"

"Yeah…" he replied with little enthusiasm. "I guess so."

She focused back on Bourgain and his comments.

"We at The Wöden Group are very excited to have this opportunity for expansion into the United States. Thanks to the influential, forward thinking minds who helped make this happen." While it was subtle, Bourgain turned his body slightly toward Rudy, who was still standing behind the podium.

Jane immediately did a comprehensive search for "The Wöden Group, Belgium" and found their company's website. After scanning page after page, she still couldn't figure out what they did, except that their motto was, "The forefront of innovative science begins here." Buried deeply at the bottom of one page was a single link titled, "Vaccine research." She clicked the link and found a page that had fewer than two paragraphs. It stated that The Wöden Group "was focused on pioneering research into cutting edge vaccine technology." But aside from a few fluffy statements that followed, it appeared that Wöden's interest in vaccines was either still in development or not their main objective. So why in the hell did the CEO fly over from Belgium to stand in front of a desolate swath of grassland in northeastern Colorado and wax poetically about the "natural beauty" of this area?

Then a light went on in Jane's head. The only controversy Dora Weller ever dealt with was her denial of a Biotech firm's desire to buy up grassland. She sided with the eco-crowd's demands to keep the land away from "those damn capitalists." While Jane was a proud capitalist and avoided being in the same breathing space as the eco-Nazis she loathed, there was something about the smoothness of Bourgain's statements that concerned her. It didn't take her long to uncover an article that mentioned Dora Weller and Wöden in the same paragraph. Two years prior, Weller had rejected the final plan from The Wöden Group to purchase one thousand acres in northwestern Colorado for "research purposes."

Jane searched valiantly and found nothing that explained what kind of research was planned. Nothing on Wöden's site was explanatory. In fact, there were links on their site that had more photos than text. It almost felt to Jane as if the website was there because the company felt they had to have a presence on the Internet but they weren't about to divulge much more than pabulum. While Bourgain continued to take questions from reporters and answer them with well-crafted but benign responses, Jane clicked on all the links again on Wöden's site and only looked at the photos.

Most of them looked like stock shots, including images of beakers in a laboratory, flowers in a meadow and a sun rising in the distance across a field. She clicked again on the vaccine link and focused on the three photos that were there. One was a syringe filled with a yellow liquid. "Jesus," Jane said out loud. She flashed on the discordant hallucination she had after being knocked out by S.B. She could still see it clearly as if the scene were presented in front of her. How strange, Jane mused. When she'd blacked out in the past due to too much booze, her hallucinations never gelled long enough for her to have a cogent memory when she awakened, let alone have a crystal clear recall of the event hours later. But sitting on the bed in that motel room, Jane could easily close her eyes and generate the scene as it unfolded. The floor was littered with hundreds of plastic syringes, all filled with a golden serum. And there was the old man standing at his desk, looking at Jane and holding the white binder with **IEB** written on the cover.

Jane continued to click on every link on Wöden's website and she was about to give up when she spotted an innocuous image that made no sense. It didn't fit. But there it was. It was a photo of a goat in a grassy field, staring up at the camera. There were no other animals featured on the entire site. She re-read the company's motto: "The forefront of innovative science begins here." But there was absolutely nothing that linked what those innovations were and why they included a single photo of a goat in a field of grass. The news confer-ence ended and Jane stared at the walls. She cautioned herself to not read too much into all these strange syncs. But ignoring a sync or odd coincidence was also not something she favored. She'd learned the hard way that sometimes the truth is standing right there in front of you, but you can't see it because you either don't believe that truth can be that obvious or you choose not to see it. But either way, it never stops the truth from operating and continuing to its logical conclusion. It was like a morbidly obese woman looking at her body in the mirror and seeing a healthy person staring back. She could deny she was dangerously fat all day long but when her heart gave out after the third rack of pork ribs and she was gasping for her last breath, the only thing standing between her and the afterlife was the truth.

Turning back to the TV, the scene cut back to the newsroom and the anchor desk.

"Officials tell us that they still believe escaped fugitive Harlan Kipple was involved in some manner with the Weller shooting," the anchor reported as the same shot of Harlan in the crowd was shown again. "However, sources close to the investigation are telling us they are not ruling out the possibility of an accomplice."

Jane's jaw dropped.

"Police are asking anyone who was at the scene and who was taking cell phone video to please contact them with any footage of the event."

For a dead woman, she was suddenly becoming a potentially lively suspect.

CHAPTER 17

How in the hell was this possible? Jane turned off the television and sat with her racing thoughts. She was witnessing chaos unfold and seeing first-hand the manipulation of lies and half-truths in order to condemn an innocent man. And now they were seeking an accomplice of Harlan's? What was going on here? Were they going to ID Jane or some other innocent soul? If it was Jane, how would they explain her "death" and now resurrection? The whole thing defied logic and yet there it was. The first article she found online that mentioned an accomplice was followed by over five hundred comments, all of them basing their opinions on false information. But that didn't stop the armchair jockeys from firing off a damning missive from the comfort of their desktop computer. Reading through the top rated comments, it was clear to Jane that Harlan's name was forever ruined. He'd been effectively turned into an evil scourge, with people fantasizing about "taking him out" and "doing the world a favor." One man wrote with impeccable spelling and grammar, "If that peace of shite had himself an acomplis, than that pirson shuld dye 2." Great, Jane thought. If she was discovered to be that "acomplis," the idea of being taken out of this world by someone that stupid made her shudder.

It also made her angry and a boiling fury began to roll inside her. Except for a few conspiracy type websites she found, nobody was giving Harlan the benefit of the doubt. He'd already been tried, convicted and sentenced to death. Romulus looked to be pulling the strings on this fiasco, feeding false information to the media who seemed to have forgotten how to investigate a story. And there *was* a story here. But how would it get out to the public? If the mainstream media outlets had been methodically corrupted to this extent, what chance was there to push the truth forward?

Harlan emerged from the bathroom. Still just wearing the overalls and no shirt underneath and with a cleanly shaven head that sported four noticeable cuts from the razor, he looked like he should be sitting on a ramshackle porch down in the Bayou, shucking corn.

"Well? What's the verdict on my new look?" he asked her.

She had no clue how to respond. "Let's hope the flannel shirt dries soon and you can find the hat I bought you." Checking the time, she let out a hard breath. Hank was probably heading out soon to purchase the cell phones and other items. It would take him about two and a half hours if he drove like a demon and three hours if he kept the rental van under eighty miles an hour. Knowing Hank, he'd show up with the hood of that van hot as a pistol.

Finding one of the pine needle beers, she handed it to Harlan. "Here."

"Kinda early in the day for that, don't you think?"

"Thought it would relax you. And maybe I can get a contact high."

"You tryin' to get me drunk, Jane?"

"No." She replaced the beer in the case, feeling stupid for offering it to him. She went over the plan again with Harlan, making sure he understood everything. "Don't open this door for anyone unless you hear my name," she counseled him in a grave tone.

"I won't, Jane."

The hours passed and Jane tried to rest but her mind wouldn't stop chasing down options of how to extricate Harlan from this mess. Yet, every prospect she considered led to ten more complications.

"Know what I'm thinkin'?" Harlan said out of nowhere.

"What's that?"

"After you see Hank, we oughta just take off and head to New Mexico."

She crossed her arms over her chest. "And do what?"

"You *know* what, Jane."

"It's not happening, Harlan. I'm not seeing her. She's probably not even at the halfway house anymore," she added, knowing full well Wanda was scheduled to be there through the week.

"You gotta see her, Jane! She's family."

"She's not family. The only family I have is a younger brother. And he's sitting in the Amazon jungle right now with his new wife enjoying a shamanic cleansing celebration." As crazy as that sounded, Jane figured Mike's plans for his day were infinitely more satisfying than her intended strategy.

Half an hour later, her cell phone rang. "Hey, there," she answered.

"I'm sitting here in the parking lot. Where are you?" Hank stated.

"Go to the front office and check into room number fifty-one."

"Where are you?"

Knowing

"I can't check into the room. Remember? I'm the one with no cash? Room fifty-one. I've already scoped it out. It's private. Call me when you get there." She hung up before he could respond.

Harlan stared at her silently.

"What?" she asked him, irritated.

"How come you can't be honest with him?"

"Oh, Jesus, Harlan. I'm not even going to answer that question."

"Maybe if you told him the truth, he could—"

"What? That I'm harboring a fugitive? But don't worry, because he didn't do all the shit they're saying he did. Really, Harlan? *Really*?"

He studied the carpet silently. "How do you play someone you love?"

"I'm not playing him," Jane stated, nervously getting up and discreetly checking out the window.

"Yeah. You are. It's not right."

She let out a derisive snort. "I'm doing this for you, Harlan. It was time to do something desperate. We were sitting ducks in that car. And no money? What am I supposed to do, huh?"

He considered it for a few seconds. "You don't set up the people you love, Jane."

She nodded. "Okay." She checked out the window again. "So, maybe I don't love him?"

He eyed her like a hawk before walking over to the window. "Don't do it, Jane. *Please* don't."

"Don't do what?" she asked with a flinty edge.

His eyes filled with tears. "Don't turn into one of them. You got a good heart."

She smiled in a dismissive manner. "What's that gotten me, huh?" She turned back to the window. "You do what you have to do in this world, Harlan." Anger rose in her throat. "I'm trying to fucking save your life! Does that count for anything?!" She moved back into the room. "Stay away from the window!" she ordered him.

Harlan sauntered back to the bed and sat down. He stared at her as she avoided his eyes. After several tense minutes, her cell phone rang.

"Yeah?" she answered with a quick clip.

"Okay. I'm in room fifty-one. Where are you?"

"Be right there." She hung up and scanned the room for her leather satchel. Finding it, she stopped, took a breath and gathered her racing thoughts.

"Don't use the phone or leave this room," she quietly offered, without looking at Harlan. Collecting her overnight bag, she took another necessary breath to calm her mind and walked out the door.

She was careful not to make a lot of noise as she walked the thirty-foot distance to room fifty-one. Jane was shaking as she rapped on the door. Hank swung the door open and paused for a moment. She wasn't sure what to make of it so she waited, staring at him with lying eyes.

"Jesus, Jane," he reached out and grabbed her, pulling her into his room. He drew her toward him and passionately kissed her. Coming up for air, he glanced at her up and down. "You look like hell, Chopper," he stated, using his pet name for her. "What happened to your lip?"

She weakened as she dove into his blue eyes. "Stop talking, would you?" Tossing her satchel and bag on the table and chairs by the window and drawing the front curtain, she tugged at his denim shirt and eagerly kissed him as if they'd been apart for decades. God, it was like coming home, enveloped in his arms and feeling secure for the first time since they parted.

His face colored with worry. "Please, Jane. Tell me what's going on."

She undid his belt and unbuttoned his jeans. "Not now. Please."

Their clothes quickly littered the floor and they crawled under the covers. Like excited teenagers, they consumed each other, moving in perfect harmony and reaching feverish crescendos that felt as if the angels were conducting their erotic symphony. As they melted into a divine rhythm, Jane felt as if she merged into his heart. Within that place, she soared in the exquisite beauty of that singular moment, willing it to never end. She felt his essence inside her and as her body relaxed for a brief moment, she forgot all the struggles, the fears and the strategies. In that moment, there was only sweet peace and devotion.

Hank kissed her gently as he rolled onto the bed, drawing the covers toward them. He might have been thirteen years older than Jane, but to her, his body and mind seemed twenty years younger. However, the easygoing guy she knew was not completely there. His face was mapped with apprehension and prickles of fear.

"You were right," he finally said, turning on his right side and looking at her. "I *did* get your message." He reached under the covers and cupped his palm on her breast. "I kept telling myself it wasn't real. But every time I started to worry about you, something inside of me put out the fire."

"Where'd you feel it? Your head or your heart?"

Knowing

Hank gave the question a serious moment of contemplation. "My heart. My mind chewed it but my heart digested it."

Jane stared at the ceiling, blown away by his comment. "The heart and the mind," she whispered.

He drew his finger between her breasts. "Hey," he said, reeling her back into the moment. "I need to know, Jane. What happened?"

She'd rehearsed it in her head so many times over the past few hours but for some reason, it was all garbled now. Each time she reached for the lie, it eluded her.

"Jane?"

"Got a cigarette?"

"I don't smoke. And last I heard, you quit."

She managed a weak smile. "Right. I forgot."

He waited. "You're stalling. Why?"

Why wasn't this easier, she wondered. She turned to him. "I found my car."

"You're kidding. Where?"

"A few miles from the Quik Mart."

"Where is it now?"

"I got it parked a block west of here in a wooded area. If you know what you're looking for, you can't miss it."

"Jane, you have to get it wiped for prints—"

"He wiped it clean. Totally clean. And he took everything in the car except my badge, and pistol. My bag and satchel were in the trunk."

"Wait a second. It's been four days, Jane. How does your driver's license show up at a bus explosion?"

She turned back to the ceiling. "I'm not sure. When I found the car, he'd already changed the plates. The right rear tire had a flat. It was out of gas. So, I trekked back to the Quik Mart and bought a couple gallons and I guess it was either on the way there or back that I somehow dropped by license." She let out a tired sigh. "By the time I got to the car and filled the tank and changed the tire, all I wanted to do was get on the road, find a gas station, top off the tank and keep going to New Mexico."

"Okay," he quietly offered. "I still don't understand why you didn't report it?"

She turned to him because she could tell the truth for a moment. "I didn't know Harlan Kipple stole my car. I wasn't listening to the radio. Jesus! I just

246

found out in the last twelve hours that I died at some bus explosion." She shook her head and stared back at the ceiling. "I just needed to get out of town."

He never took his eyes off her. "So, how's Wanda?"

She swallowed hard. There was no way she was going to concoct a story that wild. "I haven't seen her yet."

Hank studied Jane's face. "Uh-huh. So what have you been doing for four days?"

"Jesus, you sound a fucking cop."

"That's ironic. Because you *don't* sound like one."

She turned to him. "What's that supposed to mean?"

"Your story has more holes than an old t-shirt."

Jane gathered some attitude. "I didn't know I was being interrogated."

"Jane, please don't make me pick apart your story."

She threw back the covers and sat up in bed. Maybe, she thought, if there was greater distance between them, she could lie more convincingly. "I can't believe this—"

He sat up. "That makes two of us. Let's see, you don't report the theft because you didn't know it was Harlan Kipple who did it—"

She spun around to him. "I wanted to get back on the road and not have my car impounded for who knows how long while they sort it all out."

"But you said you didn't go to New Mexico. And if all he left you was your gun and your badge, that means he took your computer. The one with all your case files? If Kipple has your computer, he has access to hundreds of sensitive files. That alone would make you report it."

She turned away as her heart raced. Her mouth went dry. She could fabricate another story that her computer was in her bag or satchel but she quickly realized she didn't bring it with her from the other room. "Those files are backed up three different places—"

"That's not the point, Jane, and you know it." He waited. "You want me to continue?"

The walls were caving in quickly. "Continue what?"

"How about the fact that the bus crash was more than twenty miles from the Quik Mart? Didn't you think I might look into that? You said you lost your ID between the Quik Mart and the car and you said that was a three mile trek."

Knowing

Jane stood up and slid her shirt over her head. "You know, Hank, you should shut down The Rabbit Hole and get back into fraud investigation. I think you miss it." She plopped her bare ass on a chair and stared into the wall.

"Come on, Jane. Where have you been staying at night? Don't they have televisions? Phones?"

"I've been living in my car, okay? Remember? I got my cash and credit cards stolen—"

"Yeah. How'd that go down?"

"What do you mean?"

"How'd you get ripped off?" His tenor was direct and impatient.

"I was parked in a vacant lot, trying to get some sleep and I hear a knock on the window and there's a guy with a gun, demanding my wallet."

"You know, I realize we haven't known each other a long time but I would bet my sports bar that if you slept in your vehicle overnight in a vacant parking lot, you would have one eye open and your hand on your gun."

God, he was right. That's exactly what she'd do. "Well, I guess I fucked up then."

"And still, you don't report the theft? Wow. Remind me to start ripping you off."

"I've had a shitty four days, okay?"

"Right. Who smacked you in the mouth?"

She was about to blame the vacant parking lot bandit for it and changed her mind quickly. "Nobody smacked me," she said proudly. "It happened when I was changing the tire."

"Four days ago?" he asked calmly.

Right away, she saw the problem with her lie. "It keeps breaking open. That's why I asked for the antibiotics."

"The *fish* antibiotics."

"Yes."

"Normally, people go to doctors and get antibiotics that are made for humans."

"That fish stuff is the same exact shit. And it's cheaper."

"Great tip. I'll mention it to the next survivalist I meet. But as far as I know, you're not one of them."

"Oh, fuck. I'm the original survivalist."

"You know what I'm talking about, Jane. Somehow, over the last four days, something's happened to make you not want to get too deep into the world. I'd like to know what that is."

She shook her head. "So, a person just can't take off anymore? Is that what I'm hearing? Is that what this world has come down to? You just can't say, I need a break and disappear for a bit? There's got to be a mystery attached to it?"

He observed her with precision. "Considering your luck over these last few days, I'd say the gods are working against you. None of what you're telling me makes a damn bit of sense. You want me to believe that for four days, you had no clue that they liked Harlan Kipple, a high profile criminal, for your car theft?"

"Yes! That's exactly what I'm telling you!"

"Never turned your radio on in the car?"

"That's right."

"And you don't care that your computer is in the hands of a killer?"

She studied the floor. "Yeah, like he could even figure it out," she mumbled.

He looked at her carefully. "What does that mean?"

She turned to Hank. "Back when he was first arrested after the motel incident, it filtered down to us that he was pretty much an idiot."

"Funny. You never mentioned that to me."

"I didn't think it was important. Lots of comments are made about lots of perps. And this is *not* about Harlan Kipple."

"What is it about?"

"It's about me getting some space."

"I see. So you never intended to go to New Mexico?"

"Maybe."

"Who are you wanting to get some space from? Me?"

She paused a little too long. "Perhaps…"

"Humph. Okay. You need some time away. But then you call me for help. That's not your M.O. When you decide you want space from somebody, you'll die before you call them at three in the morning for help."

Jane felt her lower lip trembling. "Maybe I was desperate. Ever consider that?"

He eyed her carefully. "Yeah. You were desperate. I get that. I want to know why you're desperate. I want to know why you need a rental when you've got a perfectly good vehicle parked in a wooded area a block from this place? The only reason you'd ask for a rental is because you know your Mustang is on the radar. And why ask me to get you a van that blends in? Didn't you mention to me that the day you drove a van was the day you officially gave up on life? I believe your exact words were, 'If I ever decide to buy a van, shoot me.'"

Jane was operating on fumes. "It's a *rental*. I'm not buying it." She stood up and marched across the room with no place to go.

There was a thick, horrible silence between them. Jane felt her soul being ripped out.

"If you wanted to get away, why didn't you just say it? Why tell me to check on Wanda's location? Why did we make all those calls to confirm her background? You not going to New Mexico makes no damn sense. You're the type of person who makes a decision and follows through to the bitter end."

"And how do you know this?" she asked with a nasty edge. "How long have we known each other, Hank? What? A month? Actually, a little less than that."

"I know you and you know me," he stressed. "We obviously have a strong enough connection that I knew you weren't dead."

"Yeah, well," she turned away. "You don't know everything."

He waited and when she didn't move or speak, he spoke. "*So tell me.*"

It was pointless but her pride prevented her from admitting it. She flung her shirt off. "I'm taking a shower." Storming into the bathroom, she slammed the door.

Standing at the sink naked, she gazed at her reflection in the mirror. At first, she didn't recognize herself. Her eyes held a steely coldness. She turned away from the mirror and then back, hoping to see warmth reflected back at her. But it wasn't there. How many dark holes had she fallen into when she was a drinker? And how many of them did she crawl out of and, each time, leave a part of herself behind until she was left with only a skeleton of her existence. It had taken her two years of struggle to finally retrieve all the parts of herself that mattered and feel somewhat whole again. But now, here she was, and the woman in the mirror was shattered. It was astounding how quickly she could go backward and lose the ground she'd fought so hard to conquer. What was next? She'd already started smoking again. Was liquor just a heartbeat away?

She heard rustling outside in the room and wondered if Hank was leaving. He'd say goodbye, wouldn't he? She turned to the closed bathroom door and waited for him to knock or turn the knob but nothing happened. Okay, fine. If that's the way he wants to end it, she could handle it. She examined her lip in the mirror and chastised herself for trying to convince him it was four days old. She always thought her stories through when talking to the hardcore perps and was able to creatively back up her lies. But the task was more difficult when she lied to someone she cared for.

Turning on the shower, she got in and held the vibrating pulse of the water against her spine. She closed her eyes and imagined herself far away from there, cocooned in an empty fortress. It was there that safety resided. Apart from the masses and the petitions for her service, she could exist with a modicum of sanity. The hot water pounded against her skin in a syncopated rhythm. She pressed her eyes closed even tighter and continued to visualize her uninhabited sanctuary. The pulsating friction drew her into the beat until she felt hypnotized and as if she were floating from the room. In the distance, another sound merged. It started gently but grew with intensity. As it came closer, she recognized it as a drum beat. With her eyes still closed and lost in the moment, the drums became louder until that's all she could hear. Just as it reached a fevered crescendo, the sound of a young child's terrified scream broke through. Jane opened her eyes and pulled her body out of the hammering stream of water. For a second, she had no idea where she was. Turning off the faucets, she pressed her back against the tile as the water spiraled into the drain. Looking around, she felt trapped. She whipped back the shower curtain and secured a heavy towel around her body. Leaning over the sink, she wasn't sure if she was going to vomit or pass out. After a minute, she wiped off the steam from the mirror and checked herself one more time. Her hope was that the water had washed away the coldness in her eyes. But it was still there and unbroken.

"Hey, Jane!" she heard Hank call to her from outside the door.

"What?" she shouted.

"We have to talk."

She stood up, securing the towel around her wet body. Taking a deep breath, she swung open the door. "I've already said everything I'm—" She stopped and froze. Hank was calmly seated at the round table in front of the window. Across from him in the other chair was Harlan. Locked in Hank's right hand was the 9mm and it was pointed at Harlan's head.

CHAPTER 18

Jane stood there dripping wet, speechless and shaking. "What in the hell—"

"You said for me not to open the door unless I heard your name?" Harlan offered in a strangely relaxed manner. "He put the key in the lock and when it clicked, he called out that 'Jane' was lookin' for me." He shot Hank a look. "So, I come to the door."

She glanced at Hank. He might have retired from the force years before, but like all cops, he never lost his edge. His blue eyes were hard, angry and confused.

"First I checked your wallet in your leather satchel," Hank stated, never lowering the gun on Harlan. "The credit cards were all there. Then I found the 9mm. It's not your service weapon. And then I found the room key. And since you got up here so quickly after I called you, I knew the room wasn't far away." He turned to Harlan and then back to Jane. "I figured you had another guy stuffed away. I just didn't think it was *this* guy."

It took Harlan a few long seconds to feel the insult. "Hang on, Hank. Don't judge me 'til you hear my story."

"I know your story," he replied in a frosty tone.

"No. You *don't* know his story," Jane stated, carefully covering her body with the towel.

"Jesus, Jane!" Hank exclaimed. "I found this just now in your satchel," he waved Harlan's fake ID in the air. "Hartley Llewellyn, eh? And yours?" He held it out. "Anne LeRóy? And this one? Wanda Anne LeRóy? Both have your photo on them. What in the fuck is going on here?" He brought out his cell phone. "One call, Jane. One call and this is over."

"*Don't!*" She moved toward Hank. "He's innocent!"

"Prove it!" Hank rejoined.

"After my car was stolen, I walked to the bus depot and got on and then transferred to the *Anubus*. The one that exploded? Before we took off, there was a girl on the bus who knew Jaycee. She's the black prostitute Harlan is accused of killing." Jane continued, giving Hank an overview of everything. "The kid was heading to Denver to talk to PD about what she knew. She wanted to clear Harlan's name."

"So why didn't she?" Hank asked.

"She found out that morning that Harlan had escaped from custody. She freaked out and wanted to get out of town, because she said she knew he wasn't running from the cops. He was running from the people who set him up. I believed her. She had nothing to gain from telling me that story. And she knew she had everything to lose because she kept mentioning a red-haired guy outside the bus who was acting suspiciously. It was the same psycho she met in the back of a limo and who later paid her off after she lured Harlan up to the motel room. She was convinced he came there to kill her. And obviously, the poor girl was right!"

"What? Jane, this is sounding sketchy as hell—"

"I'm telling you the fucking truth! If I hadn't walked off that bus, I really *would* be dead."

"Why *did* you walk off that bus?" Hank asked.

She let out a tired breath. "Fuck if I know. I just…I felt sick…I smelled death…"

"You smelled death?" Harlan interjected with a curious expression.

"Yes. I didn't know I was smelling it until everything went nuts. And then I realized that somehow I sensed it before it happened."

Hank considered her comments. "So you witness this whole nightmare and *still* you do nothing?"

"It was fucking chaos, Hank! Bodies everywhere! And then I sneak a look over and I see the same red-haired freak she was talking about, leaning on his black sedan and *calmly* watching the whole massacre. It didn't take me more than a few seconds to figure out that if I so much as lifted my head, I'd be dead. So, I waited for him to drive away and then I did the first thing that came to my mind. I tossed my license."

Hank never let the gun waver from Harlan's body. "You knew exactly what you were doing, Jane."

She stared at him, shaking. "Put the gun down, Hank. He's not going to hurt you. Believe me, he doesn't know how to hurt a soul."

"Because he's an idiot?" Hank asked. "Isn't that what you called him?"

Jane felt her world crumbling.

"How many sides of the fence are you playing here, Jane?" Hank asked.

"I'm not playing anyone," she softly replied.

"Well," Harlan interjected, "to be truthful, I did tell you that it wasn't fair what you was plannin' with Hank." He turned to Hank calmly. "I thought she needed to be up front with you from the get-go but I think she was worried you would do what you're doin' right now. As far as her callin' me an idiot, I guess that's between her and me. It's not like I ain't heard that one before."

Jane stood straighter, re-securing the towel around her body. "Put down the gun, Hank. Do you honestly believe for one second that I'd get involved with a killer?"

Hank stared at her. "It wouldn't be the first time."

She looked at him in stunned silence. Every cell in her body vibrated with ire. "You know exactly what I mean."

"And so do you. You couldn't see it back then, maybe you can't see it now."

"Jesus Christ. I'm trying to save his life!"

Hank leaned forward. "What about your own life, Jane?! Does that count for anything? You have people who genuinely care about you. Did you see Weyler on TV when he announced you were dead?! He was a damn mess! Don't you care about that? What if your brother gets wind of this when he's coming home from his honeymoon? How's he going to react? Thought about that? What are your plans? I brought you five hundred bucks. How long will that last you? How far can you drive your non-descript van before you run out of gas and money? Then what? Skip to Mexico? Are you going to abandon Harlan or drag him along?"

"Stop it," Jane insisted.

"I'm asking you serious questions, Jane! It's not too late to get the authorities involved and sort through all of this—"

"The authorities can't fix this! And it's not the authorities I'm worried about!" She took a much-needed breath. "Look, I've done a lot of work on this case over the last four days and I just need a little bit more time to sort everything out." She stared at Hank with conviction. "He did not do what they are saying he did. He had nothing to do with Jaycee and he had nothing to do with Dora Weller's shooting."

Hank lay the gun on the table. "Holy shit...They think *you're* the accomplice?"

"No, they don't have a name. And I don't think it's the cops who are feeding that story to the media—"

"Jane, you're starting to sound—"

"I know how I sound, Hank! I get it! I sound fucking nuts! Harlan was not involved in Weller's shooting. *I* wasn't involved in Weller's shooting. But the next time Weller's puppet replacement gets on the tube to make a statement, check out the line of people behind him. Look for the red-haired guy in the dark suit. It's the same fucker from the bus crash *and* it's the same guy who's disguised in a videotaped interview and who claims he saw Harlan rip off my car. I can verify the guy in the video was nowhere near that Quik Mart. Check it out for yourself! You've got a good eye. You should be able to see the similarities immediately. Harlan knows him by the name of Rudy. He was with him at the hospital when he got his heart transplant. He's basically been monitoring Harlan and setting him up before Harlan came out of anesthesia." She took two deliberate steps toward Hank. "I've done my due diligence, Hank! I know what I'm talking about. I might sound bat shit crazy but, goddammit, if you'd seen and heard what I have over these last few days, you'd be standing right here, pissed off that anyone wanted to stop your forward progress."

Hank leaned forward, burying his head in his hands. "Oh, Jesus, Chopper." After a few seconds, he came up for air. "They can't call you dead *and* call you an accomplice."

"I bet they can figure out how to do that. Any story worth fabricating is worth the time to get it right. They'd say they made a mistake about my premature death and then like me for a shooting I had no part of. Just like they pegged Harlan for smashing the head of that prostitute. Don't you see? That's why I have to figure this out."

He regarded her with caution. "There's something else you're not telling me."

"There's a lot of shit going on, Hank. I'm just covering the basics here."

Hank bored into her eyes and turned to Harlan. "What's she leaving out?"

Harlan looked at Hank, giving the question serious deliberation. "I like to eat raw eggs." He thought a little more. "And I never liked Italian but now I'm partial to it. And pine needle beer. Damn, I *love* that pine needle beer."

Jane nodded. "That basically says it all right there."

Hank turned back to Jane. "You still haven't told me what your plans are."

Harlan piped up. "I was askin' her the same question earlier, Hank."

Jane felt like the odd man out suddenly. "There are certain…forces at work here that are requesting certain…things…that I need to clarify before I can answer what the master plan is."

"You sound like a politician, Chopper. Why aren't you telling me what you know?"

"Because you wouldn't understand."

"Really? Am I an idiot too?"

"I didn't say that. This is just a little outside of the scope of what we normally deal with."

"I see," he said, seething. "So, I'm good for a three a.m. call and a two hour plus drive in a rented van with food and money and disposable cell phones—"

"That's not true!"

"That's what this looks like. If I hadn't snooped through your stuff and found the key to your room, I would have left here suspicious, but not onto you. You never would have given Harlan up. So, which one of us would look like the fool?"

"I'm not trying to turn you into a fool—"

"Well, you pointedly told me that your Mustang is parked in a wooded area that's one block west of here! I know what's coming next, Jane. You want me to drive that car back to Midas. You want me to either wait until night or figure out back roads to stay off the highway and avoid detection. You want me to put my ass on the line for you. Given the situation, it takes a fool to do that. You want me to pretend none of this happened. You want me to go about my days and ignore the fact that I know you didn't die in a bus crash and that you're out on the road with a wanted fugitive and I'm the one who helped you get there. Only a fool would do that for you, Jane."

Jane looked at him, eyes welling with tears. "So, be my fool."

They stared at each other in heartbreaking silence. Harlan stood up and walked to Jane.

"I think you and he need to be alone," Harlan whispered to her.

She never took her eyes off Hank. "Go in the bathroom and close the door."

Harlan obliged.

After another hard minute, Hank finally spoke.

"I think I get it, Jane. You're only really friendly with people you can control."

Her gut clamped down. "No. That isn't true."

"It is true," he replied quietly. "You control your brother but you can't control his new wife, that's why you like to visit him when she's not there. You don't have any problems with Harlan because he's not that bright and he does what you tell him to do. As long as you're in control, you can somewhat function. But when you don't have the reins in your hand, you lose your reference point. And, God forbid, anyone tries to control *you*. You'd just tell them to 'fuck off,' and walk away. It really must have taken a lot for you to call me. I bet you rehearsed what you were going to say for at least half an hour." He looked at her with sad eyes. "What do you want, Chopper? I don't mean in the next day or two. I mean what do you want? You want to keep running even when this is over? The world's not big enough for you. You can't run long enough or far enough because when you land, you're still standing with yourself."

Tears streamed down her face. "Maybe I don't know how to live unless I can control the outcome."

"Maybe you just don't know how to live."

That hit her hard. She wiped the tears with the back of her hand.

"I thought you were done with all the fighting," he gently added. "But I guess it's embedded in you."

She stood straighter. "That fighting kept me alive."

"And eventually, it will kill you." He observed her. "But I don't think you really care about that. As long as you have someone to save, you can get through the day. But if somebody tries to save you, you push them away because you don't believe you're worth saving."

She bit her injured lip in an attempt to feel the greater pain. But no matter how hard she dug into the cut with her teeth, the pain in her heart overwhelmed.

He looked at her with pleading eyes. "Why do you make it so damn hard to love you, Jane?"

There was lingering silence until Jane worked up the courage to speak. "How do we rescue this day?"

Hank stood up. "We don't."

Waves of regret rippled through her. "I can't..." She stopped herself. "What does that mean?"

"It means I'll be your fool one more time." He dug his hand into her leather satchel and recovered the keys for the Mustang. "There's a cell phone I bought you with a yellow stripe down the back. I got the number for it. I'll call and leave a message on it when I get back to Midas." He brought the van keys out of his pocket and lobbed them to her. Lifting his small overnight bag off the floor, he walked to the door. "Be safe, Chopper," he said without turning around and walked out the door.

Knowing

For a moment, there was nothing. Just a blank space she occupied with orbits of life circling but never touching her. She was drawn into the bottomless pit and felt the pull to fall deeper. *Safety.* What an exceptional concept. What a luxury granted to so few.

She grabbed her clothes and threw them on before tapping on the bathroom door and freeing Harlan. He wandered into the room, looking lost.

"He seems like a real nice guy, Jane. How'd you two meet up?"

"Not now, Harlan," she said softly, walking to the window and peeking outside the curtain. She forced the logical side of her brain to kick into gear. "We're going to stay in our room tonight. We need the rest. We've been pushing it too hard."

"He's pushing it."

Jane turned to Harlan. He was pointing to his heart.

"It's always been about what he wants," Harlan continued. "From the second I woke up, there's been two of us in my body. And until I find out what he needs, I'll never be able to rest. I'll never be safe."

She looked at Harlan with callous eyes. "Safety is a fucking illusion. We crave it but it doesn't exist. You come into this world screaming and you go out begging. And in between, you find whatever cushion you can to fall back on. You're born, you work, you die. The end."

Harlan regarded her with trepidation. "Hell, Jane. That's depressing."

"It's the truth, Harlan." She swept up her bag and satchel from the table and chair. "Either accept it or live in a fucking fantasy world." She turned back to him. "Come on."

He held back. "We got two rooms," he said with a shrug of his shoulders.

"I have to keep my eye on you," she stressed.

"I ain't goin' anywhere, Jane."

"You wandered off before—"

"That ain't gonna happen again—"

"Harlan, for God's sake, would you just—"

"No," he said, his voice raising an octave. "You told me to start taking initiative."

"Oh, God, stop bringing that up—"

"Well, too bad. I just did. Which room do you want?"

She tried to convince him for a few more minutes, even stooping to tempt him with a deluxe pizza she figured she could furtively buy at a local take out joint. But even the promise of far too much cheese and pepperoni wasn't enough to sway him. Finally, realizing it was pointless she acquiesced. It was agreed she would return to their room and then retrieve him in the pre-dawn light. Checking the small cooler that Hank delivered, she pulled out a dozen eggs, and enough lunchmeat and cheese to keep Harlan somewhat sated until morning. Hefting her bags and the one that Hank dropped off across her shoulder, she rolled the cooler to the door. "I can't change your mind?" she asked, almost desperately.

"See ya before the sun rises," he said, waving her off and turning on the TV.

Jane opened the door and quickly slid the "Do Not Disturb" sign outside before returning to her room. After letting the bags fall where they chose, she lay back on the bed. God, a cigarette sounded good, she thought. Digging into her satchel, she retrieved the pack and slid out a fresh one. But when she couldn't locate her lighter, the whole process became more trouble than it was worth. It was a fractal moment that represented the last four days. Three steps forward and two steps back. Sitting up on the bed, impatience crept closer. That was always a dangerous guest to Jane's party. Once impatience shadowed her door, one thing was certain. Growing umbrage would show up next and the two of them would start a fight where Jane would have to intercede. But when impatience refused to listen, she always had to muscle it into submission. After kicking impatience's ass, she allowed growing umbrage to hang out a little longer and party. And that is where she stood at that exact moment. She was tired of being restrained and at the whim of everything out there that was determined to thwart her progress. She would be heartless. She would "drive the wedge" and face the darkness head on. She had a new vehicle and a fresh fire in her belly.

Standing up, Jane looked at herself in the mirror above the bureau. She checked her lip one more time, found the fish antibiotics and popped one capsule. As she washed it down with water, Jane returned to her reflection and ran her hands through her tangled brown locks that skimmed just past her shoulders. Without hesitating, she reached into one of her bags and, finding a pair of scissors, lopped off four inches of hair. As she stared at the fallen strands of hair that now mingled with the motel carpet, there was a sense of renewed control. Jane continued the drastic makeover, carefully following the cut edge around her head until she had a modified bob that fell just under her chin line. Putting down the scissors, she shook her head back and forth, feeling free from the excess weight. She looked different and she liked it. But she could still recognize herself. Rifling through the bags she removed from the Mustang, Jane unearthed the black hair dye she'd originally purchased for Harlan. "Cleopatra Black," the box called it. She'd never colored her hair in thirty-seven years, even when wisps of gray invaded her crown. But two hours later, there she was, looking back at a woman she didn't know. The eyes were familiar but the rest was still foreign. Without the gray, she figured she could pass for thirty in a dimly lit room. And if she had a surgical eye lift and got those bags removed, she'd not only look younger, she could disappear into another person. What if she lost fifteen pounds? Or twenty? That would be easy to do. In the space of two months or fewer, she could completely transform herself and recede from the storms of life. The original Jane Perry would always be lurking in her heart but the revised edition would be what the public saw. Hank was wrong, she counseled herself. She knew of places that were far enough to run to. The world wasn't too small yet.

She checked the time. 3:11. "Give me a break," Jane mumbled to herself. This was getting old. Even the clock wanted her to visit Wanda. It was too early to sleep, even though she felt fatigue worm its way into every bone in her body. Falling back on the bed, she agreed to a short nap. Within seconds, Jane was hovering above her body. Suddenly, she felt as if she were trapped inside a salad spinner, holding onto the sides for dear life. The spinning finally stopped and she hung in space, free floating in pitch darkness. A cascade of letters fell around her, forming words and then rearranging themselves to form different words. The word "Romulus" stretched in front of her. Seconds later, the letters spun in a counter-clockwise circle. They stopped and spelled out the illogical, "Smromul." Then one by one, each letter spun toward Jane's face, landing separately as if each individual letter was standing on its own square. The letters, "SMROMUL" lit up in a bright light and then dimmed as others shone brighter. Once only the brightly lit letters were left in view, a four-letter word remained: SOUL.

She felt someone behind her and quickly turned around. There was a blurred, male face in the distance but she could see he was terrified. The glint of a pistol reflected against him. He turned to Jane and even though she couldn't make out who he was, she sensed his eyes. *Stolen.* That's the only word that made sense to her and yet it made no sense whatsoever.

She heard her name whispered and turned around again. Nothing.

"Jane."

She twisted around once more. The darkness filled with a pink light that morphed into gold and then emerald green. There was a sense of great love and heartbreak simultaneously.

"Jane," the voice whispered again.

She awoke with a shudder, expecting to see someone standing over her. But all she saw was a darkened motel room and the digital time of 6:21 in the evening. Turning on the light, she found a piece of paper and jotted down the word, "SOUL." Her hand shook as she put down the pen. The room felt like a vacuum and she needed air. Grabbing a cigarette from the pack, she finally found her lighter and walked outside. Standing on the balcony, she lit up and took in a good hit. And then another and one more. She regarded the smoking cylinder as if it was a foreign object. She was supposed to quit. Maybe she did have a death wish, as Hank stated. It wouldn't be the first time she'd entertained the exit options. It wasn't as if she'd never loaded the gun or drawn it toward her mouth. Life had been a stern taskmaster and only through work had she found a reason to keep going. Without that stabilizing force, Jane would cease to exist. It provided her with duty and contribution and through that, a right to breathe and take up space. The thought never crossed her mind that contentment was another option or that it could co-exist within her framework. As she'd said to herself many times, where is the struggle within contentment? What is there to fight? If anything made her want to take the final trip, Jane figured too much contentment was the ticket.

But there were moments over the last month when that beast of contentment reared up and embraced Jane without asking permission. With nothing to fight against, she was lost. Each time she'd strike out, the pleasure of the moment subdued her aggression, until she was numbed into satisfaction. And there was only one person responsible for that and he was hopefully already back in Midas at that moment with her classic ride stowed safely away in his locked garage.

Jane extinguished the cigarette on the balcony and returned to her room. She found the yellow disposable phone with the stripe buried under another bag. She didn't hear it ring and he promised to call so she'd know he made it home without incident. Checking the voicemail, she was stunned to see she had one message. The message played but there was only silence. Then through the quiet, she heard a whisper: "Jane."

She waited as the silence trailed again.

Knowing

"Jane," Hank whispered. "I'm here." The waves of silence pressed on. "And you're not." He hung up.

She turned off the phone, telling herself she wanted to conserve the battery. After staring at the phone for a little too long, she slid it into her leather satchel. Her stomach grumbled and she realized she'd hardly eaten a thing all day. Opening the cooler of food that Hank delivered, she found a plastic container at the bottom. Attached to it with a rubber band was a handwritten note: "IOU 1 De-Luxe Hot Dog." Inside the container was a hearty serving of Hank's spectacular chicken salad, along with a cloth napkin and stainless steel cutlery. "Somebody needs to take care of you," he told her a few weeks before. Nobody had ever made a comment like that to her. *Nobody*. But he was somehow brave enough to see beyond the veneer and even more courageous when he suggested they were a good fit. Jane looked at the chicken salad for half an hour, feeling sick to her stomach one moment and then desperately hungry the next. By the time she'd finished the last bite, there was still a gripping emptiness in her gut.

Before turning in for the night, Jane re-packed everything and, one by one, hauled each bag down the stairs and into the van. She nicked two pillows and a couple extra blankets from the closet in the motel room and fashioned a place in the back of the van for Harlan and she to lie down. When she was finally satisfied with everything, Jane re-parked the vehicle on the side of the motel, next to the stairway so that all Harlan would have to do is walk a few feet out the door and down the stairs before he was secreted in the vehicle. All that was left to do was to trash the cell phone she used to call Hank in a dumpster she found a half block away and return to the motel room for more rest until their early morning start. But sleep was fitful and far from restful. And while she couldn't remember anything, she awoke at five the next morning covered in sweat and with the sense that something had drastically changed.

Working her way out of bed in the darkness, she crept to the curtained front window and peered outside. The only light came from a streetlamp that cast an eerie orange glow over the edge of the motel parking lot. She showered quickly and dressed, covering her damp, newly colored hair with her ball cap. Quietly stealing the fourteen steps to Harlan's room, she softly knocked on his door and said her name. He opened it almost immediately, but when he caught a glance of her dark, shorn locks, he slammed the door shut.

"Oh, fuck," Jane mumbled. "Harlan!" she said in a forced whisper. "*Harlan*! It's me! Jane! Open the door!"

He cracked it open three inches and peered out. "Oh, hell, Jane. I didn't recognize you. You look like the little Chinese waitress down at The Pancake Shack." He grabbed his few things and walked out the door. "Why'd you do that?" he whispered.

"I didn't want you to have all the fun," she whispered back, leading him back into her room. Once inside, she locked the door with the chain and glanced outside through the crack in the front curtain.

"What's goin' on, Jane?"

"I don't know," she guardedly replied, cheating another glance outside.

"See someone?"

"No. But something isn't right."

"How do you know?"

She felt into the moment, attempting to decipher if the threat she perceived was close or further away. "I can't explain it, Harlan. My mind gets these...impressions...That's the best way I can describe it."

"Okay. So now what? The sun'll be up in less than an hour."

Jane closed her eyes, trying to focus on the strange sensations. But nothing was coming through except for the fact that they had to book it out of that place right away. "Put on your ball cap. There's a security camera in the corner of the parking lot." She carried everything left over from the rooms to the van by herself before retrieving Harlan and slipping him into the back of the van. Jane slid the gearshift into neutral and glided down the driveway and onto the street before turning the ignition.

"See anyone, Jane?" Harlan called to her from the back of the van.

Scanning the immediate area, all was clear as far as she could tell. "We're good for a bit, I guess."

"Can I ask you a question?"

"I guess," she replied, paying more attention to the landscape around her.

"What does 'Chopper' mean?"

Jane sighed. She hadn't thought about Hank in nearly an hour. "It's just a name he came up with."

"What's it mean?"

"One day he said I reminded him of those 'helicopter moms.' You know? The ones who hover over their kids? He claims I do the same thing when I'm working a case."

Harlan considered it. "Chopper...Yep. He's right. It fits you."

Jane rolled her eyes, not needing to hear from the peanut gallery.

"How many miles are we putting on this thing today?" he asked, preparing his pillow and blanket to his liking.

"Only a few."

"Huh?"

"We're going to pay Gabe's right hand man a visit. Monroe is his name. That ring a bell to you?"

He was silent.

"Harlan? You hear me?"

"Yeah."

"Well? Yes or no?"

There was another heavy pause. "Yeah…it does ring a bell but I can't pin it down, Jane."

"Good or bad?"

"Both."

She nodded. "Figures."

Before the sun rose, Jane found a twenty-four-hour drive-thru and purchased a large coffee and breakfast burritos for both of them. Pulling over in the parking lot, she checked the map that Hank left on the passenger seat. Sheldon Springs was pretty easy to navigate since the town was a blip on the map and there were nothing but ranches and a few small family farms surrounding it. If Monroe lived outside of Sheldon Springs in the middle of BFE, as John Burroughs stated, it shouldn't be difficult to determine which house belonged to him.

Driving west, they cleared the town within five minutes and passed several miles of raw land with "For Sale" signage. The sun's morning golden rays illuminated the passenger side mirror, casting fresh light on the new day. After half a mile more, she spied a long dirt road that led to a modest home in the distance. Jane checked the mailbox for any sign of Monroe's name but the box was blank and the only mail inside was addressed to "Resident." Looking around the vast, empty skyline, Jane figured it was a worth a shot to roll down the dirt road and check it out. But as she inched down the road and came up on the house, the scene that unfolded was shocking.

Standing on the screened-in front porch was a skinny man in his late twenties. He was staring with terrified eyes at the van and in his mouth was the business end of his .45.

CHAPTER 19

Jane and Harlan got out of the van as the skinny man kicked open the screen door on the front porch and stood on the top step. He frantically moved the pistol to his temple.

"I'll pull the trigger before you do!" he yelled at them.

Jane put her hands up. "No guns here. We're not here to hurt you."

Harlan seemed to be transfixed by the guy. "It's okay." He took a step toward him. "*Capisci?*"

The man's mouth dropped open. He let the pistol fall to his side and took his finger off the trigger. He never took his eyes off Harlan the entire time, hypnotized and unable to speak.

"What's going on?" Jane quietly asked.

"It's okay, Jane," Harlan told her without turning away from the man.

The man lay the gun on the ground. "Oh, my God." He crouched on the dirt, looking up at Harlan. "Jesus. Sweet Jesus." He gently walked toward Harlan, tears welling in his eyes.

"Are you Monroe?" Jane carefully asked him.

He was still focused only on Harlan. "Uh-huh. That's what they call me." He looked Harlan up and down. "Oh, God, man. How'd you do it?"

"How'd he do what?" Jane asked.

Monroe glanced her way. "Who are you?"

"Jane. How'd he do what?"

Monroe returned his comfortable yet spellbound stare toward Harlan. "He's in a body like the postcard."

In a body like the postcard. Oh, hell, Jane pondered. It appeared that Monroe was indeed Gabe's former crazy sidekick. She watched him carefully. He was wiry and the flyaway strands of brown hair on his head stood up like spikes, making him look like the cartoon version of someone who had either been electrocuted or startled. His olive drab t-shirt hung on his body as if his shoulders were a wire hanger barely able to support the weight of the material. A pair of heavy canvas pants were held up with a belt that was a little too big to fit through the loops, causing it to twist and bend as it circled his waist. On his feet, Monroe wore regulation military boots that probably still had the sands of the Middle East and mysterious territories embedded in the stitching and laces. While peculiar, his personality was not offensive to Jane. Monroe wasn't all there but he didn't belong in a mental institution. He was what most families refer to as "pleasantly eccentric and harmless." His green eyes were alive with anticipation and welcoming. But they were also dimmed with sadness and memories that Jane figured lay in the suburbs of his mind. Knowing the gritty life he and Gabriel led, she was certain Monroe had seen and done it all. And while the stain of it remained, it hadn't yet plucked the last remnant of humanity from his heart.

"What do you mean 'in a body like the postcard,' Monroe?" Jane carefully asked.

Monroe smiled, fear completely absent. "Come on in, I'll show you." He turned, leaving his gun on the ground.

"Hey!" Jane called to him, pointing to the weapon. "You forgot something."

He playfully slapped his forehead. "Ah! Right!" He retrieved it. "I'm just so in awe, man." He tripped up the few stairs that led them into the screened front porch.

Jane and Harlan followed Monroe through the front porch and into the main house. It was a modest two-story abode, packed to the gills with odd pieces of mismatched furniture, boxes, documents strewn every which way and several banks of computers that were either turned off or else featured a screensaver. One such screensaver was a breathtaking photograph from NASA of the Orion Nebula. Another screensaver showed a valley on Mars where curious outcroppings rose in the distance. A third screensaver was another NASA shot of the moon, showing the wheel markings left over from a past mission to the planet. On the far wall, Monroe had spray-painted, "**Be difficult. Choose Freedom**," in yellow and red paint. Instead of pictures on the wall, Monroe apparently preferred cork pegboards. They were everywhere, and on each board was a series of postcards from all over the world. Staring at the mass of them, Jane thought it looked like a frenzied way to display your vacation shots and world adventures.

"Welcome to my nightmare," Monroe said. "Please come in and have a seat." He offered them a seat on a tan corduroy couch that was in desperate need of both deep cleaning and new springs. When he spoke, he focused on Harlan more than Jane. "You want some water, coffee, tea, absinthe?

"*Absinthe*?" Jane asked.

"Yeah," Monroe said, breathlessly.

"No, thanks," Jane said. "Kinda early in the a.m. for that."

"I got some weed. Never too early for that."

"We're good," Jane assured him. "Back to that postcard—?"

"Oh! Yeah!" Monroe frantically searched through two desks full of boxes and piles of papers. "I keep it in a special place," he excitedly offered, opening and closing drawers in his search. "But the special places keep moving, ya know? Has that ever happened to you?"

Jane could see him spiraling out of control. "Slow down, Monroe. It's okay. We're not in any rush here."

"Yeah, yeah, yeah. But I gotta show it to ya," he mumbled, continuing to lift up stacks of documents in his quest. "Mary had a little lamb…" he said to himself, as if the words were a comforting mantra. "Mary had a little lamb… Ah!" he shouted, crossing over to a wall across the room. Removing the peg-board, he uncovered a metal plate with a lock. He brought a pick out of his pant's pocket and expertly picked the lock, opening the metal plate and bringing out the few contents from the secreted hole.

"You always carry a pick in your pocket?" Jane asked Monroe, as he returned.

"Of course," he said offhandedly.

"Why don't you have the key to that lock?"

"It got stolen when I had a break in. I have a lot of break ins. I'm real popular," he said with a strange guffaw. "Ha! Not really!" he quickly added as he started to rock back and forth.

Harlan leaned toward Jane. "We got a key in my bag of tricks."

"Ha!" Monroe shouted. "Bag of tricks! I like that."

"No, he's right, Monroe. It's an old key but we don't know what it belongs to."

"Well," Monroe replied, still rocking back and forth, "I'm sure it doesn't fit that lock. I ain't accusing you two of stealing it from me! I wouldn't do that!"

Jane reached over to him and touched his arm. He jumped as if he'd been shocked. "It's okay, Monroe," Jane assured him.

"You can't touch me like that!" Monroe stated, pulling away from Jane.

"I'm sorry."

"I got triggers, you know? You gotta watch out for them. My mind's got a lot of buried land mines." He continued to rock back and forth gently, staring at the postcards in his hands. "No, I know, I know, I know. You don't, don't, don't, don't have it in you."

"Have what in me?" Jane asked.

For the first time since their short meeting, Monroe made eye contact with Jane that was meaningful. "The...ev....ev....evil," he stammered.

"You're right. I don't. And neither does Harlan," she said, pointing toward him.

Monroe smiled broadly. "*Harlan*? Ha! Oh, wow. What a name, man. Nice to meet you, Harlan." He held his hand out to Harlan who grasped it tightly. Monroe didn't let go as he stared into Harlan's eyes with a mixture of sadness and disbelief. "Oh, God, man," he whispered as tears welled in his eyes again. "I miss you. It's a fucking jungle out here without you." He tried to manage another smile. "*Capisci?*"

Harlan never took his eyes off Monroe and seemed to understand him. "*Capisci.*"

"What do you have there?" Jane asked, pointing to the postcards.

"Oh, yeah! Right! You gotta remind me sometimes more than once. I have a little problem, you know? My head? It's all jumbled. Too many different people hidin' out in there, you know? Ha! But I know I can trust you. I wouldn't have if he hadn't of told me about you."

"I'm not following you," Jane said calmly, doing everything possible to not rile him.

"I'm not following you either! I've been right here the whole time! But that's not to say they ain't out there, ya know? Followin' us? Watchin' us? Listenin' to us? I don't sleep a lot but I hear 'em in my sleep, ya know?" He turned to Jane. "You hear 'em in your sleep?"

Jane knew from past experience that when you indulge the psychosis, the psychosis always wins. But somehow, she had to figure out how to uncover the truth that was buried beneath the insanity. "Yeah. I do. But I don't know what it means. That's why we need your help."

Monroe became very serious. "I *know* you need my help. And I'm here for you." He turned to Harlan. "*Whatever you need.* You can stay here for as long as you want. I got enough food stored away for the Apocalypse. I've always been here for you, man. You know that." He seemed hypnotized suddenly.

"Monroe?" Jane said in an attempt to jar him out of his trance.

"What?"

"The postcards?"

"Right! We'd send postcards back and forth to each other. And we'd collect 'em too, wherever we went. Real low tech, considerin' right? But it was so low tech, nobody caught on. Isn't that *crazy*?"

"Yeah. Crazy," Jane offered. "Can I see the postcard?"

He nodded. "It's this one," he handed it to Jane.

The card showed a portly farmer standing in his field. His head was bald and he wore denim overalls with a flannel shirt. She showed the postcard to Harlan.

"Damn, Jane," Harlan murmured. "This photo looks kinda like me right now."

"Well, of course it does!" Monroe exclaimed. "That's what he was trying to tell me when he gave it to me."

Jane leaned forward. "When you say 'he,' let's be clear who we're talking about."

Monroe sat back, confused. "*Gabe!* Who the hell else would I be talking about?"

"And he gave you this postcard for what reason?" Jane asked.

Monroe stared at Harlan. "So I would know him when I saw him again."

Jane's head spun. "Hang on a second. That's simply impossible."

"You never met Gabe, did you?" Monroe quizzed her.

"Not in the flesh, no."

"Well, if you had, that little postcard is just the tip of the iceberg! Ha!"

Jane glanced down at the farmer's image on the postcard. It didn't add up. It was clear to her that, for whatever reason, Harlan was given Gabriel's heart at the last minute. The entire thing seemed like a spontaneous decision by the surgeon who performed the transplant. But instead of it being an unplanned selection, as she believed, here was a nutcase telling her it was actually providence that stepped in. And the whole thing had seemingly been predicted before it happened.

She leaned forward, handing the postcard back to Monroe. "You realize that Gabe is dead, right?"

Monroe smiled, showing plenty of teeth. "Yeah, right." He winked toward her in a dramatic manner.

"No, Monroe," Jane counseled. "He really *is* dead. He was killed nineteen months ago and they transplanted his heart into Harlan's chest."

"Wow. That's fucking beautiful, man." He looked at Harlan with awe. "And that's exactly the way he would have done it too."

"What do you mean?" Jane asked. "You're saying he planned this?"

"With Gabe, nothing is off the table. He may not have planned it ahead of time, but I guarantee you, he had a guiding hand in it after they took him out."

Jane felt like she was swimming inside a disturbed mind and trying to stay afloat. "How could he have a guiding hand, Monroe? By that point, he was on life support."

"Oh, life support? That's even better. His soul was cruisin' 'round that hospital looking for the right fit." He held up the postcard with the farmer. "Looking for the guy he already met." He leaned forward toward Harlan, speaking in a tone that inferred confidentiality. "You know, I bet he hung out with you afterward to make sure you were okay. That's the kind of guy Gabe was."

Harlan nodded. "He did. I thought it was a cop sittin' by my hospital bed. But it was him, wasn't it?"

"Ha! A cop! Love it! He'd laugh about that! Oh, yeah, it was Gabe. No two ways about it. It'd be just like him to watch over and protect his new vehicle."

"His new vehicle?" Jane asked with an incredulous tone.

"Yeah!" Monroe replied, seemingly more relaxed by Jane's presence. "And what a vehicle he chose!"

"Why do you think he picked me," Harlan asked, becoming more intrigued.

"It was destiny, brother. You betcha! Gabe talked about destiny with me, among many other things. He used to say, there's fate, destiny and karma. Fate is the son of destiny. Destiny is written in stone but fate is more forgiving and can alter based on your deeds. Karma is what you earn based on how well you accept your destiny. But in the end, time, God and karma tend to solve everything."

Jane took it all in. "That's not exactly the type of conversation that an assassin and his…assistant…typically have."

Monroe didn't seem offended by the reference. "Oh, I know that! I've worked with a few shooters during my time with the group and Gabe was head and shoulders above all of them."

"Can I ask you when he got into all this stuff?" Jane inquired.

"I think it was always there inside him. But when he left the group, he started taking it more seriously." A profound calmness came over him. "He stepped away from this world and spent three years hiking and walking on foot, hitching a ride when he could, working odd jobs, doing seasonal work.

But for the first nearly five months, he went into complete isolation. When he came out, I was the first person he looked up. He told me he'd been holed up all winter in a cabin that was off the grid. You have any idea what it takes to do something like that? But he did it and when I heard from him again, he sounded totally different. He said he started eating only raw foods. And I'm not talking vegan shit, man. He was still eating meat, but it was *raw* meat. Even raw eggs!"

Harlan shot a glance toward Jane.

"I thought he'd gone off the deep," Monroe continued, "but he was saner than anyone out there. Gabe said when he left that cabin, he felt like he was part of the earth again. He said he was purified. He called that shack 'his desert,' and he emerged from it a new man. He told me he was 'rehabilitated.'"

Harlan turned to Jane. "What'd I tell ya? Didn't I say this heart was 'rehabilitated'?"

She nodded. "Yes, Harlan. You certainly did."

"It's true, man," Monroe interjected. "He proved that he couldn't be broken by them. He had mind-bending abilities before he left the group but after that, he honed those gifts with razor-sharp precision. He used those gifts when he needed to during his sabbatical and it made him much more powerful than they could *ever* wish to be. When they figured that out, they had to kill him because you can't have anyone on this planet more powerful than they are."

"Wait a second. That can't be the reason they took Gabe out. I get that he had 'mind-bending' abilities. Wouldn't that be a useful skill for his covert employment, instead of a detriment? You don't kill a man simply because he has a unique gift that other soldiers don't have."

"You kill him if you see that man as a threat!" Monroe relaxed a little more, seemingly comforted by discussing his dear friend. "Gabe was a student of the mind and how far you could push it. Maybe they were afraid of all the things he was able to see. You know? Not just the behind their curtain, but behind the veil? Know what I mean? Or maybe," he offered, seemingly trying to dive into Gabe's thought process, "he worried that somehow his abilities could be manipulated for their benefit. Maybe they could fuck with his head and rewire it somehow, making him a truth teller of what world leaders were saying behind closed doors. I realize that sounds a little sketchy, but the possibilities are endless with these people. If you can dream it, they can build it and make it happen with better precision than the sun rising and setting. They have access to the greatest minds on this planet. I kid you not. If you even knew some of the rooms I've walked into and the people who've been in those rooms, you would shit your pants." He paused, taking a breath. "Look, Gabe was *never* a company man. Even when he was embedded in a job, he was his own man. His allegiance was only to himself and those he trusted and cared about. He'd protect you and guide you toward the next place, even when you thought it was all over and your number was up. He was the guy you want at your back because he *knew*. He *knew* how to keep you safe. And when you have got nothing and you think the gig is up, feeling safe is priceless. But maybe they thought he was too much of a loose cannon. If he didn't like what you were doing, he let you know about it. He never backed down from any fight. If anyone could do it, Gabe would be the one to fuck up their ability to keep their secrets. Loose cannons are only effective when they hit their target. If you can keep them from doing that, you win. Problem solved."

Jane leaned forward. "Look, Gabe obviously discovered something of great importance. Their greatest asset turned into their greatest liability. I think he wanted to expose something he uncovered. I mean, there's a limit, right?"

"A limit?" Monroe asked.

"Yeah. A limit to what a truly honorable person will agree to do. Even the most courageous soldiers who have seen and done everything have a line they don't cross. It's different for every single one of them, but if you're the least bit human and your soul hasn't been destroyed, there *are* places you won't go, no matter what somebody orders you to do. Based on what you've told me and what I think I know about Gabe to this point, I have a feeling that his murder was directly related to some plan he was going to disclose."

"Well, hell, what's that got to do with his heart ending up in another man's body?" Monroe asked.

Jane sighed. "I don't have a fucking idea."

Monroe pondered. "Maybe, it's not one thing. Maybe what Gabe knew and the heart transplant were two separate things?"

"They *have* to be connected, Monroe," Jane stressed.

"Why? 'Cause that's the way you want to control your investigation?" Monroe shook his head. "You need to open your mind more and explore the options here."

"I don't have time to do that!" Jane argued. "For all I know, Romulus is already onto us."

"Hang on, you don't have time to find out the *truth*?"

"Jesus!" Jane exploded. "You sit there and act like I've got a task force behind me, helping me sort out the minutia. I don't even have a fucking office! I have a van with a laptop and two disposable cell phones. If you know something that will help me decipher this mind fuck of a case, please share it!"

Monroe thought long and hard before he spoke. "Gabe got into exploration of the levels."

"The levels?"

"Of consciousness," he replied as though it was obvious. "That's the future, man. Forget space exploration. The mind is the next frontier. You want *real* power in this world? Own your own mind. Exploring the mind is a person's God given right. And that ain't easy to do when everything around you is programmed to destroy it. I'm telling you….consciousness and how to manipulate it is the future. That was Gabe's passion. He tried to teach me all the different methods he learned. Mediation, sun gazing, moving a pencil with just your mind. I never figured out how to do that one."

"But Gabe did," Jane assumed.

"Yep.

"Wow," Harlan said in wonderment.

"But," Monroe continued, "he always said there was a dark side to the coin."

"Like what?" Jane asked.

He hung his head. "Most of what he said I don't understand—"

"I don't give a shit. Just repeat to me what he told you!"

Monroe appeared to pull up the conversation from an old file in his brain. "Consciousness can be corrupted for someone else's gain."

"That's it?" Jane asked, her irritation growing.

Monroe focused and gradually recalled the information. He spoke as if he were in a trance. "The heart of a person's mind can be corrupted, exploited and manipulated in order to gain power for those who don't possess the heightened awareness."

Jane let it percolate. "The heart of a person's mind," she repeated. She remembered the old man from her vision who held the white binder with IEB written in the front. *The heart and the mind*, the old man stressed to her. The chances of that strange reference and now this information nearly coinciding had to have value. "What does that mean, Monroe?" She leaned closer to him. "Come on. Go deep." She felt a moment of angst, acting like a handler and forcing this delicate soul to tromp across his already traumatized mind. "Pull up the information. You can do it."

He willingly took several shallow breaths as if "go deep" was an order he never refused. When he finally spoke, it was as if he was reading the words in the air. "He said knowledge might be power, but higher consciousness is the gold standard for acquiring that power. When you have the ability to see a lie or hear a truth simply because your mind is wired to receive that input, you have massive leverage over somebody else who doesn't possess that capability." He hung in the ether, reciting from a script only he could see. "The fruits of consciousness cannot be reserved for the few who believe they are owed that gift." He emerged out of the trance and turned to Jane with fear tracing his face. "Gabe wanted to leave a legacy. But more than anything, he wanted to stop those bastards." He looked at her with terrified eyes. "Whew! It just got hot in here!" Monroe exclaimed. "You feeling hot?"

"No," Jane said.

"Jesus! I feel like I'm on fire."

Jane needed to keep him on point. "How was he planning on stopping Romulus from what they were planning?"

Monroe got up and opened a window. "I don't know and that *is* the truth. But Gabe never set out to do something he wasn't going to finish." He stood in front of the open window and let the cool air hit his body. "Romulus has their hands in a lot of pots. Private military contracting is just one division of the group. Basically, if you know about it, they're involved in it. And if you *don't* know about it, they are *still* involved in it. Ignorance of something does not prevent it from still operating on full tilt." He turned to her, lifting his t-shirt to cool off. "Gabe and I saw and did a lot of things during our time together. I hope when it's my time to leave this world, God understands that everything he and I did was because we didn't know the whole story and because we didn't have any choice." He sighed as he leaned against the wall. "When they're feeding you those frequencies 24/7, it's hard to not be under their thumb."

"What frequencies?" Jane asked.

Monroe walked toward her and sat down. He twisted around and pointed to a spot in his neck that was red and scarred over. "See that spot right there? That's where Gabe dug it out of me. After his five month sabbatical in the mountains, he came to see me in the flesh one more time and he told me he was going to make me free. He'd dug it out of his neck the day he took off and once he got unplugged, he said he'd been resurrected. So, I figured, why not?"

Harlan turned in his chair. "Check this out, Monroe." He pointed to the same spot on the back of his neck. "It feels like I got something stuck under my skin."

"Ha! That's priceless, man! Yep, yep, yep. That's where he had it. That's where we all have it."

"Have what?" Jane asked.

"The microchip. What'd you think I was talking about?"

Jane stared at him. "Please tell me this is a joke," Jane said.

"Hell, I *wish* it was a joke. Did you know there are idiots out there right now who are voluntarily allowing themselves to have a microchip injected in them? And it's all being done under the bullshit guise of 'safety' or 'health protection'. Shit, they brag about the chips they put in animals and how great it is because you can just wave a wand and locate the owners. People think that's a modern miracle of science." He rolled his eyes. "People are fucking stupid! Modern science is so far *beyond* microchips, it's not even funny. But that doesn't stop some people from wanting to jump on the ol' chip wagon. Let me tell you, as somebody who lived with a fucking chip inside of his body for way too many years, I can attest to the fact that it's not cool or inventive. It's fucking crazy! And I *know* that you already think I'm crazy so me saying that to you won't have much of an effect. But I'm here to tell you that it's *fucking crazy!*"

Jane recalled a comment that John Burroughs said to her. "You lost your connection?"

"Humph," Monroe snorted. "I wouldn't call what I had injected in me a connection! It was a leash made of steel chains. When Gabe cut that chip out of me, he helped me unhook the controlling voice in my head. That was the first step. You gotta get unhooked from the matrix. But he couldn't hang out with me long enough for me to get straight again. Whew! I'm a mess in there!" He pointed to his head. "He said it took him a while to unhook himself after he cut it out. A lot of old memories came flowing back, he said. Stuff that he'd compartmentalized and forgotten. He had some caverns in there from his past where he didn't like to go but he went there and came out a better man. He said he could finally *think* again, after getting rid of all the static in his brain. He told me it took him months to find himself. But his cell memory finally kicked in after a bit and slowly, he remembered who he was and what he came into this life to do." He looked at the floor, somewhat saddened. "I'm still waiting for that to happen to me. And I hope I can find myself again before they kill me. But, just like you two, I don't know how much time I got left. My future is so uncertain, I stopped buying green bananas."

"Why haven't they killed you yet?" Jane asked.

"When I feel them coming, I take off and ride it out until they leave. Somehow, at least up to now, I get warnings. I can't explain except that I just know they are close by. It's the same feeling I get that tells me Gabe is protecting me too." He turned to Harlan. "Just like he protected you when you were in the hospital? Sitting by your bed? Yeah. He does that for me too." He turned to the screened in front porch. "Sometimes, I think I see him standing sentry out there at night. And even if I'm just imagining it, it gives me peace. I know that as long as he's out there, I'll be safe. But I know he can't do it forever."

"So, you haven't worked for Romulus since—"

"Since Gabe cut the chip out. That was about four years ago."

"If you don't mind me asking, how do you support yourself without Romulus?"

He smiled a sad smile. "The bank of Gabriel."

"I don't understand," Jane said.

"I was plucked out of college by the group because of my ability to break codes and hack into any computer system and fuck it up. I got straight A's and was on the Dean's List," he said proudly. "I had a full scholarship to any Master's program I wanted in computer sciences. But Romulus offered me a shit load of money to do that first job and I was too stupid to realize it when they sucked me in. It's like your first dose of heroin, you know? The first dose is always free. It's all the ones after that that cost too much." He studied the ground. "Years later, my job title changed. I was Gabe's front man. The set up guy? I'd go ahead of Gabe and set up what he'd need to do the job. I'd hide notes, directions, money, all over hell and back. Then I'd send him coded messages to let him know where to look. When he and I agreed to get out, he told me he'd take care of me. And he meant it. He'd send me a coded message and I'd go to the location and dig a hole at the exact point and there would be a piece of PVC pipe wrapped in duct tape and inside would be separate stacks of money. Sometimes, it was thousands of dollars. And he seemed to always know when I was running low because I'd get a message and, damn, he'd save me again!"

"Bank of Gabriel," Jane mused. "I like that. We should all be so lucky to have a friend like that."

"He was my brother in spirit. The one I never knew I needed? He saved me from my past and gave me the feeling I could have a future that wasn't dependent on the length of my kill sheet." He let out a hard breath. "But I don't think that's going to happen now that you've shown up. You two being here is a sign. He came back just like he said he would. So all that's left for me to do is to help you out and then wait."

"Wait for them to kill you?" Jane asked. "Why would you do that?"

"It's my destiny. I knew I wouldn't make it to thirty. Most of us never make it to thirty. They embed a suicide switch in our programming. It usually clicks on around age twenty-seven and goes into full gear before thirty. I think Gabe felt it coming on right before he hit thirty, but he was smart enough to not flip the switch. It's a real strong trigger for self-destruction. It's hard to override their system. Your desire to implode is greater than your desire to live. And when it gets too much, *you* take care of business. One less problem they have to deal with. It's quite efficient programming, huh? The computer destroys itself and everything in it. *They* don't have to lift a finger."

"But you cut out your chip," Jane offered. "So, you're not hooked in to their end game."

"If I kill myself now," Monroe said with authority, "it's on *my* terms, not theirs." He wiped his brow. "Damn, seriously, you don't think it's hot in here?"

"No, it isn't," Harlan said.

"Shit, I feel like I have flames dancing on my bare flesh." He got up again and stared out the side window.

"What is it?" Jane asked.

"They're out there."

Jane got up and moved to Monroe's side. She peered out the window but all she saw was acres of farm and ranch land with not a soul in sight. "Is this your paranoia talking?"

"No, ma'am. This is experience talking." He scanned the area one more time. "Nobody's ever met the guy at the top of the pyramid. Nobody knows the names of the few who protect him. But all I know in my heart is that he's indestructible."

Jane shook her head. "I don't understand how any person or small group got this kind of supreme power that overrides everything rational."

"It's a good question. It didn't happen overnight. I heard that Romulus has been hiding in plain sight for centuries. Pulling the strings and making us think we are in charge of our own future."

"We *are* in charge of our own future."

"You sure about that?" Monroe asked, with a crooked grin. "How can you be so sure that what you believe and what you desire has not been programmed into you by everything you encounter on a daily basis? If every choice you are given is not a choice at all and really just a pre-digested preference that was created for you, how would you feel? We have the *illusion* of choice because no matter what we choose, the game never changes. The wheels always keep moving in the direction that suits the ones who are designing the wheels. If they don't want that wheel to travel somewhere, they make damn sure it's designed so that it doesn't roll there." He cocked his head to the side. "If they want you to be afraid of something that's not even a real threat, they can do that too. Oh yeah, there's *nothin'* more compelling than a *perceived* threat, especially when you're the one in control of creating that perception!" He turned to the side in contemplation. "You know, Romulus does have one downfall. They can't generate anything on their own because they lack sanity and humanity. They don't create anything except chaos. Everything they own, they've stolen. Essentially, they exist by sucking on the souls of others."

Jane nodded, recollecting her dream. "The word 'soul' exists within the word 'Romulus.'"

"You saw that too, huh?" Monroe replied with a sly grin.

"It was pointed out to me," Jane stated.

Monroe meandered back toward them. "It ain't a coincidence. But the joke's on them because they have no soul. They have the heart of a lizard and the breath of a devil."

"Fuck 'em," Jane stated.

Monroe glanced at her. "It's easy to say that when you haven't dealt with them directly."

"I have! I'm deep in their muck right now, Monroe. They want to kill Harlan because they think he knows something."

Monroe looked at Harlan. "He doesn't know anything. But his heart does."

Jane had to wrap her mind around the fact that the only person who finally understood what was going on just happened to be mentally unfit. "You said Gabe wanted to leave a legacy?" She pointed to Harlan. "*That* is his legacy, right there!"

Monroe moved away from Jane and plopped his skinny ass on his chair. "What are you going to do if you find out what that heart of his is trying to tell you? You going to expose it?"

"That's what Gabe wants, isn't it?" Jane replied.

"Why?" Monroe asked gently. "Why put your ass on the line for a dead man?"

She glanced nervously toward Harlan. "Harlan isn't dead yet."

"I was talking about Gabe."

Jane considered the question. "Well, Gabe is inside of Harlan. So, I guess it's one in the same. I save one, I save the other."

"Why don't you just go back to your life and forget about all this?"

"Because I don't have a life!" Jane stated, shocked somewhat that she was admitting that to a stranger. "The only life I have is in saving other people."

Monroe looked at her perplexed. "*Really*? You're all alone?"

"No, she ain't," Harlan suddenly interjected.

"Shut up," Jane whispered toward Harlan.

"Don't tell me to shut up," Harlan retorted. "She's got a real nice boyfriend. She just doesn't want to believe it."

Jane spun toward Harlan. "That boyfriend had a 9mm pointed at your head."

"Yeah, well, I already forgave him for that." Harlan stated in a stern tenor. "You should too."

Monroe popped out of his chair again. He began tapping his head with the tips of his fingers. "I've got places to go and people to be."

Jane stood up. "Hey, come on! I thought you were going to help me out." She observed him and realized he'd split and another personality took over.

"I need to do my rounds." He picked up two rifles and shoved his .45 pistol down the front of his sagging trousers. "*By myself.*" His voice was strict. "You can look at or read anything you want. You can eat whatever you find. You can even play games on my computers. You'll never get past my firewall so I'm not worried."

"When are you coming back?" Jane asked.

"Couple hours. Maybe more." He grabbed a clip and shoved it into his pocket.

"What if you don't come back? We'll be sitting ducks."

"Gabe has watched over you two so far. Hopefully, he's still up to the job."

CHAPTER 20

For the first hour of Monroe's absence, Jane sat on the screened porch and waited. Harlan, on the contrary, built himself a thick sandwich, knocked back half a dozen raw eggs, two bottles of pine needle beer and settled his ass in front of Monroe's giant computer. He was still sitting there playing Tetris when Jane finally walked back into the house. She heated up a can of clam chowder she found on a shelf in Monroe's sparse kitchen. Returning to the living room with the saucepan of chowder and a large spoon, she ate a few spoonfuls before setting it down and collecting the remaining four postcards Monroe retrieved from the hidden wall safe.

She cleared a space on Monroe's cluttered desk and laid them out. Checking the back of each card, the only handwriting was Monroe's address and a circled number in the space where the message would normally be written. The numbers began with "2" and ended with "6." The card with "2" on the back featured what looked like a city park, with beautifully manicured lawns, playground equipment and a baseball field. Turning the card over, the imprint on the back read: "O'Rian Park in the small town of Helios, Colorado, is a popular center for family gatherings and sports activities." Jane remembered seeing a map amidst the clutter and once she found it, she opened it up and laid it on the floor. From what she could tell, Helios was in spitting distance of Monroe's dwelling.

Looking at the card with "3" on the back, the photograph was a family farm with rows and rows of verdant produce ready to be harvested. She turned the card over. "*The Green Goodness* CSA is located in the San Luis Valley, resting in the Sangre de Cristo mountains." This was the same CSA mentioned in the Eco-Goddesses newsletter Harlan kept in his mysterious burlap bag. Jane ran out to the van and brought back the burlap bag, Harlan's notebook and her leather satchel. Fishing out the newsletter from the bag, Jane turned the pages until she found the large black and white photo of the fifty people standing in front of a field of vegetables. The caption beneath had crammed the names of the CSA members so tightly that it was nearly impossible to discern any of them.

"You see a magnifying glass anywhere around here?" she asked Harlan.

He was deeply involved in his computer game. "Hang on. I finally got to level twenty five."

Jane waved him off and started hunting through drawers until she uncovered a photographer's loop. Running the loop across the caption, she read each name until she came to one that was all too familiar: Werner Haas. "Shit," she said standing up and staring at the photo. Counting the people in the photo from left to right in that line, she held her index finger on the face. Pressing the loop against the photograph, there was Gabe. It was exactly what John Burroughs told her. He could blend in and play any part he wanted—a priest, executive…or CSA farm worker.

She snapped up the third card that had "4" circled on the back. But Jane noticed right away that there was no title or explanation of the photo as the other postcards. The scene was strange, depicting a rugged view of a mountain top meadow. To the left, was an old, rusty windmill and to the left of that was an "X" written in black permanent ink. Above the "X" were the words, "You are here." Jane flipped the card over again, thinking maybe she missed some minute description of where this was located but there was nothing there.

Jane retrieved the fourth and last card. The number "6" was circled on the back. Where was the card with number five, she wondered? Everything she had in her hand was what Monroe removed from the hole in the wall. Figuring she'd go with what she had, Jane looked at the front photo. It was an adobe shrine in northern New Mexico called El Santuario de Chimayo. The sloping adobe wall at the front of the sacred church opened to a modest entrance that led visitors down a weather beaten pathway and toward the shrine. On the back, it read: "The Santuario de Chimayo is a historic shrine of New Mexico that draws hundreds of pilgrims annually. It is considered a consecrated location for healing the spirit, the body and the mind."

Jane looked at the photo again. She'd heard about Chimayo many times from her brother who was fascinated by all things "woo-woo." He called it the "Lourdes of the Southwest" and he had good reason for it. People made pilgrimages from all over the world to walk the short distance into the chapel and then into the modest side room where a small pit in the floor, known as *el pocito*, holds the "holy dirt" which many believe has remarkable curative powers. Visitors return to their homes with a bag of this holy dirt and report that miracles occurred in their lives shortly thereafter. Terminal illnesses went into remission, marriages were saved, couples were able to conceive, and, yes, people could walk again. The chapel at Chimayo is filled floor to ceiling with crutches brought there by believers as evidence that a miraculous healing occurred for them.

Jane laid out the four cards and looked at them again. But the fact that the order started with "2" and not "1" bothered Jane. Spying the lone card of the farmer in overalls that resembled Harlan, she picked it up and turned it over. There was "1" on the back. Setting it down in the first position, it felt to Jane as if the cards represented a collective pathway. Why else would Gabe number them? The first card established Harlan's arrival. To Jane, it made peculiar sense that Gabe somehow knew all of this would occur and wanted to give Harlan and her the guidance they would need to complete their journey. Accepting that theory, Jane deduced that their next stop would be locating O'Rian Park the next day. But in the meantime, she would continue to take Monroe up on his offer to read and look at anything she desired.

She roamed the periphery of the living room, reading and looking at the various postcards that were tacked onto the boards in thick layers. She'd pull one off a board and Jane would find three more hidden underneath it. One card had a single quote across the front: "WE DON'T HAVE HOAXES ANYMORE. WE HAVE ENGINEERED MISUNDERSTANDINGS." Jane smiled and continued to remove one card after another until she found one that made her take a break. It was a vintage reissue of a card that sported a 1966 ice blue Mustang on the front. Pulling it off the board, she turned it over and saw that it was unused. How odd, she thought. Staring at the depiction of her cherished ride, her heart sunk. She wasn't sure if it was the damn car she missed or the guy who drove it away from her.

Tucking the card into her jacket pocket, she perused a few more pegboards of cards before noticing that one board stood out from the wall more than the others. Jane lifted it off the two screws and set it down, exposing another secret compartment. She tapped the door of the compartment lightly several times, testing its security. Either it wasn't locked correctly or the lock had been compromised because the door opened. Jane turned to alert Harlan but stopped before uttering a word. He was onto level thirty-three and there was no way he could be ripped away from that achievement. Reaching into the twelve-inch square hole, Jane removed a single, plain, 8 ½ x 14 inch envelope that felt somewhat weighty. She turned back to Harlan who was still engrossed in his game and then quietly walked into the kitchen with the envelope.

Jane unhooked the envelope flap and lifted the contents onto Monroe's cluttered kitchen table. It was a stack of 8 x 10 inch color photos. The first photo showed what appeared to be an African tribal village from the air. The photography was well done with vivid colors and crisp images. The second shot was taken closer to the ground but still in the aircraft. Jane turned over the shots to see if there was anything written or stamped on the backs but they were blank. Each subsequent shot seemed to tell a chronological story of walking into the village, showing lattice-roofed mud huts and young children. Jane stopped and pulled up the two shots of the lattice-roofed huts. They were identical to what she saw in her strange and disturbing vision. Remembering how that vision ended with a horrific scream from a child, Jane steadied herself. She snuck a peek outside the kitchen door to make sure Harlan was still occupied before returning to the photographs. There were several shots of children that appeared to be between the ages of two and six, dressed in their native garb. One child, a boy, wore a unique horn necklace around his neck. He smiled at the camera, holding out his hand.

Jane felt her mouth go dry as she turned to the next photo in the stack. There was a close-up of the same young boy with the necklace around his neck. But in this photo, his skull was split in two down the middle and pulled apart. It was clear that the brain had been removed from his cranium. Jane took several steps backward, pressing her back against the wall. She'd seen thousands of gruesome, murderous crime scene photos that involved children and infants but somehow, this felt different. *This* shot seemed to have surgical precision. She felt sick to her stomach as she moved back to the table. The next twelve shots would have challenged hardcore detectives who'd "seen it all." Each one was worse than the one before. Every photo featured a close-up of another child under the age of six with his or her head split open in the exact manner as the one before, and each child had their brain removed.

Jane collected all the photos and shoved them into the large envelope. She sat down and tried to catch her breath and steady her nerves. One of the postcards Gabe sent Nanette Larson featured children in the Congo dressed in their native garb. Jane easily recalled Nanette's comment about how, less than a week after receiving the card, she saw a story on the Internet about a coup in the Congo where tribal leaders were slaughtered, along with many children. But if this was connected to that massacre, where were the shots of the tribal leaders? Wouldn't a tribal leader, Jane reasoned, be more valuable as some sort of photographic "kill prize" rather than a child?

Then her mind drifted to another disturbing yet probable connection. Suddenly, Patsy Cline's "Through the Eyes of a Child" took on a sinister twist. Jane wracked her brain trying to come up with a suitable explanation for Harlan being compelled to include that song in his burlap bag. The only thing she could come up with was the abject terror in their young eyes right before they were killed. But that ran counter to the lines in the song that spoke more positively about "what a wonderful world it would be" to "see the world through the eyes of a child." Jane scooped up the envelope and walked back into the living room. She started to put the envelope back into the hiding place but pulled it back out, closed the steel door and replaced the peg board on the wall.

After finishing her soup and grabbing a few stale chips, she walked out onto the screened in porch, sat in a comfortable recliner and waited. Occasionally, she dozed but quickly stirred at the softest sound. Harlan eventually joined her, bringing her a sandwich and then a bowl of ice cream from a carton in the freezer. And together, they waited. As night confiscated the daylight, Jane and Harlan pulled a couple blankets closer to their bodies. Two more sandwiches later with a pine needle beer for Harlan and a soda for Jane, they were still waiting. Jane had already chewed the skin nearly off one thumb and was working on the other one when she heard footsteps disturb the gravel pathway that lay cloaked in darkness in front of them. She slid off the recliner and stood up as Harlan followed suit. Out of the April shadows, Monroe appeared, looking tired and troubled. Harlan relaxed but Jane stood as if a steel rod replaced her spine.

"Where in the hell have you been all day?" Jane exclaimed.

Monroe opened the front door and rested his two rifles and .45 on a small table. "You know, I don't even know your name," he said with an eerie calm. "Should I just call you 'mom?'"

Jane wasn't sure what new personality had taken him over but it seemed to be a laid back one. "My name's Jane and I'm nobody's mother."

"Could've fooled me," Monroe mumbled under his breath.

Harlan shot Jane a half-smile of agreement. "I need to talk to Monroe. Alone."

Harlan worked his way around chairs and back into the house. "Damn, brother. I'll say a prayer for you."

Jane waited until Harlan was in the house and out of earshot. "Sit down."

Monroe held firm. "You know, this is *my* house, right?"

"*Sit down*," she firmly repeated.

He ran his fingers through his tangled hair. "Oh, man. Shit just got real." He planted his ass onto the recliner across from Jane.

She grabbed the envelope and threw it at him. "Yeah, shit just got *way* real!"

Monroe didn't touch the envelope. "This was hidden in my wall."

"You said I could read or look at *anything*. And I didn't have to pick a lock to get it. Don't act so shocked, Monroe. You expected me to find it. That's why you were gone so long. You wanted to give me lots of time. I've been waiting for you for almost nine fucking hours. I'm not sure who you are used to dealing with but—"

"Gabe didn't do it," Monroe suddenly interrupted in a low, modulated voice. He looked Jane straight in the eye. "You thought he did this?"

"I don't know what to think anymore."

"Wow. Even after everything I told you about him and what you probably already knew, you still thought he was capable of this," he flicked his middle finger against the envelope. "Is that what your mind told you or is that what your heart told you? The heart and the mind are two separate elements that can often work against each other."

Jane regarded Monroe with a puzzled expression. The syncs between the worlds were beginning to collide.

Monroe flung the envelope on the floor. "Jesus, how could you believe Gabe had a hand in that? I think the trickster got hold of you."

"What's that?" Jane asked, sitting down.

"He's within your head and outside of it. He enjoys making you suffer and his only goal is to destroy you. He hates those who love you so he feeds you lies and dismisses those who tell you the truth. He makes you doubt what your heart tells you and then whispers what you want to hear. His biggest fear is that you will wake up, so he waits for you in the darkened shadows and demands that you sleep. He needs to keep you enslaved. He's gotta keep you afraid, addicted and unsure of yourself so you are paralyzed to act. He gains his strength by making sure you are weak." He looked at her. "Weak enough to believe that the heart of the man inside your friend's chest could even conceive of this, let alone do it."

From what Jane could tell, it appeared that a sidewalk philosopher was now living inside Monroe. "Fine. Explain why you have those photos hidden away."

"I was doing a job for Romulus and needed some codes. I got sent a link that wasn't encrypted. That never happened before. Somebody slipped up, I guess. But I saw what I had and it was like a door swung open and I ran right through it and hacked into their system. I knew alarms would go off somewhere so I blew through what I could, transferred the data, yada, yada, yada, and got outta there. From the files I was able to steal, I could only decode three. Two of them were no big deal." He pointed to the envelope. "That was the third file. There were no dates on it so I have no clue when they were taken." He rubbed his face, obviously in great distress over the photographs. "I only showed those to two people…You're the second one."

"And what did Gabe say?"

"That he had no information about it. But that he was going to check it out. Look, part of what he and I used to do is help destabilize governments or groups or powerful officials. And lots of people die when you do that and it's awful and gruesome. But this? If this was done to destabilize another fucking tribal whatever in the armpit of Africa, it wouldn't look like that! You would have bodies heaped into mounds and a chaotic mess of gunshot wounds, high-impact attacks, machete slashes, decapitations, and on and on. What do we have here? We have a handful of later shots where you can see the elders of the tribe in the background, laying every which way on the ground but no close ups of them. From what I could tell when I zoomed in on the shots of the older people, none of them had their heads cracked open. But when you really look at the photos of those young kids, I think their heads were cracked open surgically."

Jane scowled. "Jesus Christ, Monroe. You're saying they were alive when this 'surgery' happened?"

"Yep. That's what I'm saying."

"For what purpose?!"

"There's only one season to pick apples. But when it comes to organ harvesting, every day yields a new, fresh crop."

Now the philosopher was becoming obscure. "What the fuck—?"

"Oh, haven't you heard?" he asked offhandedly. "We are no longer people. We are potential harvesting machines. Parts is parts and we are the sum of our parts. And some parts hold more value than others. And the younger you are, the more likely those parts will be healthier and less likely to have significant problems."

Jane pointed to the envelope. "Brains? I've never heard of a brain transplant."

"I haven't either."

Jane waited, expecting him to continue. "And?"

"Well?"

"No," Jane stated with a sweep of her hand. "You can't sell that to me. No way!"

"Well, if they're not transplanting it, there's only two things I can think of. Either they are selling it for food," he said cringing, "or they're working with the cells or the tissue in some sort of medical experiment. And since Romulus isn't hurting financially, I don't believe they are selling it for food."

Jane pondered for a long minute. A strange memory suddenly crept into her consciousness. "You know, when I was a kid, I read one of those ghastly fables that told the story of an ancient warrior who cut open the chest of a still dying soldier and ate his beating heart. There was something about consuming his soul along with the warrior's courage that sprung through his heart at the moment of his death." Jane considered it. "It was believed that a golden light entered his body as his soul ascended and that if you could capture the tail of that light within the still beating heart and eat it, you would hold the light of God's immortality and be able to travel through all the worlds that parallel our universe. Immortality and the ability to space travel at will. That was what they craved in that fable. So, what type of power does Romulus crave?"

"Nothing short of everything," Monroe shrugged. "Complete and utter power and control over everyone and every living thing. And they are willing to go as long as it takes for it to happen. They're in no rush. As long as they keep the world off balance, they're happy."

"Okay. What does it take to strong arm that kind of ultimate power away from the people?"

"Not sure."

Jane cocked her head to the side. "You capture the hearts and minds of the populace. Then you turn on them. And through one, you destroy the other.

Through rejection of the heart, you kill the mind. Through sole submission of the mind, you kill the heart."

He nodded. "They steal your mind through your heart. Control one and they'll make you doubt the other."

Jane suddenly understood the possibility that the hearts and the minds meme that began with the old man in her vision could actually represent two separate discoveries that Gabriel uncovered. Flashing back to the first vision she had where she followed behind Gabe and watched him kill the old man, he first examined the files on the man's desk, separating out various files that he seized. He then turned and crossed to the file cabinets, removing the white binder with the IEB inscription. Jane had linked the two together prior to this point, but now she was open to the concept that there were two diverse issues at play here.

"You know the organ transplant business is *big* business with the elite around the world," Monroe said matter-of-factly. "If they have the money, honey, they'll hire someone to do the crime."

"What kind of crime?"

"Stealing organs out of a body and selling it to the highest bidder. I set up a job once for a guy who was hired to get a young, healthy kidney for a diplomat."

"Hang on." Jane sat up and faced him. "If he's not a surgeon, how'd he 'get' the kidney?"

"Oh, there was a surgeon there. We paid him off too. Unless he talked. They don't like it when people argue with them. You do what you're asked to do and you spend the rest of your life trying to forget it. Hey, Romulus isn't the only one involved in organ harvesting. There are wealthy individuals who broker overseas deals. They find a young, strong man or woman who has the organ they need and they make a private agreement. Problem is, the donor is usually poor and destitute. So, getting some good money for a kidney looks like a decent trade. But what they don't understand is that more times than not, they'll be opened up and the surgeon gets what he needs and then does a hack job sewing him up or doesn't give the person adequate drugs to prevent infection. Then the donor dies. But so what, right? They got what they wanted. Moving on. Nothing to see here, folks. It's happening every day of the week, all over this fucked up world. Like I said, we're just two-legged vehicles that carry spare parts for those who need an upgrade when their hardcore lifestyle turns on them."

"That's insane, Monroe."

He leaned forward, his eyes equally insane. "I *know* that. I'm trying to get you to understand that these people are beyond cold blooded. They are soulless, Jane. They have more money than God, but they keep wanting more. *More of everything.* All they need is to keep us dumb, hopeless and stupid so they can keep the cream for themselves. You know, I'd feel sorry for Romulus if I didn't want to see them all dead and burned up in a holy fire of retribution. It's tough because I wish I could warn people and tell them what I've experienced. But I can't. And they wouldn't believe me anyway. It's like teaching a goat to sing. It's a waste of time and it annoys the goat."

"You mean a pig?" Jane corrected him.

"Nah. A goat," Monroe said with a wink toward Jane.

Jane wasn't sure what to make of the goat comment but let it go. She let him know that she reviewed the remaining numbered postcards Gabe sent him and that she would take them with her and then return them.

"They belong to you and Harlan," he said with precision. "That's who Gabe meant them for."

"I talked to a woman who received a postcard from Gabe before he left the company. It was a photo of tribal children from the Congo. Why would he send her that card?"

His interest showed. "Not sure. I think as he started to see more shit he didn't agree with he wanted to expose it but he knew he couldn't. So, maybe sending the postcards to the woman was his way of getting the info out there and off his chest." He pretended to appear more casual than he was truly feeling. "Which woman are we talking about?"

"Nanette Larson."

"Humph. Okay." Suddenly, he became taciturn.

"'Humph. Okay?' What does that mean?"

"Nothing."

"Bullshit."

"Drop it," he said with a sudden edge. "Gabe made it clear that nobody crossed the line into his personal life. With him, there were places you didn't go." He reclined on the chair, drawing one of his rifles closer to him. "There were dark holes and regrets that he built steel walls around. I think it had to do with love and family." He caught himself. "Shit. I've said too much already."

Jane observed Monroe and the way he fidgeted nervously with his rifle. It was obvious to her that he was about to split again. While his mind decided which personality to call up next, she decided to use his transitioning time to get cogent information. "He had a girlfriend, didn't he? *More* than just a girlfriend, in fact."

"I never said that."

Jane sank back into her recliner. "Sure you did," she said off handedly.

He turned toward her sharply. "I *never* said a word about Marion."

Jane smiled and glanced his direction. "Until right then."

Monroe bit down on his lip. "*Fuck.* I lost Situational Awareness again. Shit! This is why they keep me behind the computer and out of the main theater."

The mysterious "M" in Harlan's notebook now had a full name. "You know Marion?"

He sat up and draped his legs over the chair. "Drop it, Jane!"

She observed him again and rested her head against the back of the chair. "Interesting. She's very special, isn't she?"

"I mean it!" His voice sounded manic. "Stop it!" He began rocking back and forth. "Please. I'm not kidding. This is not funny."

"Okay, okay," she said, holding her hand in the air. "It's dropped." She watched him and waited for the next inhabitant to take him over. Within seconds, his visage altered and he had the appearance of a square jawed, tough army grunt. She pulled her leather satchel toward her, along with the burlap bag and the black notebook. "I need you to look through this bag and notebook for me. See if you pick up on anything important with your keen military eye."

Monroe spilled the contents of the burlap bag onto the floor of the porch. He laid them out in a straight line and stared at them. Picking up the bottle of sandalwood oil, he opened it and gave it a good sniff before putting a drop of it on his arm and massaging it in. He lifted up the *Yogi* book and smiled. "This guy was intriguing."

"You've read it?"

He nodded. "That's affirmative. Gabe gave me a copy. He talks about the spiritual mind. He who controls the mind, controls everything. You give away your mind, and you become nothing but a pawn for them to play with." He picked up the Easter card with the Angel Gabriel. "Now, that is a good one, Gabe. Nicely done."

Jane watched him peruse the items one by one. There were no questions about why Harlan collected all of this or whether Jane was "imagining" it meant something. There was just pure acceptance and for the first time since her journey began, she didn't feel crazy. The irony didn't escape her that a crazy guy helped her feel normal. Right at that moment, she didn't care what alter was operating inside the poor man. "Thank you," she softly said.

He looked up at her. "For what?"

"For believing me. You have no clue what that means to me."

"You're welcome." He continued looking at the items. "You know, that's how they keep their power, Jane. What they do is so mind-boggling and improbable that you'd have to be crazy to believe it's really happening. And yet? It's going on right now, somewhere in this world. Somebody is being sacrificed so someone else can prosper." He picked up the pinecone and the bag of pine nuts. "Redundancy. It's like code. You look for stuff like that." He regarded the pinecone as if it were a skull in a lab setting.

"Gabe would only drink pine needle beer, imported from Scotland."

"Another sync. So what does a pinecone mean? Pine nuts? Pine beer? They're just symbols that represent something else. But it's the power we give to those symbols that makes them so compelling." He lifted up the lapis stone with the Eye of Horus engraved in gold paint and stuck it up to his eye, giving him a very distorted visage. "It's repetitive."

"What do you mean?"

"Something about this bag of stuff is repeating itself." He slid *The Q* magazine out of the way, along with the Easter card. He focused on the key and set that to the side. Picking up the Eco-Goddesses brochure and Blue Heron card, he tossed them to the side, followed by the Patsy Cline tape. But then he retrieved the cassette and placed it next to the pinecone, pine nuts and lapis. Staring at the tiny bottle of sandalwood oil, he gently set it next to the pinecone. Finally, he laid the *Yogi* book next to the pine nuts. "The pinecone pile is a repetitive code. Yeah, yeah, okay, he's being repetitive for a reason. That's how Gabe operated. When he was explaining something to me, he'd tell it to me three different ways with three different analogies. Eventually, it made sense. I think that's what you have here." He opened the notebook and flipped through the pages.

"See anything in there that stands out?"

Monroe turned the pages. He came up on the page that was filled with the number seventeen and the number thirty-three below it, both with a single accent mark after the number. "Humph."

Knowing

"I met a nurse from the hospital where Harlan was in recovery after his surgery. She had a tat on her wrist of a dove and "17:33" underneath it. But I can't believe that she was a big enough player in this to earn a whole page in that damn notebook."

Monroe stared at the page as if he were deciphering the most complex computer code. "Like I said, Gabe often told the same story more than one way. If you take off the accent marks, you could read it this way. Gabe was born on the seventeenth of February and he died when he was thirty-three."

"Maybe it's a time code? There's gotta be a reason why Harlan wrote it like a fraction without the line between them."

"No, you wouldn't write a time code like that."

"Seventeen has been popping up a lot. You have any idea why that is?"

"There are a lot of numbers and sequences that come up all the time. And while it's true that math holds the hidden code of our world, I'm not sure every single one of them has a sinister meaning."

"Maybe it's not sinister. Maybe it's just trying to lead me somewhere. That sequence has to mean something or I wouldn't have found that nurse with the tattoo."

"Right. Because every single thing you've done has been predestined."

"I didn't say that."

He continued to peruse the book. "It's scary, isn't it? Understanding that you have no control over your life and the way it plays out."

"You do have control. You just have to take it."

He smiled. "Control is a complete illusion, Jane. Unless you're like Romulus and believe you're a god."

She hesitated before speaking. "You let Romulus control you."

He looked up from the book. "You're right. But Gabe never allowed it."

"Gabe's dead. They won."

He turned around to make sure Harlan was nowhere in earshot. "As long as Harlan is alive, Gabe is also alive."

"You think that's what Gabe wanted? Really? Living out the rest of his 'life' in someone else's body?"

"For awhile…Yeah."

"You mean, until they kill Harlan."

"I mean…until Gabe decides it's time to abandon his host."

Jane's head spun. "Wait, what?"

292

"When the journey is over, there's no need to keep driving the bus." The notebook slipped out of his hands, opening to the center and the page with the single "IEB."

Jane was still trying to sort through Monroe's logic regarding Harlan's possible demise. "You have any idea what 'IEB' stands for?"

He shook his head. "It doesn't match anything I've run into." He turned suddenly, grabbing his rifle and pistol. "What was that?"

"I didn't hear anything," she said, scooting down on the recliner. "Listen, back to what you were—"

He motioned for her to be still and stay quiet as they sat there with the spring wind blowing through the screen. As hard as she tried, Jane couldn't sense anything that was off. She turned to Monroe. He had his pistol raised to the side of his head with the butt pointed toward the roof. And in that second, she recalled her odd vision where she saw the blurred image of the man with the gun by his head. *Stolen.* That's the word she came up with then and now she understood it. He didn't own his own perceptions because all those horrific years had robbed him of his ability to see clearly. His observations and reactions were now tainted with the stain of so much trauma that a sound of a water droplet against a pipe became a reverberating echo that triggered an over reaction.

Hyper-vigilance. Jane had danced with that beast many times, beginning when she was a young girl. It's waiting for the other shoe to drop and wondering if it will be a slipper or a boot. It's coming up with five different exit strategies in the space of four seconds. It's taking "What if?" to levels that defy rational thinking. It's learning how to take shallow breaths, because inhaling too much air will create an explosion where all the pieces of your shattered life will be tossed into the wind and scattered for miles. It's the ultimate control game and the one who chooses to play it, is always the loser. But no matter how many times the cycle spins, the one in the hot seat always forgets that most times, whatever one fears usually doesn't happen. But that doesn't matter because it means that the odds of something really big happening the next time are increased. And so it goes. The waiting, the measured relief and the anticipation of the next blow.

Jane had done that a million times and because of it, she could easily see the shared suffering in similar individuals. Eyes would connect across a crowded room and while the two of them might never say a word to each other, the dialogue of suffering was present and connected them. It was always in the eyes—the windows to the soul. Through the orbs, Jane sourced her comrades, even if they were wearing veils of deception. It was why she loved to see comic actors play serious roles. That was the only way she could see the brutal pain in the actor's eyes that first molded him and forced him into the role of a funny man so he could escape the brutality. It was that uncut, almost too-hard-to-look-at torture that grabbed her and made her not want to turn away. The recognition was a shared secret between the two of them and every time she watched one of the comedic movies in a darkened theater, she was aware that no one else in that room truly comprehended the depths of despair that was required to pull off the role.

There are scars that can't be physically seen. There are wounds that never bleed. Jane determined that in this life, one's path could be delineated down to two factors. One is the kind of trauma you experience. The second is how you choose to deal with that trauma. Those two factors had charted Jane's course and colored the palette that had framed her life. She'd learned that when the trauma doesn't own you, it can't control you. But being able to unhook your psyche from the oily memories of darker days is a rare gift that isn't bestowed on many. Looking over at Monroe, waiting like a spaniel on point for the mysterious sound to manifest that only he could hear, she recognized a kindred spirit. He wasn't even thirty years old but the damage that had been done to him would take several lifetimes to undo. And sadly, whoever he really was on that day when he was plucked out of college and recruited into Romulus was long buried under layers of PsyOps, trauma-induced schizophrenia.

He was done for the night. He detached himself from the conversation as his mind roamed the dirty corners where the monsters hide. Monroe slowly worked his body back onto the recliner and, rifle by his side and pistol at the ready, he closed his eyes and fell asleep. Jane quietly collected the envelope, sliding it into her leather satchel and replaced the items into Harlan's bag. After gently removing the black notebook from underneath Monroe's recliner, Jane sunk into her chair. Pulling the blanket over her body, she willed herself to sleep.

When she stirred the next morning, she heard the lyrical tweet of sparrows welcoming the new day. Opening her eyes, she saw Monroe standing up, facing the screen and the rising sun. She watched him tilt his head backward and draw in a deep breath. Then, with eyes wide open, he looked directly into the golden light that spilled up and over the distant low-lying hills. In a voice almost impossible to hear, he repeated the prayer that Harlan chanted whenever he was in trouble. "I will face the darkness, but I will not let it become me. Fear may be present but it will not possess me. I will face the darkness, as the knowing light within my heart and mind leads me home. And once again, I will be free." He held his focus of the morning light, only blinking twice.

"Hey," Jane said softly so as not to startle him.

"Hey," he replied, never taking his wide eyes off the rising sun.

"Aren't you afraid of burning your cornea?"

"No," he whispered, as if speaking too loudly would ruin the moment. He continued to stare. "The first light of the day and the last light are safe to gaze into. Gabe taught me how to do it. He said the Egyptians did it. Books will tell you that they worshipped the sun. But that wasn't exactly true. They'd bend their heads upward at sunrise and sunset to receive the energy and reboot their mind's eye. They knew a lot more than history books like to talk about. Ancient knowledge is sacred and only those who have the understanding or the ability to convert the knowledge into substance are allowed to discuss it and teach it."

"Gabe told you that?" she whispered.

He closed his eyes and after a few seconds, turned to Jane. "You don't throw pearls before swine. You don't try to educate somebody who is stupid or shallow because they'll never get it, even when they are surrounded by it. You only put your energy into the people who can make a difference." He turned back to the sun. "You noticed that the sun is whiter these days?"

It appeared to Jane that whatever character was inhabiting him at that moment was pretty mellow and forthcoming. "Whiter?"

"I talked to a guy who was in his 70s and he told me the sun used to be warmer. Have more of a yellowish, golden glow. Now it's like white lightening. Stark. I told him I think it's because back in the day, we remember everything in a warm wonderful glow and now we're starting to see the stark reality of our collective situation." He looked at Jane. "It's as if the sun is sending us a message."

A thought crossed her mind. She located the greeting card that protected Gabe's photo and held it out to Monroe. "Check this out, would you?"

He took the card and opened it. "Wow," he smiled, pointing to the radiating gem in the center of the Pharaoh's elongated head. "Ajna!"

"What's that mean?"

"No, no. That's what you call this." He pointed to the gemstone.

Knowing

"The jewel is called an Ajna?"

"No, no!" he said with impatience. "The point where it's located. Right here," he touched his index finger to the middle of his forehead.

Jane felt a sudden jolt. While it wasn't identical, the movement of Monroe's finger to his forehead was similar to the old man in her vision. "Ajna…" Diving into her satchel, she withdrew Harlan's notebook and nervously flipped through the pages until she found the one. The word, "Agna" stood out in the center of the page. Jane had interpreted Harlan's poorly written "j" for a "g." She poked her finger on the page. "Look at that! It's right there."

Monroe grinned. "Yep. Sure is." Opening the card, Gabe's photo dropped out. He retrieved it and sadly stared at his friend's face before reading the inscription.

"That photo was taken when he left on his three-year journey. And that's part of the prayer that Harlan repeats."

Monroe's face softened. "He said he was given that prayer by a medicine man he met. It was a prayer of protection from evil to be said aloud whenever you were in danger or when you were about to die. It was thought to free one's heart so that if you perished, your heart had already gone ahead to find your soul's place in heaven."

They heard a tap-tap at the door. Monroe suddenly jumped to attention as Harlan waved at both of them before sleepily retreating into the bathroom.

"It's just Harlan. It's okay."

"That's affirmative!" His voice strangely changed, along with his facial expressions.

"At ease, soldier."

Monroe relaxed and turned to Jane. "I know who he is, ma'am." He glanced at the photo envelope in Jane's satchel. "And it all makes sense now why they framed him like they did." He looked at Jane. "He was found in bed with a black woman whose head was smashed open with her brains coming out."

Jane couldn't believe she didn't make that connection. "Shit. You're right!"

"That's what they call 'humor' and the rest of us call 'fucked up.' That's a signature—"

"Yeah, yeah. I know, I know. I think it also means there's a solid link between Harlan's framing for the murder and whatever those photos are connected to."

"Same meme. Yes. I'd concur on that."

Jane wasn't sure which one of Monroe's alter personalities would show up next but the vibe was getting *über* militaristic. Before he revved it up and told her to drop and do ten, she figured it was time to exit the location. Excusing herself, Jane gathered everything and packed the van. She took a quick shower and changed into a pair of black jeans and a light blue turtleneck. When she returned to the porch with Harlan, Monroe was standing guard at the door with his rifle cradled in his arms.

"Thank you for letting us stay here, Monroe," Jane offered.

"My pleasure, ma'am," he said, spinning around on his heels and saluting her. "You can stop by any time." He swung open the screen door, holding it open for them.

Jane and Harlan walked to the van and Harlan got inside. After closing the side door, Jane turned back to Monroe. "Hey, I meant to ask you. Do you know the name of the medicine man that Gabe talked to?"

"No, ma'am. Gabe just said he was the medicine man next to Haas."

Jane took two steps forward. "Next to *Haas*? What? What does that mean?"

"I'm telling you all I know, ma'am," he stated, staring straight ahead and never making eye contact with Jane.

"Wait a second, the name Haas is important. Haas is mentioned in an ad on page 17 of an old issue of the '*Q*' that I found. The ad referenced a hit on him. I need to know who he is and why Gabe would adopt his name."

"All forward!" Monroe yelled in a sharp, military bark. He clicked his heels together and readied his rifle.

As much as she wanted to pursue it, there was no way he could maintain any cohesive conversation at this point.

"Please take care of yourself," Jane quietly said to him.

"Yes, ma'am!" he replied, never making eye contact. "And may I offer you this: trust no one. Sometimes, you can't even trust yourself which can make life quite interesting."

She managed a weak smile and drove down the gravel road. When she reached the highway, she took one last look back. He was still standing there, like a frozen solider waiting for the sun to warm the battlefield before his next fight.

CHAPTER 21

Harlan located his anti-rejection drugs and popped his morning dose. "Well, that was different," he deadpanned.

"It's *all* different, Harlan."

"He's kind of a whack job, Jane."

"I know. But you'd be surprised how many 'whack jobs' have turned out to be my best sources over the years." She turned to Harlan who was already pleasantly ensconced in the back of the van. "The next time someone tells you hell doesn't exist, remember Monroe. That son-of-a-bitch will never be free."

Harlan thought long and hard about his time with Monroe. "What does *capisci* mean?

"It's Italian for 'do you understand'?"

"Is that so? Never heard the word until it left my lips."

She sunk her hand into her satchel and pulled out the postcards. Pulling the first one off the pile, she laid it on the dashboard. "Next stop, O'Rian Park."

They drove east and then north up the two-lane highway, past acres of farmland where the soil was waiting patiently for the first seeds to be sown. The spring air held the fragrance of renewal as thousands of weeds, grass, flowers and trees awakened once again and remembered their purpose. Jane turned on the radio and found only a few stations that weren't burdened by static. Vicki Lawrence's version of "The Night the Lights Went Out in Georgia" came on.

"Hey," Harlan chirped from the back of van, "don't move the dial. Would you please listen to the words of this song and tell me what the hell it's about?"

"Not now, Harlan."

"Can you explain it then?"

Jane listened to the words that she'd heard dozens of times over the years. After one minute, she was lost. "It's about revenge."

"Well, no joke, Jane. I know that 'little sister' gunned down her sister-in-law and 'that's one body that'll never be found' but I can't figure out the rest.

Who's that 'Amos boy Seth?' And why didn't Andy want to kill him first? I don't get it."

"Can we please focus on what's in front of us? Let it go. A lot of songs don't make any sense." She checked the side windows. "I still don't get why you chose 'Just in Time' back at that bar."

"*I* didn't chose it, Jane."

"Yeah, *he* did. I want to know why?"

"You want to know why and I say, 'why not?'"

The song ended and the top of the hour news began. "In local news, it was announced today that Colorado will be hosting three hundred very special guests from Scotland this year. But these visitors are four-legged critters and their new home will be acres of grassland in northeastern Colorado. So, don't be surprised when you're driving up in that part of our state and you see several hundred goats, happily chewing away to their heart's content."

Jane tuned out the rest of the news. It was far too much of a coincidence. That ground had to be the same grassland that was turned over to The Wöden Group and announced at the recently televised press conference. To anyone else, the news of three hundred goats meant nothing. If anything, the listeners probably smiled, relieved because three hundred goats was a better deal than another oil and gas rig eyesore. But something felt completely off to Jane. She was all too familiar with what information is released to the pubic and what is held back. It happened all the time during high profile murder cases in Denver. A rep from DH would stand at the microphone and appear to be forthcoming with details of the latest killing. But Jane would watch it and tick off the multitude of holes in the announcement. They always held information back but if the news conference was spun correctly, viewers would walk away believing they'd heard the whole story. From that, people would move into their day repeating the half-story to others and before long, it was an accepted "truth." Only the ones whose ears were trained to know how a murder case really rolls would recognize the gaping holes in the story that trains could slide through.

And that's exactly where Jane was at that moment—staring at the holes in the story about the happy goats eating grass in northeastern Colorado. Clearly aware of the power players who were involved in this acquisition, Jane found the story seriously troubling. But with nothing to link it to, all she could do now was file it away and hopefully bring it back up when the pieces fell together.

Knowing

Within less than half an hour and just shy of 9:30, Jane entered Helios, Colorado, a quaint town with a village ambiance. In the center of the main street was a beautifully designed roundabout with a manicured grassy center and a playful statue of children playing with a kite. Realizing that O'Rian Park shouldn't be hard to find, Jane swung the van down a street that paralleled Main Street and easily saw the park at the end of the road. It was a fairly large area for such a small town, and its mature landscaping and rolling grassy hills made it a desirable destination for families and others who wanted to bask in an architect's adaptation of nature. A ring of parking spaces, allowing easy entrance from any angle, encircled the park. In the far right hand corner was a baseball field that doubled as a T-ball field for youngsters. About twenty mothers congregated in the center of the park doing yoga while a group of toddlers and preschoolers played off to the side with a caregiver watching over them.

Harlan edged closer to the front of the van, supporting himself against the back of the passenger seat. "Drive around the park, would you?"

His voice sounded different to Jane. "What's going on?"

"I've never felt anything like this before," he said, in reverie. He flattened his palm against his heart. "My heart…"

"What about your heart?" Jane asked with concern as she continued to troll the parking lot.

"It's bursting, Jane." He moved closer to the front.

"Hey, hey, hey! You can't do that. Come on!" She looked at him and all she saw was a man with a purpose. "Talk to me, Harlan. What is it?"

He waited, his eyes constantly focused on the women in the center of the park. "This is real, Jane. This is *too* real." He slumped behind the passenger seat.

Jane braked quickly and put the van in park. She spun around. "You okay?"

He held his heart with his huge palm. "I can't explain it, Jane. I've never felt this kind of…"

"This kind of *what*?"

"Love…" He seemed unable to rectify his emotions. Lifting his large frame up, he looked outside the window. "Keep drivin' around, would ya?"

Jane obliged. As they moved closer to where the women could be seen better, Harlan told her to stop the van and park it. She agreed and stared at the yoga group, scanning them for anything that stood out to her. Seven of the women were pregnant, six were over the age of seventy and four were in their teens. "Seventeen," Jane said. She was so focused on dissecting the scene that she didn't hear Harlan open the side door of the van. It wasn't until his feet were planted on the ground that she turned. "Oh, shit! Harlan!" she yelled with an urgent stage whisper. "No, no, no!" She struggled with her seatbelt and that gave Harlan just enough time to move onto the grass and start toward a large stand of towering aspen trees that formed a small grove.

Freeing herself from the seatbelt, she rushed out of the van and stopped quickly, not wanting to attract attention. She could vaguely see Harlan in the grove, which gave her momentary solace that he wasn't standing out like a sore thumb. Moving toward the trees in a pseudo casual manner, Jane stood near him. She looked at him and saw a visage that didn't belong to Harlan. Within that short walk, he'd been transformed. And although she couldn't be certain, she felt as if she was standing next to someone else.

"We can't be out like this," Jane whispered to him. "Come on."

He didn't budge. "We came here for a reason, Jane."

"I know, but I can't risk anyone—" she saw the yoga group break up and collectively roll up their mats.

Harlan drew in his breath quickly and grabbed his chest.

"What?" Jane tensely asked. "You having a heart attack?"

He was unable to speak and simply replied to her with a shake of his head.

Jane turned back to the yoga class. A brown-haired woman in her late thirties broke away from the group, carrying a mat under her arm. She appeared to be about eight months pregnant. She waved at a pickup truck that was just pulling into the park and carried an eager Australian Shepherd in the bed. A man who looked about forty got out of the pickup with a frisbee and let the dog out of the bed. The dog happily ran toward the woman who greeted it with a warm welcome. As the man sauntered toward her, she smiled and gave him a quick kiss on the lips before motioning that she would be right back. She headed in their direction, walking up the slight incline and past the grove, retrieving her car keys from a side pocket in her yoga pants. Harlan watched every second of every motion she made. The woman opened her car door, a modest Toyota Corolla, tossed in the yoga mat and locked the door. Walking back into the park, she stood just outside the aspen grove and searched for her partner and their dog.

Harlan moved toward the edge of the grove, his eyes focused so intently on the woman that Jane thought he would never emerge from it. Jane gingerly crept behind a trio of aspens and observed the scene. There was nothing else to do now except wait and watch it play out. She watched the woman cautiously. Now that she was closer, Jane could see her much better. She wore a simply wedding band and no other jewelry. There was a calm and kind light around her that was intoxicating. When she moved, she walked with gentle steps and a tender spirit. And somehow, she was familiar to Jane. With that realization, a pungent perfume of roses enveloped her senses. She was catapulted briefly back into the vision she had when she held Harlan's hand back at the tiny cabin. Jane recalled inhaling the same fragrance as she stood inside a small house with lots of windows that allowed the breeze to waft through. She remembered the sound of a man and woman whispering and kissing in another room and the sense that the love they were making was of the highest expression. Turning back to the woman on the periphery of the aspen grove, she somehow knew in her heart this was the woman on the other side of the wall in that house. She was Marion.

As if Jane's mind sent that sudden recognition out into the park, Marion turned and peered into the grove. Without one bit of fear, she seemed to know and she took several steps toward the trees. Jane swallowed hard and waited. Harlan never moved a muscle but kept his eyes lovingly focused on her. With one hand cupped on her protruding belly, she took several steps closer and met Harlan's eyes.

Harlan began to hum so quietly at first that it was nearly imperceptible. But as he continued, Jane recognized the tune. "Just in Time." She thought he was singing it to her back at the karaoke bar. How foolish could she be? she told herself. Marion walked into the grove, shaded by the towering branches and catkins that hung from the buds. Her eyes filled with tears as she stood there fixated. She turned briefly to Jane, her hazel eyes acknowledging her, and then returned her heart's focus to Harlan. Still holding her belly with one hand, the tears rolled down her cheeks as she reached out to Harlan, brushing her fingers against his cheek. Her hand drifted to his heart where she rested her hand, pressing it lightly into his body. She closed her eyes and smiled as tears continued to fall and drift down her face. Opening her eyes, she took a deep breath.

"I've been waiting for this day," she whispered to him, her hand never moving from his heart. "I still have the note you gave me. It's tucked away where only I can find it. 'Til our hearts meet again, you'll know me in the strangest of faces.'" Marion managed a sad smile.

Harlan's eyes swelled with tears as he placed his hand over hers. "Thank you."

"Marion?" the voice called out from the park.

She didn't seem to hear it. Jane stepped forward.

"You have to go," Jane whispered.

Marion didn't move.

"Marion?" Jane said, seeing her husband and their dog start up the incline toward the aspen grove. "You have to leave now. Please!"

Marion stepped back, never taking her eyes off Harlan. She touched her heart as if to say "goodbye" and walked down into the park to meet her husband.

Harlan immediately collapsed on the ground, sobbing uncontrollably. Jane quickly walked behind him, crouching down and wrapping her arm around his shoulder.

"I've never felt anything like that in my whole life," Harlan cried. "*Never*. That's more than love. I can't even put it into words. It's like seein' yourself in another person's eyes and knowin' you've found the missin' piece." He got hold of himself. "Have you ever felt that, Jane?"

She wiped away a tear that appeared out of nowhere. "I don't know."

He turned to her. "You'd know it if you did."

They waited until no one was around before returning to the van. They drove in silence for several miles, heading southwest toward the next destination. As her mind began to move back onto the case at hand, she chided herself for not bringing up the mysterious Werner Haas name to Monroe when he was somewhat able to respond in an intelligent manner. She pulled the van over to the side of the road and announced to Harlan that she was returning to Monroe's house with the idea of getting to the bottom of his "Haas" comment. Just as she started to pull the van away from the shoulder, she saw a police car in the far distance zooming up behind her with lights flashing.

"Shit," Jane whispered.

As the patrol car moved closer, she could hear the siren piercing the air. Scanning the area, she tried to come up with a suitable escape but fell short each time. The siren screamed with a harsh tenor. She looked into her side mirror and watched the black and white, powering toward her van. "Please, God, no," she whispered. Jane closed her eyes as if to block it out and felt the air shift as he burned rubber past the van and continued at breakneck speed down the highway. Letting out a sigh of relief, she stuck the key back into the ignition and then stopped again when she spied a fire truck barreling down the highway, with lights flashing and sirens blaring. That truck was joined by two more. As they passed her van, she started feeling ill and lightheaded. She turned the key and tore onto the highway, shadowing the fire trucks on their ten-mile rescue. When she crested the farthest hill, thick black smoke billowed into the bluebird sky. Two miles later, she slowed down. The patrol car, followed by the trio of fire trucks, turned onto Monroe's road and set up a perimeter around his burning house. Harlan crawled to the front of the van and took in the scene.

"Damn, Jane. You think he set it?"

She nervously checked out the surrounding area, recalling the ominous sight of Rudy calmly standing by his sedan as the *Anubus* blew up and watching the aftermath. "No, I don't." She checked her side mirror and spun the van around, blazing down the highway in the opposite direction.

"What does this mean, Jane?" Harlan asked nervously.

She stared straight ahead, silent.

"*Jane*! What's going on?" he said again with more firmness.

"I think they might be onto us."

"The cops?"

"No! Romulus!"

She drove like a demon, heading southwest. Harlan hung on for dear life.

"Jane! Slow it down, would you? We don't to attract unwanted attention."

Jane let up on the gas and slowed down to the speed limit. "He knew it was going to happen, Harlan. Remember? He kept saying he was so hot? He even said he felt like he was on fire." *What in the hell was that*, she thought. Precognitive sensations? Feeling the future before it happens? As much as Monroe did in his short life, he didn't deserve this kind of death. The poor guy probably only had nineteen or twenty years of somewhat normalcy before he got sucked into Romulus and destroyed forever. He'd been discarded because he was another liability. He was taken out in the same measured manner as when you set a mousetrap and then dispose of the dead mouse while you're chatting on the phone. It's a great approach unless you are the mouse and you trip that trap. Jane said a quiet prayer, asking God to watch over him. She drove for another two hours, staying off the main road.

Arriving back in the heart of the Sangre de Cristo mountain range, Jane turned onto none other than Highway 17 and headed north. Twenty miles later, she found a vacant rest area that had access to free Wi-Fi. Since they had the parking lot to themselves, Harlan got out of the van to stretch his legs and use the public restroom. Jane paced around the grassy islands, still shaking internally from the events of the past few hours. Instead of cogitating on the breathtaking experience between Harlan and Marion, Jane had to put that aside as thoughts of their safety moved to the forefront. Harlan came out of the bathroom and headed back into the van, keeping the side door open. He lay back, flipping through one of the Q magazines before drifting off to sleep.

As his snoring hit levels that could shatter glass, Jane scooped up her laptop and leather satchel, grabbed some lunchmeat and cheese and crossed to one of the nearby grassy islands. Seated under a tree, she typed "Ajna" into the search field. Choosing the first link, she read that, "According to the Hindu tradition, the Ajna is the sixth chakra. It is positioned in the brain, directly behind the eyebrow center and known as 'the mind's eye.' Its activation site is at the eyebrow region, in the position of the 'third eye.'" Scrolling down, Jane continued to read. "Ajna is also known as the 'eye of intuition.' But it is much more than that. It is considered the bridge between the various spiritual worlds as well as the point that, when activated, can link two people and allow them to communicate, no matter the distance." A quote at the bottom of the page read: "He who masters the power of the Ajna, masters his life through clarity of sight. He who masters clarity of sight, holds more power than all the riches of the world combined."

After grabbing a few pieces of meat and a slice of cheese, she brought out the greeting card with the Pharaoh picture on it. She typed in the quote at the bottom of the card and found that it was actually only a partial quote of a larger one: "The light of the body is the eye: if therefore thine eye be single, thy whole body shall be full of light. But if thine eye be evil, thy whole body shall be full of darkness. If therefore the light that is in thee be darkness, how great is that darkness!"

Thine eye be single, Jane focused on. She thought about the lapis stone with the single Eye of Horus. But to Jane, Ajnas and chakras were spiritual concepts with nothing physical to support their existence. She certainly didn't deny the power of intuition because she'd used it far too many times on the job. If there was something physical that was connected to this ethereal belief, it would lend more credibility to the idea. Without giving it any thought, she did a search for the "Physical third eye."

Strangely enough, there *was* a physical third eye and it was called the pineal gland. Jane clicked on the first link and sat back. At the top of the page, was a subsection of the brain, illustrating the location of the reddish-gray gland. The size of a pea, the pineal sits in the center of the brain between the two hemispheres. It's an endocrine gland responsible for melatonin production—the hormone that regulates sleep/wake cycles—and is recharged by sunlight. As important as that function is, the spiritual implications associated with the pineal gland were much more intriguing.

Jane scrolled down the page and took in a quick breath. "The word *pineal* comes from the word *pinea*, which means pinecone." And there was a photo of a perfect pinecone to drive home the visual shock.

The pinecone was apparently the "hidden symbol" that represented the pineal gland. Suddenly, it was starting to make strange sense. Monroe was right. Gabe was being redundant with the pinecone, pine nuts, the book and the Eye of Horus lapis but she couldn't make a pineal connection between the sandalwood oil and the Patsy Cline tape. A quick check discovered that sandalwood oil is rubbed on the "third eye" to activate intuition. That left only the odd cassette tape with the highlighted song, "If I Could See the World Through the Eyes of Child." She recalled how Monroe first set the tape to the side and then reconsidered. That told her that it might not be directly connected with the pineal but it was linked in some manner.

Reading further, Jane learned that esoteric and "mystery" schools throughout history venerated this tiny but powerful gland, calling it "the seat of the soul" and "the eye of God." Philosophers and students of mysticism waxed poetically about it. Plato stated in *The Republic* (Book 7) "the soul…has an organ purified and enlightened, an organ better worth saving than ten thousand corporeal eyes, since truth becomes visible through this alone." Rene Descartes taught that we had a body and a soul and that the soul functioned in "the innermost part of the brain." The pineal gland appears in the human embryo around forty-nine days of gestation. This was the exact number of days the Tibetans believed was required for one's soul to incarnate into their next body. Jane discovered another pineal reference in the Bible that was startling. While open to interpretation, in Genesis 32:30, there was the line, "And Jacob called the name of the place *Peniel*: for I have seen God face to face, and my life is preserved."

Jane learned more information from a website that featured chapters from an Indian spiritual book. When one spiritually "awakened" the pineal gland, it was thought to bring about mastery over the mundane life, elevating one into a realm that few people know exists. Reading further, it sounded like a club with a handful of members who had the ability to see what others could not, to delve into the cosmos with precision and return with higher knowledge that could change the course of human history. Maintaining activation of the pineal, Jane learned, is thought to confer "eternal youthfulness" since it works in harmony with the hypothalamus and our biological clock that helps determine the aging process. On the bottom of the website page, there was a quote from "The Sleeping Prophet," Edgar Cayce that caught Jane's attention. "Keep the pineal gland operating and you won't grow old — you will always be young."

And it appeared that youth had the advantage when it came to this mysterious gland. Up until of the age of six, it was believed that the pineal functioned without interference, allowing a child to "see" and know things that others could not. But something strange happened at the age of six. The gland began to calcify, growing a crust around it that eventually blocked its function completely. Thus, after age six, the silver cord between the worlds was cut with no access to one's spiritual source. However, Jane read, "There were those who were able to keep the pineal operating after age six and well into their older years through deep meditation. These rare people were known as Masters of their Destiny."

Jane learned that, during meditation, their trigger mechanism for pineal activation was a piercing point of blue/indigo light that often physically appeared as a single illumined dot in one's line of sight. Known by some as "the blue pearl," seeing it was acknowledgment that the pineal had been "turned on." Jane suddenly made the startling connection between what Harlan called the "blue light special" that he experienced before he scribbled in his notebook. And yes, she saw that same point of blue light when she held Harlan's hand that night. It was overwhelming to her—to have this otherworldly experience *first* and then read later about a specific element she'd seen in that vision. The confirmation was staggering. As much as she'd tried her best to push away the incredulous nature of this case, there was always a part of her that needed verification that what she was feeling and seeing was genuine and not some delayed flashback from her youth or a lingering side effect of PTSD.

She continued to locate page after page of information on the pineal gland. This "bridge between the worlds," was apparently a major player at the time of death. The theory was that upon death or in near-death experiences, the pineal gland excreted a huge amount of a chemical known as *Dimethyltryptamine* or DMT. Some scientists who studied DMT theorized that it was responsible for the blast of blinding light that people mention who have died and come back to life. Within that light, one progressive theologian wrote, was "the light of God" and the ability to become one with "the source." To travel into that rarified sphere and commune with the angels was the gift everyone received upon their exit from this life.

But the light wasn't an idea born out of someone's imagination. Information had been collected from hundreds of people who had been clinically dead. Many of them reported seeing an enormous flash of bright white light upon the tremor of death. But none of them feared it. In fact, they bathed in it and even mentioned a "loving voice" that communicated with them without words. When asked how they conversed, the answer was always the same: "With my mind's eye."

Another article postulated that when a person has a near death experience brought on by a terrorizing act, such as an attempted murder, the blast of DMT into the pineal gland is overpowering. It was, Jane figured, as if the terror that preceded it needed to be cushioned and blanketed to absorb the shock when the soul re-entered the body. Whatever the source or trigger, it was clear to Jane that DMT was a powerful chemical that the pineal gland was programmed to consistently produce on cue.

Finishing the meat and cheese, she sat back, scanning the desolate highway. From what she could ascertain, three themes were at work: death, connection with "a God source" and regeneration. But there seemed to be a concerted effort to keep this information out of the mainstream. There certainly wasn't a lot of media coverage about this pea-sized gland, where the masses were alerted to its potential power. Except for exploitive entertainment that is easily dismissed, there were no talk shows that seriously discussed how to harness one's intuitive talents, activate the mind's eye or how to project oneself into five dimensional reality. That kind of instruction was left to the Saturday evening soirees or "salons" where men with jeweled turbans lead small groups through meditations. But for most of this world, it was a well-kept secret. And she understood why that had to be. As Monroe so deftly said, "Ancient knowledge is sacred and only those who have the understanding or the ability to convert the knowledge into substance are allowed to discuss it and teach it." That was followed up by his remark that you don't waste your time on those who can't begin to comprehend the complexities and profound possibilities. It was casting "pearls before swine." She realized he was probably talking about the manner in which Romulus looked at the populace. Glaring down at us from their gilded palace, Jane envisioned them separating the cream from everyone's jar, leaving a watery, opaque film that never satisfied. If we were to them as Monroe suggested—just links in a chain that were easily manipulated, molded and controlled—it made sense that this kind of secreted wisdom was removed from the mainstream consciousness. Furthermore, Jane surmised that to release that kind of knowledge on a grand scale could easily compromise Romulus' agendas. As she'd been told, they hated spontaneity. And a populace that was awakened and aware of their vast individual potential was not an asset. To Romulus, it was the greatest danger they could ever imagine.

Jane returned to her computer and continued to research the pineal gland. But when she searched for images, she was staggered by what she found. There seemed to be an oddly frequent addition of a pinecone motif within sacred or religious settings that spanned the centuries. A staff of the Egyptian sun god Osiris had two "kundalini serpents" that entwine and face a pinecone at the top. The Greek God Dionysus is also depicted carrying a staff with a pinecone at the tip. Many Roman Catholic architectural designs, especially in sacred settings, incorporated a pinecone in their motif. The Pope carries a staff with a pinecone directly above where his hand is positioned. And if that isn't enough, the largest pinecone sculpture in the world is featured in Vatican Square in where else but the "Court of the Pinecone." Researching further, pinecone images had been featured for centuries in rugs, clay pots, paintings and other artistic pieces in ways that suggested the artist placed it there *deliberately* to symbolize the pinnacle of wisdom. For anyone "in the know" who understood the spiritual code, the recognition of the symbol was always a quiet reminder of their secret knowledge. Power had to be contained in order for it to be controlled by a few. And in case any of them forgot, there was a language of visual reminders that harkened back to the knowledge they so desperately guarded. He who held the key to the ultimate knowledge of our universe would triumph beyond everyone else. And through that triumph, immortality would be guaranteed through the bloodline that protected their secrets.

Jane sat back, feeling the bark of the tree dig into her spine. She thought about the photos she found in Monroe's hiding place. Since she'd given up believing in coincidences, she felt there had to be some kind of significance. After all, besides her, Monroe only showed the photos to Gabriel. And then Gabriel sent that curious postcard to Nanette featuring children from the

Congo. Coupled with the way in which Harlan was set up with the slaughtered prostitute, then taking into consideration the symbolic meme of the pinecone, et al in his burlap bag that directed her to the pineal gland, Jane had no choice but to link them together. The minute her mind agreed to that concept, she flashed on two sentences she'd just read about the pineal gland being open and receptive in children between birth and age six. She then remembered Monroe's observation when he looked at the bodies of the slaughtered elders in the Congo village and how they were heaped together. The children, however, had been laid out carefully and photographed with clean surgical cuts into their cranium and their brains removed. Jane couldn't believe what she was beginning to formulate. It was like nothing she'd ever encountered in her often-grisly career. She'd met her fair share of psychopaths who sliced and diced their victims with no remorse. She even remembered a guy they nicknamed "Carl the Cannibal" who killed his wife, then sliced her open and dined on her organs before calling 9-1-1. But Carl and the other nutcases had no other agenda to their insanity except temporary malevolent depravity.

But this case? This felt strategized and planned with an obvious nefarious intent. And then, as if this nightmare was coalescing in a bloody pool of terror, she recalled another passage from the article that referred to DMT and the moment of death. The theory held that if someone died during sustained trauma, their pineal gland swelled with DMT and then released it at the moment of death. It was just like the deer that's shot by the hunter and keeps running, releasing its "fear" into its flesh until it drops dead. The only difference Jane could deduce was that the flood of DMT could be seen by some people as a powerfully "positive" phenomenon. However, exactly how they could exploit it was still unknown to her.

She turned off her computer and let out a deep breath. Harlan was still snoring loudly in the back of the van. But she was able to tune it out as she took in the surrounding area. Jane noted a bronze plaque fastened to a nearby rock with an inscription that explained the section of road in front of her was a "memorial highway" dedicated to a fallen police officer. Every time she saw a memorial highway, she thought the same damn thing. It's quite the honor but it's got a Catch-22—you have to die for it to happen. It was just like people who were considered ahead of their time. Nobody really appreciated their contributions until after they were dead. She was still ruminating on these digressions when she turned to her left and saw a black sedan inch onto the shoulder of the highway, about five hundred feet from the parking area.

Immediately, her antenna went up. They were sitting ducks at that moment, with one way in and one way out. While she couldn't be sure if the driver of the black sedan had nefarious intentions, she wasn't about to be caught unaware. Without making a scene, Jane casually got up and stretched, yawning to enhance the laid back appearance. If she was being watched with high-powered binoculars, she wanted to generate the sense that she was unaware. Crossing to the van, she sauntered to the open side door, which couldn't be seen from the sedan's point of view, and quickly slammed it shut. Circling back to the driver's seat, she caught a glimpse of the sedan rolling off the shoulder and back onto the highway. She swung her ass into the driver's seat and secured her seatbelt, alerting Harlan to wake up and buckle in.

Her heart beat like a bongo as she backed out of the parking lot and started toward the exit. The sedan moved closer. That's when she saw the blackened windows. It never attempted to pull into the lot, but rather, trolled closer staying in the right lane the entire time. The sedan moved well within eyesight of Jane in the driver's seat.

Without moving her lips, she spoke to Harlan. "Get...back..." Inch by inch, she reached into her satchel and removed the 9mm.

Harlan's breathing became rapid. "Damn, Jane. I sure don't like this one bit."

"Really?" she said with a sarcastic tenor. "I love feeling as if I'm about to die."

The sedan slowed but never came to a halt. And then, as if the driver received an urgent call, the darkened vehicle spit gravel from its rear tires and charged up the highway. Jane kept the pistol close by and turned left, adjusting her driver's side mirror and keeping her eyes peeled for any action coming up behind her. After twenty-five miles and no sign of the sedan anywhere, she calmed down enough to quit the shallow breathing and take in a deeper gulp of air.

"You think that was them?" Harlan asked her, wiping sweat beads of fear from his forehead.

"I'm not sure. I don't know whether my paranoia is getting the better of me or not." She turned on the radio in an attempt to find a station that would take her mind off the gravity of her situation. It was the top of the hour and just in time for the local news program.

"We have breaking news to report in Colorado. Sources tell us there was a three-alarm fire at an abandoned residence outside of Sheldon Springs.

Knowing

Authorities are reporting that alleged killer and fugitive, Harlan Kipple, was killed in the blaze."

Harlan lurched forward, grabbing the back of Jane's seat. "What the hell? Jane, what's goin' on?!"

The reporter continued. "Sources report to us that it appears he traveled to Sheldon Springs and barricaded himself in this vacant structure. For reasons we do not know yet, we are told he booby-trapped the shelter with explosives and apparently set those off this morning, creating a massive explosion that was felt several miles away. Mr. Kipple's body was burned beyond recognition."

"Tell me I'm dreamin', Jane. Please, tell me I'm dreamin'."

"It's not a dream, Harlan. It's a fucking nightmare."

CHAPTER 22

She turned the channel and found another station reporting the same bogus story. That station featured an interview with a local police chief who wasn't on the scene but was relaying information to reporters.

"It's always tragic when someone feels the need to self-destruct in such a violent manner. Our prayers go out to the family of Jaycee Cross and we hope this incident gives them some closure in the death of their loved one. Unfortunately, we'll never know why Mr. Kipple chose to do what he did. I know we've spent nearly one week stretching our resources to locate and apprehend Mr. Kipple and we are sorry it had to end in this violent manner. However, I want to thank everyone for their dedication in working to stop Mr. Kipple from committing any more vicious crimes. I also want to add that while we will also never know Mr. Kipple's motive for the Dora Weller shooting, we can confirm that based upon video tape and cell phone coverage given to us, he did, in fact, act alone."

Harlan swallowed hard. "They're takin' you off their hook, Jane."

"Yeah, well, I'm already dead. Remember?"

"Then how come they even brought up an accomplice in the first place?"

"Plan B. You always keep something in your back pocket just in case you need it for leverage. They've obviously got their plan in place now and they don't need me to resurface in order for them to carry it out." She turned off the radio.

"So…what does this mean?" His voice was laced with terror.

"They called you dead before you actually died," she said shaking. "It's what they do. It's like a formality or a ritual. They did it to Gabriel. When he left Romulus, that was the day everybody in the company believed he was killed."

"Hang on, hang on! If the *cops* think I'm dead, then that means I can't *ever* come back to my life! Is that right?"

She understood the implications. "Yes," she softly replied.

Knowing

He pushed himself forward, resting on the front center console. "*Jane*? What does that mean? Where am I supposed to go? How can I make a livin'?

She gripped the wheel tighter. "You don't."

Harlan looked at her, his eyes getting wider with each stunning realization. "So, I was right. I *am* a dead man, ain't I? I've always been a dead man since this started. I bet from the minute they stuck his heart in me, they've been plottin' my finish."

She suddenly felt an understanding so strongly, she couldn't ignore it. "They know that you know," she said quietly.

Harlan was still reeling from the news report. "Huh? What?"

"Somehow, they know that you know."

"Know what?!"

"That you understand what's going on."

Harlan screwed his face into a ball. "But I *don't* know! I don't have a clue!"

She pulled the van over to the side of the road. "But I'm starting to, Harlan. I don't have everything figured out, but I don't think it's going to take much longer to sort it out."

"And then what?"

"We see where we are when that happens. If it's possible, we haul our asses back to Denver and we lay our cards on the table and see where it all falls."

He looked at her with sad eyes. "You didn't believe a word you just said."

He was right but Jane wasn't giving in. "Look, Gabe has given us a course to chart with those postcards. The next one is the CSA and—"

"No, we can't go there! We gotta get outta this state. Let's go to New Mexico. That's on Gabe's postcard list!"

"First off, they will find you anywhere we go. You can escape to an island in the South Pacific and they'll find you. And secondly, Gabe numbered the cards for a reason—"

"And one of the cards is missing. Come on, Jane! I can't hitch my future on a bunch of numbered postcards!"

She spun around to face him. "*Really*, Harlan?! You've been hitching your future for the past week on a burlap bag full of miscellaneous items and a black notebook with chicken scratch. And somehow, we've made progress! We're figuring this out!"

"*You* are figurin' it out. Not me."

"I...we...same thing." She gripped the wheel and stared into the blue, cloudless sky. "We're going to that CSA."

"I didn't think I could show my face, Jane."

She turned back to him. "You're dead. They killed you. You're free now."

He regarded her with a mixture of gratitude and fear. Opening the side door of the van, he got out, slid it shut and opened the passenger door before wedging his large posterior in the front seat.

"How does the view look from freedom?" she asked.

Harlan glanced around. "I like it, Jane," he offered with a shy smile. "But I still don't know how we're gonna convince people that I'm not Harlan Kipple."

"You've got that fake ID, remember? Hartley Llewellyn is your name."

"But my head ain't shaved in that ID photo."

"Photos change. You can manufacture a good excuse for just about anything. Look, they are already building your myth. We just capitalize on it." For the next few miles, she explained the "myth building" process she'd seen repeated over the years. Jane noticed a disconcerting "pageantry" that was born from any major news event that featured an alleged killer. It appeared to be second nature now and part of the news media approach that promoted a high profile story and embedded it into the collective consciousness. It was then transformed into a peculiar "entertainment" that the audience was trained to expect and loved to participate in. If the killer was given a clever title the public could sink their teeth into, all the better. "The Sixteenth Street Killer" or "The Smiling Rapist" propelled the suspect into an elevated stratosphere of macabre notoriety. No matter how viscerally disgusting the crime, the public needed to weigh in, if only to log onto an Internet forum and post their opinion on what should be done to the killer. Consider it a refined version of ancient gladiators with a cyber twist. As the old saying goes, "Opinions are like assholes—everybody's got one." And, over the many months, with their investment of time and energy, the public begins to feel oddly connected to the case, with some actually so involved that they become obsessed with the daily twists and turns. And yet, between urban legends, rumors, law enforcement "leaks," innuendo and outright lies, the killer's life and criminal aptitude were sometimes so ridiculously fabricated that Jane had to stop and remember that the truth she knew was nothing like the public's perception.

However, if the "pageant" ended on a sour note and the killer was taken down, the "myth builders" were brought in to tweak and propagate a convincing story that sounded realistic but usually suffered from the absence of the truth. As she'd commented many times before, the further you get away from the facts, the easier they can turn into a myth. It wasn't enough to have a short gun battle where the perp was immediately slain. No, now that he was dead, anything could be written or said about the individual to make the final moments of his life more gripping. Depending upon how the media and others wished to spin the story, stories could easily emerge that speciously referenced "tense moments" and "frantic negotiations" that never occurred. If necessary, artificial "heroes" would be concocted to feed the imagination of the captive public. If the suspect had been drawn as an extremely dangerous maniac, it wasn't outside the scope of reason to create a dramatic demise that buoyed the public's need for "justice" and "revenge." In this way, the greatest pageant of all—death—could be embraced by hungry viewers who needed to see visual proof that "the bad guy" was dead and that "goodness" had triumphed again. Including non-stop footage of the killer's last stand was always effective, whether it was a gun battle inside a structure, a standoff on a lone country road or a building ablaze in the middle of nowhere. The whole point, from Jane's point of view, was burning the perceived image of the killer into the mindset of the viewer. How that perception was handled, depended upon how well the myth sold.

Using the obvious mythical information she'd already heard on the radio regarding Harlan's alleged fiery demise, Jane could easily take it apart. How would a "fugitive on the run" be able to travel to Sheldon Springs with enough explosives in tow to rig an abandoned house so that the explosion was heard "several miles away?" Where did he buy these explosives? *How* would he buy them? He had no cash when he ran from the hospital. If he found them at the location, what were they doing there in an "abandoned house?" Who owned the structure? And no mention was made as to how Harlan even traveled to Sheldon Springs. Claiming that his body was "burned beyond recognition" was salient as it made it impossible to refute the findings. And furthermore, tying Harlan to Dora Weller's attempted assassination based upon a "belief" that he must have pulled the trigger because he was there at the time, didn't wash in Jane's world. As far as Jane read, there were no eyewitness testimonies that said they saw Harlan pull the gun that was used in the shooting. But none of these questions were important anymore. Harlan was now "dead" and "one more bad guy was in hell." She fully expected the myth builders to concoct a continuing fable that would effectively put to bed all the public's questions with reasonable answers that sounded plausible. Since Jane felt most of the public had lost their ability to critically think and use common sense, the myth would gain momentum until the lie became the truth. Eventually there would another high profile murder case that usurped this one. The book would be closed and all that was left would be a string of inaccuracies that passed for fact. Like stories that end up in history books, most are varnished, colored and usually sterilized to paint a portrait of the event or individual in the manner in which the designers of history want the memory to be preserved. And in Harlan's case, Jane understood that his page in that book would be brief, violent and epically false.

Harlan listened to every word and took strange solace in knowing what he was up against. "Okay, Jane. You said somethin' about capitalizin' on it?"

"Yeah. If the television says you're dead, then you're dead. We can walk into that CSA today and if anyone says you look a lot like 'that guy who killed that girl,' you can look them straight in the eye and tell them that people mistake you for the actor John Goodman all the time."

"But they don't."

"But they *could*. It's a game of lies, Harlan. You have to play along."

"You gotta have a good memory to be a good liar."

"No. You gotta have a good reason to keep lying and you have that… *in spades*." She checked the map. "We're only about five miles from the CSA. There's a nylon head wrap buried in that yellow bag back there. I wear it when I run sometimes. Find it and tie it around your head. It'll be one more distraction to make you look different than the photos they've been showing on the news."

He headed into the back of the van. "This should look interesting."

Jane sat back in her seat and glanced out the window. A red-tailed hawk tore across the sky, seemingly on the prowl. But Jane suddenly realized that the imposing hawk was actually being chased by a tiny sparrow. As she watched the scene play out, she saw how the hawk was trying to worm its way into the sparrow's nest in the nearby tree. Sparrow was adamant and each time hawk swept in for the kill, she chased him away. Finally, she came up behind hawk in an aerial pursuit that looked as if she was engaging him in battle. After a momentary tussle, hawk had enough and swooped around the tree one more time before disappearing into the blue sky.

Her cell phone rang. The sound startled her since only one person had the number.

"Why ain't you answerin' that, Jane?" Harlan called out to her.

Jane stared at the still-ringing phone. "I can't talk right now." She turned back to him with urgency. "Come on! We have to get going."

Knowing

The phone continued to ring.

"You know, if it weren't for him—"

"I don't want to hear it, Harlan! You find the head wrap?" she asked with irritation.

He slammed the back door. "Got it."

Δ Δ Δ

Two miles before reaching the CSA, Jane turned onto a dusty gravel road that was barely wide enough for a large truck. Modest farmhouses dotted the road, separated by wide-open fields that stretched for dozens of acres. Rolling down the windows, Jane let the scent of newly turned rich soil and manure permeate her senses. She loved the aroma every spring. It was like breathing in renewal and the promise that anything could be made right with new seeds and fresh dirt.

But the bucolic banquet was cut short. Glancing in her side mirror, Jane caught a glimpse of what looked like a black sedan. She checked again and it was gone. Slowing down, she pretended to be searching for the CSA, but the entire time her eyes were keyed on that mirror.

"What's up, Jane?"

She wasn't going to say a word to him. "Nothing."

A mile later, they easily found the driveway that led to the CSA. A line of twenty cars and trucks with license plates from all over the country were parked alongside the narrow road, some angled toward the bar ditch. Groupings of festive balloons and ribbons were tacked to a large round wooden plaque that welcomed visitors to "opening season" at The Green Goodness CSA. Locating a parking spot fifty yards from the driveway, Jane handed Harlan his fake ID and they anxiously walked down the road and up the driveway. Neat rows of white hoop houses lined both sides of the gravel path, nestled between quarter acre plots of soil waiting to be seeded. Two John Deere tractors that looked a little worse for wear were stationed midway up the driveway, next to several wooden sheds and finally a barn that appeared to have been built when FDR was in office. The closer they got to the split-level house, the more they could see the small crowd gathering on the curved lawn that circled the two-story house. A woman who was in her mid-forties and sported a mane of salt and pepper hair, stood atop a sturdy apple crate, addressing the assembly. She wore a cheerful pink cowboy shirt under a pair of clean overalls. Her husband stood next to her, feet firmly on the dirt, letting her do all

318

the talking. He looked affable enough to Jane, but also a bit weak with his angular frame and irresolute vibe. Seated at a picnic table in the side yard, Jane noticed a brown-haired girl about fifteen with jeans and a tight-fitting sweater texting on her cell phone. A slender, spry boy, who looked about eleven or twelve, stood nearby tossing a stick to a black Labrador. His crown of brown hair looked like it hadn't been combed in quite some time and his white shirt had plenty of grass stains ground into it. From the manner in which these two conversed, Jane was certain they were siblings. A long table covered in red gingham fabric held bowls of salads, bite sized sandwiches, chips and salsa, platters of fresh fruit and pitchers of water and coffee. Harlan wasted no time heading for the food, scooping up nearly one-fifth of a platter of bite-sized sandwiches in his huge hand.

Jane looked at Harlan and realized the navy blue head wrap made him look like a hardcore biker from the neck up. "Let me do all the talking," she whispered to him.

From what she could tell from the woman's effusive greeting, the gathering was an annual "spring event" where volunteers or those seeking agricultural internships visited the CSA and spent a three-day weekend getting a taste of farm life. The woman gave a brief overview of their property, pointing to a field next to their farm where visitors could park their vehicles and set up camp. A line of five porta-potties stood at the ready downwind. On the other side was a trio of camping showers, with an old pipe carrying water from a large tank into the cubicles. Various classes, which the woman called "learning opportunities," would be offered throughout the three-day period, which guests could attend at their leisure. Since there were only four slots available for the eight-month internship program, it seemed to Jane that this was an audition weekend where the family could get to know each prospective trainee and vet them. The woman really got excited when she announced that everyone was invited to a "slow cooking" night of "food, festivity and friendship." Jane had no clue what "slow cooking" was but it sounded like another gimmick to pacify the Greenies. Frankly, she was always under the impression that "slow cooking" was when the prep cook smoked too much weed. No, this was definitely not her gig but she knew she had to figure out why Gabriel sent them there.

She continued to observe the crowd and farm when she turned around and looked down the long driveway. The hood of a black car could easily be seen inching up the narrow road, stopping just short of the CSA. The trees and

Knowing

bushes along the road blocked the full view but Jane could hear the throaty motor running in the distance. She hadn't recalled hearing the same sound coming from the black sedan that Rudy drove but it didn't matter. Moving nonchalantly, Jane gently encouraged Harlan to walk to their right and obscure themselves in front of a stack of hay bales. But the movement seemed to catch the eye of the woman standing in front of the crowd. She turned to Jane and clasped her palms together with a huge smile on her face.

"Oh, my!" She waved enthusiastically toward Jane and Harlan. "So happy to see you here!"

Jane managed a weak smile as the crowd turned around in unison and stared. Harlan was just finishing off his last fistful of the finger sandwiches while Jane gave a little wave to the woman. The woman wrapped up her presentation as Jane turned around. The black car was gone. A pitter-patter of applause issued forth as the group streamed toward the food table. Jane was just about to step aside when the woman in the pink cowboy shirt and overalls walked up to her.

"Iris!" the woman exclaimed, holding out her hands to Jane. "I am *so* glad you finally came to visit us!"

Jane stared at the woman. "Well, why not?!"

"Your brother described you to a tee! Right down to your outfit and your cute hairstyle and jet black hair! That's what he called it. Jet black, just like Cleopatra's."

Jane's heart pounded.

The woman took Jane's hand in hers. "How is your brother doing? I have to tell you that Werner was one of our favorite interns!"

"Yes, well, he thinks a lot of you too. He made a point of sending me a postcard of your place—"

"I know! I'm the one who gave it to him, silly! He said he wanted to send it to his big sister, Iris. Although, in all fairness, he made a point to say you were *much* more like a mother to him."

"Did he?" Jane countered. "Well…that Werner…we're not that far apart in age, you know?"

"I think it had more to do with your mothering vibe," she said with a sweet smile.

Harlan stepped forward. "I can vouch for that one!"

The woman was a bit taken back as she looked at Harlan. "I'm sorry, I don't know your name."

Jane spoke up. "He's my—"

"Husband," Harlan said, extending his hand to the woman. "My name's Hank."

Jane froze but her neck was still able to turn to him and glare.

The woman shook his hand. "Well, Hank! Nice to meet you. My name's Blythe." She observed him a little more carefully. "I don't mean to be rude, but did anyone ever tell you that you look a lot like that—"

"Actor John Goodman?" he quickly interjected.

"Well, no, actually I meant—"

"I get it *all* the time," Harlan interrupted. "'Can I have your autograph, John?' Sometimes, I just sign it to get rid of them."

Blythe offered a warm smile to Harlan, quite taken by his charm. "Oh, Hank. You're just a big teddy bear, aren't you?"

Harlan wrapped his big arm around Jane's shoulder. "Well, ain't that somethin', honey. That's what you call me too!"

Jane felt the muscles in her face tighten. "Oh, yeah. I sure do."

Blythe's fifteen-year-old daughter bounded toward her, tears streaming down her hormonal face. "*Mom!* You said I could go to Tami's house tonight. She just texted to say *her* mom said that *you* said *I* had to stay *here* for the dinner! That's *not fair!*"

Blythe attempted to calm her daughter but the soothing words fell on deaf ears. The girl, named Blossom, became increasingly emotional and exaggeratedly dramatic until Jane worried she would collapse to the ground and have a full-blown temper tantrum. Jane looked off to the side. A short, wiry guy in his late sixties hung close to the main house, smoking a cigarette and peering around. Something about him sent Jane's antenna on high alert.

"Excuse me one second, kid," Jane said in a dismissive tone before turning to Blythe. "Who's that?"

Blythe turned. "That's Jude. He's been with us for years. He lives in a small cabin out back. Jude's a jack-of-all-trades which comes in really handy around here." She looked at Harlan. "I bet you're a jack-of-all-trades too, Hank!"

He nodded. "Yes, ma'am. You need somethin' done, I'll help you out."

Jane smiled, pulling Harlan toward her. "Let's not get ahead of ourselves, okay?"

"Hey, sweetheart," Blythe said, "we're like a big, *happy* family around here!"

Knowing

"I hate you, *Mom!!!*" Blossom screamed. "I can't *believe* you don't care! What *am* I to you *anyway*? Just another person to plant another *stupid* carrot? I will *not* be your *slave!*" With that, she ran crying into the apple orchard, all pistons firing on high drama and theatrical acumen.

Blythe turned to them. "You have kids?"

"Not a chance," Jane stated.

The rest of the day was spent visiting with the other guests and making light of the fact that Harlan looked so much like the "guy who killed that girl in the motel and died that morning." Every time somebody made the comment, he was quick to tell them his name was Hank. And each time Jane heard that name she stiffened. But by late afternoon, Harlan had the crowd laughing with his silly jokes and card tricks. Jane observed all of it and shook her head. He never told her a silly joke. He never showed her a card trick. Suddenly, he was the belle of the ball and she was the hapless sidekick.

Finally, Jane had enough. She returned to the van to organize the vehicle and figure out how to turn it into a temporary camper. As she pulled the van into the grassy field next to the CSA, she caught sight of Jude watching her every move. He looked like one of those creepy little parasites that lurked around the soup kitchens on East Colfax in Denver. Broken by years of alcohol and drug abuse, Jude was your typical poster boy for what hard living does to a body. Happy-go-lucky Blythe and her weak-chinned husband didn't have a clue about that reprobate. It was so typical, Jane mused. The "granola crowd," as she called them, were deliriously unaware or simply disbelieving that people like Jude were potential liabilities. All Jane had to do was take one look at him from a distance, and she had his number. What was so startling to her was that his game was so poorly carried out. As she moved bags in and out of the back of the van, she easily saw Jude traversing the field back and forth on the other side of the fence, checking a few sprinkler heads along the way for show. Finally, he did his best "casual stroll" toward the fence line and stood there, staring at her.

"Something I can do for you?" Jane asked, with her guard up.

He said nothing at first. Now that he was closer, she realized he appeared a lot older than she first thought. He was what Jane called "an operator," but one that hung on the bottom rung of the ladder. If he were involved in drugs, he wouldn't be the one with the bag; he'd be the one waiting in the car to pick up the guy with the bag. Jude was not a guy motivated by morality or religious fears. His sole motive was greed and his avarice knew no bounds. She was certain he'd sold his soul, humanity and any straw of integrity to the first bidder who threw him a few bucks to buy a bottle of whiskey and a pack of cigarettes.

"So, you're Werner's sister, huh?" he asked, squinting even though the sun was behind him. His voice had a squirrely quality to it.

"Yeah. That's right," Jane replied, turning to him and closing the side door. "You knew Werner when he worked here?"

Jude didn't answer right away. It was as if he either didn't hear it or chose to give it a lot of thought before replying. "Yeah...I knew him..."

It seemed like a loaded answer to Jane.

"What happened to him?" Jude asked, curling his upper lip.

"He's overseas right now. Working for a relief organization."

Jude stared at her, cocking his head. "Is that right?"

She looked him straight in the eye. "Yes. That's right. Why do you ask?"

He regarded her with a strange glower. "Just checkin'." He turned without saying another word and ambled back across the field toward the main house.

It was just strange enough to make Jane return to the van and remove the 9mm before holstering it in the waistband of her jeans. Covering the pistol with her leather jacket, she locked the van and headed back to the house.

For the next few hours, guests were encouraged to pitch in and help prepare the evening meal. Harlan continued to be the reliable jokester, entrancing the crowd with his genuine affable nature. Jane watched it from the comfort of a side room off the kitchen. In the space of a few hours, he'd captured them hook, line and sinker with his stories and musings on life. When he told the group that he sometimes sold firewood in the winter to make ends meet and that he got the most calls when he put an ad in the paper for "free range, grass fed firewood," they exploded in fits of laughter. A transient sadness fell over Jane. She'd been so tuned into keeping him alive and safe that she'd never taken a spare moment to see him through the eyes of a stranger. He was very kind, she decided. She even noticed him innocently flirting with a forty-something, single woman in the group. It was clear that the group looked at him as someone who was "safe" and easy to talk to. The irony of that realization wasn't lost on Jane.

Before sitting down to the meal later that evening, Blythe gave an ad hoc introduction to "slow cooking." From what Jane could muster, the idea had to do with "communing" with your food, feeling "connected" to your meal, taking the time to appreciate the work that went into cultivating and harvesting the food and approaching the meal with "focused, conscious intent." It sounded like a lot of work to Jane. She couldn't argue that it was important to be conscious when you ate since most of the people she'd seen passed out weren't interested in eating. For someone who was used to cooking *and* eating out of the same saucepan and then placing said saucepan on a beat up oven mitt instead of a placemat, Jane was patently aware that this dinner would force her far out of her comfort zone. She didn't trust the "Greenies," as she called them. She also referred to them as "Eco-Nazis" but she wasn't going to let that one out of the bag. There was just something quite *eco-smug*, Jane decided, about people who believed in "conscious eating" and "intuitive cooking." And when she looked up at a banner that was strung across the kitchen that read: "We support the Sustainable Eco-Aware Local Farmers co-op," she smiled. Their acronym was SELF. To her knowledge, there was no "me" in "community."

When Blythe happily went into way too much detail about each item on their dinner menu, Jane gazed at the family's old time glass bottle collection and read a handful of the many homey plaques that cluttered their walls. One plaque definitely caught her eye. It was an illustration of a pointing hand aimed at an "X" and the words, "You are here." It was similar to the postcard in Jane's possession that came next in the sequence. Perhaps, she pondered, Gabriel mimicked the plaque on purpose when he used the same words on the postcard? If she was right, maybe there was something of worth in the plaque. It was difficult to read because part of it was hidden in the shadow of a ceiling beam. Peering at it closer, she was able to make out the wording: "You are here: 37° 59' 56" N / 105° 54' 36" W. Jane stared at it, trying to figure out if there was any hidden meaning.

"Iris?" a voice said.

Jane turned to the group, unaware of anything that had been said.

"Sweetheart?" Harlan said, pulling out his chair across the long table from her. "They want you to say the prayer that Werner used to recite." His eyes showed a moment of trepidation.

Jane looked at Blythe and her husband, who looked like a wet lap dog as he stood in the background and blended in. "Which prayer was that?"

Blythe stepped forward. "He said it was a family prayer he'd learned as a child."

Harlan regarded Jane with a look of uncertainty.

"Oh, right. That one." She cleared her throat and waited for the prayer muse to show up. Somehow, she knew that "God is great, God is good" wasn't going to cut it. All eyes were upon Jane, including Blythe's young son, who stood off to the side by the stove with a curious look. Jude sat on a stool at the far end of the table, wearing a smirk on his weathered face and waited for Jane to speak. She let out a breath and closed her eyes. The words suddenly came to her. "I will face the darkness, but I will not let it become me. Fear may be present but it will not possess me. I will face the darkness, as the knowing light within my heart and mind leads me home. And once again, I will be free... Amen." She opened her eyes. Every eye in the room was upon her.

A lone tear drifted down Blythe's face. "Beautiful, Iris. Just beautiful. And you said it perfectly. I could almost hear Werner's voice in yours."

Jane smiled. "Yeah. I get that a lot."

Everyone took a seat and dug into the first course, which appeared to be a medley of corn, green beans, fava beans, jalapenos and tomatoes. Slow cooking also involved slow eating. At least that's what Jane discovered after devouring her first course and sliding her plate to the side before some of the others had finished filling their plates. Blythe set a huge platter of freshly baked bread on the table and was in the middle of telling the group how it was pre-baked in an authentic outdoor clay oven and then finished off in a solar oven built by a group of unwed mothers, when Blossom emerged at the top of the stairs, screaming.

"I cannot believe I am part of this family!" Blossom bellowed, her whiny voice hitting decibels that would startle a laying hen. "Nobody cares about me! *Nobody*!"

While the rest of the group remained taciturn, Jane matter-of-factly stood up and dished herself another serving. "Don't know how you got the tomatoes to taste this fresh in April," she offered.

Blossom pounded down the stairs and when she reached the kitchen, she abruptly crossed her arms across her teenage chest. "Why won't anyone listen to me? If you push me, do I not fall? If you cut me, do I not bleed?"

Jane plopped down in her seat. "If I shoot you," she mumbled under her breath, "will you not shut up?"

Blythe suffocated a chuckle, as did a few of the visiting guests. Jane noticed that Blossom's little brother was looking at her with a huge grin pasted on his face.

Blossom swung around and, with hands on her hips, approached Jane. "That's *not* funny!"

"No, Blossom, actually it was. But what's even funnier is the way you're acting, with the emphasis on 'acting.' You make Sarah Bernhardt look like a shy recluse."

Blossom's mouth dropped open and she ran screaming up the stairs and into her room with a defined slam of the door.

Jane furrowed her brow. "She knows who Sarah Bernhardt is?"

Blossom's brother piped up. "That's what Werner used to call her all the time."

Jane sat back. "Is that so?"

Blythe brought out a few more platters. "It's amazing how in tune you and your brother are, Iris. Tell us how he's doing."

Jane was glad she had a prop of food in front of her. After taking a bite and chewing it slowly, she sipped some water. "He's overseas right now...in Africa, actually. He's working at a relief center there for tribes who have been displaced."

Blythe frowned. "Displaced? Come on, Iris. You know better than that. 'Displaced' is a nice word for 'violently overthrown' or 'slaughtered.'"

Jane nodded. "Yeah. It's a nightmare over there. But that's where Werner's heart is right now." She glanced at Harlan who smiled.

Blythe sat down at the head of the table, serving herself a plate. "You know, Iris, Werner never said you were married. How did you and Hank meet?"

Harlan looked at her. "You know, I'd like to hear that story again, Iris."

Jane took another slow bite of food and looked across the table at Harlan. "I met Hank when I was working up in Midas, Colorado."

"Werner never mentioned what you did for a living," Blythe said.

Jane let out a slow breath. "I was doing fraud investigation at the time for an insurance company. One day, I went to lunch at this sports bar on the main drag called The Rabbit Hole. And the guy behind the bar was Hank. I later found out that he owned the place and that he used to be a cop, who also specialized in fraud cases."

Harlan never took his eyes off Jane, drawn into her story and fascinated.

"What drew the two of you together?" Blythe asked.

"Oh, that's easy," Jane smiled. "Hank knows how to build the best hot dog you've ever tasted. And he makes a mean chicken salad too."

"Well, food is, of course, important," Blythe declared, "but I was more interested in what drew you and Hank together emotionally."

Jane swallowed hard. "I don't know how to answer that." She struggled as all eyes were pinned on her. She kept her focus on Harlan. "I suppose it's because Hank is the only person in this world who really gets me. I'm not used to that. I'm used to the fight...so, having somebody look at you and all you see is love coming back feels strange to me. I don't have to worry about him going out on me. I don't have to question his integrity. He's solid and he's dependable." Jane felt the emotion ball in her throat. "Maybe in time, I'll figure out what I did to deserve that."

The room was silent. Jane took a sip of water and prayed to God that someone would speak up.

Blythe leaned across the table toward Jane. "Beautifully said, Iris."

Harlan winked at Jane. "I second that."

For the next three hours, the meal continued with one platter of food after another brought out and "eaten with purpose." People talked and laughed and exchanged opinions on the world's news reports. Gradually, groups naturally began to form of likeminded individuals, with Harlan attracting more women to his satellite group than the others. Jane glanced across the room to Blythe's young son. His focus lingered on her a little too long before he purposely got up, grabbed a jacket and walked outside into the night air. Jane waited a few minutes, before quietly removing herself from the kitchen and sneaking outside without anyone noticing.

The air was chilled and befitted a heavier jacket. With no streetlights around and the moonless sky above her, Jane crept slowly across the yard, trying not to fall over the scattered hay bales.

"Hey," a voice softly said.

Jane turned to the sound. "Where are you?"

"Wait a second until your eyes get used to it," the boy said.

She stood in the cold, her fingertips feeling the sting of the night air. Plunging them into her jacket pocket, she began to make out a few outlines of farm equipment and buildings. Gingerly moving around the hay bales, she crossed next to the boy. He leaned against a post and stared into the clear night sky.

"Do you know where Orion's Belt is?" he asked her.

"No. Is that why you wanted me to come out here?"

He kept his head tilted up toward the starry sky. "Nah."

Jane waited, feeling the cold creep closer. "Well, okay...happy stargazing." She started off.

Knowing

"Werner and I were good friends. Even though I was only nine when he showed up, he always talked to me like I was older. He worked here two years in a row, during the whole season, so I got to know him real well. And one thing I know is that he's an only child." He turned to Jane for the first time.

She walked back to his side. "That's odd. He told your mom he had an older sister."

He smiled. "I know. He told me the truth. He told her something else."

Jane started to speak when the boy "shushed" her quickly.

"Don't say a word," he whispered in her ear.

Jane heard the faint crack of footsteps coming from the side of the house.

The boy whispered in her ear again. "Follow me. Be *quiet*."

Jane moved behind the boy and down the long driveway. When they reached the road, the boy checked behind them to ensure their privacy. "He'll be down here any second," he whispered.

"Who?" she whispered back.

"Jude."

Jane nodded. "Right. I already have him pegged."

He regarded her carefully. "I need to show you something. Got a flashlight on you?"

She shook her head and walked with him to the van in the field. Once inside, she grabbed a blanket and covered both of them. The boy climbed into the passenger seat and scanned the darkness around him.

"I don't know your name," Jane said.

"Sage. Yours?"

She contemplated honesty but fell short. "Anne. Anne LeRóy."

He looked at her with penetrating eyes. "That's not your name," he stated.

She met his stare and raised it. "That's what I want you to call me."

"Fair enough." He looked out into the coal night. "It is kinda funny, you know? You calling yourself Iris and Gabe calling himself Werner."

Jane wrapped the blanket around her chilled hands and lap. "Okay. So you know about that. What else do you know?"

"That I'm supposed to help you. That's what he told me," Sage offered, turning around and looking closely into the distance.

"Why do you keep doing that?" Jane asked.

"Why do you think?"

Jane nodded. "Okay. So what is Jude's problem?"

Sage sighed. "Whoever was after Gabe, got to Jude first. Then Jude sold him out."

Jane felt her blood boil. "What was he worth?"

Sage shook his head, showing disgust. "Thirty bottles of Silver Whiskey. It's Jude's favorite."

"Right. Jude's a real connoisseur."

"He'll sell you out, too. You and your friend."

Jane turned to the boy. "To *who*? You got names?"

"No. Gabe never mentioned names on purpose. He told me that if anything happened to him, it was meant to be." He swallowed hard, staring into his lap. "He's dead, isn't he?"

"Yes."

"I knew it," Sage whispered, trying to hold back his tears. "I don't want to know how it happened, okay?"

Jane nodded. "Okay. So Gabe said you were supposed to help me?"

He got a hold of himself. "He told me to wait for the day when his older sister, Iris, showed up. He said when that happened, the 'wolf was gonna be at the door,' and you had to work quickly. It was like his own little...prophecy. But he was right on with everything else he ever told me so I believed him." He turned to Jane with a shrug of his shoulders. "And he was right again."

Jane looked at the kid in shock. Her head was spinning with a million thoughts and fears. "The wolf at the door" had to be either Rudy or Romulus. "You said you had something to show me?"

Sage nodded. Reaching into his inside jacket pocket, he brought out a folded postcard and handed it to Jane.

She turned on the interior light and looked at the card. It was the exact one she had that came next in the sequence. Jane turned the card over. Gabe wrote three words on the card, "YOU'RE NOT DREAMING." She felt dizzy, even though she was seated.

"You okay?" Sage asked.

"No. But it'll pass." She looked at the photo again. "You know where this is?"

"Yeah. It's way up on the mountain, about five miles east of here. It's where Gabe used to camp during his days off."

Jane tried to work out the timing of everything in her head. "When did Gabe give you this postcard?"

"He didn't. I found it about nineteen months ago."

Jane realized that was when Harlan had his transplant surgery. "Nineteen months…so, you didn't see him?"

"No. Jude sold him out in late August of that year and when Gabe got wind of it, he left. He showed up again here the night of September 15th. I found it slipped under my bedroom door in the morning."

Jane couldn't believe what she heard. "Wait, you're saying Gabe broke into your house and left this without anyone knowing he was there?"

He twisted his face into a questioning smirk. "That was the *least* of his talents. You never knew him?"

"No."

"Oh…wow…okay. Then you wouldn't believe it."

"Try me. You'd be shocked what I believe these days."

He gauged her sincerity before he spoke. "He taught me how to meditate. My parents were okay with it since it was hippie enough to be cool but not creepy enough to be dangerous. And they loved Gabe."

"So you learned to meditate and then what?"

He resisted answering.

"*What?*" Jane stressed.

"I moved a spoon on the kitchen table."

Jane shrugged her shoulders. "So what?"

"With my mind."

Jane sat back. "Oh. Yeah. That is different."

"You don't believe me! See! I should have never—"

"I believe you," she interjected.

He looked at her closely. "You really do, don't you?" He thought about it. "You're not gonna ask me to prove it to you, are you?"

"No. You're not Barnum, I'm not Bailey and this ain't a circus."

"Huh?"

"Never mind." She slid her hand into the side pocket of her leather satchel, removing the postcards. Finding the one that matched Sage's, she held it up to him. "There's more proof, just in case you need it."

He nodded.

"So, are you going to show me where this place is?"

"Yeah. But not tonight. Maybe tomorrow? We can take the 4-wheeler up there. Your van will make it if the roads are okay but if we get a rain, probably not."

"We're doing this tomorrow, Sage. You say the word and we go."

He looked around. "I swear to God he's out there watching us."

"I know the feeling, kid."

"No, I really mean it. He's watching us. I just know."

Jane sighed. "That's your third eye working overtime, kiddo."

He smiled. "Hey, can I ask you a question?"

"Sure."

"Gabe slid something else under the door that night. But I don't really know what it means." He reached up to his neck under his t-shirt and pulled a pendant out, strung on a piece of leather. "Any ideas?"

It was a tiny bronze pinecone pendant.

After Sage returned to the house, Jane stayed at the van and waited for Harlan. Hours passed and he finally showed up with three covered dishes of food in tow. For twenty minutes, he told Jane about all the stories he heard and how much fun he had.

"And you know what?" he asked her, crawling into the back of the van. "I finally figured out what happened to that Amos boy, Seth."

"Who?"

"The song? Remember?"

"Ah, right." Suddenly, Jane felt out of the loop again.

"I feel like I've been let out of prison, Jane!"

"I see that."

"I never met that many folks who wanted to talk to me. I swear this heart is a chick magnet."

She pulled a blanket out of a bag. "Maybe it's not your heart, Harlan. Maybe they just like you."

He considered it. "Nah. It's him. It's all him."

She removed the 9mm from her waistband and locked it in the glove compartment.

"Hey," Harlan offered, a bit sheepishly, "about what happened at the table regardin' how you and Hank got together and—"

"It's fine. Don't worry about it," she replied succinctly.

"I'm just sayin'—"

"Really, Harlan, we do not have to talk about this. Put it to bed."

He leaned closer. "What happens at the CSA, stays at the CSA."

"That's highly doubtful." She told him about her short but informative visit with Sage and their plans for the following day. Harlan wanted to come along but Jane instructed him to stay at the CSA and "work his magic" to deflect her absence. "And whatever you do," she cautioned him, "do *not* get into any conversations with Jude. That son-of-a-bitch sold your heart out." She explained everything she knew about the little weasel. When she was done, she thought Harlan was going to find him and pummel him into organic compost. "We have to be smart, Harlan," she warned. "You can't give that s.o.b. more ammo to hurt us."

"I don't get it, Jane. Why would Gabe purposely lead us here if it was a set-up with Jude?"

She'd already contemplated that question. "Maybe there was no way around it. Maybe in order for us to find out what the next postcard reveals, we have no choice but to put up with the lowlife." The comment seemed to appease Harlan but Jane still questioned the obvious complications. It almost seemed to Jane as if the entire process had to take place in order for the intended ending Gabe set forth. It was that kind of theorizing that kept her mind fitful and apprehensive. She needed to occupy her mind with something besides imminent danger. Digging around in the van, she came across a piece of paper at the bottom of the cooler Hank delivered to her. Unfolding it, she recognized the writing in Patois, a somewhat sloppy French dialect popular in the Caribbean islands.

It read: "*Mwê ni èspwa pou la yonn kilès ki sa fè mwên tjè feb antyè ankò*." Jane already knew the translation that was written beneath it: "*I hope for the one who can make my tender heart whole again.*" She'd found the odd phrase in a diary during her last case and asked Hank to figure out the translation. She stared at the small piece of paper, realizing that she wrote the words in Patois at the top and Hank wrote the English translation. It was akin to a love letter, Jane reasoned, with the phrase echoed back to her. Nobody could ever accuse Jane Perry of writing a love letter but there it was in her hands. He put it at the bottom of the bag on purpose so she'd find it after she pulled out the chicken salad. But by that time, vitriol had robbed her of a peaceful parting.

"I got a question for you, Jane," Harlan asked, setting up his bedding for the night. "You think Marion loves her husband the way she loved Gabe?"

Jane considered it. "No. I don't. But I think Gabe was the kind of guy who was only meant to live a short time. People like Gabe who have that kind of intrinsic power don't last long. They burn up in their own orbit. This world can't contain people like Gabe because they can't be shoved into a neat little box that satisfies the status quo." She looked out the window. "You know what I bet? I bet Marion has something of Gabe's that she deeply cherishes."

"Like what?" he asked, popping the cap off another bottle of pine needle beer.

Jane wasn't sure where this was all coming from. "I don't know. I just have this feeling, you know? In my gut?"

"Maybe it's another one of them postcards?"

"No. It's not that," Jane stated, still staring off into the night sky. "It's much greater than that. It's her connection to Gabe."

While Harlan finished making his bed and enjoying the beer, Jane found her cell phone and checked the voicemail. He didn't speak at first and the dead air worried her. But after a few seconds, she heard Hank's voice.

"Hey…look, I don't know where in the hell you are right now. I hope to God you're safe." He let out a sigh. "Okay, here's the deal. I took the bait and I checked out the videos of the red-haired guy you mentioned. You're right, Jane. You hear me? You're *right*. The guy at the Quik-Mart and the guy standing behind Crandall are one and the same. And based on the background scenery I blew up in the screen capture, the Quik Mart in the shot is not the same one where you got your car ripped." He let out another frustrated sigh. "I don't know what to make of it, but I think you stumbled on something pretty damn deep. Please, Jane…please be careful. Don't just…don't disappear on me."

The call ended abruptly. Jane hit the REPLAY button and listened to his message several more times before turning off the phone and drifting off to sleep. She felt herself falling into a deep, resonating slumber. Then, as if the poles shifted, she quickly found herself standing in a long, sterile hospital ward. On either side, were glass-walled rooms with tightly drawn gray curtains. There were no doctors or nurses but Jane could feel the fears and hopes of the patients on the other sides of the glass walls. It took her a few seconds, but she realized there was no sound around her. Even her footsteps on the shiny gray floor fell like cotton balls on a pillow. The farther she walked, the longer the aisle became until it was a never-ending stroll into nowhere. Then, in the distance, she heard the distinctive sound of wheels on a cart rolling across a vinyl floor. The whir of the spinning wheels increased as Jane spun in circles, attempting to source the location. Finally, the wheels came to a halt. Jane turned and saw an empty stainless steel gurney in front of her. A beautiful long, shiny ponytail of red hair sat on the left. On the right, was a single, empty syringe. She picked up the syringe and questioned whether it belonged to the others she'd seen carpeting the floor of the old man's office. The second that image came to mind, she dropped the syringe, realizing this wasn't a dream. Layers of clear, critical thinking aren't usually present when one is in a dream state but at that moment, Jane was considering end runs and assorted game plans she usually reserved for her daytime reality.

Suddenly, she heard a team of footsteps moving closer behind her. She turned and looked into the gray haze that filtered closer to her body. The steps became more pronounced as fear gripped her hard. The haze grew denser until it swallowed her body and choked her. Struggling to breathe, Jane gasped once and then again. Risking it all, she took in a deep breath and opened her eyes. The starry sky out the front window of the van lay directly in her sight. She sat up with a start, checking to make sure Harlan was still there. He was sound asleep, softly snoring on his side. It took her another two hours to fall back to sleep.

The next day started early. Awakened by the loud sound of an iron dinner bell triangle at six thirty, Jane and Harlan sleepily made their way to the camping showers before the happy band of other guests were out of their tents and vehicles. With no hot water, Jane realized where Gabriel might have gotten his idea to end his shower with a blast of icy water. It was certainly bracing and an easy way to speed up the crew so they didn't linger under the showerhead.

After a breakfast of oatmeal, poached eggs and one of the best bowls of raspberries Jane ever tasted, the guests broke up into small groups and busied themselves with the free educational opportunities. Harlan eagerly chose a class on "Building Better Soil With Waste" because as he said to the crowd, "I just love the smell of cowpies in the mornin'." Jane grabbed her third cup of coffee in a paper cup and ducked outside. She hadn't seen Sage that morning yet and began to worry that something was wrong. Strolling into the front yard, she scanned the second floor of the main house, searching for any sign of movement.

"Whatcha lookin' for?" Jude said.

Jane spun around, shocked that he crept up on her so quietly. "Nothing," she replied with an abrupt sting. "I'm just looking."

He gazed at her a little too long before talking, taking snips instead of drags on his ash-laden cigarette. "Why aren't you in one of the classes?"

"I thought maybe you were teaching something."

"Me?"

"Yeah. What's your specialty around this joint?"

He regarded Jane with his squinty eyes. "Well, I figured your brother would have let you in on that talent."

Jane wanted to grab his wiry neck by his tattered collar, pound his head into the welcome sign and stab him in the neck with a pitchfork. But she had to play this one closer to the vest. "He did, actually." She moved a few inches toward Jude. "And he gave me a message for you. He told me to tell you to 'fuck off.'" She turned, heading down the driveway. "And you know my brother. He said it in twelve *different* languages!"

Jane expected the cancerous tumor to follow her but, thankfully, he stayed put. By the time she got to the road and turned around, Jude was walking back into the house. Noticing a Wi-Fi antenna on a nearby house, she wondered if there was a possibility of stealing some Web time on her computer. She started toward the van when she heard the throaty engine of a large car coming up the road behind her. Jane turned and saw an old black Lincoln Continental with blacked out windows driving toward her. It was the same sound of the motor from the black car that appeared to be hovering close by when they arrived the day before. She turned in the direction of the van in the field and quickened her step. With each hastened punch of her cowboy boot in the dirt, she could hear the rapid acceleration of the Lincoln. She only had another thirty feet to go when the car swept up on her left side and veered in front of her. Jane stopped, reaching in her waistband for her weapon before realizing it was still locked in the van's glove compartment.

The darkened passenger window slowly rolled down as the male driver, dressed in all black, leaned toward Jane's direction. "Get in."

CHAPTER 23

Jane jogged to the left but the driver gunned the Lincoln in reverse, blocking her escape. She hefted her body across the wide trunk, skimming as fast as she could against the hot metal, before falling somewhat short of her dismount. Stumbling, she raced toward the mouth of the field where the fencing opened up but the Lincoln easily turned and lurched forward, blocking the entrance to the field. Jane turned, looking down the road and tried to figure out where to run when the driver rolled down his window.

"What in the hell are you doing?" he asked her in a firm but somewhat off-hand tone.

He was a tall man, Jane deduced, with olive pockmarked skin, broad shoulders and a shock of black hair. His dark eyes were focused and showed hints of past cruelty. His vibe was "all business" and cutting to the chase.

"What in the hell are *you* doing?" she retorted.

"You getting in?" he gruffly asked.

"Why should I?"

"Because I'm the medicine man."

Jane felt a shock travel up her spine. "Where are you taking me?"

"Jesus, you have a lot of questions. Come on. Get in. There's not a lot of time left."

Jane glanced around the area, checking to see if anyone was watching. Finally, she walked around the long car and got inside. The upholstery was crimson red leather and the interior of the automobile looked as if it had been well taken care of over the many years. He turned around and drove back up the road and onto Highway 17.

"You got a name?" Jane asked.

"Call me Saul."

She looked at him with his Mediterranean appearance. "You don't look like a 'Saul.'"

He smiled and remained silent.

"You know who I am?" Jane asked.

"I know you're the one I need to talk to."

"You want my name?"

"I couldn't care less about your name. All I need from you is your help." He gunned the Lincoln up to ninety miles an hour.

Jane held onto the door handle as it moved like an ebony bullet across the flat highway.

"Why are you called The Medicine Man? You make potions?"

He smirked. "No potions. The real medicine…the *true* medicine, is in the mind."

About five miles later, he slowed and turned right onto an unmarked, one lane road. The Lincoln's tires spit gravel and dust as Saul zoomed down the path. In the distance, miles of desolation lay wide open. Jane flashed on a somber image of her being led across this uninhabited territory and shot once in the back of the head.

"I have no interest in killing you," Saul declared. "That's the last thing I'd do."

Jane had to check herself. "I never said that—"

"You thought it," he said off-handedly, "don't bother denying it." He bore to the right again and drove up to a tall steel gate. "And I'm telling you that you've got nothing to worry about from me." He stopped the car. "It's the others you need to be concerned about." Saul reached under his driver's seat and removed a small remote. Clicking the red button toward the gate, it lumbered open, sending whining echoes across the open space.

Jane fully expected to see a massive house or structure on the other side. But all that lay there was an enormous spate of raw land surrounded by a twenty foot electrified fence, with concertina wire curling over the top. Saul drove into the property and parked, turning off the engine. The steel gate closed behind them.

Saul turned to Jane. "Ever seen a Kansas dugout?"

"I don't think so," Jane replied cautiously.

He smiled. "This is nothing like that." He punched a green button on the remote and the car began to sink into the ground.

"Jesus!" Jane yelled. "What's going on—?"

"Relax," Saul said with a grin. "Enjoy the ride."

Jane held on as she watched the blue sky above her pull farther away. Inch by inch, the Lincoln sunk deeper into the ground. It was quickly clear to Jane that they were positioned upon some sort of hydraulic elevator that reached deep underground. Gradually, they were swallowed and surrounded by concrete walls on all sides. When they reached about one hundred feet below the surface, the elevator came to a slow stop. Saul pushed a yellow button on the remote and an enormous steel door that stretched three times the width of the Lincoln, opened up like a garage door. On the other side, it looked like the scene from "The Wizard of Oz" when Dorothy emerges into Oz and everything turns to brilliant color. Saul drove forward down a short paved road lined with brilliant lights and what sounded to Jane like a babbling brook.

"What the hell is this?" she asked, her mouth agape.

"I call it home." Saul rolled the Lincoln to a stop and parked. "Come on. Follow me." He led Jane to a large wall that appeared to be dirt. He located a brown metal plate that blended into the façade. Opening it, he punched in a series of numbers and stood back. What appeared to be dirt was actually a clandestine door that slid open to the right. Jane followed him through.

She stopped as he turned to close the sliding door and stared at the scene in front of her. Above her head were a million pinpoints of light that illuminated into a blue Colorado skyline. It was so realistic, she had to make sure that it wasn't actually the sky seeping in from aboveground. In front of her, stood a modest house, complete with a healthy looking lawn, exterior lighting and a small waterfall that cascaded into a koi pond.

"I seriously do not get this, Saul." She was trying to take it all in while simultaneously wondering if she was dreaming.

"You're *not* dreaming," Saul said, catching her thought.

Jane looked at him, shocked. "Those are the same three words Gabe wrote on a postcard."

Saul smiled with genuine sincerity. "He and I thought a lot alike. Come on in. And wipe your feet, would you? It's a bitch to keep this place clean."

Jane followed Saul into the living room of the one-story house. It was appointed with beautiful mahogany antiques, all polished to perfection. The temperature felt perfect—not too hot or too cold. In the center of the room, attached to the twelve-foot ceiling, were dozens of various sized crystals, illuminated by a large arch of light that hung above them. As they softly rotated against a gentle breeze that issued forth from tiny holes in the ceiling, the spectrum of refracted color bounced across the white walls and filled the entire space with an intense energy.

He offered Jane a seat in a rich leather chair as he sat across from her on a small leather couch with enormous mahogany armrests. A modest coffee table separated them. To his left was a small side table that held a trio of books with the bindings facing out. Watching him stretch out his long legs and push up his black trousers, Jane figured Saul was about sixty, even though there wasn't a bit of gray in his black locks.

Jane let out a low breath. "Quite a place you got here. Ever miss having neighbors?"

"No time for chit-chat. We don't have a lot of time left—"

"You said that already," Jane replied, still trying to rectify the last twenty minutes of her life.

He leaned back in the sofa, draping his left hand over the armrest. "Can you imagine having everything you've ever feared or been conditioned to fear being conquered?"

Jane shook her head. "No. I can't."

"Well, that's what I did. And I taught Gabe how to do it. When the student is ready, the teacher will come."

"I don't understand."

Saul edged forward and turned in his seat so that she could see the back of his neck. "You see that?" he asked, pointing to a tiny dot on the right side of his neck. "I dug it out long before Gabe dug his out."

Jane felt her mouth go dry. "Oh, shit. You're one of them?"

"No. I *used* to be one of them." He sat back again. "I got out, I stayed out and I'm still alive," he declared with a sense of pride.

"Living underground…"

"I like it. I've always been fond of the earth and now I'm part of it."

"I don't mean to get in your business, Saul, but this place must have set you back a few bucks."

"I was in their game for a long time. Did a lot of big jobs. It built my bank account but it broke me. I've spent every second since then making amends."

"Was one of those amends helping Gabe when he got out?"

Saul nodded. "He found me."

"How?"

"On another wave of reality."

"Right," Jane said with a nod. She was beginning to accept that while some actions cannot be rationally explained, it didn't change the fact that the results of the unseen feat still materialized.

"I finally met him in the flesh just over three years ago. He stayed down here with me for a while after getting wind that the company was closing in.

He said he'd uncovered information during his last hit and he wasn't sure how to handle it."

"Hang on. Why wouldn't he know how to handle it? I thought Gabe was an all-seeing prophet!"

"Gabriel was a human being and he'd be the first person to tell you that! He lived in this world just like the rest of us. He knew what childhood innocence felt like. He understood anger and aggression. He knew what it felt like to plot a man's death and follow it through. He felt lust but he also experienced great love for a woman. He regaled in triumph and carried the burden of massive defeat. Regret, deep depression, questioning life's purpose, walking around in an empty shell…he lived all of it. And when it was the right time… when he knew he couldn't continue the life he'd led any longer, he committed his soul to the unknown…to the death of everything he thought he knew. And he walked into it with his eyes and heart wide open. When he emerged after three years, he knew what he had to do. He also knew the price he would pay. But by that point, he'd already died a thousand deaths. As long as his death was pure and final, he had no quarrels."

"So, Romulus really didn't know who they were getting when they recruited him."

"They knew who he was and what he could do. Gabriel was a god to Romulus. And Romulus loves their gods. He was their rising sun. They put him through the most intense training and testing and he never broke. They shot him full of LSD, cocaine and heroin, fed him Psilocybin mushrooms and he was still able to function and not give away company secrets. That's unheard of! He was extremely comfortable worming through heightened realities of consciousness. He was measured as a "P7"—that's known as a Psychic Conduit. And he could do that without artificially altering his consciousness. He could easily feel other people's emotions and hear their thoughts just like you and I listen to the radio. He saw auras around people so he always knew what type of person he was up against. But after he left Romulus, he took all of those talents to a different level." He eyed Jane carefully. "He went through his own death. He experienced it as if it was frighteningly real. He felt every stab of pain and when his life force was snuffed out, he went through the light and he was told his destiny. When he came back into his physical body, he was committed to following what he had been told to the letter."

"Told by whom?"

"By the pool of infinite wisdom and compassion. Call it God, the Universe, the Source, whatever works for you. The point is, everything he saw regarding his death came to pass. I was with him the whole way. He told me what he saw but he also left some things out because he still needed to confirm a few key points first in the physical reality. He was mired in that process right up to the end. The last week of his life, he traveled all over this state, building more connections and putting as much as he could in place before they found him. He knew he was running out of time. It was coming up on the 22nd of September. The Autumnal Equinox. The beginning of the season that marks the souls' harvest. Gabriel had taken out enough people on that date so he knew what it meant. It's a powerful time to die in their world." He looked off to the side. "They always get off on that kind of symbology. With them, it's all about symbols, numbers, dates and places of power on this earth. With them, a profane act done at a sacred location magnifies the destruction, lifting it into another stratosphere." He became strangely sad. "If people only knew the things we did and what is still being done...Jesus, I'm telling you, I think the shock alone would destroy people's belief that good ever existed." He looked up at her, his eyes clear and focused. "But good *does* exist. They want to convince you otherwise. But I'm telling you, there is *still* light in this world. And as someone who has seen and been part of so much darkness, that should tell you a lot."

Jane's head whirred with too many questions. "I don't get why I got pulled into this chaos. He was talking to you on a regular basis about what he found. Why didn't he choose you?"

"Think about that for a second. I got out of the company years ago. You think I might be a pretty big fish to reel in? Besides, I don't have the freedom of movement you have."

"If you can talk to people at a distance, mind-to-mind, you have a lot more freedom of movement than most people!"

"You are correct. But the footwork still has to be done. And you and Harlan were the foot soldiers that Gabriel chose."

Jane was taken back. "How do you know about Harlan?"

"Are you serious?" Saul asked.

"Point taken."

"Gabriel chose you. He also chose Harlan." He looked at her sternly. "But *they* did not choose Harlan."

Knowing

Jane shifted in her seat. "Right. Somebody else was scheduled to get Gabe's heart but the doctor on call said they weren't as seriously ill as Harlan."

"The operative word in your sentence is 'scheduled.'"

"I'm not sure I understand what you mean."

"Gabriel's heart was scheduled for transplant on September 22nd, the same day he would be killed."

Jane stared at Saul in total disbelief. "No. I don't buy it."

He sat back and observed Jane. "Do me a favor. Go over to that bureau and open the top drawer."

Jane turned to her right where an ornate bureau stood. She crossed to it and opened the drawer. "Holy shit."

"Holy shit, indeed. Go on. Bring it over here."

Jane was still unable to fathom how this was possible. Staring back at her was the infamous white binder and those bold red letters, IEB.

"Come on!" Saul said with urgency.

Jane removed the binder from the drawer and moved back to the chair. She placed it on her lap, still staring at the three letters.

"The Project went through different names," Saul explained. "First it was called Project Bennu. That's the Ancient Egyptian bird that's similar to our Phoenix. It was the sacred bird of Heliopolis. It's also a symbol of the rising and setting sun. Next, they changed the name to Project IEB."

"What does IEB stand for?" Jane asked.

"It's not an acronym. IEB means 'heart.' That's another reference to ancient Egypt. They believed our heart was the center of all consciousness. Upon death, instead of saying someone 'passed away,' they'd say his 'heart departed.'"

Jane carefully threaded the pieces together. "So, if the heart is truly the center of consciousness and if your heart doesn't die with you, but is transplanted instead…"

He waited. "Go on…"

"Then you can live on in someone else's body."

"No. Your consciousness lives on."

Jane nodded. "Well, I can't argue with that. But why is that such a bad thing? From what I've seen, it can be life changing for the recipient. And Gabe's heart? Well, who in the hell wouldn't want his heart?"

He nodded. "Yes. *Who* in *hell* would want it?" He leaned forward, clasping his hands in front of him. "Open the binder. You'll find the third and final name for their Project."

Jane's stomach churned as she turned the front cover over and read the black typed lettering on the front page. "PROJECT GABRIEL." She looked up at Saul.

"*He* was their project," Saul stated. "From the moment they recruited him, Gabriel was *always* their project. To them, he was perfection. A god among men. They put a lot of time and money into this one. And they always got whatever they wanted. *Except* for this time. *This* time, Harlan got what they desired the most."

Jane stared at Saul, suddenly understanding. "And now they want it back."

Saul nodded.

Jane felt dizzy and wondered if she would pass out.

"You'll be fine," Saul interjected. "Let it pass." He regarded her with a stern eye. "You've got work to do. Use your mind to get over your matter." Saul leaned forward. "*Did you hear me?*"

Jane came back into herself and steadied her nerves. God, if she ever needed a cigarette, it was now.

"Hold off on the nicotine for the time being," Saul offered, prying once more into her head.

Jane looked down at the binder. "There were two distinct things Gabe found. The second one was this binder. What was the first thing?"

Saul sat back. "That's what Gabriel was working on when he was killed. He was very close to delivering it but there were still pieces he couldn't pull together. That's where you come in. You must follow through with everything you've been given, in the *exact* order in which it was given to you."

"Wait, wait, you said he was very close to 'delivering it.' What does that mean?"

"You'll figure it out."

"Jesus Christ! You gotta help me! This is not a fucking joke to me!"

"It's not a joke to me either!" he yelled. "But Gabriel chose you and Harlan to play this out to its conclusion."

Irritation rose up. "You know, when I hear that Gabe delegated all of this in some cosmic court, I feel like I've lost complete control of my life!"

He shrugged. "So what? Deal with it. If he didn't think you were capable of what you have to do, he never would have given you the job. Situations will unfold and everything will become evident to you as it occurs."

She bored into his eyes. "You know everything that is going to happen, don't you?"

"Not everything."

"Tell me what you know."

He jabbed his finger at Jane. "It's *yours to do*, not mine!"

Jane ran her fingers through her dyed hair. A thousand images and words crashed inside her head, all competing for her attention. Then, one comment came to the fore. It was Monroe's odd statement about "the medicine man next to Haas." She looked at Saul and then turned her attention to the table next to him on his left side. Three books stood upright. The one closest to Saul was authored by Werner Haas.

"It's about damn time," Saul stated, turning to his left and handing the book to Jane.

Jane turned to the back cover and felt her heart fall. The black and white photo of Werner Haas was the old man Gabe assassinated. "Why did he kill him?"

"It was just another job. But then everything changed when he realized he'd killed the man who was hired to design *his* death and, shall we say, rebirth."

Jane flipped through the pages of the book. It was a scientific tome that was far too complex. "Who was this Haas?"

"He was a Belgium scientist living and working in Scotland. He'd long been ostracized from his post at the University due to his controversial ideas. They even wiped his name from all the scientific literature he took part in."

"Why?"

"He wasn't a traditional scientist. Instead of following the conventional heroes, he was drawn to the likes of Nikola Tesla. Haas studied energy, just like Tesla, but the type of energy Haas was interested in couldn't be photographed in a thunderbolt of light. He was obsessed by the energy you cannot see but that exists nonetheless. And as he became increasingly demented in old age, his experiments caught the company's attention. He was just the kind of twisted genius they needed for their research. But as brilliant as Haas was, he should have known his alliance would end badly. All loose ends have to be swept up, you know?"

Jane nodded. "All witnesses need to die." She glanced at the book again. "This is way over my head, Saul. Can you at least give me a nutshell explanation of what this old guy was into?"

Saul leaned toward Jane. "He theorized that the energy from one person could be given to another. It wasn't a gigantic, speculative leap. While academia doesn't accept it, real life examples exist where transplant patients often feel strange or different after their surgery, feeling the cellular energy of their donor. Using that as his foundation, he accepted that there was a clear transference of awareness and perception from one body to another. Haas sought to develop a way that could capture that consciousness in its purest form and transfer it to another human being."

"My God, he sounds like a geriatric Frankenstein."

"Haas would have loved that association. I think he'd lost his soul at the end. I'm not sure you can do what he did if you have a shred of conscience left."

"If Haas was so evil, why in the hell did Gabe use his name?"

"Maybe to remind him of the kind of evil he walked away from? Or perhaps to draw your attention to that name?"

Jane turned to the side, desperately trying to patch together a plan. "What do you know about the Congo?"

"I know it's a place where hope doesn't exist and where people are looked on like cattle. Bred and slaughtered at the whim of those in charge."

"And when they die, nobody cares," Jane surmised. "Nobody misses them because even their families are killed alongside them."

"Commodity is the word you're searching for. We're all commodities to them. We're only as useful as what we can offer them. As destructively brilliant as Haas was, he wasn't above them. They used him and when they were done, they eliminated him."

Jane considered it. "But Gabe wasn't only a commodity to them. They obviously didn't want to eliminate him completely. Through his heart, they could still benefit from him. Just exactly what are they expecting to get from that heart?"

"Everything. Look at your friend, Harlan. If he was a different person, if he was more aware, if he had an understanding of how to manipulate that heart inside him, he could potentially be a very powerful man."

"*Potentially*. It's all theory, Saul."

"Not necessarily. You've been given enough proof that what I'm telling you is accurate. And the company never worried about having to support their theories. They don't have any corporations to answer to or investors to impress. It's a game for them but they take that game *very* seriously. They will continue to take as many lives as necessary to achieve whatever they want."

"And you're trying to tell me that Gabe had enough ammo to stop their train?"

"Not completely." He considered his words carefully. "He wanted to shine the light on them because the more light you push into the darkness, the less power it will have. And through that, the dominos can begin to fall until there's so much light on the truth that it can't be ignored any longer. Gabriel's intention was to push over the first domino."

"And now that's *my* job?"

"Consider yourself the domino pusher."

Jane felt every wall in that underground cavern closing in on her. "What if I say no? What if I choose to disappear?"

Saul sat back and observed her. "You could do that. You could run and keep running. But it wouldn't be freedom you'd be feeling."

"I'm fucked either way?"

He smiled. "Something like that." He reached into the side table's top drawer and pulled out a deck of Tarot cards. "Do you know the allegory of The Fool that's told through the Tarot?"

"No."

Saul went through the deck, pulling out the twenty-two Major Arcana cards. He laid them out on the coffee table. "The first card is The Fool. The story that continues through the successive cards involves his spiritual journey. He meets his teachers," Saul pointed to the The Magician and The High Priestess cards. "Later in his journey, he finds love," he said as he pointed to The Lovers. "As he evolves on his journey, he discovers his power and his strength. But then he has his dark night of the soul." Saul touched The Hanged Man card. "And from that, a purely spiritual death," he pointed to The Death card. "He learns temperance before he encounters The Devil, the evil within all of us. From there, his world crumbles. And the towers of ego he's built collapse in total destruction." He held up The Tower card. "His life is obliterated. The slate is wiped clean. At that point, he could choose to die. But instead, The Fool selects the spiritual path. The Tower Card is the sixteenth card in the deck. The seventeenth card is The Star."

Jane picked it up. The illustration showed a woman bent on one knee over a body of water, holding two vessels of water. One foot is firmly in the water and one is on the earth. Her right hand pours the water into the pond while her left hand pours water onto the ground. Seven white stars and one larger yellow star hover above her head. "What does this mean?"

"There are a lot of interpretations. But I see it as a portentous card. It speaks of renewed hope and purpose. Rebirth. Some believe it represents the beginning of higher consciousness or the pathway that leads to that place. It's the first card toward the end of The Fool's journey that moves him closer to the light." He dealt The Moon and then The Sun cards. "And finally to the sun. After that, there is Judgement and, finally, The World." He lay the cards out and sat back. "But the higher enlightenment begins with the seventeenth card."

"So what does seventeen mean?"

"You seeing it a lot?"

"Lately, yeah."

"I don't know that it means anything by itself. It's what it attaches to that seems to have the deeper context. King Tutankhamen was wrapped in seventeen sheets. The Parthenon is seventeen columns long. Beethoven wrote seventeen string quartets. In the Bible, the seventeenth book is the shortest. In the exact middle of the Bible, you'll find the 117th Psalm, which is also the shortest. The Great Flood started on the seventeenth of the month and Noah's Ark landed on Mount Ararat on the seventeenth. There are seventeen muscles in the tongue. Japanese Haiku contains seventeen syllables. The U.S. Navy had seventeen battleships in service when the Japanese attacked Pearl Harbor. The White House is on the seventeenth street in Washington and there are seventeen methods of strangulation. Those are just a handful of examples I can offer you. It's not a magical number but whatever it touches, in whatever shape or form, seems to carry with it a lingering echo that is not quickly forgotten."

Jane stared at The Star card. "Enlightenment." She looked at Saul. "It's not for the queasy or the narrow minded, is it?"

"Sure it is. It's for everyone. And all you have to realize is that it is already present within you and just needs the proper spark to ignite your mind." He leaned closer with an uncompromising expression. "Enlightenment is our birthright. And God help you if you let them take it from you."

His words chilled Jane. "Can I take the binder with me?"

"No. You don't need it. You already know that part of their plan. Your job is to complete the second part. And you only have days to do it."

"How many days?"

"Two or three at the most."

Jane turned away, defeat filling every pore.

"*Yes*," Saul stressed. "You *can* do this. You can't give up." He reached across the table and grabbed her hand, protecting it in his. "They can't win. Did you hear me? I was part of their sickness. I know what they dream about and, believe me, it's a nightmare."

"If it's even possible, I could *maybe* stop one of the sick experiments. But from what I understand, Romulus has their hand in every facet of the world. Anything I help bring out will be a drop in the bucket. They'll just shove it under the rug and keep moving forward with the thousand other plans they've got going."

"You're not supposed to stop everything. All you have to do is get the information to the right people so that the light can finally be shed on these pricks."

She sighed. "I don't know, Saul. I'm kinda tired of feeling used, you know?"

"The difference is you're being used for a good purpose."

"Uh-huh. Notice how the word 'used' is still in there?"

He peered into Jane's eyes, hypnotically securing her gaze. "How do I compel you?"

"Tell me the truth."

He smiled. "Interesting choice of words there. Truth? Whose version do you want?"

"How about the one that's closest to being accurate."

Still grasping her hand, he nodded. "I'm afraid they've made the answer to that question more difficult. You see, we're surrounded by lies. You truly have *no* idea how deeply those lies are rooted in our history, religions and spiritual lives. Any supposed truth, for what it's worth, is getting harder to find. Pretty soon, you won't recognize the truth when it walks up and slaps you on the head. *That's what they're counting on.*" He leaned a few inches closer. "How can I get this across to you?" His tone became alarming. "Their lies have become deeply embedded in the fabric of this world. And those who speak the truth are disavowed or destroyed. That's how *they* remain in control.

Believe me, I spent enough time on their side of the fence to understand how they've achieved it."

"Well, go on then. Tell me how they did it."

"They lead the ignorant from one disillusionment to another. They tease you with the next best thing that has a shelf life of six months. They quell your hysteria with drugs while your petitions remains unheard because of their blatant disinterest. They distract you with daily doses of 'bread and circus' so that you're looking the other way when they make their bold moves. They make you doubt your own feelings and distrust your intuition when it's screaming at you to get the hell out! Because you know what? Somewhere down deep inside all of us…somewhere that hasn't been napalmed by their propaganda, there's still an ancient awareness that *knows*. Even though everything around you appears ordinary and business as usual, that primeval cell inside you has the ability to see through their veils of deception. And when the few wake up and *see* the lies—when that light turns on—they want to shout from the rooftops! 'Look! Look over there! See that? Did you see it?' But they turn around and nobody's listening to them. They stare into the eyes of their friends and family and all they see are blank orbs and lost souls shaded by the façade of competence. So, they think, 'No, no, no. Can't speak up. Better to be safe and stay silent.' And so they do just that. They stay silent because they're terrified of being separated from friends, locked up or shunned by their family. That's a potent fear right there. They stay silent because they believe no one else out there has ever seen what they have seen or felt what they have felt in the deepest core of their soul." He took a breath. "And *that* is how the liars remain in control. Through one's silence and fear of alienation, the truth is buried deeper under the soil of fabrication and deceit. Chaos rules because eventually, it's easier to cling to whatever debris is left than to walk into the storm, taste the rain and greet the thunder with your fists balled and your courage lit like a fire that will never be put out." He let go of her hand. "And that, my dear, is why you must not give up."

Jane felt her world collapse around her as Saul walked with her to the Lincoln and then rose back up on terra firma. They drove in silence until he was a city block away from the CSA. Putting the car in park, he motioned for her to open her door. "No need to attract attention."

Jane got out and looked around. "You think they're watching us?"

Saul glanced around the area, sniffing out the unseen with his eyes. "Not right now. But they're close."

349

Knowing

She leaned into the car. "Aren't you going to give some kind of parting warning like everybody else has?"

He looked her straight in the eye. "No warnings. When the time comes, you'll know exactly what to do."

He turned the Lincoln around and disappeared down the dirt road. Something about his last words left a sterile sting against her heart.

CHAPTER 24

By the time Jane hiked back to the CSA, the classes were just breaking up and guests were taking advantage of the short recess. She didn't have a hard time locating Harlan; she could hear him delighting the group with another story.

"I got a ticket in the mail once from one of them cameras that snapped me goin' over the speed limit. You know what I did? I mailed *them* a photo of my hundred-dollar check!"

Jane waved toward Harlan.

"Hey there, honey!" he said, hugging her around the shoulders. "I just learned four more ways to compost."

Jane pulled him aside as casually as she could muster. "Something's come up. We gotta get outta here this afternoon."

Harlan's mood sobered up fast. "Why wait?" he whispered. "Let's do it now."

"No. I have to do the damn cards in order—"

"Huh?"

"The kid. He's going to take me to the location of the next card. I'll find whatever I need there and then we can take off." She spied Sage standing to the side. "Gotta go." Jane turned around and meandered around the visitors toward Sage.

"Where you been?" Sage asked urgently, keeping his focus in front of him. "I spent the morning keeping my ear to the ground to make sure Jude stayed away."

"Well, if you pressed your ear a little harder, you might have heard me."

"Huh?"

"Do I hear the *vroom-vroom* of a four-wheeler in my near future?"

They agreed that Jane would nonchalantly walk down the driveway and up the road where Sage would meet her on the four-wheeler. Less than half an hour later, he showed up and Jane hopped on the back of the ATV. He navigated toward Highway 17 then turned onto the byway that paralleled the highway. Less than one mile later, he turned left and kicked the puppy into the next gear. For three miles, they traveled up a bumpy, hard-packed mountain road with no guardrails or regular maintenance. Sage expertly avoided the many potholes as they ascended a steep hill that crested into a shallow valley where the road dead-ended.

They got off the vehicle and Sage led Jane two hundred feet across the grass and down a short hill where a babbling spring brook wound around a clump of aspens. It must have been an idyllic escape for Gabe, Jane mused, with a summertime panorama of wildflowers blanketing the surrounding meadows.

"That's where the cabin was," Sage said, pointing to an empty spot across the creek.

"What happened to it?"

"It got burned up in a wildfire right after Gabe left." He stared at the empty spot. "Gabe always said that fire was purifying. So when that thunderbolt sparked the grass and the fire broke out, I was the only one who really got the message." He pulled the postcard out of his jacket and held it in front of him, to his right. "See it?"

Jane easily made out the weathered windmill on the left where "X" marked the spot. They trudged through the moist ground but as they moved closer, the wet earth turned to mud, almost causing Jane to slip several times. Finally, they reached the windmill. Seeing that the "X" was exactly to the left of the windmill, Jane slipped across the muddy slope and scanned the immediate area. "There's nothing here!"

"It's gotta be there!"

"What am I even looking for?"

"I guess you'll know it when you see it," he said with a shrug.

Jane peered into the muddy swath of land that lined up with the windmill. Nothing. She decided to walk the path, feeling with the tip of her cowboy boot as she inched along. Fewer than five feet in, her boot scuffed against a round metal sign the size of a dinner plate. The bright yellow sun symbol caught her eye. Wiping off the mud from the metal, there was the marker: "SUNNY & SON FARMS—SPUD-TASTIC POTATOES SINCE 1937."

"This is it, Sage!" Jane looked off to the side. Lying next to the base of the windmill and covered with heavy burlap was a shovel. She started for it when Sage let out a quick whistle. She looked over at him.

He discreetly pointed behind him, toward an upper ridge that rimmed the valley. Standing in full view was Jude, with his ATV close by.

Jane's blood boiled. "What in the fuck is he doing?"

"Shit," Sage whispered, kicking the soil and pretending to look out over the valley. "He took the four-wheeler up the shortcut. You can't dig anything up now."

Jane's patience was wearing thin. "Listen to me, kid. My friend and I have to get outta here no later than tonight."

Sage thought about it. "He's going to be perched up there, waiting for you."

Jane ruminated. "Does he miss any meals?"

"Never."

"Okay. I'll figure this out."

They headed out of the area, toward the four-wheeler.

"Hey, I got to tell you something," Sage offered. "I don't know if it means anything but I heard Jude talking on his cell phone this morning really quietly."

"Yeah…"

"He never talks on his cell phone. The last time he did that was right before Gabe took off."

Jane's mouth went dry. "Fuck…"

"You really do need to get outta here."

"I can't leave without digging up whatever is underneath that dirt."

A hard south wind swept quickly through the valley, signaling an approaching spring rainstorm. They got on the ATV and drove away. Jude stayed put, never once taking his eyes off of them.

Once back at the CSA, Jane asked Sage to drop her at the van. He sped back to the main house as Jane trudged through the soggy field. The pitter-patter of rain spat against her leather jacket as she unlocked the passenger door. But it was already unlocked. Her heart raced as she dove into the van. Quickly opening her satchel, she found the postcards in the same place she left them. From what she could tell, they hadn't been disturbed. Digging into the center of the satchel, she felt around for the envelope of photos that Monroe gave her. Finding it, she pulled it out and lifted out the photos. They were all there. Checking the glove compartment, it was still locked and didn't look as if it'd been touched. Unlocking it, she pulled out the 9mm. That's when she spied her wallet sticking out from under the passenger seat. Grabbing it, she looked inside. The five hundred dollars was gone. Her two fake IDs had been removed and carelessly put back. Jane felt the tension mount. Suddenly, somebody rapped hard on the passenger window. Instinctively, she grabbed the 9mm up without even looking and pointed it.

"Whoa!" Harlan yelled, holding up his hands and taking a step back.

Jane unlocked the passenger door, waving Harlan inside.

"What's goin' on?" Harlan asked, his clothing wet from the rain.

"We got ripped off." She showed her empty wallet. "And he figures I'm either Anne LeRóy or Wanda LeRóy."

"He who?"

"Jude. The creepy little fuck is onto us." She momentarily considered telling him about her disturbing visit with Saul but decided against it.

Harlan glanced around in the back of the van. "Oh, hell, Jane."

She turned. "Shit!" All the bags in the back of the van had been opened and pawed through. Clothing, blankets, gear for the car, flashlights, food and more was strewn every direction. "Jesus. What in the hell did he take?"

Harlan hefted his body back into the van and feverishly searched through the chaos. "Aw, hell, Jane. He found my bag of stuff and threw it everywhere. Looks like he ripped off my ball cap with the lights—"

"What about the notebook?"

He rummaged through the piles. "I don't see it, Jane!" His voice became frantic as the rain pounded harder on the roof of the van.

"Calm down, Harlan."

"Looks like the son-of-a-bitch stole the Vicodin."

"Figures..."

"Oh, no....oh, God..."

"What?"

Harlan held up the two empty prescription bottles of his anti-rejection drugs. "He tossed them, Jane! I can't live without them!"

Jane darted out of the van and swung open the back door. The rain pelted her face as she sorted through the mess. "What's this?" She held up a prescription bottle.

"That's the Valium. He must have missed it."

Jane quickly shoved it into her jacket pocket and crawled into the clutter, searching for any sign of his pills. Coming up empty, she jumped outside. "He had to toss the pills somewhere. Tell me their colors."

"One capsule is light brown and cream. The other is a light purple tablet."

They searched the surrounding area.

"I found two purple ones!" Harlan exclaimed.

Jane discovered three of the brown and cream capsules but one of them was already halfway dissolved and useless. After half an hour, they were able to gather only six of the tablets and three of the purple tablets, enough to last Harlan three days.

Harlan looked at her with dread. "Jane, what in the world am I gonna do? I'm dead without these drugs."

"I'll figure it out, goddammit!" She ran her fingers through her black hair. "First things first." After giving it serious thought, she devised a precise plan for later that night. When she told Harlan her plan, he regarded her with slack-jawed awe.

"Damn, Jane. I hope I never get on your bad side."

By dinnertime, both of them were ready to see the CSA in their rear view mirror. But Jude was nowhere to be found. It was hard for Jane to believe he was still sitting on that ridge in the pouring rain waiting for her to return. Darkness had already descended as the group grabbed their plates and made their way down the food line. Sage hovered close by but kept his mouth shut. Jane was impressed by his ability to stay so cool, while still being aware of her situation. As the guests filled their plates, Blythe reminded everyone of "The Singing Bowls" meditation that would take place after the meal. From what Jane gathered, seven glass bowls representing the seven chakras would be "played" as they "sang" and the vibrations would "clear the cloudy corners" of everyone's body. As much as Jane had misgivings about the New Age world, Blythe's "singing bowls" were the perfectly tuned foil she needed.

Ninety minutes later and bloated from too much gluten-free pasta and three-bean salad, Jane and Harlan were still waiting for Jude's arrival. Blythe instructed the group to file into the room just off the kitchen and sit in a circle. Sage ducked away and up the stairs, hanging on the landing for a little bit, before retreating into his bedroom. The outside kitchen door opened and Jude walked in just as Jane carried her plate and cup to the sink. She pretended to be preoccupied with the dishes but she saw every move the skinny little asshat made. He was wet and covered with mud from the soles of his boots to his knees. She wasn't sure whether he got his ATV stuck on the trail or if he just barreled through muddy runoff. Either way, he looked fit to be tied as he scooped up what was left of the food, slammed it onto his plate and sat down at the long table. Harlan eyed Jane and she tilted her head toward the meditation group. Reluctantly, he followed the other visitors into the next room, closing the door behind him.

Jane felt her body shaking but not from fear. All she wanted to do was wrap a belt around Jude's scrawny neck and pull it tightly until she pressed the last peep out of his throat. Instead, she crossed to the thermos of spicy, hot apple cider and poured it into her mug.

"Might ask me if I'd want a cup," Jude declared with a slimy tenor.

Jane turned. "Who do you think this is for?"

He eyed her carefully. "Why you being so nice to me?"

"You're wet. You must be cold. Figured you'd want something hot." She set the mug in front of him.

Jude shoved a mouthful of food into his ragged little mouth and washed it down with a gulp of cider. "Ain't even that hot!"

"You got a lot of complaints, don't you?"

Gradually, a strange tone began to emit from the next room. Jane likened it to an armada of alien spacecraft hovering above the farm as their galactic engines whirred. With each passing second, the tones increased in intensity. Part of her wanted to lay back, relax and let the mesmerizing droning pulse from the "singing bowls" sweep her into dreamland. But focus was paramount right now. She got up and poured herself what was left out of the coffeepot. After a few good swigs of black coffee, she felt more centered, even as the buzzing hum grew louder and deeper. Jane moved to the side and reread all the homey plaques she'd already committed to memory. Looking at the "You are here" plaque again with the longitude and latitude written out, a piece of the puzzle possibly clicked into place. Once she got back to her computer, she could verify it.

"You know," Jude said, after fifteen long minutes of slurping his food and cider, "for someone who don't look like they know their way 'round a kitchen, you sure are hangin' out in this one a long time. Don't you have someplace you need to be?"

The cycling droning tones from the "singing bowls" deepened. Jane pulled out a chair and sat down across the table from Jude. Turning back to the wall, she checked the clock.

"Whatcha doin'?" he griped, plowing the last bite of food into his mouth.

"How was your dinner?"

He regarded her with an indifferent sneer. "Why you care?" Downing the last drop of cider, he slammed the mug on the table and wiped his mouth with his filthy hand.

"Did you grab everything you wanted?"

He squinted his eyes toward her. "What in the hell is up with you?"

She leaned forward on her elbows. "I'm asking because I see you got what you wanted out of our van."

Jude casually yawned in a dismissive manner, sliding his plate and cup to the side. He smiled, licking his thin lips as he tipped his chair back. "Yeah? What proof you got?"

Jane looked at him for a hard minute. She was reminded that people really *do* take on the grime of their connections. Experience really does wash over each of us and color the unseen aura that shadows and compels us. She leaned closer to him. "Let me ask you something. How long have you been a piece of shit?"

He righted his chair. "You got a lot of nerve, bitch," he said with a lazy drawl.

She felt her blood boil. "You know what? You're right. I do. I got a lot of nerve. And when someone corners me, I fight back." She stood up, checking the clock one more time.

"Why you keep lookin' at that damn clock?"

Jane glanced around the room, making sure they were alone. She maneuvered around the long table and stopped directly behind Jude. Leaning closer to him, she spoke clearly above the din of "singing bowls." "I'm waiting for it to kick in, Jude."

"What kick in?"

Jane reached into her pocket and slammed the empty bottle of Valium on the table in front of him. "You missed this one when you ripped the Vicodin. There were nineteen pills in that bottle. And now those nineteen pills are percolating through your stomach and into your failing liver where they will surely not succeed."

Jude turned around in his chair, eyes wide as saucers. "Are you batshit crazy, woman? That's a fuckin' overdose!" He started to stand up but wobbled as the room spun around him.

"Yeah, it's a fuckin' overdose." Jane snatched up the empty orange prescription bottle and shoved it in her jacket pocket. Without any effort, she slammed Jude's bony ass back into his chair. "I figured you had it coming after what you did to us...and our other friend?"

The pulsating sounds from the adjacent room intensified until it felt as if they were swimming in the center of a swarm of bees. Desperate, Jude put his index finger down his throat. Jane grabbed his wrist, twisted it and pulled it out of his mouth.

"No way, you son-of-a-bitch. You're not getting out of it that easily."

Jude tried to fight her but the Valium was quickly creeping up on him. He fell back into his chair. Spying his dinner knife, he grabbed for it, but Jane was way ahead of him. She skimmed it down the long table before reaching into her rear waistband and revealing the 9mm. With his collar in a vice grip, she pressed the tip of the pistol into his temple.

"Did you call them?" she said to him, inches from his haggard face. "Did you give us up?"

Jude glared at Jane, moving in and out of consciousness.

"What were we worth to you this time?" she spat at him, tightening her hold on his collar. "Talk to me!" She slapped him hard across his face. "What are you gonna get out of this deal, asshole! Another fucking case of whiskey?" She yanked up on his collar, moving her finger to the trigger. "Tell me, you motherfucker!"

His face was turning beet red as she slapped him again, leaving a palm print against his cheek.

"*What did you tell them*?!" Jane yelled, pulling the gun off his temple and aiming it in the middle of his forehead. "Tell me before you fucking die!"

"No—" Sage softly said.

Jane jerked backward, letting go of Jude and looked up on the landing. Sage stood there, eyes pleading for her to back off. The pulsating hum reached an almost deafening drone. Jane glanced down at Jude. He'd collapsed over the table and was barely conscious. She bent down so he could easily see her with his one open eye.

"As you drift off to sleep right now," Jane whispered into his ear. "Know in your heart that you're gonna wake up in hell." She shoved the pistol in her waistband, buttoned up her jacket and waved goodbye to Sage.

He raced down the stairs. "I'll drive you up on the four-wheeler!"

"No. I'm not dragging you into this any more!"

"The rain makes that road almost impossible to drive up—"

"Enough!" Jane stated. "You stay here. And if I catch you up there, I'll shoot you," she said flippantly. She jutted her chin toward the meditation room. "Go in and get him for me."

Sage obliged. Jane double-checked Jude's status, holding a stainless steel spoon under his nose to confirm he was still breathing. Harlan quickly walked into the room, followed by the kid.

"Damn," Harlan said, his head swirling, "you pulled me out of there just in time. I thought I was gonna shapeshift."

Jane motioned Harlan toward the back kitchen door. He glanced over at Jude.

"Come on, Harlan! Let's go!"

He raced outside. Jane turned to Sage and thanked him before following Harlan into the darkness and pouring rain. Reaching into her pocket, she pulled out a small flashlight and they raced as fast as they could to the van. Soaked to the bone, Jane sped out of the field and back up the dirt road toward Highway 17. Turning on her high beams, Jane retraced their earlier steps and came to the bottom of the hill that lead up to Gabe's location.

"It's gonna be slick as snot, Jane!" Harlan yelled above the din of pelting rain on the roof.

"Do we have a fucking choice?" she yelled, sticking the van in reverse. Rolling it backward twenty feet, she kicked it into gear. "Let's see what this vanilla van can do."

She gunned it, fishtailing immediately and sliding sideways fifteen feet. It lurched to a halt and started to sputter.

"You know," Harlan suggested, "sometimes the softer approach is best in situations like this. Push the accelerator *gently*." He looked at her. "You know how to do that, right?"

Righting the van, she gathered her thoughts and lightly tapped the accelerator. The van moved forward, sliding just a bit before Jane was able to smoothly correct the direction. Midway up the hill, a torrent of muddy water poured down the side embankment, forcing her to hug the other side of the road. Slowly and steadily, she kept moving forward and crested the hill. Not wanting to risk getting the van mired in the muck, she turned it around so it pointed downhill. Racing across the drenched meadow, Harlan and Jane located the "Sunny Farms" metal sign with the flashlight. They took turns digging into the soaked earth, pulling up clumps of roots and grass shoots.

Knowing

Finally, the shovel tip hit a large metal box. Harlan reached into the hole and drew up the heavy, locked box.

Racing back to the van, they got in and secured the box. Jane slid it into low gear and gingerly worked her way back down the quickly disintegrating road. After catching a rock that pitched the vehicle sideways, Jane slowly eased the van back into place and continued inching down the treacherous incline. She drove for another few miles before finding a pullout off Highway 17 and parking.

Turning on the interior light, they examined the unearthed mystery. It looked like it might have been used as an ammo box during a past war, with its olive drab color and multiple dents and scratches. A simple combination padlock was the only thing between them and the contents.

"I say shoot the son-of-a-bitch off," Harlan chimed in.

"Wait. Just try one combo. How about zero, one, seven."

Jane shown the flashlight on the lock as Harlan spun the dial around and back. After coming around to seven, he lifted the hinge and it opened.

Harlan handed the box to her. "You look through it. I'm too nervous."

Jane pulled the box closer and opened the lid. A letter-sized white envelope sat on top of the contents. Attached to the envelope was a square sticky note that had a small drawing of a pinecone in the upper left corner. On it were the handwritten words, "Thank you, from the bottom of my heart." She showed it to Harlan.

"Who do you think he's writin' that to?" he asked.

Jane opened the sealed envelope and brought out the contents. "It's five, one-hundred dollar bills."

"That's impossible, Jane," he said, stunned. "How could—"

"Bank of Gabriel? Remember?"

"Yeah, but how could he know—"

"Oh my God," Jane mumbled. She lifted a heavy, boxed and wrapped package out of the box that measured twelve inches square and eight inches high. Fingering the edges of the package, Jane knew exactly what was inside. "It's more cash. *A lot* more cash." She carefully unwrapped it and they stared at the box of greenback. "There's gotta be more than half a million dollars here."

"What's that?" Harlan pointed to a folded note attached to one of the piles of cash.

Jane opened the note. Inside, she saw two words: "FOR MARION."

"Look at that, Jane. Is that not a beautiful thing he did?"

Jane didn't say a word. Her head was spinning with options.

"Jane?" He looked at her with a questioning glare. "There's more in there."

She handed the block of cash to Harlan and pulled out another postcard. The photo looked like your standard, bucolic, rustic Colorado ranch barn. Something about the photograph was reminiscent to Jane. She showed it to Harlan.

"Oh, hell, Jane. That's the place with the tall grass. When I—" he caught himself. "When *he* was a boy and nailing that rabbit? That's the barn I seen in that vision."

Jane agreed. She recalled seeing the same barn in the identical scene when she forced herself into Harlan's altered world. Quickly turning the post-card over, there was a "5" circled on the back. It was the missing card from the series. To the right was a name and address. The name was Iris Cristsóne. And based on the address, that barn was fewer than three miles away, just off Highway 17.

CHAPTER 25

The cloudy night hampered their short drive, as the moonlight fought through the haze. The storm died down, leaving a soft mist in its place. It was closing in on eleven and Jane was forced to slow down and stop at every highway turnoff to check the road numbers. After finally locating the approximate exit, Jane turned off the highway. Even surrounded by the coal black evening, the area felt strangely familiar.

"You feel anything?" she asked him.

"Yeah. Remember that sadness I felt during the first part of our trip?"

"I do. I'm feeling it again right now myself."

Jane parked the van and got out, walking to the fence line. She recalled Blythe's statement about how Gabe went out of his way to say his "sister Iris" was "*much* more like a mother to him." His sense of humor, Jane decided, was as ambiguous as he could be. Gazing into the near distance, she saw a familiar barn. The field in front of her was where they picked the wild asparagus. And it was in that barn where the young girl gave her the food and the clothes still on Harlan's back. She was suddenly reminded of a quote from T.S. Eliot on a card she was given a couple years before. "And the end of all our exploring will be to arrive where we started and know the place for the first time." As if on cue, the thick clouds moved away from the moon, allowing the blue light to illuminate the ground.

Jane walked to the corner of the dirt road that led to Cristsóne farm. She felt the sadness in her heart deepen. Harlan got out of the van and joined her. He stared down the dark road as a swell of emotion balled in his throat.

"That's home," he said, choking up. "He...he brought it home for safe keeping."

"What's left in your bag of tricks?"

"Just the old key I found on the ground that doesn't unlock anything."

"Get it, would you?"

Harlan returned to the van and found it. Turning back, he saw the strangest thing. "Hey, Jane! Check out the name of the road."

Jane looked up. The weathered sign read: Perry Ridge County Road 017. Somehow, she'd missed that the first time they motored down this way. Instead of coming up with a suitable explanation for this coincidence, she calmly returned to the van and took their destiny into her hands.

She drove as far as she felt was safe, keeping the headlights off. Once in front of the large farm, Jane parked the van off the road. Moonlight danced across the metal roof of the large barn, making it easy to locate. Sliding through the barbwire fence, Jane and Harlan moved quickly across the barren field. Coming up on the large rear door, Jane unlatched it and they went inside. She found the light and turned it on. Harlan immediately appeared overwhelmed.

"Hey," Jane said softly. "Don't cut out on me now."

He turned in slow circles, scanning the upper levels where the last bales of hay stood waiting. "I used to play up there." His voice was distant and overcome with emotion. "When I'd hear my mother coming, I'd sit in that corner over there and stay real still. That's the first time I made myself invisible…"

Jane gently approached him, resting a firm hand on his shoulder. "I need you to tell me where he put whatever it is we're supposed to unlock."

Harlan stood quietly, glancing around the area. He moved purposefully to the side of the large opened door where stacks of grain bags lay against the sturdy wall. He hefted one bag after another off the stack, piling them behind him. "Look, Jane."

Jane came forward and saw the peripatetic "Sunny Farms" metal sign attached to the wall. "Oh, hell. Not another dig."

Harlan found a shovel and started to stab the ground when Jane stopped him.

"Check that out," she said, pointing to a hinge that poked out from under the sign. She lifted the metal sign off the wall and discovered a ten-inch square door with a latch. Opening it, she removed a 9 x 16 inch metal box that required a small key to unlock it.

Harlan held up the old key he found on the road. "That's too big."

"Looking for this?" a soft voice asked.

Harlan and Jane spun around. A tall woman with a shock of white hair stood at the far door, supported by her walker. She looked to be in her early sixties but was very frail, painfully thin and hooked to a small, portable oxygen tank that hung on the front arm of her walker. A heavy, barn jacket covered her chest over a long gray nightgown.

Knowing

Moving closer, she stopped in the center of the barn, struggling to breathe. She held up a tiny metal key in her bony fingers. "I've wondered who would show up ever since he left it here." She rolled a few feet closer to them. "I don't have a gun. Unlike my son, I never believed in them. So, if your intention is to kill me, do it quickly."

Jane looked at her. "Iris?"

The woman nodded.

"Why did you come down here? Why didn't you call the cops? Somebody else could have been in here. Somebody who actually *did* want to hurt you."

Iris relaxed a bit. She glanced at Harlan and then back to Jane. "I don't care if I die. I welcome it." She studied the ground. "I've wanted to die for years."

Jane watched the pain engulf Iris. "Ever since he left home?"

She nodded, her lower lip trembling. "Seventeen years ago, almost to the date." Her mind fell back into a shattered memory. "He never said goodbye. He didn't leave a note. He was here one day and gone the next." She looked at Jane. "We could never contain him. He was our only child but he didn't feel as if he came from us. We didn't understand him and we thought that if we tried to control him more, he would come around to our way of thinking. But that never happened."

Jane moved closer to Iris. "Yes. It actually did happen."

Iris regarded Jane with a questioning stare. "I don't understand."

"He walked away from the violence. He holed up in a cabin for many months and he found himself again."

Tears welled in Iris' eyes. "When?" she whispered.

"About four and a half years ago."

Iris steadied herself, clearly stunned by the news. Jane brought a folding chair over to her and helped her take a seat.

"Where was the cabin?" Iris asked, tearfully.

"Three miles east of here," Jane softly stated.

Iris looked off to the side as a wellspring of grief overwhelmed her. "He told me I was imagining it…"

"Who's that?" Jane asked.

"Oscar. My late husband. I'd tell him that I'd come down into the barn and I could feel Gabriel here. I'd call out for him but he'd never respond. It reminded me of how he liked to play the 'invisible game' when he was a child. He'd tell me he could stand right next to me and I wouldn't see him. Of course, I didn't believe him then. But I realize now, if anyone could do that, he probably could figure it out." She pulled a tissue out from her sleeve. "When I found that box and the key on top of it, I knew I wasn't imaging his visits. But I never told his father about it. He would have told me to throw the box into the pond, without even opening it. That's why I hid it away and kept the key close by." She shook her head. "Oscar never forgave Gabriel for leaving like he did and pursuing the life he chose. And the years of absence just made it worse until he dropped dead in the field from a heart attack." She sat back, looking at Harlan and Jane. "I wish...I wish Gabriel would have come out of the shadows when he'd stop by. I never got to tell him that I forgave him."

Harlan walked over to Iris. Kneeling next to her on one knee, he clasped her left hand in his. For a moment, she didn't turn to him. Then, as the scent of familiarity blossomed, she made eye contact. Staring into his eyes, her face softened. She drew her right hand to her heart and held it there, as if to steady herself against the unseen current. The longer she looked into his eyes, the more her body melted into the chair.

"What's happening?" Iris said, barely audible.

"You don't have to suffer anymore," Harlan said, his voice momentarily sounding strangely different. "All that's over now."

Iris collapsed in Harlan's arms, sobbing uncontrollably. After a long minute, she pulled back and brushed her hand against his chest. She fell into his eyes. "If I didn't know any better," she said, trailing off. Wiping her eyes with her tissue, she let out a long breath. "It's done," she stated with a gentle nod of her head. She pressed the key into his hand. "Go on. Before they find you."

Harlan stood up, not taking his eyes off Iris.

"Go on," Iris insisted. "I'll be fine."

Jane tucked the metal box under her arm and tugged gently on Harlan's sleeve. Once they returned to the van and got in, Harlan gazed back to the barn.

"She won't live much longer," he said pensively, handing the tiny key to Jane.

Jane drove several miles down the frontage road before turning into a pullout and parking under the cover of a large tree. Her plan was to hang out there for the night and figure out the rest of their trip in the morning. While Harlan busied himself laying out his bedding and reorganizing the chaos that Jude created, Jane sat in the front seat staring at the locked metal box.

Knowing

"You gonna open that or what?" Harlan asked. After being met with silence, he piped up again. "What are you afraid of? That this nightmare is comin' to an end? I sure ain't! I say open that damn box and let's get goin' to New Mexico."

"Who says we have to go?" her voice was eerily distant.

Harlan tossed down his pillow and crawled forward toward Jane. "Because we got one more postcard. Ain't you the one who wants to do everything in order?"

Jane mumbled her words.

"What's that?" Harlan asked, leaning closer.

"It's a fucking trap," she stated with authority. She turned to him, eyes on fire. "Chimayo? It's a trap. They're waiting for you there. Why in the hell would I lead you into that? After everything we've been through, trying to stay alive, dodging cameras and cops and red-haired fucks in black sedans? Why in God's name would I do that?"

"Because that's exactly what Gabe wants."

"Really? Well, you know what? Fuck Gabe."

"Jane—"

"No. I mean it. Fuck him. What did he ever do for me except complicate my life, fuck up your life and turn our realities into Swiss cheese? *Fuck him*! I will not let those bastards kill you. You have a life, Harlan. It's time to live it."

"And how in the hell am I supposed to do that now, after all that's happened?"

She tapped the muddy box with the toe of her cowboy boot. "We got at least five hundred thousand dollars sitting right there. That'll buy us a shitload of freedom."

Harlan pulled back, screwing his face into a frown. "He marked that for Marion—"

"She doesn't need it—"

"She's got a baby on the way—"

"That's not my responsibility, Harlan."

"Well, I don't care. For whatever reason, Gabe wants her to have that money and he's askin' you to take care of it for him."

"You know, for a guy who is supposedly all knowing, Gabe sure had a hard time getting his shit together at the end." Her tone was unforgiving and cruel.

"*Jane*—"

"Don't you think? Running out of time and hiding all these cards and money and whatnot all over hell and back. If anything, I wouldn't call him 'second sighted,' I'd call him shortsighted."

"Jane, stop it! This ain't about you and it ain't about me neither."

"Right. It's about a dead man. *A dead man*, Harlan."

"Stop it! He's as alive as ever." He looked at her more closely. "Whose side are you on?"

"What kind of a question is that?"

"How come you ain't answerin' it?"

She derisively laughed. "Don't try to be a cop, Harlan."

"Well, maybe one of us here needs to be a cop and remember what we're workin' toward!" He leaned in closer. "I don't like what I'm seein' in those eyes of yours."

"What's that?"

"Cold-heartedness, for starters. Hatred. Resentment. And just plain meanness." He eyed her with greater precision as concern quickly clouded his face. "I'm thinkin' about Jude right now. I have a feelin' you probably enjoyed doin' that to him."

She turned to him with a callous expression. "You're right. I did. After what he did to Gabe and most likely repeated for you…yeah, I did enjoy it."

"Where's that bottle of Valium?"

Jane brought it out of her pocket and slapped it into Harlan's palm.

"Okay. Now, where are the pills?"

She smiled.

"*Jane*? Where are the pills?"

There was an uncomfortable pause before she reached into her other jacket pocket and pulled out a handful of light blue tablets. "Count 'em, if that makes you feel better."

Harlan counted each one as he dropped it back into the bottle. "Seventeen."

She nodded. "And two in his nasty little gut. When he wakes up tomorrow, he'll hopefully be rockin' a pretty bad headache." She noted a strained expression on Harlan's face. "Don't look at me like that, Harlan. I've gotten you this far and I've done it staying smart and strong. Frankly, I've always found it odd how some people are scared of strong individuals. I've never been inspired by weakness. You do what you have to do in this world. If you don't, they'll eat you alive." She eyed the money-bomb box. "It's time we started thinking about what's best for us."

Knowing

"Really? I see. So, what's your plan, Jane? You gonna disappear?"

"*We* are."

"No! *Not me.*" He turned and crawled back into the rear of the van. "You can drive me to New Mexico and let me out at Chimney-O. Then you can be on your way if that's what you still want to do."

Jane found a cigarette and angrily got out of the van. By the time she'd burned it down to the butt, she'd calmed down a little but there was still enough boiling rage bubbling underneath. Feeling inside her pocket, she brought out the key. The minute she turned that damn lock, she knew there was no going back. Part of her wanted to know what Gabe hid in there and another part willed herself not to care. Crawling back into the van, she glanced back at Harlan. He was fast asleep and practicing another round of mouth breathing. She gazed at the large moneybox. Leaning over, she lifted the lid and pulled out the smaller envelope of cash. As she removed the crisp bills, something fluttered out of the corner of the envelope. Shining her small flashlight on the floor near the accelerator pedal, Jane retrieved a round sticker the size of a quarter. After closer inspection, she realized it was a band-aid and the topside sported a cheerful drawing of a smiling rising sun over a green hillside. Jane stared at that damn thing far too long, her mind tossing around various possibilities for its proposed usefulness. *Shit*, she thought to herself. Gabe had drawn her in again.

Slipping the band-aid into her jacket pocket, she pulled the locked box toward her. Setting it on her lap, she faltered before sliding the key into the lock and turning it. Inside, was a large legal-sized brown envelope, secured with a wax seal. Breaking the seal, Jane slid out a stack of stapled documents. At first glance, most of the documents were scanned from computer files, but there were also a few handwritten pages, along with some typed passages. The top page was handwritten in ballpoint pen by Gabe and seemed to be a letter of intent. It was addressed to "To Whom It May Concern."

"Please combine this documentation with the photographic evidence and any corroborating verification you have gathered, as methods most likely have advanced since I left this here. I trust you to deliver this package to the individual on the enclosed letter in a timely manner. This is the only copy available. Many thanks, Gabe."

Jane re-read his note several times and each time, she felt a growing indignation take over. Here was a dead man trying to clean up his loose ends and needing Jane to complete that circle. She was nobody's minon and, yet, curiosity took charge. She began reading. The whole thing sounded like science fiction, but, sadly, their plan was deadly and devastatingly serious. Gabriel had painstakingly gathered together covert files from Romulus' databases as well as supporting evidence from various sources and outlined what could only be described as the most hedonistic attempt at usurping psychological control over the masses. And, like everything Romulus conceived, it came at the expense of someone else. The problem was that, in this case, that "someone else" was a child.

From what Jane was able to ascertain amidst the mix of scientific documentation and the observations that Gabriel established, Romulus had hired Werner Haas to investigate how to take the consciousness from a human organ and cleanly transfer it into another body. However, it was determined by Romulus that the "sanctity" of the donor and their specific organ must be "compliant with the proposed agenda and meaningful outcome of the experiment." Jane knew that whatever words were chosen were done with purpose. The word "sanctity" seemed out of place. To her, that implied purity and even a sacred quality. But as the hours passed and she read every document, Jane agreed that "sanctity" was indeed a requirement.

It was given a title. "Project S.O.U.L." [Sourcing Optimal Uncalcified Light]. For all intents and purposes, it was a mining expedition, with the "mining" taking place in the deepest caverns of the brain. And the treasure they were after was none other than the human pineal gland. Based upon compelling studies that were included in the packet, the "health" of one's pineal gland determined one's ability to see outside of himself and potentially perceive every secret in the universe. But after the age of six, as Jane learned from her previous research, this tiny endocrine gland became encrusted with calcium until it gradually grew inactive. But the next line on the page really got Jane's attention.

"Imagine being able to see through the eye of a child?" the document read. Suddenly, the song on the Patsy Cline tape made twisted sense. However, instead of "eyes" as Patsy sang, this document specifically mentioned the single "eye." And *this* "seeing" was about *perception* and awareness, rather than visually acuity. To "see through the eye of a child" was Romulus' objective with their experiment. To accomplish it, they needed two things: "a young pineal gland from a pure subject and an application method that was painless and effective to administer the serum." As Jane read further, she felt like she'd been sucked into the middle of a nightmarish scene. According to

Haas' typed notes, "the most advantageous environment to remove the child's pineal gland is during periods of heightened trauma and terror, thereby allowing a massive flow of DMT to saturate the gland and *optimize* it." Jane read the sentence again. "Optimize?" she said aloud. Jane immediately thought about the photographs of the children in the Congo village, with their clean, surgical cranial incisions. It was beyond anything she could have envisioned. But she was also reminded of a term Saul used when he talked about the way Romulus looked at the populace. "Commodities," he told her. "We're only as useful as what we can offer them."

The fact that the macabre idea was even discussed, let alone put into action by locating a distant tribe and using them as part of the experiment, showed Jane that there were no limits to what "the company" would do. It seemed that Romulus truly was into "capturing the hearts and minds" of the populace to use for their own "vision" and benefit. And, she theorized, through that stolen insight, they hypothesized that through regular "doses," they would enjoy immortality along with infinite power over the populace. But the further she read, the more she wondered about the second part: how the "imprint of the pineal," as they called it, could be easily taken into their bodies and utilized. Turning the pages, she found a document titled, "The Serum."

Scanning it, Jane realized that when Gabriel put together his investigation, the process used to take in this "insight" was still on the proverbial drawing board. But one paragraph caught Jane's sharp eye. It discussed the possibility of an injection. However, because that involved a certain amount of discomfort, it was proposed that a less invasive method should be explored. The last line of the paragraph sent a chill up her spine. "Our goal is to make this therapy effortless. If it were possible to accomplish it from drinking a daily beverage that masked any peculiar flavors, this would be the preferred method of administration."

"Holy shit," Jane mumbled as she ruminated about the land grab in northeastern Colorado. There had to be a connection. Jane recalled the comment from the CEO of The Wöden Group at the news conference and how he thanked the "influential, forward thinking minds who helped make this happen." *Forward thinking*, Jane thought to herself. The more she mulled over a nefarious association between The Wöden Group and Romulus, the faster the pieces began falling into place. And the biggest piece of all was the announcement of those three hundred "very special" four-legged guests from Scotland who would be grazing on their grassland.

While she couldn't be certain, Jane began to formulate a theory. They wanted an "effortless" way to administer their dose and suggested that a "daily beverage" would be the preferred method. Jane stared into the darkness that circled the van. "Goat milk," she said. It wasn't that far fetched. She'd already seen how science had the capability to breed a "spider goat" by genetically altering a goat's embryo with the DNA of the spider. When the goats lactated, they produced a spider milk protein that was converted into a silk fiber, stronger than Kevlar. Was it possible, she wondered, to somehow genetically alter a goat's embryo with the fluid from the young pineal gland, create a mutated "pineal goat," thus producing the ultimate delivery system for the most powerful milk on the planet?

But, like everything else they devised, the milk would only be reserved for them. It was strange, Jane thought. Here was a group bent on exploiting consciousness because they didn't have the God-given abilities or the inclination to study and develop their own intuition. They wanted the quick fix—the one-step solution to enlightenment. And they were willing to hire as many brilliant people as it took to advance the process. But once their usefulness was drained, they were eliminated. She recalled *The Q* magazine's page seventeen "ad," dealing with the hit on Mitchell Cloud. Somehow, he must have secretly been part of their early process. When he died, the press referred to him as "the eccentric microbiologist who was obsessed with goats." Such a dismissive, throwaway line that the public chewed and spit out, Jane mused. But if they'd known the depths of Cloud's "obsession," she didn't think they'd trivialize his life's work.

And Werner Haas? Yes, he had to die too. They couldn't have a major player like Haas still sucking up the air when they launched the final stage of their experiment. Romulus could have sent anyone to kill him but they sent Gabriel. Perhaps, they truly did not understand how deeply Gabe was connected and wired into the unseen world. Maybe they never thought he'd go through Haas' files or open the cabinets and gather data. Maybe, Jane wondered, because Romulus lacked what they coveted—a heart, a soul and clean, pure insight—they made a cardinal mistake and hired the one man who would attempt to bring them down.

Combing through the last pages, Jane found a cover letter addressed to Jim Baptíste at the *Denver Post*. It was dated three days before Gabe was killed. In it, Gabe reiterated their previous telephone and email conversations and thanked John again for having the courage to look into this story. "Courage,"

Knowing

Gabe wrote at the end of the letter, "comes from the Latin root word *cor*, which means heart. I hope your heart is strong, Jim." Turning over the large folded envelope, Jane noticed that Gabe addressed it already with no return address and seventeen, one-dollar stamps. Either Gabe thought mailing costs would skyrocket by the time she found this or he was sending her a not-so-subtle message.

Turning on her computer, Jane checked on the next puzzle. Using the Congo as her template, she searched for the degrees, minutes and seconds of both the latitude and longitude coordinates that mirrored seventeen degrees north and thirty-three degrees west. She arrived at one location: Jomba. It was located just west of the Ugandan border in what looked to be a remote and isolated territory.

She brought out the ghastly photographic evidence of their "experiment." They would certainly lead credence to Gabe's assertions. Sliding the separate envelope with the photos underneath her packet, Jane rested her head on the seat. She was exhausted and felt the strain beginning to weigh heavily on her. Sleep hovered close by and she willingly succumbed to it.

When she awoke the next morning, Harlan was gone. Looking down at her lap, the stack of documents and the envelope of photos were also missing. Jane burst out of the van, spinning in circles in search for Harlan. She called out and heard nothing. Running over a short hill, she found him. He was seated cross-legged with his eyes closed and allowing the morning sun to warm his face. Next to him were the envelopes, along with a large map and another folder. She approached him carefully, not sure if he was aware of her presence.

"I hear you," he quietly said.

"You scared the shit out of me…again…"

He turned to her, opening his eyes. "Were you ever gonna tell me about this? Or did you think I was too dumb to understand it?"

"I was going to wait for the right time," she stated, hunkering down on the ground.

"When? When you figured I evolved more?" He turned away. "I'll be honest with you, I don't get half of what's written in there. But I sure as hell catch the gist. Them photos sure drive the point home." He let out a tired breath. "So, I guess we gotta find ourselves a post office."

"Not yet.

"You waitin' to collect more facts?"

"No."

"Then why are you waitin'?"

"I'm not sure."

Harlan showed irritation. "Okay, check this out," he drew the map closer to him, laying it flat on the ground. "Based on the address you got for Wanda—"

"What—?"

"Would you let me finish before you jump my shit?" He opened up the separate folder that held Wanda's photo and information. "Based on where you think she is right now, we have to go right through her location in order to get to Chimney-O."

"Chimayo."

"Whatever. The point is, you are seein' your sister."

"*Half*-sister."

"Whatever." He stood up and looked at Jane, studying her face. "If you're gonna disappear, you owe it to yourself to at least find out what she looks like. If you don't do that, it'll dog you forever, Jane."

She turned away. "That's exactly what he said to me before I left."

"Hank?"

She nodded.

"Smart man," he said, walking back to the van.

When she returned to the van, Harlan was swallowing his morning dose of drugs. "We have to make one stop before Wanda. It'll be quick."

The drive to New Mexico would take just under three hours. But thirty minutes later, and five minutes before nine o'clock, Jane rolled into the last small town in Colorado she could find that had a pharmacy. Parking across the nearly empty street, Jane observed the brick building and vacant lot. While Harlan chowed down on a breakfast of leftovers from the CSA, Jane kept her eyes peeled on the pharmacy. A small Prius rolled up and parked as a gray-haired woman in her early seventies got out of the car. She unlocked the front door and turned over the "Open" sign in the window.

"I'll be right back," Jane said, lowering her lighted ball cap over her forehead.

"What are you doin', Jane?"

"I feel a cold coming on. Maybe they'll have some Vitamin C."

She slipped out of the van and, glancing around the area, crossed the road and walked into the pharmacy. The older woman was in the far back, behind the glass window. Jane locked the front door, before turning the "Open" sign around to "Closed." She eyed the lone security camera in the corner of the room. Spotting a complimentary tea and coffee island, she grabbed the large dishcloth that lay under the coffeemaker. Keeping her head down and avoiding looking directly into the camera, Jane climbed up on a chair and slung the dishcloth over the camera.

"I'll be right there!" the woman called out from the back.

Jane jumped down, securing her hat lower on her forehead. Taking a deep breath, she steadied herself and approached the window. The gray-haired woman walked to the window with a cheerful smile.

"What can I do for you, sweetheart?" the woman asked Jane.

Jane reached behind her body and pulled out the 9mm from her waistband. Aiming it squarely at the woman's head with both hands, she stared her down. "Open the door, or I'll kill you."

CHAPTER 26

The woman moved her hand along the edge of the counter.

"Stop it!" Jane yelled. "Do *not* push the panic button or I will shoot you!"

The woman took a step back from the counter with her hands held up. "I didn't push anything, sweetheart."

"Stop calling me sweetheart and open the fucking door!"

The woman never took her eyes off Jane as she crossed to the side door and unlocked it. Jane turned the knob and, keeping the pistol on the woman, closed it behind her.

"It's okay," the woman gently said. "You don't have to do this."

"What?" Jane snapped.

"If you need help, I'll help you."

"Where do you keep the stock?"

"In the back room but—"

"Shut up!" Jane yelled. "Show me the room!"

She led Jane around a counter and through a back door with Jane staying several feet from her.

"Okay," the woman said nervously, "here we are."

Reaching into her jeans' pocket, she brought out a piece of paper and handed it to the woman. "I need as much of that as you have in stock."

The woman read the names on the paper and looked up at Jane with a quizzical expression. "These are anti-rejection drugs."

"I know! Give me all you have!" she demanded, shoving the gun closer to the woman.

"I'm sorry, sweetheart…I don't have these in stock."

"You gotta be fucking kidding me!"

The woman's face changed from frightened to compassionate. "I can get them for you."

"*When?*"

"I'll make some calls. It'll take about five hours to get them couriered up here—"

Knowing

"I don't have five fucking hours! I need them *now!* This minute!" The desperation in her voice was palpable.

"Sweetheart, I want to help you—"

Jane charged toward her, grabbing her from behind and wedged the 9mm against her head. "Stop it! You gotta have *something* in this place that'll work. Give me some fucking generics, I don't care!"

The woman grabbed the side of the shelf. "Please…please…I know you're desperate…but please don't make a bigger mistake." With that, she began whispering The Lord's Prayer.

Through the haze of tension, Jane left her body and stood to the side. There she drifted, shadowed by a cloud of malice and falling into the void. She didn't recognize her own face as it twisted into a malevolent expression. All that was left was for her to submit and allow her conscience to be seared forever. She could sense how easy that would be and she knew if she yielded to the potent demand, there was no going back.

"Give us this day, our daily bread," the woman whispered. "And forgive us our trespasses…"

Jane moved back into her body as her eyes welled with tears. Glancing to the shelf next to her, she was oddly attracted to a bright yellow box.

"As we forgive those who trespass against us," the woman continued. "And lead us not into temptation, but deliver us from evil…"

Jane reached over and grabbed two of the boxes, shoving them into her pocket. She loosened her grip on the woman and stepped back. "I'm not gonna hurt you…"

The woman turned around to face her. "If you're in trouble…let me help you."

Jane moved to the door. "God, I wish you could," she mumbled before walking into the front room and out the door.

By the time she reached the van, sweat beads were rolling down her face.

"You got a fever, Jane?" Harlan asked her as she turned the van around.

"No worries, Harlan."

They drove for the next couple hours nearly in silence. All around her, she felt the world pulling away as if it was about to take a long rest. Then she questioned if perhaps it wasn't the world that was moving away, maybe it was she who was disconnecting from the planet. The feeling stunned her, giving her pause as she contemplated her mortality. The longer she drove south into New Mexico, the more she questioned if she shared a mutual destiny with

Harlan. Was their bizarre meeting meant to end in a hail of bullets? If so, what was the point of everything that happened during the last week? If death was assured, then how did she measure her life up until that point? It was in that staggering moment, that she realized she hadn't allowed herself to really live until only the last few weeks. And even then, she was still a complex work in progress. How could a benevolent God snuff out her life when she was just beginning to figure it out? That seemed a pointless venture on His part. But then the thought crossed her mind that perhaps she'd learned everything she needed to learn and her time was up. On reflection, that also seemed absurd, especially since she was of the opinion that enlightened souls don't manhandle elderly women, demanding drugs. So, if she wasn't going to die, what was this feeling? Looking around at the miles of tan and ochre stained high desert, it was still present. There was a heartbeat of sadness but also of reconciliation and renewal. It was the peeling away of the old and the dying, melded in the realization that time was speeding up and each minute was precious. There was chaos in the air but there was wisdom to see it for what it was and not be paralyzed by the fear. As she continued down the windswept highway, she likened the barren landscape to the blank canvas her life had now become. It compelled her as much as it scared the hell out of her.

They drove into the small town of Esperanza, New Mexico just as the clock tower in the town square struck noon. The place looked like an adobe wonderland with one terra cotta structure after another. The New Mexican flag—featuring an ancient Zia symbol that represented the sun—flew proudly above the clock tower. The only information Jane had on Wanda was the location of her halfway house and the restaurant where she worked. Her anxiety turned into panic as she rolled the van in front of the halfway house and parked. Harlan held the open file in his hands, checking Wanda's mugshot against the stream of faces around them.

"She's not here," Jane quickly suggested.

"Give it time, Jane. It ain't like you called her ahead of time and told her to wait at the curb."

Harlan suggested they drive the short distance to the restaurant, which took all of three minutes, including parking. After half an hour, Jane was ready to call it a day when a woman walked out of the restaurant and headed around the corner into an alley that framed the building.

"Jane? That's her!"

Knowing

Jane felt her heart shudder. "Yeah. I know." She pulled the 1967 black and white photo of her mother and Harry Mills out of the file and grabbed her wallet. "I'm doing this alone, Harlan." She got out of the van and walked with hesitation to the mouth of the alley. Peering midway down the alley, she spotted Wanda edging closer to the side and then hiding quickly behind a huge commercial dumpster.

"Shit," Jane murmured, figuring her timing couldn't be worse. She jogged down the alley, slowing her pace as she moved within twenty feet of Wanda. The first thing she saw was Wanda's waitress cap peeking out from the top edge of the trash. The second thing she heard was the frantic flicking of a butane lighter. "Hey!" Jane shouted.

Wanda slammed her body against the large metal container and spun around. "Who's there?"

Jane was taken back by the voice. It sounded rather weak. "Wanda LeRóy?" she asked, realizing she sounded way too much like a cop.

There was a slight pause. "Yes?" she said, still obscured.

Jane's mouth went dry. "Come out, would you? I need to talk to you."

Wanda carefully slipped out of the shadows. She wore a soft pink uniform and a nametag with a pink ribbon and tiny brass angel glued on it. Her dirty blond hair was swept in a neat bun, exposing her ten earrings in one ear and seven in the other. Looking down at her fingernails, they'd been chewed to the quick. Her teeth were stained with nicotine and in desperate need of a dentist. She looked underweight to Jane, as her uniform hung a little too loose around her waist.

"What's going on?" Wanda asked in a soft voice.

Jane stared a little too long. "What are you smoking?"

"You a cop?"

"You doing drugs?" Jane quickly asked.

Wanda brought out cigarette and lighter. "Yeah. Nicotine. It's the hardest one to quit, you know?"

"Yeah. I hear you."

She tilted her head in a puzzled manner. "Who are you?"

She hesitated again. "Jane. My name's Jane." She couldn't stop staring. It was jarring to her, but at the same time, mesmerizing. It was strange and yet familiar. They were the same height and, looking into Wanda's eyes, she couldn't help but see a reflection of herself. It was in the way she licked her lips and looked off to the side when she answered a question. And there was the sigh. Somehow, across the channels of space and time, her other half had learned to sigh exactly the way Jane sighed in pitch perfect harmony. Wanda's body was ravaged by time but her mind hadn't agreed to it. She could still talk herself into believing she was twenty-one years old and invincible. Somehow, even after all the abuse from the drugs and the hard lifestyle, Wanda hadn't lost that optimistic spark. It was still there in the corners of her eyes, battling for dominance.

"What do you want?" Wanda asked.

Jane swallowed hard as she held out the photo. "The woman on the left…" She hesitated, realizing she hadn't rehearsed a damn thing. Of all the meetings to come to unprepared, this wasn't the one.

"What about her?"

"Her name…Her name is Anne LeRóy."

Wanda's eyes widened. "What?"

"That's your birth mother. And the man next to her is Harry Mills. That's your father." She handed the photo to her.

Wanda stared at the photo, her body gradually shaking.

"Please don't tell me you need a drink." Jane nervously said. "Are you okay?"

"No. I need to sit down," she faintly said.

They walked down the alley and across the street to a small park. Taking a seat at a picnic table, Jane waited until Wanda calmed down.

"You going to ask who I am?"

Wanda looked at Jane, her brown eyes studying every line and crease. Finally, she replied. "I think I know."

"You know?" Jane asked, skeptically.

"I've been looking for you my entire life," she said as her eyes teared.

"I don't understand."

"When I lived at the orphanage, it was pretty bad. On visiting day, I'd get all dressed up in a fluffy dress that was only reserved for that occasion. And I'd sit perfectly still in the front window seat. And I'd wait. When the lady who ran the place asked me who I was waiting for, I told her I was waiting for my sister to show up. Of course, she laughed at me and told me I was an only child and that nobody was ever going to come for me." A tear rolled down her weathered face. "But I never stopped waiting. I just knew. I can't explain it. Somehow, I'd meet the part of me that I always knew existed and I would know her when she showed up." Wanda gave the photo another good gaze. "She looked like a lot of fun. Was she?"

"When she conceived you, she was having a lot of fun. By the time I was conceived five years later, the only 'fun' was in dysfunctional." Jane observed her. "I think maybe you got infused with that early lighthearted quality and I got stuck with the miserable end."

Wanda looked up at her. "Are you miserable?"

The question came out of left field. "Isn't everybody nowadays?"

"It's a choice though, isn't it?"

"Oh, fuck. You're in AA, aren't you?"

"Yeah. It's part of my probation. Why?"

"Because I can name it and claim it with the best of them." She spied the cigarette pack. "You mind?" Jane took out a cigarette and lit up. "I'm only going to have three puffs."

"I say the same thing," Wanda smiled, taking a drag on her cigarette and admiring the photo of Anne again. "What was she like?"

"I never knew that side of her," Jane offered, pointing to the photo. "By the time I showed up to the party, she was pretty beaten down. I realize now that part of that had to do with you. She used to stare out the kitchen window a lot. I thought she was trying to figure out how to disappear from my father. But now I wonder how many times she was thinking about you and wondering where you were at that moment."

Wanda choked up. "That's when she and I were thinking of each other."

"Why do you say that?" Jane took another hit.

"Because I'd be walking along and for no reason whatsoever, I'd think of her. I had no idea what she looked like but I knew her by heart. And I'd wonder at that moment, now why in the world did that thought pop into my head right then? That's when I realized it popped into my head because I was catching her thought on the wings of the angels." She leaned closer to Jane. "I'm very intuitive. I sense you are, too?" She smiled. But a shadow of sadness quickly overcame her. "When did she die?"

"When I was ten."

She was taken back. "And I would have been…"

"Almost fifteen."

"Fourteen. Yeah. I remember. I changed right around that time. I'd been doing okay up until then but I recall just losing my anchor, so to speak—"

"You did…so to speak." Jane shook her head, sucking in another dose of nicotine. "My fourteenth year didn't turn out so great either. You lost your anchor and I lost my mind. I've been looking for it ever since."

"You didn't lose your mind," Wanda said with a wry grin. "You lost your heart. Don't worry, I get them confused too."

"What do you mean I lost my heart?"

"Your willingness to love. Your fear that if you love too much, the fall will destroy you. The knowing that losing the one rock in your life can change everything and leave you paralyzed to the point where love becomes too fraught with peril. Believe me, I get it. But what are the options, right? Living alone? Hangin' on by a thread? Counting the days until you drop from this world? No, I don't care what the question is." she said wistfully. "Choose love as the answer."

"Sounds like a bumper sticker."

"It's the way I live my life. I've made a lot of bad decisions, I grant you that much. But I've loved and I've lost and I've loved again. It's easier to slay a dragon than it is to love another human being with every fiber of your soul. To give that much, to risk that much, is more than most can handle." She set down the photo. "You know what I think? I think people are afraid their reserves will become exhausted and a big hole will form in their heart. They're afraid that nothing will come to fill that empty space. And just the *fear* of that possibility is enough to make a strong person run from a chance at happiness."

Jane sat back, taking a hard drag on the cigarette. "How in the hell did you figure all that out?"

"I've had a lot of down time, so to speak, over the last twenty-two years. Lots of time to lay on a cot and think."

"And that is what you thought about?"

"It beat thinking and talking about what the other inmates were focused on. I tell you what, Jane, if I had to listen to one more story about victims, I'd carve a spoon into a knife and shank a fellow inmate just to have my ass thrown in solitary and get some peace and quiet."

Jane looked at her and couldn't help but smile. It sounded exactly like something she would say. She took another drag.

"You know, you've hit that more than three puffs. It's such a bad habit," she offered, taking a puff.

"I noticed," Jane smiled. "But you're just worried about my welfare, aren't you?"

Knowing

Wanda grinned as she played with one of her many earrings. "They call me the little mother over at the transitional housing center."

"Is that right? You like to hover over people?"

"I guess." She thought about it. "I think one of my problems is I'll take care of everyone else but I won't take care of myself. I have a hard time believing I'm worth it. Does that make any sense?"

Jane took a hard drag before crushing out the cigarette on the picnic table. "Too much sense."

Wanda glanced at the photo again before returning her attention to Jane. "How'd you find me?"

Jane gave her the condensed version of how it all went down, leaving out the parts she felt were too hard to believe. "It was around the fifth of this month when it all came together and I found out where you were."

Wanda looked stunned. "The fifth? You're kidding?"

"No. Why?"

"That's the day I left prison. I walked outside and my heart swelled. I'd felt so alone up to that point but then, I remember so clearly walking down that path and out of nowhere, I actually felt this strange sense that somebody out there cared. Like somebody was looking for me. I didn't know it on that day but it was you. I could feel my life starting to come together, even though I didn't know how it was going to happen. I felt it in here," she touched her heart. "I would finally have an identity." She reached forward, grasping Jane's hand. "Do you have any idea what this means to me? To have this confirmation and realize that everything I felt as a kid in that damn orphanage was real. That my heart wasn't lying to me after all?"

Jane nodded. "I do," she whispered.

Wanda checked the time on her watch. "My break's almost over. I can't be late getting back. The job's part of—"

"Your probation. I know. I understand how it works."

Wanda didn't move. "I'm not gonna wait tables forever. I'm just gonna do it until I find my purpose." She smiled. "My sponsor told me something the other day that really stuck. She said, 'Through work, you find your purpose. But through love, you find salvation. And through that salvation, you rediscover your purpose." She looked at Jane. "Now *that* is a bumper sticker." She swung her legs on the other side of the bench.

"Hang on a second," Jane said, opening her wallet and bringing out the fake ID. "I had this made for you." She handed it to Wanda.

382

"A fake ID?" she said with a grin. "I've had a few of these."

"This one's different," Jane said, pointing to the wording on the ID. "It says, 'Wanda Anne LeRóy.' That's so you'll know your mother's first name. Check out the address. 'Three eleven' is your birth date and 'Harry Mills Street,' that's so you remember your father's name. 'Midas, Colorado' is where I was when I discovered you."

"Who's that in the photo?"

"That's me, prior to my makeover. And 'January 11, 1972' is my birthday. Just in case you want to send me a birthday card," she said with a wry expression.

"And how would I do that?"

Jane thought about it. "I'll send you my address."

Wanda's face saddened. "Right. Okay." She looked off to the side. "I gotta go." She got up and started off.

"I'm a cop," Jane said.

Wanda stopped and turned around. "Is that right?"

"And my life is pretty complicated right now."

"I see. Well…when it gets less complicated, look me up again, okay? You obviously have the ability to track me down." She turned.

"She loved you, Wanda," Jane loudly stated. "Please know that. You were loved from afar. You may not have felt it, but—"

"I did. I felt it." She looked at Jane. "I'll think of you, too. And hopefully you'll know it when I do." She turned around and walked out of the park.

Jane sat there for another half hour, waiting. She waited for answers that never came. Her mind was as blank as the miles of desert that stretched around her. She waited for direction but nothing happened. Saul assured her that when the time came, she'd know exactly what to do. But sitting there with the spring sun beating on her face, she was clueless. Her mind was toast. All the strategies and clever manipulations had vanished. What was left was an aching heart that willed her forward, even though she had no idea where it would lead her.

Returning to the van, she found Harlan seated in the passenger seat, staring out the window. Propped up in front of him on the dash was the last card.

"You okay?" he asked her.

"I will be."

He turned to her. "I want to go home, Jane. It's time."

"Home?"

Knowing

He nodded, reaching for the postcard of Chimayo. "Home."

The eleven-mile drive took twenty-two minutes as the road narrowed and they snaked along Highway 76. The territory turned rural with low rolling hills and the occasional house tucked to the side. When they drove up to the adobe chapel, the parking lot was full. A crowd mulled around the front entrance and inside the front patio area. This was a good sign, Jane told herself. Sliding her 9mm in the rear waistband of her jeans, she got out of the van and walked alongside Harlan. As they wove in and around the tourists, Jane's eyes never stopped observing everyone. She was keyed into locating black suits but she knew they could have sent anyone to do the job. So, she started looking for faces that she felt held bad intentions. But every face she stared into seemed to hold pain and hope in one breath. They were all looking for a miracle as they reverently filed into the church. Some of them took a seat and cried; others knelt in prayer.

"Over here, Jane," Harlan whispered to her, pointing to a side room.

She followed him up a short incline and ducked through a narrow entrance. The room was small and packed with visitors. In the center, was a hole about eighteen inches across that was called *El pocito* or "the little well." Inside, was the coveted sand every pilgrim wanted to take home from Chimayo. As guests knelt by the "miracle sand," they filled their plastic baggies and crossed themselves, giving thanks to God for the gift. The crowd dispersed and eventually, Harlan and Jane were alone. Harlan removed his head wrap and, twisting it into a modified knapsack, he bent over and scooped a handful of sand into it. Jane watched as he gently secured it and then tucked it in the pocket of his overalls.

"It's magic dirt, Jane," he said with a soft smile. "And as long as you're holdin' it, you can be invisible."

She regarded him with a curious face. "Invisible?"

"That's what you need to be, right?"

Jane knelt by the pit of dirt. She cupped a handful of the sandy soil and let it filter through her fingers. Standing up, she touched his shoulder. "Let's go."

"But there ain't nowhere else to go, Jane. This is the end of the road."

She fought back emotion. "I won't leave you, Harlan. I don't care what I said. I won't leave you for the wolves."

He looked off to the side, lost for a moment in another world. "I know you'll do right by me, Jane. I know I can count on you."

Jane turned to Harlan. His voice was completely different. "Harlan?" she asked, sensing another soul.

He didn't turn to her.

"*Harlan*," she said with more effort.

He looked at her. "I'm here, Jane. Come on."

They moved through the crowd and back to their van. Jane made a visual sweep of the surrounding area, even checking beneath the van for anything that looked out of place.

"Come on, Jane," Harlan insisted, hefting his frame into the driver's seat.

"You're driving?"

He nodded. "I figured it was about time."

He drove down the soft dirt road and back onto Highway 76.

Jane checked the map. "If you turn right, we'll eventually get to Taos."

"Nah," he softly stated. "I'm turnin' left."

Seven miles down the road, Harlan pulled over to the side and parked the van. He stared in front of him for a few long seconds. "I gotta use the facilities."

Jane looked around the uninhabited area, dotted with sagebrush and the occasional piñon tree. "Sure. It's as good a place as any. I'll go, too."

Harlan got out and walked around the rear of the van, stopping at a narrow path that led up to a clump of bushes. Jane chose another path and started toward it.

"Hey, Jane."

"Yeah?"

"I'm glad I jacked your car at the Quik Mart. That was the best day of my life." He pulled the sack of dirt from his pocket. "It's gonna take a lot of courage." With that, he gently lobbed the bag of sand toward her.

She caught it and watched him walk up the hill and disappear behind the bushes. Looking at the bag, she considered walking back to the van and securing it. But instead, she tucked it into her rear jeans pocket, just beneath the 9mm. She hiked up the rocky path that led to a stand of trees. Ducking behind the trees, she looked around the dry landscape. The wind blew gently, bringing with it the scent of earth and promise. In the distance, she heard a muffled pop that sounded like a car backfiring miles away. A raven swooped across the sky, circled three times above her head and then landed on the branch of a piñon close to where Harlan was concealed. She watched it, drawn into its aggressive *caw*.

Knowing

"Harlan?" she called out. There was no response. Reaching into her rear waistband, she removed the pistol and stealthily crept closer to the clump of bushes. Holding the gun with both hands and one finger on the trigger, she peered as best she could through the thicket in an attempt to locate him. "Harlan!" she called out, inching closer. When she heard nothing, she leapt forward.

He was gone. Jane raced down the short incline, skidding to a stop when she spotted their van. Half a mile down the road, she saw the black sedan burning rubber and speeding away.

CHAPTER 27

Jane tore down the dirt path and into the van. Keeping enough distance between herself and the sedan, she followed it, hitting speeds of eighty miles an hour down a forty-mile-per-hour road. The bags and loose items in the back slammed against the van's interior with each tight turn. Occasionally, she'd lose sight of the sedan but then catch a glimpse and muscle forward. When they reached the outer boundary of the town limits, the sedan slowed and expertly navigated in and out of traffic. Jane tried to stay close but she couldn't match the sedan's intricate moves. Straining her neck, she watched as the sedan pulled out of traffic and turned right, ascending a short hill.

She lay on the horn until the cars in front of her moved to the side. Powering ahead, Jane skidded around the right hand corner and accelerated up the hill. The black sedan was nowhere to be seen. Rolling past every parking lot and business on the street, she frantically tried to locate the vehicle. Finally, at the crest of the hill, she looked down into the wide valley in front of her. Less than one-quarter mile away on the left hand side, stood a six-story, brick building with a large blue Caduceus. Jane pressed the pedal to the floor and raced toward it. Circling the top parking lot, she still couldn't locate the sedan. Speeding down the ramp to the underground levels, she peeled around the tight corners, winding the van like a corkscrew into the bowels of the medical building until she reached the final level. Nothing. No sedan. And yet...she could feel him.

Suddenly, she heard a "ding," and turned to the side. A service elevator's doors opened. She rolled the van into a parking spot and waited for a few seconds. The doors never closed and the "ding" rang again. Jane got out of the van. She adjusted her 9mm in the back of her waistband as her hand brushed against the bag of dirt. The elevator bell "dinged" once again with urgency. Jane shoved the bag back into her jeans' pocket and entered the elevator. The sixth floor button lit up as the doors closed. Holding on tightly, the elevator zoomed toward the top level, rattling and moaning the entire way. The doors opened and Jane quickly stepped out into a dimly lit, wide hallway, lined with medical carts, trauma beds and wheelchairs. She could hear the rumble of activity on the other side of the wall as she moved fast toward the far glass door.

Taking care to not be seen, she poked her head up and peered through the glass. It looked like a thriving hospital unit except for the fact that there weren't any patients. Then, crossing from one side of the large unit to another, she saw Rudy. He was speaking to someone out of her view in what looked like a demanding manner. Suddenly, he turned toward Jane's direction. She ducked away, pressing her back against the wall to the side of the door. She reached into her waistband and drew out the 9mm. Her heart raced as footsteps moved closer. The door swung open. Rudy took one step into the area, his silver plated pistol with a silencer extended in front of him.

Taking another step forward, the door closed behind him. It was over, she told herself. All he had to do was turn around. If she shifted the gun from her side, he would catch the movement and kill her before she had a chance to shoot. She could feel the weight of the bag of dirt in her back pocket. Her heart pounded so hard she was afraid it would explode. Rudy took another two steps to his left and then twisted around, his gun pointed directly at her head.

She waited for the flash of the gun with her eyes wide open. But as she stared into his eyes, she realized he couldn't see her. He gazed all around her, sniffing like a dog on the hunt. She held her breath as he took several steps closer. His shock of red hair and pale flesh seemed to intensify the darkness of his black suit and tie. Staring into his absent eyes, Jane tried to detect a sliver of humanity. But mercy had left him long ago, replaced by a depraved cunning that operated more like a machine than a human being. At that moment, the machine was breaking down as it searched through the vapor and came up empty. Rudy lowered his pistol, holstering it and, after taking one more spin around the dim hallway, he exited back into the hospital.

Jane inched closer to the glass above the door and caught sight of Rudy waving forward someone on the left side, out of Jane's view. She watched as a gurney was rolled in front of him. Whoever was under the covers was awake and moving their feet. However, their head was obscured. Two more men, both redheads, entered the hallway from the side. They were also dressed in black suits and ties. The men approached the gurney with deep reverence, leaning forward and nodding their heads before saying a few words and stepping back. Rudy pointed down the hallway away from Jane, directing the person pushing the gurney.

As the gurney moved forward, Jane took in a quick breath. A woman in her mid-forties lay on the gurney. Several of her long wavy red strands of hair peeked out from her surgical cap. Jane flashed instantly on her disturbing vision and realized that the scene in front of her was identical. From the shiny gray floor to the empty hospital and now to the tendrils of red hair, it was now imprinted in reality. The only thing missing was the syringe that lay on the gurney in her vision. She patted her jacket pocket and removed the two bright yellow boxes she stole from the pharmacy. Opening them, she removed two syringes and read the name of the drug: epinephrine hydrochloride/1:1000 ratio. The stunning realization hit her as she dropped the syringes to the ground and backed up.

"No..." Jane whispered. Looking through the glass, she watched as the woman was wheeled down the long hallway and disappeared behind the double doors. Suddenly, a force moved behind Jane and surrounded her. It compelled her forward, even when common sense argued against it. She picked up the syringes and opened the door. As she walked forward, everything around her slowed down as she moved closer to the double doors. She smelled a sickly scent when she arrived on the other side—a mixture of decay and death that seemed to even permeate the vinyl floor. Glancing from side to side, the curtained areas with vacant beds stood as silent witnesses to the malevolence Romulus had been planning for years. Walking farther, she saw one red-haired man in a black suit sitting in front of a curtained, glassed in room. She stopped in mid-step and realized he didn't turn toward her. Jane stepped forward again and he still didn't move.

She continued until she reached the curtained door that was half-open. The man never moved a muscle toward her. Jane slipped through the open door and walked into the anteroom just off of a surgical room. A line of stainless steel sinks sat against the far wall with a glass window circling it that gave a full view of the operating theater. She moved closer and saw Harlan propped up on a gurney, plugged into tubes and a heart monitor. A young man in scrubs stood near the gurney, checking Harlan's vital signs. Pressing her face to the glass, Jane watched helplessly as she saw the clean bullet hole between his eyes. His pallor was deathly gray and his body lifeless. The man in scrubs exited through a side door, leaving Harlan alone.

Jane quietly opened the anteroom door and solemnly walked to Harlan's side. The heart monitor beeped with measured precision in the background as a machine helped Harlan take in each breath. Jane lay her hand over his and closed her eyes. She willed herself to see whatever chose to appear but there was nothing. With her hand still resting on his, she leaned closer to his ear. "Can you hear me, Harlan? Lift your finger if you can." She waited but nothing happened. And then, on cue, his heart monitor sped up just enough before returning to a regular beat. The force around her enveloped her tightly with urgency. She leaned closer to his ear again. "You're safe." She waited, as her eyes welled with tears. "And you're almost home."

She brought out the first syringe, spinning the dial to deliver the full dose. Jane swallowed the pain balling up in her throat as she released the drugs into the tube. "I will face the darkness," she whispered through her grief, "but I will not let it become me. Fear may be present but it will not possess me." Reaching for the other syringe, she turned the dial and plunged the needle into Harlan's heart. "I will face the darkness, as the knowing light within my heart and mind leads me home. And once again, I will be free." She watched the monitor continue to beat in precise beeps and then begin to quickly falter. Every part of her wanted to stay in that room to see it through to the end, but the compelling influence that held her protectively in his arms demanded her to leave. As she walked like a ghost from his room, she never looked back. The sound of the monitor rang like a siren as she walked through the door and back down the elevator. When she reached the van, a surge of energy moved through her body that brought her to her knees. It was as if the breath of life was yanked from her chest and left a cavern in its place. Unremitting anguish wrapped its tentacles around her as she sobbed like a child.

Minutes later, she crawled into the van and sped up the spiraling cement structure until she blasted into the sunny street. From there, Jane drove north until the van was operating on only fumes. Finding a cheap hotel, she locked herself in the room. She couldn't get the scent of death off her skin. Stripping off her clothes, she stood under the hot shower water, begging to feel clean again. The specter of loneliness hung close by with its unforgiving heart. By the time she crawled into the bed, the exhaustion overwhelmed her and with no effort, Jane quickly fell asleep.

Δ Δ Δ

She awoke just before dawn. Slipping out from the sheets, Jane peeked through the curtains as the sun's rays washed across the eastern plains. She dressed and walked outside into the cool daybreak. Standing there, facing east, she tilted her head and opened her eyes to the new light. Holding her gaze, she felt the warmth enfold her and penetrate her core. The world awoke around her, unaware that a mortal tragedy had taken place. All around her, the gears of life began to spin and groan. As the sunlight infused the streets and painted the buildings, life began again with the potential that this day would have to better than the last.

She checked out of the motel, filled the van's gas tank and dumped all the food out of the cooler save for a block of cheese and some fruit. Finding Harlan's bag, she sorted through it. She tossed everything except for the vial of sandalwood oil and the *Yogi* book. But looking into the dumpster, she retrieved the pinecone and the greeting card with the Angel Gabriel. She buried the bottle of Valium deep under the heap of garbage and then dug her hands into her jacket pockets. After removing wrappers and sundry trash, she found the folded postcard of the '66 Mustang that she pinched from Monroe's pegboard. Stuffing it back into her pocket, she felt around for what was left and brought out the band-aid with the smiling rising sun face. She started to flick it into the trash when something held her back. Putting it back into her pocket, the last thing she removed was the headband filled with dirt, still stuck in her rear pocket. Jane stared at it, not sure what to do. Back inside the van, she laid the headband on the passenger seat and organized the rest of the paperwork. Glancing at the moneybox, Jane formulated her plan. It was a fresh start, she told herself. Soon the weather would warm and life would once again flourish. And in time, optimism might bloom.

Rolling out the map, Jane searched for the next destination. Once her conscience agreed, she continued north, before jogging slightly to the west. Ninety minutes later, she stopped the van and studied the group of women in the center of the park. The yoga class was just about to break up as she climbed out of the vehicle and walked onto the grass. A group of young toddlers played and laughed nearby. Hovering near the stand of aspens, she waited for Marion to ascend the hill.

"Marion," Jane called out.

Marion stopped and calmly looked at Jane. "Hello," she said with a smile. She glanced around the immediate area.

"He's gone," Jane quietly said.

Marion's face fell as her eyes drifted to the side. "I don't want to know." Jane nodded.

"Is that all you came to tell me?" Marion asked.

Jane shook her head. "I have something that belongs to you." She crossed to the van and brought out the wrapped box. "Gabe asked me to give this to you," she said, handing the package to her.

Knowing

Marion ran her fingers across the top, easily identifying the contents. "Oh, my God. Are you sure?"

"I'm positive. You'll see your name on a note in there."

Marion was silent for a minute as the shock set in. "I don't even know who you are. Did you work with Gabe?"

Jane thought about it. "Yes. For one week. I got to know him quite well. He never gave up. He was dedicated to the extreme, but you already know that." She stared out into the park. "He wanted to leave a legacy and hopefully that package will allow that."

Marion turned to Jane. "A legacy? He told you that?"

"In a roundabout way, yes."

She smiled. "In a roundabout way? Yes, you did know Gabe."

"Marion!" a woman's voice called from the park below.

Marion turned and called out to the woman who was encircled with toddlers.

"We've got a little guy here with a scraped knee!" the woman yelled back to her.

"Send him over!" Marion called back.

Jane watched as a child who looked to be a little over three years old charged up the grassy hill. As he ran closer, Jane noticed the thick black hair and the purposeful way he moved forward. By the time he reached his mother's side and looked up at her with his crystal blue eyes, the connection was certain. Jane looked down at his knee with the minor wound.

"I've got something for you, kid," Jane said. Bringing the rising sun band-aid out of her pocket, she peeled the backing and placed it across the scrape.

He looked at her with an understanding far greater than his years.

"You're going to be just fine," Jane offered to the boy.

Marion smiled. "What do you say to the lady, Gabriel?"

Jane caught her glance.

"Thank you," the boy said with a strong voice.

Δ Δ Δ

By the time Jane arrived at the main lobby of the *Denver Post*, the offices were almost closed for the day. She'd penned a quick note and attached it to the top of the packet. Without giving her name, she wrote Mr. Baptíste a quick overview of the contents and implored him to research the deaths of Mitchell Cloud and Werner Haas, along with a strong suggestion that he investigate Jomba as evidenced by the photos. She included *The Q* magazines in the package, briefly explaining the mysterious ads on page seventeen. Finally, she gave him a breakdown of the land owned by The Wöden Group in northeastern Colorado and her theory about the goats and their intended use. Handing the packet over to the front desk, Jane asked them if she could buy a postage stamp from them.

Outside the building, Jane found a mailbox. Bringing out the postcard with the Mustang on the front, she addressed it to Morgan Weyler at Denver Homicide. She jotted only a few words on the back but it was sufficient. Paraphrasing a line from Mark Twain, she wrote: "Rumors of my death are greatly exaggerated." Sliding the card into the mail slot, she realized her job was finally complete.

But as Jane stood there, the hole in her heart was palpable. Surrounded by spectators moving quickly around her, she'd never felt so alone. She gazed into their faces and saw a myriad of emotions. While most of them looked grim and carried the world upon their tired shoulders, there were a handful who somehow still knew how to smile even though the day was dying. How was that possible, she wondered? Couldn't they see the decay and turmoil? How could they remain so confident when all around them was falling into darkness? Was it really a choice, as Wanda suggested. Was it faith and, if so, was it strong enough to recognize what needed to be done? Or was it a knowing that in the end, when the game is played out, we all return to where we began and acknowledge that the journey was hard but necessary. And maybe at that point, the masks are removed, the secrets revealed and the burdens lifted. Perhaps, Jane thought, the apocalypse of our collective hearts didn't have to come to pass.

She continued northwest and arrived less than two hours later. Turning off the ignition, she saw the light on in the front room. She walked toward the house and stopped. It was a choice, she told herself. And it would be the second most difficult thing she ever did. But she wouldn't have to knock. Somehow, he just knew and when he opened the front door, she was standing there waiting. Without a word, she handed him the poem written in Patois. He glanced again at the translation, "I hope for the one who can make my tender heart whole again."

Hank pulled her toward him and held her against his chest. "You're safe, Jane."

She gave in for the first time. "I am."